For Jill Dando.
An everlasting friend.

ONE

'Bugger London.'

Peter Amadeus swore softly to himself as he stepped out from beneath the shelter of the theatre doorway and into the semi-darkness. Shaftesbury Avenue was under assault from the rain and was on the point of surrendering. Gutters ran with garbage and puddles like oil slicks were collecting on the cracked pavement. Even here, in the heart of the West End, it seemed that London was falling apart. Its streets echoed to the constant noise of nothing, while strangers huddled inside their cars, cutting corners so they could be the first to arrive at the next traffic jam, sounding their horns in impatience as they splashed down life's muddy road. No one gave a damn about anyone else. That's what life in the city was all about.

He lit a cigarette, drawing deep on nicotine and dank night air. The evening lights reflected from the damp roadway, forming a chorus line of red-and-yellow neon that danced around the soaked shoes of two figures beside a taxi. They were coming close to blows. One door handle, two hands. Raised voices. A dispute over occupation rights. Wars had been started for less, Amadeus supposed, but only by politicians.

Beyond the battle, on the other side of the Avenue, Amadeus searched for signs of his country, the homeland for which he had fought and on more than one occasion almost died. He found a Turkish restaurant, a Balti house, a pizzeria and three Chinese wok shops brushing up against a branch of his own bank that recently had been taken over by the French. There may be some small corner which was forever England, but it wasn't here.

He'd been right first time. Bugger London.

Black fingers of rain began to burrow their way behind Amadeus's collar. He shrugged, welcoming them like old friends, stamping impatiently as he waited for his wife. Marriage, he had long since concluded, was much like an examination of his prostate, something that left him wanting to be on his own for a while. She was still inside the foyer where he had left her, cheeks flushed, voice trilling as though in the heat of sexual excitement, launching opinions on a tide of gin-and-diet-tonic about a performance that had pitted two notorious thespian queens against each other, locked in a battle for inclusion in the Birthday Honours List. The only sort of combat they were fit for. And as close as she'd got to an orgasm in years. Unless, of course, she'd been . . .

Suddenly he felt the blood drain from his cheeks, overwhelmed by one of those fleeting moments of honesty that left him feeling physically sick. Who the hell was he to sneer at others? Amadeus was nothing but a paper warrior, whose weapons were bulldog clips. Whose battlefield was a bursar's desk at some inconsequential fee-paying school in the suburbs, whose only recent victories were against misdirected invoices, and whose Commanding Officer was a woman intent on exacting exquisite revenge for the years she'd spent following in the dust of his career. A once-and-would-be man who now smoked too much and swore too little, who over-tightened his belt and whose bed was as cold as an Arctic foxhole. Who found himself lingering outside playhouses like some cuckold in the rain.

He needed more narcotic. He lit another cigarette. He wasn't to know that it was a cigarette that would change the course of his life.

Life disgusts Amadeus – no, it's worse than that. He disgusts himself or, more precisely, is disgusted at what he's become.

His mind wanders. He's no longer on the steps of the theatre but back behind his desk in the office at Aldershot where he commands 3 Para. He distrusts this desk, indeed any desk, and despises the fact that so much of modern soldiering is fought from behind barricades of paper. It's one of the reasons why he leads from the front, hoping to leave much of the paperwork scattered in his wake. This is also why his battalion will follow him anywhere, for Amadeus is a soldier's soldier.

Yet some pieces of paper refuse to be ignored.

After months of deliberation, the Defence Council has reached its judgement. The Army has been weighed in the scales that balance political convenience against the many bad cheques signed by politicians at election time, and it has lost. An Army that once ruled a quarter of the globe and refused to bow to Thug or Zulu or Hun is to be brought to its knees by a mixture of recession and the awesome incompetence of its political masters, who have ordained that an entire third – the legs, one arm and both balls – is to be hacked off. Discarded. The letters of redundancy have just arrived by courier. They are sitting on Amadeus's desk, accompanied by details of the appeals procedure and glossy brochures about how to survive in the life ever after. More worthless paper.

It is Thursday. The letters are to be locked away in the regimental safe waiting for distribution to the miserable wretches concerned on Monday. Amadeus, of course, has been told that he is entirely bombproof, that his exceptional military record stretching from the battlefields of Goose Green to Bosnia and the Bogside means that his position is beyond question. They can't touch him.

So why is his own name on one of the envelopes?

They'd avoided him after that, all his colleagues and fellow officers who had any part of the decision and who might have been able to tell him why.

Why? Why me?

In fact, it was true, Amadeus had been bombproof, right up until the very last moment. The computers of the Directorate of Manning had whirred and identified the targets for redundancy by age and by rank, and Amadeus only just crept into the zone. When the

Army Establishments Committee had sat in deliberation, they'd even asked Amadeus to give evidence.

Perhaps his evidence had something to do with it. The five members of the committee had sat like hooded crows in Historic Room 27 on the third floor of the Ministry of Defence, beneath chandeliers that hung from a magnificent stucco ceiling and lit walls crowded with oils in gilded frames. They were here to discuss economies. Cuts. Surrender. The chairman was a brigadier with a reputation for soaking up whisky in much the same manner as a teabag soaks up hot water, a process that afterwards left them in much the same condition. The only traces of colour in his face were the red rims of his eyes and the reflection of last night's decanter that still clung stubbornly around his cheeks.

'I'm still not sure, Colonel Amadeus, why you insist that an air mobile brigade couldn't be commanded by another cap badge. Perhaps a Royal Marine, say, rather than by a Para officer.'

'I would have no problem with that.'

'Really? But I thought you'd just been telling us at some length and with considerable vehemence why putting a Royal Marine in charge of a parachute unit would be tantamount to disaster.'

'But the Parachute Regiment is not an air mobile unit, Brigadier. We're air-*borne*, part of the airborne brigade. The sort of rapid deployment unit that took the Rhine crossings and Goose Green and –'

'Yes, yes! A slip of the tongue, Colonel, you know what I mean!'

'You ask me how we might make economies in

5

the Parachute Regiment without undermining its effectiveness. I tell you it's not possible. Our political masters cut the Army by a third in the 1990s, yet they kept tasking us to do more. Not just in Northern Ireland but Cyprus and Bosnia and Kosovo and Timor and Angola. And now they want to cut another third? It's madness. Madness! They'll be able to fit the entire British Army inside Wembley Stadium and still leave plenty of room for the other team's supporters. Although come to think of it, we might have to leave the tank outside.'

'No need for impertinence, Colonel.'

'My apologies, sir. Must have been a slip of the tongue.'

The brigadier's red eyes flashed mean and filled with the desire for retribution. 'Let me return you to the issue. Economies have to be made, those are our instructions. So the armed forces must become more flexible. After all, since the end of the Cold War there's no longer a need for great standing armies –'

'Which is why we need to be more flexible and mobile. Which is why we need the Paratroopers.'

'The threat is more "up and down", if you like, I'll grant you that. Yes, more flexible, I agree. So why not use the Territorial Army to plug any gaps at a time of occasional crisis?'

God, watching this man fumble with his brief was like watching a child play with a loaded pistol in the school playground. 'The Territorial Army, sir?'

'Yes, the Territorials, Colonel.'

'You mean the same Territorial Army that the Government cut in half only three years ago? It would be easier to plug the gaps with traffic wardens. There's more of them to spare.'

'Take care about your tone, Colonel. We have a job to do here. It may be distasteful but do it we shall.'

'So who's going to stand up for the Army, then?'

'I resent that, sir! I'll have you know that my ancestors fought at Waterloo.'

'On which side?'

The brigadier was out of his chair as though a grenade had rolled beneath it. 'Enough! We've heard enough from you, Colonel. Evidence over!'

Typical of bloody Amadeus, they all said, and smiled. Yes, somebody had to stand up for the Army. Amadeus was safe.

Until the last minute. For it was only at the last minute, as the main outlines of the recommendations were being prepared for consideration by Downing Street, that someone remembered the Prime Minister had a constituency interest, a Royal Marine base on his doorstep, and a majority that was anything but robust. So the Royal Marines had to be spared. The outlines were redrawn and an additional lieutenant colonel from the Parachute Regiment was put in the slot instead.

Amadeus.

They couldn't tell him that, of course, couldn't even hint they'd destroyed his career for the convenience of the Prime Minister, so many of them simply avoided him. They left it to a wretched captain to meet him when he travelled up to the Personnel Centre of the Military Secretariat in Glasgow to exercise his right of appeal. (He was meant to be seen by a colonel, equivalent rank, but the colonel in question had heard of Amadeus's reputation for being bloody-minded and had suddenly discovered a mountain of urgent paperwork to sort through. So he'd delegated and the captain had drawn the short straw.) The Personnel Centre was next to the bus station, a place which came complete with its full quota of derelicts and dossers, men with outstretched hands and reluctant eyes who had been unable to manage some transition in their lives. Former soldiers, perhaps. As Amadeus passed them by he wondered with a flash of alarm whether he might even have served with some of them. Yesterday's heroes. He hurried on, ashamed.

The Personnel Centre was gaunt, built of red brick, economic, cold. This was where he had come to argue for his life. Inside Amadeus found nothing but a heartless open-plan room with cheap industrial screens providing the only means of privacy. He also found the shifty little apple-polisher who passed as a captain in the New Model Army.

The captain had Amadeus's file open in front of him. Twenty-five years' worth of bravery and dedication. Top in 'P' Company. Director of Infantry's Prize at Platoon Commander course. His tour with the SAS out of Hereford. Instructing at Sandhurst. And the battles – the South Atlantic, the Gulf, the Balkans. The season ticket to Northern Ireland and the Queen's Gallantry Medal that went with it. Even the little details like Warren Point, where he'd shovelled what was left of his companions into plastic bags after the bomb. Everything was there. Not many files as thick as that in this place.

'You've done extremely well, sir,' the captain began. 'I see from reports that you've had an excellent career . . .' The captain read on, prattling, patronizing. Anything to avoid looking Amadeus in the face. 'A difficult matter, sir. But you see, a decision had to be made. And I see you have a problem with dyslexia.'

'It's only a problem if you can't tell the difference between an order to shit and shoot, sonny. Haven't made that mistake yet. So how about you?'

'Sir?'

'You ever had an order to shoot?'

Flustered, the captain pushed a piece of paper across the table. 'If you want to go through the formal appeals process, Colonel, you will need to fill in this form.' More nervous shuffling of papers. 'And I've got some additional details of the assistance we offer with reset-tlement, just in case.' At last the captain summoned up the courage to look into Amadeus's slate green eyes. 'Do you need any help filling out the form, sir?'

Amadeus picked up the form, and with it a glass of water. His mouth had suddenly gone dry. And as he read, and sipped, he realized something had happened to him. Tiny almost imperceptible waves upon the water in the glass were catching the light from the overhead bulb. As he watched, transfixed, he thanked all the gods that the bumped-up little creep of a captain couldn't see what had happened.

For the first time in his life, Amadeus's hand was shaking.

*　　*　　*

He is back outside the theatre, in the rain, feeling homeless in his own homeland. In a moment of silent fury he tosses away the half-burnt cigarette, the cigarette that will change his life, then in considerably less silence he mouths a curse more suited to a sergeants' mess after the beer has run out. As the wind carries his curse away into the raw night, a figure darts from the shadows, barely dodging the front end of the now-departing taxi and forcing it to a sudden halt. The brakes screech in protest but the figure pays no heed. It is a figure that belongs to the night, of no definable appearance, swaddled in a grime-streaked blanket. A man, by its size, bent and scurrying awkwardly, with no apparent care in the world other than to retrieve the still-smouldering cigarette from the damp, evil pavement.

From beneath the blanket a thin, bone-filled hand reaches out to snatch up its prize. Eyes flicker, yellow in the night and on fire. A stare is held. A glimpse of recognition passes.

Then the eyes are gone.

Amadeus freezes, paralysed by memories of another life. Another place.

Mount Longdon in the Falklands, on the march to Stanley. Amadeus no more than a first-flush lieutenant, a Para platoon commander on a night assault in the swirling snow, up against Argentinian lines that were well dug in. In the dark it had come down to hand-to-hand combat, bayonets and guts. A lot of

10

guts, mostly theirs. Sleepless for three nights. Exhaustion to the point of hallucination. And carelessness. When he'd jumped into the trench he'd assumed that the spic was dead, like the other three, killed by his grenade, and so he'd turned his back. That was when he had seen those eyes, and the man, advancing on him through the darkness and snow with murder in mind and a bayonet already caked in blood. He remembered a lunge, a scream, another gut-spilling twist of the blade.

But no pain, not for Amadeus.

Behind him the Argentinian, rifle still clenched in his hands, had fallen dead.

'Behind you, bastard!' Amadeus had heard. 'Why, there are Welsh Guardsmen out on this fucking hill and the sheep have all scattered or been blown to buggery. No telling what those Welsh fairies might get up to without their sheep. So remember. Watch your bleedin' back, you stupid bastard. Sir.'

And with that the eyes were gone once more, away on their mission of murder.

The eyes had belonged to Scully. 'Skulls.' Albert Andrew. At that time a camouflage-covered, crap-chewing corporal, and later the Regiment's finest and most formidable Sergeant Major with an MM, a QGM and a mention in despatches as proof, and a portrait hanging in a position of honour in the mess. A man who had risked his life on occasions beyond remembering in the service of his country.

A man who now values his life as no greater than a discarded cigarette butt.

*   *   *

11

Scully.

They'd betrayed him, too.

One minute he had been sitting in a bar off a cobbled backstreet in Osnabrück, having a last drink before being sent out to Kosovo, the next he'd been spewing his mince and tatties into his partner's hands, his leg and his career shattered by a coffee-jar bomb. Kids' stuff, those bombs. A simple affair, nothing more than a glass jar filled with scrapyard confetti and a compression detonator, and the top screwed on. The coffee jar had been thrown from the back of a motor scooter which disappeared into the night even before the coffee jar had hit the floor. The one brief sighting of the bombers suggested they were teenagers. Truly kids' stuff. When the glass broke less than a dick-length away from Scully's right foot, the detonator had decompressed and exploded, and the confetti – sharp, murderous chunks of metal with razor teeth – had chewed a path halfway through his leg. All in a day's work for a Para keeping the peace on the streets of Djakovice or Pristina, perhaps, but not in a backstreet bar in Germany, not when he was off duty. Which is why, when they decided they had no further use for a soldier with only one leg, they offered him their very best wishes but no compensation beyond a meagre disability payment. They argued that Osnabrück wasn't a war zone, the sort of place where you budget for a heavy cripple count. Hell, he was off duty. Drinking! Couldn't expect the Treasury to pay for every last damned scratch. It was unfortunate, of course, and unexpected, but that's what goes with being a soldier. Have to expect the unexpected. Of course, the two youths on the scooter might have been members of the pro-Serbian Prince Lazar terrorist group that was chucking bombs all over the place. That was entirely possible, but not provable. So, sorry, Skulls. Now, if you'd actually reached Kosovo, that would've been different, and Northern Ireland, too. Part of the home country. Sensitive. Soldiers weren't supposed to get blown up and butchered on home turf, so if Scully had copped it there he'd have got a thousand pounds a stitch.

But Osnabrück wasn't the Bogside. Scully hadn't been an innocent victim. He'd simply been . . . well, unlucky. Wrong place, wrong life. A trooper with a bad break. And only one leg. As if he'd fallen down stairs on a Friday night. And if they paid out to every soldier on the basis of bad luck, where would the System be?

So Scully's career had disappeared, and with it his wife. Then Scully, too, shortly after that.

Until tonight.

Amadeus was about to launch himself after the RSM, but now his wife was at his side, dragging him back, as always she dragged him back. Anyway, Amadeus knew there was little point in pursuit; if Scully didn't wish to be found then he would not be found.

Suddenly Amadeus found himself overcome by a feeling he could only describe as envy. Envy of Scully, of this man in the gutter. Of his freedom, his ability simply to be able to disappear and leave the whole miserable mess behind him. God's bollocks, it had come down to that. He was jealous of a fucking tramp.

His wife was summoning him, demanding he find a taxi. The call of duty. At one point in the Gulf War, during his tour with the SAS, Amadeus had been leading a Scud hunting patrol and in the darkness of the desert night had stumbled across a recce company of Iraqis. They shouldn't have been there, according to the oxymorons at Army Intelligence, and even if they were they shouldn't have offered any resistance, certainly not a firefight. With only seven men Amadeus had captured forty-three Iraqi regulars – forty-nine if you counted the body bags. Stopped an entire Iraqi company. For that they'd given him the Military Cross. Now all he did was stop taxis. Two young women brushed by, arm in arm, their young faces full of life. They were laughing – not with him, not even at him, they simply hadn't noticed he existed. To them he was just another anonymous, middle-aged man stuck in a crowd. A cold, sodden cloak of self-loathing suddenly wrapped itself around Amadeus's shoulders. He found himself reaching for another cigarette, his hand shaking, the cigarettes all but tumbling from the packet.

Then the loathing overwhelmed him. His hand clenched tight and, with all the strength he could find, he crushed the pack of cigarettes as once, when his rifle jammed, he had crushed the neck of an Iraqi conscript until the terrified eyes had begun to bleed in their sockets. All in the service of his country. A

14

country that no longer wanted him, and thousands of others like him, like Scully. A country whose leaders had betrayed those who had served them most loyally.

He spilled the offending cigarettes into the gutter, slamming his heel down and grinding them to pulp underfoot. He didn't want them any more. What he wanted, what he truly bloody wanted out of this mess, for himself, for Scully and all the others, was . . . what? Not their careers back, not even justice, it was surely too late for that. But perhaps an apology, an acknowledgement that they had been treated wrongfully, that all this cut and slash had gone too far. Belated recognition that they were men. Of valour, and of value. Not to be discarded like some cigarette pack in the rain.

It wasn't much to ask for, an apology, but to men of honour even a small sign of contrition can heal so many festering wounds. Amadeus stood in the rain, at one of those turning points that mark a man's life and throw his future unto the hazard, looking up and down this foreign-infested street, and decided upon his course. It was time for action, in the tradition of any wronged British soldier.

He would write a letter. To the *Daily Telegraph*.

Less than half a mile away from the cracked paving stone on which Amadeus stood resolving to change the world, Thomas Goodfellowe was entering upon a personal crisis of his own. The rain had hesitated and he decided to avoid the scramble for taxis in New

Palace Yard after the House had adjourned. With a wary eye cast at the low clouds swooping overhead, the Honourable Member for Marshwood unlocked the chain securing his bicycle – it wasn't safe nowadays, even left in Speaker's Court – and resolved to risk the ten-minute ride back to his apartment in Chinatown.

He needed the fresh air. The last two hours had been spent in the manner of a small schoolboy on detention duty, wriggling in discomfort on his seat while he endured a debate about the war against drugs. The war was going exceedingly well, according to the Minister, a former car assembly worker by the name of Prosser who had MUM tattooed on the knuckles of one hand and DAD on the other, a diminutive man who kept rising and falling on the tips of his toes as though peering over the top of a trench under enemy fire. Drug seizures had declined sharply in the last year – proof positive, in the Minister's view, that the smugglers and cartels no longer saw Britain as a soft touch, scared away by sniffer dogs and the force of his own Napoleonic will. His new shoes squeaked in acclamation.

Trouble was, this was the self-same Minister who, a year previously, had bobbed up and down at the Despatch Box to claim credit for a sharp *increase* in drug seizures, 'unambiguous evidence,' he had claimed at the time, of his 'commitment in the war against these weeds of evil'.

Fair enough, Goodfellowe had concluded, consistency in politics was usually nothing more than evidence of a closed mind, but in Prosser's case it

16

seemed scarcely a mind at all. The man hadn't the wit to appreciate the absurdity of his logic, nor the grace to laugh it off when it was brought to his attention. Goodfellowe had done so, brought it to his attention, intervened in jovial fashion to remind the House of the words the Minister seemed to have lost somewhere along the way.

The Minister, however, had been unappreciative. His eyes narrowed, his knuckles cracked, Mum had chased Dad around the Despatch Box and Goodfellowe had been reduced to parliamentary pulp. Such was the prerogative of Ministers. And the lot of backbenchers.

Goodfellowe had shuffled tediously through the final Division Lobby feeling much like a cow passing through the gates of a milking shed. It had been a long night and several of his colleagues were showing unmistakable symptoms of 'the staggers', the parliamentary equivalent of BSE in which the victims stumble aimlessly about their democratic duties, particularly after a heavy dinner – although the political variant of the disease rarely proved fatal. Many members had been known to survive in that condition for years. Thank God they had the Whips to prod them along and to take over when their own faculties failed.

Particularly Whips like Battersby.

Battersby was an oversized man with a figure like a deflating balloon and a face that brought to mind a cauliflower. A couple of outer leaves stuck out from the top of the cauliflower in passing imitation of hair. The Battersby mind could never be described

17

as broad but, in the exercise of his duties, it was extremely singular. He was what was known as the Whip of Last Recourse. It was his function to deal with those Members who had reached that point of utter confusion in which they started rambling about 'conscience' and 'principle' and refused the invitation to enter the milking shed. At that stage Battersby would reach into his badly cut and over-large jacket and pull out a little black book. The production of this well-thumbed volume was a gesture that inspired remarkable piety, for in it were recorded all the known telephone contacts for that particular Member. Starting with The Wife, of course. Then The Parliamentary Secretary. Also The Constituency Agent. In the case of an alcoholic, the book held the number of The Doctor or The AA Group, and with a gambler, perhaps even The Accountant or The Bookmaker.

But the most potent entries in that little black book seemed to be those numbers that a Member struggled to keep most private – the 'OI' numbers, as they were referred to in Battersby's shorthand. What those in the Whips' Office called 'the numbers of the night'. The places where the Member was mostly likely to be found in the hours after the sun had set. The numbers of The Mistress or The Lover.

In Battersby's book and in his meticulous script, these names were divided into two categories and marked as either 'OI-1' or 'OI-2'. These categories differentiated between 'Occasional Indiscretion' and 'Ongoing Involvement'. Of course, the collection of these numbers was more of a hobby than a necessity since all his Members had waistband pagers by which they could be contacted, but Battersby liked to keep 'that little personal touch', as he explained it.

The errant Members themselves were marked with an 'FU' designation. 'FU-1' indicated 'Family Unaware', thereby rendering the Member open to coercion. These Members he liked, even had affection for, so far as his politics allowed. But he drew the line at the 'FU-2s'. From Battersby's point of view, those marked with the awesome 'FU-2' branding were outcasts, worthy only of eternal exile or – still better – execution as soon as an appropriate scaffold could be nailed together, for it indicated the small number of Members who had not only sniffed at the skirts of perversion but who had grabbed at them and lifted them high. These were the most dangerous of parliamentary colleagues, the Members who were in the habit of *switching off their pagers*. Who were 'Frequently Untraceable'. And therefore 'Fundamentally Unreliable'. And many other things besides.

All were recorded, noted down in Battersby's lexicon of lusts. His diagnostic skills were something of a legend; a Member need only to have tarried for a few hours beneath a duvet he hadn't bought himself and Battersby would have discovered not only the number of the bedside telephone but even the tog-value of the duvet. Production of the dog-eared manual at the regular surgery he held in the Whips' inner sanctum had a similar effect to a cattle herder producing a revolver – cures amongst those beasts afflicted by the disease of conscience proved almost miraculous.

Battersby was a bully. Goodfellowe found him breathing down his collar as he waited his turn in the milking shed.

'Still shagging that waitress, Goodfellowe?' Battersby enquired, addressing the back of Goodfellowe's neck. It was meant without undue maliciousness, almost as humour, as one might have asked after a result at tennis, but Goodfellowe had already played the victim once that evening and was in no mood for a rematch.

'Did you have garlic for dinner, Alfred?' Goodfellowe responded, not bothering to turn round. He sniffed. 'Yes, definitely garlic. And Guinness.'

'Something's taking your eye off the plot,' the Whip growled, responding in kind, his tongue working around his teeth as though in search of a lost sweet. 'Must be the waitress. 'Bout time you came round, old chum, and remembered the first duty of every backbencher.'

'Which is?'

'To be loyal to his Prime Minister, of course.'

'And his second duty?'

The question seemed to startle Battersby. 'Hell, there's a second?'

Goodfellowe at last turned to face his pursuer. 'Ever wondered why they keep you in the Whips' Office, Alfie? Why they never give you a proper job or allow you out amongst real people?'

'It's because I'm loyal. An inspiration to others.'

'It's because if you fell ill in the outside world they wouldn't know whether to take you to a hospital or the Natural History Museum.'

'Don't push it, sunshine.'

'And what are you going to do? No, don't tell me, let me guess. You'll confiscate my bicycle pump? Or cover my saddle with superglue?'

Battersby remained silent for a moment. Goodfellowe was a notoriously awkward sod, a man who had a mind of his own and absolutely nothing of relevance to the Whips. No position, no ambition, nothing to lose. So no weak points, no leverage. An archetypal FU-2. And Battersby was beginning to feel uncertain of his ground. Had they really put garlic in the steak-and-kidney?

'Anyway, something you ought to know.'

'What's that?'

'The waitress,' Goodfellowe continued. 'She owns the restaurant.'

With that, Goodfellowe was gone, democratic duty done and on his way home, leaving behind him the over-ripe odour of the milking shed and savouring the fresh air – although in London everything was relative, particularly the concept of fresh air. Whitehall was still crowded with traffic grinding its way towards Trafalgar Square and even the rain hadn't managed to wash the taste of burnt diesel from the night. He spat, then spat again when he found a glistening maroon Ministerial Rover parked ostentatiously across the new green cycle lane, blocking his route. The vehicle's driver was leaning against the wall of the nearby Cabinet Office, smoking a cheap Dutch cheroot.

Goodfellowe felt his fuse beginning to burn. It

was barely a month since they had painted this cycle lane, and then only after years of lobbying. It represented a small stream of green hope washing through Whitehall. Now Ministers were using it as a car park.

Yet like all London cyclists who lived in hope of survival, Goodfellowe was prepared. Whistle to his lips, as was his custom when fighting heavy traffic, he blew to attract the driver's attention. The driver turned, stared impassively from the shadows of his wall, dark eyes unblinking, his face lit like a Halloween mask, then returned to his cheroot.

Goodfellowe blew again, impatiently, a shriller blast, but Ministerial drivers were a law unto themselves – why, they even had little silver badges issued by the Metropolitan Police to prove it. This bastard wasn't for moving. And the rain was back.

Exasperated, Goodfellowe engaged a lower gear and began to manoeuvre his small collapsible bicycle out into the roadway. But the gears were stiff, unoiled, reluctant, and the distraction caused him to be careless. He bent to his task, head down, and twitched at the handlebars, but no sooner had he moved out from the kerb than his world was all but turned on its end as he found himself hurled back towards the gutter by the bow wave of an advancing double-decker. The bus screamed past, almost brushing his shoulder. A collapsible bike pitted against fume-belching spray-spewing red-metal monster. No contest. Goodfellowe ended up drenched.

The front wheel wobbled in despair. The Ministerial driver smirked.

Suddenly Goodfellowe realized he knew the fellow. From years ago, but reasonably well. The smirk belonged to a driver from the Whitehall motor pool who on frequent occasions had driven Goodfellowe during those heady days of fame and good fortune when he'd been a Minister at the Home Office. At that time their relationship had been all smiles and shared Polo mints, larded with gossip about the fumblers and fallers in the great parliamentary steeplechase, but now the driver stared at him, oblivious and unrecognizing.

Goodfellowe could feel the rain creeping like slugs down into his socks and his shoes. His suit had about as much chance of surviving its next encounter with the trouser press as Battersby had of winning *Mastermind*. It had been a mistake to use the bike. In weather like this it made him look a prat. Hell, perhaps it made him look a prat in any weather. But that still didn't give the bastard the right to block the cycle lane!

There was some part of Goodfellowe that was Irish, on his father's side, from old Queen's County before they renamed it Laois. In spite of the English overlay, which was supposed to consign all of life's furies to safe storage in some form of spiritual Tupperware, he took immense pride in these roots, if for no better reason than that it provided an ideal excuse for the occasional outburst. He was also on a diet, nothing but salads and crackers and no second glass of wine, which would make any Celt feel irritable. So, as another bus thundered past, Goodfellowe began to feel mightily and irresistibly pissed off. The whistle fell from his lips. He stood to his full height on the pedals, and let forth a stream of foulness.

The driver looked up once more, dull eyes staring, casting around to make sure no one else was observing him. Then slowly, almost reverently, he offered Goodfellowe his middle finger.

In his capacity as the Honourable Member of Parliament for Marshwood, Goodfellowe had sworn a solemn oath by Almighty God to uphold the Crown and its laws, but here it was dark, another world, and now he was drawing alongside this bloody car. Perhaps God wasn't watching. He shifted his weight in the saddle, took a deep breath, summoned a curse to his lips. Then he was upon it!

He lashed out at the panel of the driver's door with his heel. The panel gave a low cry of abused metal, giving great satisfaction to Goodfellowe, who wobbled onwards, taking a yard or two to recover his balance. He turned in his saddle to claim his triumph.

The driver simply shrugged and returned to his cheroot. He didn't give a stuff. Wasn't his wretched car.

Goodfellowe pushes on into a night that is rapidly coming to resemble the rinse cycle of his local launderette, an awareness growing inside him of two things. The first is that he's made a bloody fool of himself – but that feeling will pass. It always has before.

The other feeling he knows will be more difficult

to handle. As a politician he is accustomed to finding self-justification for almost anything he does – hell, hadn't he just spent all afternoon voting for an Access To Welfare (Disability) Reform Bill he knew in his heart was rubbish and deeply inequitable? – but the upswell of rage about the cycle lane is more, far more, than a bruised sense of justice. What has really got him going is that the bastard driver hasn't recognized him. That's what really hurts and has got so far up his nose that it's pinching his brain. Suddenly he's become aware that he loathes his feebleness, scuttling around Westminster like a spider crab, getting soaked with every incoming tide, his only function to act as target practice for the likes of Battersby and every passing bus driver.

He wants to change the world, but before he can do that he will have to change himself.

A hot flush passes through him that is very masculine and slightly menopausal but which seems to dry his collar and warm his wet toes. He is directly opposite the Old Shades pub in Whitehall, on a night of storms and sticking Sturmey Archers, when suddenly the clouds part and everything becomes clear to him.

He knows. He hates his impotence and he hates the crumpled clothes, even more than he hates that insolent bloody driver.

It is a moment of personal conversion. Goodfellowe wants out of the laundry basket that his life has become. Before it's all too late.

TWO

Dawn had arrived gently, like a baby at its mother's breast, but already the farmhouse was alive with the noise of a new day. Magpies squabbled on the reed roof while its ancient beams, salvaged from a shipwreck on the nearby coast some three hundred years earlier, stretched in the warmth of the slow yellow sun. Somewhere near at hand a loose shutter began a quarrel with the morning breeze.

In a room at the top of the house, directly beneath the thatch, Captain Mary Wetherell (retd), formerly of the Royal Corps of Signals, lay in her bed, tracing the path of a rivulet of condensation as it trickled uncertainly down the windowpane, and identifying each and every noise, just as she had lain awake through long hours marking the noises of the night. Those noises of the dark hours had been less comforting. The screeches of hunters and the hunted. The insistent ticking of the long-case clock in the hall. The snoring of her husband.

Mary was one day into her thirty-first year. Her birthday had been celebrated – if 'celebration' were the appropriate term – the night before with a small dinner for herself and a few friends. Her husband's friends, to be precise. She had almost none of her own in this distant corner of Exmoor where the gorse and heather did battle with the sou'westerlies and on a damp day the slurry trickled in the general direction of Withypool. This was her husband's house, his world and his life, as it had been his father's before him. Something she had accepted when they had married seven months before and something that, in the loneliness of night, she knew had all been a wretched mistake.

It wasn't as if she had been a naïve spinster. There was little to be naïve about growing up in the cobbled backstreets of Burton-upon-Trent, in the shadow of the breweries and the Marmite factory with their rich, overpowering smell of yeast. Mary had been one of four sisters with a father who had a serious problem with both alcohol and employment. Too much of one, none of the other.

To say her family was dysfunctional would satisfy only the most unimaginative of sociologists. It wasn't dysfunctional, it was a disaster. When her father was drunk but still capable, which was often, he would inflict on Mary and her younger sisters, but particularly Mary, the most appalling suffering and indignities. Fuck anything at hand today, for tomorrow would bring oblivion. By contrast, her mother lived not for today but for the afterlife, being utterly devout. She was also stubbornly blind and deaf, a woman who never saw, and never heard, who refused to believe in the presence of evil even when it was sitting at her breakfast table. Life for Mary, even as a nine-year-old, was already a bitch.

When she was eighteen, shortly before she was

about to go to university, her father had come home with a drinking mate, someone to whom he had lost a substantial and ridiculous bet. Mary was supposed to be the payment. As the two men had stumbled through the front door, she had fled through the back in her bare feet. She never returned. University was out and within six months, in desperation, she had ended up at the only warm place on the High Street that would welcome her, a recruiting office, so she had joined the Army. It didn't take them long to recognize the raw but irresistible talent of their new recruit. Soon it had been Sandhurst where sheer persistence had made her runner-up for the Sword of Honour, and simple excellence had put her at the top of the academic order of merit. Then it had been Blandford (top of the troop commander course). 30 Signal Regiment at Nuneaton. Germany. Angola. Bosnia. Northern Ireland. Namibia, where she had helped plug an election structure into the creaking southern African country even as she was being shot at by rebels. No postcards home, not from here, even if there had been anyone to send them to. Then Ethiopia, coordinating food drops. Training for life, and for death. She'd discovered the stench of death in abundance on the flood plains of Bangladesh, a country which, in her view, should never have existed, and probably wouldn't for much longer if the sea levels continued to rise. Signals were 'teeth-arms', at the cutting edge of every major military encounter, and she had been there, anywhere there was a challenge, at the edge. Sometimes too near the edge.

Yet in the armed forces a woman is inevitably

a target. A target of fun, and occasional abuse, of discrimination and desires. Mary Wetherell was more of a target than most, because she was not only cropped-blonde with a figure that was athletically feminine, even in mud-washed fatigues, but she was also remarkably determined – hell, in order to survive a father like hers, you had to be. She asked for no favours, nothing more than the chance to stand and compete upon that most elusive of hallowed plots, the level playing field, and the Army was an equal opportunities employer, or so the recruiting officer had told her.

It hadn't worked quite like that. She never seemed able to shrug off the fact that most of her colleagues were men with unfair advantages like university degrees, while in turn they never seemed able to accept that she was as good as or often better than them, or to forget that she had breasts. No one ever stopped noticing that she was a woman, whether under instruction on the Staff Course at Camberley, in the officers' mess at Rheindahlen or stuck in the middle of the fratricide of Bosnia. If she eased up and was too friendly with the men, they regarded her as a regimental recreation centre, yet when she refused the first offer of a drunken fondle on a Friday mess night they called her a frigid little feminist. Bike or dike.

Never just plain Captain Mary Wetherell.

Her Commanding Officer was a particular problem. Lieutenant Colonel Abel Gittings was a very modern warrior with an OBE and MBE to show for it. That's what you get when you fight all your campaigns at what they call the 'politico-military interface' inside the Ministry of Defence rather than on a battlefield. A filthy job, he'd been known to say, surrounded by cigar smoke and politicians, but somebody had to do it. He'd fought with such skill in the Directorate of Military Operations that they'd promoted him to be Military Aide to the Chief of General Staff. You weren't going to get much farther away from the bullets than that. Chances were he'd probably survive to become a general, once he'd finished his tour as CO of Mary's regiment. Yes, a very successful soldier, was Abel Gittings.

Didn't stop him being a prick, of course, and it took a totally unambiguous prick to wander over to Mary's Troop Sergeant during an exercise on Salisbury Plain to enquire whether the troop was 'taking care of their little lady, making sure she's tucked up at night, got her bed socks on'. A few patronizing words that in a fleeting moment had destroyed all the respect she'd sweated so hard to build.

When he and Mary were alone, his eyes said it all. They wandered over her like a route march through the Brecon Beacons, marking every turn and undulation, and rarely making it as far as her own eyes.

One evening in the mess she had joined in a game of 'tunnels'. Simple rules. Pile all the soft furniture into the centre of the room to form the tunnel. Then two teams, one at either end. The object was to force your way past each other in the narrow

30

and dark confines of the tunnel, run back to the starting position and down a pint of whatever was on the list before the next member of your team took over. A relay game of high spirits and considerable quantities of alcohol. When it had come to Mary's turn, Gittings had arranged for himself to be her opponent, intent not so much on pushing past her in the tunnel as grabbing and fondling every last soft bit of her. His hands were all over her, half an arse and a full raw nipple, and when the buttons started popping she'd decided she'd had enough, even from her CO. She'd left him with a fiercely bloodied nose. Yet he'd thought it great fun. Later he bought her a drink at the bar and quietly propositioned her. 'Swift and Sure, my girl. Swift and Sure!' he'd whispered, expropriating the Corps motto.

She told him in the most lurid terms to shove his active service up his own tunnel, and had been overheard. After that it was never going to be the same between them.

Two months later the Regiment was sent on its second tour of duty in Bosnia. An O Group was called and troop dispositions were announced. Bosnia was prime posting, a real war, everyone wanted in, and Mary's troop was to be sent again.

Without Mary.

Her troop was to be deployed under the command of a different officer, and Mary was about to be reassigned. As Families Officer. She was out of the loop, sidelined, humiliated. Nothing wrong with her performance, the adjutant had told her later when she'd kicked down his door demanding to know what the fuck was going on. It's simply that the CO thinks it's time for you to move on, take the next step. *As a Families Officer?* Anyway, Bosnia was inappropriate for her. That's the term he'd used, 'inappropriate'. She hadn't needed an Army field manual to translate. Inappropriate *for a woman*. After all, the men had to keep their eyes on the enemy, not on her arse.

Gittings had confirmed these details in the mess after dinner one evening, elaborating with a few more lurid descriptions of what he thought the most appropriate position for a woman like Mary should be.

It was, of course, unprofessional for Mary to respond in the way she had but, even in hindsight, the sweet-sour pleasures of the moment hadn't lost their freshness. She would for ever cherish that look of bewilderment in his alcoholic eyes – her father's eyes – followed by the first flush of pain in the moments after Gittings had hit the floor. She had bloodied and bent the CO's nose once again, and broken a tooth for good measure, but this time without the covering screen of the tunnel. She'd thumped him out in the open, in full view of the entire mess.

'Was that swift and sure enough for you, sir?'

The matter couldn't be left there, of course, but Gittings decided against a court martial. His bloody nose had quite a history of its own, there would be too much scope for awkward questions at a trial. Anyway, Mrs Gittings had already put up with as much lurid rumour as she would tolerate about what she referred to as his 'campaigns on foreign fields'. So, instead of a court martial, Gittings had held forth about the dangers of PMT and claimed credit amongst the men for 'doing the decent thing', protecting the regimental honour by having Mary sent away. Like a leper. Which in the Signals meant a posting to a Territorial Army regiment somewhere north of Newcastle – although to cover their exposed legal backsides they'd offered her the alternative of organizing the appeal for an extension to the military museum at Blandford. She'd have preferred the court martial and a firing squad.

Within five months she had quit in despair, her career destroyed, her confidence shattered as completely as a discarded bottle.

That's why she had married Oscar. In a moment of weakness. He was a stooping gentle giant of a hill farmer, a widower with two grown sons, and a good companion. OK, so he was old enough to be her father, but he was unlike her own father in so many ways. Oscar, for instance, had worked diligently, drank in moderation on every day except Friday and showed only fleeting interest in her sexuality. She hoped that at last she had found a partner who would share her needs rather than treat her body as an excuse for violence or as a prize in some Friday-night rutting festival, but Oscar showed almost no interest at all. He had a family, had already done his duty. At last she had found that elusive level playing field for which she had been searching, only to discover that it was as empty as it was flat.

Beside her, Oscar was beginning to stir, the smell of

last night's stale cigar smoke still on him. She didn't feel like waiting for the usual exchange of greetings which were no longer meant, on her part at least – did he realize? A pang of confusion and guilt burst upon her, driving her from her bed. He wasn't a bad man, not like the others. It wasn't his fault they couldn't get newspapers delivered to such an isolated spot and had no conversation to share other than the tumbling price of milk quotas and the closure of the local post office. But it was his fault that they lived there, and her fault, too.

She stood in her bathroom shivering, and not just from the cold, failing to recognize the face in the mirror that was melting in tears at the thought of another day in their half-forgotten world on the middle of this moor, with its empty hearths and closed hearts.

She knew she would do anything for a change.

Goodfellowe was enjoying the prerogative of a Member of Parliament, exercised on days when the Government wasn't about to fall, of loitering in bed.

Not that he was idling, of course. He was preparing himself for the tribulations that lay ahead by devouring the *Daily Telegraph*. Back to front, as was his custom in matters of the mind. First the sports section, where he discovered that something called Charlton Athletic was sitting on top of the Premiership. Mystified, he rubbed the shadows from his eyes and turned to the obituaries. The Lord Drago had died, leaving no family. Goodfellowe knew him

– *had* known him – but then he seemed to know more and more of those featured in this column with every passing year. He read about a progress through the ranks of Party and Parliament that was written like the eulogy for a modern-day Alexander and was, of course, complete bollocks. Forty years ago, before they had changed the law and lowered the age of consent, Drago had avoided imprisonment only because he had once served in MI5 and had friends in necessary places – although fourteen-year-olds were still beyond the pale, even today. He should have ended up in Wormwood Scrubs, instead he'd ended up in the House of Lords, and now he had ended up dead. Goodfellowe sighed and wondered what sort of obituary he would get, indeed whether he would get one at all. He decided not to dwell and hurried on through business and fashion, discovering what he might do with his money. If he had any. Then, finally, a splendid front-page story reporting a bravura speech by Brenda, the Environment Secretary, in which she claimed to have 'honoured this Government's covenant, not just for today but with future generations,' by announcing an increase in spending on the environment. No mean achievement during these turbulent and tight-fisted times.

Sadly, as the newspaper reported with considerable malice, Brenda's rhetorical sophistication hadn't markedly improved since the days of last year's drought when she had advised the nation to 'dig deep and do whatever it takes' to conserve water, and her husband had been discovered showering with their next-door neighbour. A finger in every pie and a foot in every mouth, had our Brenda. Several pounds short of a pension.

Oh, but what would the *Telegraph* do without her? On a bad news day – no divorces, no disasters, almost a day of despair for the newsroom – they were able to reveal that Brenda's citadel had been built with bricks of straw – and not even her own straw. In fact, she had done little more than rhetorically to raid the contingency budget that had been set aside by the Ministry of Agriculture to prevent hard-pressed farmers from starving, then in a gesture too far had classified it all as environmental expenditure on the grounds that most of the money was keeping the countryside green. Or, more accurately, being poured down a hole in the ground. Too bloody blatant, even for this Government. One day it would spin itself entirely out of control.

The letters page made for scarcely more comfortable reading. Clerics featured prominently this morning, with epistles deploring everything from the inaccuracy of church clocks to the most recent outbreak of pew power in which a congregation in Durham had mounted a picket line outside the cathedral. Their objective had been to insist on a return to King James and a few snatches of traditional organ music in place of all the clapping and community kissing. As Goodfellowe was frequently moved to note, God moves in a mysterious way; perhaps it would be better if God stopped dashing around and simply rested for a while to enable all these confused souls to catch up with Him. Or Her.

Another letter caught his eye. A broadside against

the Government, damning it for its broken promises and fractured budgets, much like many other correspondents over the months, but this letter was of particular interest to Goodfellowe. Full of anger, yet written with simplicity and considerable dignity. It described the Defence Secretary as doing *'what no tyrant has been able to do since the days of the Norman Conquest, namely, single-handedly to threaten the security of the entire country.'*

That description was inaccurate, Goodfellowe reflected. The Defence Secretary was no tyrant, rather an inferior form of ministerial life who had proven himself wholly incapable of standing up to the grasping demands of the Treasury, which was precisely why he had been allowed to linger in office so long beyond the point where any signs of usefulness had expired.

'Self-sacrifice is part of the military tradition,' the letter continued, *'particularly in order to save the lives of others, but to be sacrificed in order to save the life of an ebbing administration is an extraordinary breach of faith. There is nothing in this but shame for the Government, and growing danger for the country as a whole.'*

Goodfellowe wriggled his toes in discomfort beneath the duvet. He agreed. The cutbacks had been appalling, even dangerous. He had thought so even as he'd marched through the lobby to vote for them. But what was he to do? Unlike the military, a backbencher is not immersed in thoughts about the nobility of self-sacrifice.

The letter fired its final salvo. *'For most soldiers, to be cast aside by their country is a greater humiliation than surrender. Most soldiers would prefer the simple dignity of being shot.'*

The letter was written by Colonel Peter Amadeus, MC. The Parachute Regiment. Retired. Obviously forcibly.

Goodfellowe gave a quiet squeak of surprise. 'I know this old bastard.'

'Which old bastard?'

He looked up.

It was Elizabeth.

'Nothing better to do in bed than read the newspaper?'

She was smiling. Bearing a breakfast tray. And completely naked. For a moment all his senses were filled with her, the soft curves of her body that caught the light from the window, those places of shadow and mystery, the almond-and-marzipan lips and eyes of . . . Eyes of what? He always had difficulty describing the colour of her eyes. Marmalade was about as close as he ever got. Full of sunshine and Seville. Not that he'd ever been to Seville, or had any idea what it was like. Except it produced lots of marmalade.

There were some questions he would never be able to answer about Elizabeth. Theirs was a relationship that had covered the spectrum between hell and the hurricane, and visited most of the storm centres in between. They had never fully trusted each other, since they were two people who found considerable difficulty in trusting themselves, particularly Goodfellowe, who had battled for what seemed half a lifetime to come to terms with his guilt and anger. His guilt arose because he was married to Elinor, his anger, even greater than his guilt, because Elinor was no longer, and could never again be, his true wife. Poor, tormented Elinor, locked away within the darkness of her starved mind and confined to a nursing home since the death of their son, Stevie. Not her fault. Perhaps not his fault either, but enough torment to have laid a trail of confusion upon his love for Elizabeth.

'It's Amadeus,' he announced, placing the newspaper to one side as he accepted the proffered tray. 'I know him. Or knew him, to be precise. At school. Didn't know him well, but pleasant enough. Very intense for a fourteen-year-old. Not a name you forget in a hurry.'

'You didn't enjoy school much, did you?'

'Not that school,' Goodfellowe agreed. Not any school, in truth. 'Got expelled.'

'You? Expelled?' she burbled in surprise. She perched on the edge of the bed, intent on discovering more.

'The headmaster and I suffered from fundamentally differing viewpoints.' He rallied, tore his eyes away from her body, knowing he would have to finish the story first. 'Hoare – unfortunate name for a headmaster, don't you think? Left him rather distracted, I suspect. Christened his daughter Amanda. Can you imagine her school register? Anyway, during a dull interlude in one of his lessons when perhaps my attentions were drifting, Old Hoary thought it was in order to throw his stick of chalk at me. Which is where our fundamental disagreement came into play.

Because he didn't think it was appropriate for me to pick it up and throw the bloody stuff back. Caught him smack on the bridge of his spectacles. Knocked 'em clean off. Smashed. You could hear the noise all over the school.'

'So he expelled you? For throwing chalk?'

'No, not for the chalk. It was for my artwork. As he was shaking the hell out of me for breaking his glasses, one of my illustrations fell out of a text-book.'

'Illustrations?'

Goodfellowe looked reflective, painting in the air with a piece of toast as he refreshed the picture in his mind. 'An amateurish but highly annotated illustration of a woman. Entitled "Martha".'

'Naked?'

'Of course. Vividly so. Accompanied by a brief but entertaining sexual history. One which was highly accurate too, according to fourth-form rumour. To which the headmaster, even without his glasses, took great exception on the quite narrow-minded grounds that Martha was also the name of his wife. Copped merry hell for that. Not to return after the end of the term, my parents were told. Copped a packet from the old man, too.' Goodfellowe bit into a corner of the toast, trying to avoid the thick smear of butter that clung to its surface. 'Amadeus was in the year below me. Came to say goodbye when he heard I was being thrown out. Asked for a copy of the drawing. Offered me a shilling for it. Damned decent gesture, I thought.'

Goodfellowe pulled a face.

'Unpleasant memory?' she enquired, concerned.

'No, unpleasant toast. How can you ruin toast, for pity's sake?' He dribbled crumbs onto his bare chest, which she brushed tantalizingly with the tips of her fingers, tracing the fragments of scorched bread down towards his navel.

'Why do you think I own a restaurant? It's the only way a girl like me can get a decent meal. Either that or joining an escort agency. Come to think of it, an escort agency would offer much better hours. The overheads would be lower, too.'

'In my opinion, which is anything but humble, the chaotic hours of running a restaurant are ideal for you.'

'Why?'

He beamed wickedly, pulling her back towards him. 'Because they precisely match my own.'

'You selfish bastard, Goodfellowe,' she cried, picking up his newspaper and beginning to hit him around the head.

'Don't do that! I want to keep Amadeus's letter. Invite him for a drink, perhaps. When you've put your clothes on.'

She began to laugh, like wind chimes disturbed by a summer's breeze. She was remarkably unself-conscious about her naked body, and with good reason. Even in her thirty-somethings it was still finely crafted with, as Goodfellowe had once put it, 'excellent long-term potential'. She had thought it a clumsy phrase, while he thought it summed her up exactly. So they fought a lot, misunderstood each other, had to compromise. But, as they fought, he learnt, about

41

himself, and about that other half of humanity they called Woman. He liked learning as he neared his fiftieth, almost as much as he'd done in the fourth form. As for compromise, he found it easy when he was in her bed. Elizabeth de Vries. Excellent long-term potential. A body. Brains. A superb Russian restaurant thrown in, too. What more could a man want?

Except for an uncreased copy of the *Telegraph*. He grabbed it back.

'Anyway, what does he say in his letter, your friend Amadeus?' Elizabeth asked, conceding.

'That the Government is crap. He's probably right.'

'But it's *your* Government, poppet.'

She sounded the words slowly, with a smile of saccharine, as though she were lecturing a small child, but he wasn't in the mood. Nowadays he was rarely in the mood. He had developed a fundamental humour loss when it came to this Government. His Government. A Government that was deep into its menopause and now so bereft of ideas that it had all but run out of things to leak.

'That's naïve,' he responded, he hoped softly enough to smother the sounds of his own imploding frustration.

'You vote for it every day of the week.'

'Like all women, you don't understand . . .'

'What's the matter, Goodfellowe, the only place you discover your balls is in bed?' She laughed, claiming victory.

'Ridiculous female logic.'

'Typical male inadequacy might be closer to the mark.'

'Elizabeth, you're being emotional,' he protested, knowing already that his banners were in tatters and the field was hers.

'I know I'm nothing more than a weak and wanton woman, but you aren't. So why don't you do something about it?'

The *coup de grâce*. A single blow. Delivered with unerring accuracy.

'Do something? Do something?' he repeated, as though the question was struggling to penetrate the wits of a drowning man. 'I can't! I wish I could but I can't. I'm a miserable backbencher with no power and a bike that's going rusty while these bloody Ministers . . .' He clenched the rescued newspaper in his fist as he spoke, unaware that he was crumpling it beyond redemption.

'Most of them are cock-ups scuttling around Whitehall in search of an occasion,' he continued. 'They sweep past in their Ministerial limousines, their spin doctors strewing rose petals and whisky in their way, while we are expected to stand idly by in the pouring rain and wave them onward. And, to hell with it, look what you've done to my newspaper!' he howled in the manner of some Dickensian villain.

'No, Goodfellowe, you did it. And it's my newspaper. My toast.' She picked up the tray. 'And my bed. Time to get out of it. The second shift arrives in half an hour.'

He looked at the disappearing tray with a sharp edge of hunger. Damn the diet. The toast didn't look that bleak after all. 'You know what I really want,

43

Elizabeth?' he called after her, his imagination full of the sight and succulence of a full English from the Connaught.

She turned at the door. 'I know exactly what you want, poppet,' she said with a certainty that for a moment completely overwhelmed him. 'You want to be a Minister once again.'

For a moment he was stunned. Was it so bloody obvious?

'It would cause problems for me, of course,' she continued, her lips puckering. 'The Minister's mistress. I'd become a cliché.'

'Would that be a very great problem?'

She stared at him directly, glints of orange fire in the marmalade. 'I'd manage. If that's what you wanted. In fact, old darling, I think I'd manage rather well.'

The words hung between them, persisting. It was the first time they had admitted to each other, perhaps even to themselves, that they saw their futures together, as a team. This was not easy for either of them to admit. There was something often a little theatrical about Elizabeth, like Vivien Leigh, all extravagance and dramatic passion as though she had stepped out of 'Gone With The Wind' with high cheekbones and expressive lips that could squeeze submission from almost any man. But if so much of her life was an act, it was only because, in those secret places inside, she had spent much of her life feeling inadequate. She had first learnt the mechanics of satisfying a boy at the age of fourteen. She had also learnt of the potential consequences when, once satisfied, he had simply walked away. Abandoned her to the sniggers of his friends. Made her feel like a slut. She had decided there and then that if anyone was going to do the walking away after that, it would be her. She had been walking away ever since, from her ill-prepared university exams, from her ill-starred marriage, from any sort of personal commitment she felt she could not control – until Goodfellowe had come along on his bloody bike. He was different, confusing, didn't run by the normal rules. He was both infuriating and fun. So maybe it would be different this time. Maybe.

Goodfellowe understood some of this, although he had never been allowed to penetrate behind all the layers of tinsel. It meant that his love for her could never be a comfortable matter but, hell, he'd had years of respectable marriage, done the comfort thing and collected the T-shirts, all of which were starched and ironed and filled the locked matrimonial closet. He needed something different, not order and contentment but a challenge that would strip away the restraints and leave the T-shirts crumpled and torn, something that would allow the man beneath to show through.

As he listened to her words about Ministerial office and advancement, an uneasy sensation scoured his stomach. At first he hoped it might be nothing more than the echo of an unfinished breakfast, but quickly it overwhelmed him. A sensation he hadn't felt in so very long.

Excitement.

Twisting inside him once more.

45

He had Elizabeth. And now, with her encouragement, once again he had that other inspiration missing from his life.

He had ambition.

The hour is late, well beyond evening. A solitary shaft of light cuts across the prep school lawn. The turf is immaculate, which is much more than can be said for Boris, the caretaker's cat, a ginger-walnut tom with missing ear and the look of battles past, many of which he appears to have lost. He pauses, cautious, sniffing the air in suspicion before padding across the river of light.

The old clock above the quad takes its time about striking ten, disturbing the screech owl that had found a perch on the weather vane. There is no disguising the fact that the bell is badly cracked, and getting worse. The entire clock tower is a disgrace, so dilapidated it will soon need replacing if Amadeus can find the money, or silencing if not. Another tedious battle which as bursar he will have to fight with the governors, hand to hand, a tussle that will soak up as much of his energy as did the recapture of 'Full Back' on Mount Longdon, and maybe leave as many scars.

He turns up the volume of his CD player until the voices make his office vibrate. Not a problem, since there is no one left to disturb, apart from the cat and the owls. Mozart's *Requiem*. The work of a dying man that was destined to be left behind, uncompleted. Amadeus has revisited this music many times recently, feeling its power, beginning to understand how wrathful the composer must have felt in his frustration, and sensing his fear. So much unfinished business.

'. . . *fac benigne ne perenni cremer igne,*' the chorus sang. 'Grant that I burn not in everlasting fire.'

How Amadeus loathes his job. A travesty of his talents. Surrounded by children who have no respect and teaching staff who show no interest, parading in their crumpled jackets and tatty liberalism. When he was interviewed for the post, the headmaster suggested he had no management experience. Sure, he didn't know how many paper clips he had in his desk drawer. But he had planned a Para battle group assault with eight hundred men and heavy drop kit, all loaded onto twenty Hercules that were then flown five hundred miles and dropped on precisely the right bloody spot at exactly the right bloody time so that no one drowned or broke his fucking back. That wasn't management, of course, not in Civvy Street. He'd just have to get used to such subtle distinctions. 'Look, it's an income,' the Officers Association had encouraged when they pushed the bursar's position at him. Yeah, but so was mugging grandmothers.

He took the job because there was nothing else on offer at the time, apart from the still greater humiliation of his wife's incessant nagging. And when he sat down and considered all the options, beneath all the doubts there was the bedrock of his pride. Amazing what a man's pride could make him do.

Amadeus turns from his post at the window and wanders back to his desk, a route he has crossed and

47

recrossed at least a dozen times during the evening, restless, like a refugee. From beneath the puddle of light thrown by the solitary lamp upon his desk he retrieves the copy of the *Telegraph*, tightly folded to the letter page, which contains the reply that has been printed to his own. It comes from the Minister for Defence, Gerald Earwick. He reads it again, and still his soul burns.

'. . . *distortion of the truth . . . time for the country to decide, arms or Accident & Emergency wards . . . our duty to defend our hospitals and schools, our old and infirm . . . an end to feather-bedding in the armed forces.*'

On that night in the black snow on Mount Longdon, he had watched the youthful Argentinian conscript die, Scully's bayonet stuck in an inch below his twelfth rib, the young man scrabbling uncomprehending at his emptying stomach while hope drained away between his fingers. Somehow it hadn't seemed like a feather bed.

'*We should not allow the argument to be distorted,*' Earwick's riposte continues, '*by the self-interested pleading of a small number of disgruntled former officers. The truth of the matter is simple. The nation's security remains safe in this Government's hands.*'

He reads it yet again, even though every word has already dripped like acid across his heart. The music of the Day of Judgement echoes in his head.

'*Dies irae, dies illa, solvet saeclum in favilla . . . Nil inultum remanebit,*' they chant. 'O, day of wrath, that day will dissolve the earth in ashes . . . Nothing will remain unavenged!'

Nothing will remain unavenged. Eternal words

that reach out across the ages. At last Amadeus stops his pacing. He pours himself a large whisky, a Talisker, neat, the colour of amber, sits at his desk and lights a cigarette. He drinks and inhales, both deeply. His mind reaches out to places far away but not so long ago. The slopes of Longdon with its stench of rotting fish. The drive through Sniper's Alley in Mostar, and the ridge above Konjic where death jumped out of the virgin snow. Kigali, with its piles of bodies strewn like yesterday's newspapers along the fetid roads, bloating in the sun. Places, and times, when he had been needed.

The music has stopped. The only sound in the room is that of his breathing, which is deep, as though he has been running, or is about to start. Perhaps he should put it all behind him, bury his anger and wait for salvation in the life hereafter. But he can't. Forgiving the enemy is for saints, or politicians, or oil companies. Not for him. For Amadeus, every dark corner hides an injustice, every breath grows into a sigh of protest.

And while he breathes, he will not let it go.

He sucks at his cigarette until it glows brightly, like a star shell hanging in the sky, illuminating the field of battle. Then one more drag before he grinds it out. He uses Earwick's reply as an ashtray.

As the paper curls in protest and the acrid smell of burning stings his nostrils, Amadeus makes three vows. He is not a man who takes vows lightly.

The first is that this cigarette will be the last he ever smokes.

The second vow, more difficult, is that he will drink

less. Pity, but this will be the last bottle of whisky. From this point, only an occasional glass of wine or beer.

The third, however, gives him great pleasure.

He has been trained all his life to deal with difficulty, not to turn his back and bow his head. Earwick, that bag of shit, wants a fight, so that's precisely what he'll get. But not the fight he might expect, not a gentlemanly duel in the letters column adjudicated by the editor of the *Telegraph*. This will be a different contest, on grounds that Amadeus will choose. 'Safe in this Government's hands'? We'll see. From this point on, he vows, Mr Earwick is going to be a desperately busy man.

Amadeus is back.

From within the locked drawer of his desk Amadeus retrieves a thick bundle of letters, mostly from military men, many of them old comrades, which have arrived from all corners of the country in the last few days in support of his protest in the newspaper. He reads a dozen of them yet again, and then once more, reading slowly as he tries to assess not only their wealth of support but also the strength of the passions behind them.

Letters, letters, letters! Letters have been the greatest burden of his life. Letters with his wife's overdue bills, letters of protest, of accusation, of incitement. Letters of redundancy. He hates letters, has treated them as enemies, ever since his mother thrust that first alphabet book into his hands. He tore it up, and she beat him with the book's empty covers, not understanding his problem with letters.

From another drawer within his desk he takes a few sheets of personal notepaper, sits before his word processor, gives thanks to IBM and the Almighty for voice recognition and spell-check software, and dictates three more. These are letters of invitation.

The printer gives out its strange pattern of binary bleeps and, like messages from an alien world, the letters tumble forth. He signs, stamps and with great care seals the final envelope, then runs the tip of his tongue around his lips. They feel coarse from the glue, his mouth is dry. Needs a drink. He picks up the tumbler and holds it to the light. Liquid peat. Rich. Soothing.

Oh, and as steady as sunlight!

For the first time since his discharge from the Army, his hands are still. The trembling has disappeared. As the last mouthful of whisky trickles down his throat in long farewell, he rejoices.

The music beats out. Resurrection is at hand!

THREE

'George, this is all you ever do. I watch you, your lips move as though you're talking to me, I listen, I even concentrate, but all I hear is gobbledegook. Incomprehensible nonsense about PPPs and PSBRs and OEICs and PESC rounds. Like you're still on some acid trip at Oxford. Can't you come down to earth for once? Say what you mean?'

George Vertue, the Chancellor of the Exchequer, a man noted for his East Anglian reticence and who at university had experimented with nothing more lethal than an occasional mutton biryani, winced and sought time by smoothing out some invisible flaw in the nap of the brown baize tablecloth. 'I'm trying, Prime Minister,' he replied. 'Believe me, I'm trying.'

The two sat alone in the Cabinet Room on opposite sides of the table, the leader young, with foundation still upon his cheeks and hair a suspicious shade of chestnut, the second-in-command neither young nor old, simply beyond time, with a sad, almost molten expression reminiscent of a walrus that had spent too long at Whipsnade.

'Seriously, George, we need something that's going to sell in Salford.' The Prime Minister had just returned from a tour of the north-west and was, as ever, keen to reveal his roots on the factory floor, even though in practice they amounted to little more than a student vac spent sweeping the floors of a metal-bashing operation outside Basingstoke. 'Up there,' he continued, eyes raised as though Salford were part of the spirit world, 'they think a PESC round is a day out ratting with terriers. Language, man. Language. Remember the focus groups.'

'What I'm attempting to communicate' – the Walrus counterattacked in an attempt to stifle the Prime Minister's march through the provinces – 'is that unless we do something quickly, all they'll be selling in Salford, or anywhere else, come to that, is their wives and daughters. We've got to find another five billion or else.'

'Or else what?'

'Or else our masters in Brussels won't allow us a permit to run a car boot sale.'

Jonathan Bendall studied his Chancellor, a former don, of media studies, bottle-bottom glasses and eyebrows like seaweed washed up on a shore. Depending on one's point of view Vertue was either a notoriously dour man or a cold-blooded bastard. Perhaps in the end it didn't really matter which. A Chancellor's personality always played second fiddle to his navigational skills, and right now the economy was stuck fast on a sandbank and facing an approaching riptide. Whispers of impending crisis had even penetrated behind the closed doors that led off the Treasury's endless oval corridor, and they were always the last to know.

Bendall took a classical view of such situations. If

the gods were angry, they needed placating. A sacrifice, some head upon the plate. He had a reputation for being a willing carver and had already put two Chancellors to the sword since the last election, but it had been a cut too far and now the dining rooms of Westminster echoed to the cries of angry ghosts auditioning for the role of Banquo. No, laying down the life of yet another Chancellor was no longer an option; they were in this together, up to their necks. He would have to continue to wade with the Walrus, no matter how dire it got.

'What about the Contingency Fund, George?'

'What Contingency Fund?' The seaweed wriggled on Vertue's brow. It was as close to a display of emotion as he ever came. 'The last of that was swept away during the autumn floods.'

'Nothing left?'

'Not even a tidemark.'

The Prime Minister sighed and felt the sand shifting beneath his feet. 'OK, George, so that's the bad news. What's the good news?'

The seaweed wriggled once more, but then subsided.

'Come on, George, humour me? Or do I book an appointment at the Palace this evening?'

They both knew this game. The Chancellor was a man of little traditional charm but meticulous planning, which made him an excellent player in the guerrilla warfare of Whitehall. He had a reputation for never opening negotiations without at least one hand grenade to toss across the table. The Walrus always went armed.

'My suggestion, for what it's worth . . .' – the Walrus examined his leader with an expression he usually reserved for a plate of bad oysters – 'is that we lay to rest the Youth Unemployment Programme.'

It was as if he had suggested legalizing incest.

'Scrap the Yuppie initiative? But that was a core election commitment.'

The Walrus flapped his fins distractedly, as if he were irritated by flies. 'We could always close a few hospitals, or even cut the old age pension. If you'd prefer.'

'You're kidding,' Bendall responded breathlessly, struggling to keep up. The approaching sea seemed to have become boiling hot. The Walrus smiled. It was not a natural act.

'Cut Yuppies?' Bendall continued. He drew in a deep breath. 'We'd lose the Employment Secretary.'

'A tragic loss.'

'But wait a bit.' Bendall was lengthening his stride. 'He's muttering about wanting to go at the next reshuffle anyway. So why not get in there first, bring the changes forward? Better to push him, don't you think, rather than let him jump?' Already Bendall's keen presentational nose was to the fore. It was said he could sell snow to Eskimos but his speciality was selling indulgences to the middle classes, a task he had performed with remarkable success in every region from Hampshire to the Highlands. Up to now.

'We'd need some justification,' he continued. 'Apart from the bloody obvious.'

The Walrus blew his nose on a large red handkerchief, shaking himself as he collected his thoughts.

'Well, I suppose we start by rounding up the usual suspects. You know, the competition from Eastern Europe. The financial crisis in Latin America. Short-sighted bankers. That sort of thing.'

'Perhaps we could get Brussels to bail us out.' Bendall threw the suggestion into the air to see how it might fly. 'Could we get the Commission to rule the Yuppie programme invalid? You know, not only save the money but also get a good stand-up row with the French.'

'It might be arranged.' The Walrus nodded in appreciation. 'But we'd still be stuck with a substantial increase in the unemployment figures.'

The Prime Minister brightened, as though television lights had been switched on. 'No, not necessarily. You see, I've long been of the opinion that the unemployment figures are . . .' – he paused, like a conductor with baton raised to attract the attention of the orchestra – 'that the unemployment figures are exceptionally crude. One enormous rubbish pit into which everything is dumped. Young people who've never had a proper job. The middle-aged who may never get another job. The unqualified, the infirm, the idle and apathetic.' He loved toying with phrases. Many of his policies had been built on little more than the appeal of alliteration. Phrases were so flexible. If one didn't work out, you changed it, found another. Didn't do much for continuity but made for great sound bites. 'You know, I feel an overwhelming sense of public responsibility to make sure the unemployment figures are cleaned up. And broken down. Into their constituent parts. They need to be rationalized.

56

Redefined. Redistributed. Add a few categories here, maybe take a few categories there.'

'Create so much smoke that no one will be able to see through it clearly enough to know what the hell is really happening.'

'Precisely. Just as we did three years ago.'

Their deliberations were disrupted by a knock upon the door. It swung open slowly and from behind it appeared the timid-eager face of Anita Chaudury, the Member for one of the Leicester seats and the Prime Minister's Parliamentary Private Secretary. The 'Parly Charlie' was little more than an unpaid parliamentary gofer, a runner of errands, tasks which at times were of such menial standing that in any other profession they might have led to a lawsuit, but she loved every minute of it, from making sure there was enough Frascati in the fridge to keeping her master's compact available but unobserved. It mattered not a jot to her that she had been chosen for the role solely to prop up the Prime Minister's credentials on sexism and racism, his 'double whammie mammie', as he had been know to refer to her. For Anita it was the first rung on the ladder, the pathway to higher things.

'Excuse me, Jonathan . . .' She looked flustered but couldn't hide the reverence in her voice. 'I thought you ought to know straight away. It's Sampson.'

'Who?'

She took a couple of tentative steps into the room. 'Sampson. One of our Members in Leeds.'

Bendall knotted his brow, trying to locate him. 'So what's young Sampson gone and done?'

She coughed. 'Old Sampson,' she began, anxious about the necessary correction. 'I'm afraid he's gone and died.' She made it sound as if it were her fault.

The furrows on the Prime Minister's brow deepened. 'I am inconsolable, Anita. What's his majority?'

'Over ten thousand.'

'A fine man. And a fine legacy. Arrange the usual letters of condolence.' Bendall was on the point of returning to his business with Vertue when he became aware that she was already clutching a sheaf of letters. 'Ah, you have them already. Well done. I'll sign them immediately.'

She retreated half a pace. 'No, no, Jonathan, these are . . . from the public. In response to Gerry Earwick's letter in the *Telegraph* about defence cuts. Didn't go down too well with some of the Old Contemptibles, I'm afraid.'

Bendall sat back in his chair, contemplating his assistant. 'Tell me, Anita, what did you think of the letter?'

Her brown eyes grew large, she thought she had entered heaven. She was in the Cabinet room. Her opinion being sought. On her way. 'To be frank, I thought it brutal.'

'Absolutely right. Man's a bloody Tojo.'

'It would have been better, in my opinion,' she continued, emboldened by his support, 'to have found some common ground. Conciliated. Extended the hand of understanding.'

Oh, and that's where you are absolutely wrong, Bendall concluded silently. Politics is not a game of apologies. It's war, bloody, at times bestial. No prisoners. If Earwick's remarks had been a trifle intemperate, they had at least revealed all the brutal instincts required to ward off sharks. A necessary man. Which is why, at the forthcoming reshuffle, he will be getting a promotion. While you, little Anita, will be cast adrift alongside the Employment Secretary. With a big label marked No Longer Needed On Voyage.

'Tell me, Anita, can you swim?'

'N-no,' she stumbled in surprise.

'Thought not.' He dismissed her with a wave of his hand.

'The full tide of existence is here,' Dr Samuel Johnson had once remarked about the crossroads that are now Trafalgar Square, and Goodfellowe was inclined to agree with him, although for the moment the tide seemed to have ground to a halt.

Goodfellowe had retreated in late afternoon to his flat in Chinatown in order to escape the inevitable demands of the Tea Room. He had both a diet to defend and a backlog of personal correspondence to clear and was behind schedule on both, but now he was scurrying back to Westminster, braving the evening rush hour to make the seven o'clock vote. Except nothing was rushing. As he manoeuvred his bicycle around the queue of cars waiting their turn to enter the square he found his path obstructed, the intersection jammed. From his eyrie, the figure of Nelson presided over a maelstrom of anger and abuse.

The square had been hijacked.

Goodfellowe struggled on for a few precious yards, only to find himself in the middle of a demonstration that had been planned with the precision of a Prussian cavalry assault. Several hundred eco-warriors mounted on bicycles had charged upon the enemy's divisions, taking them by surprise at a time when their manoeuvrability had already been reduced to a rush-hour crawl. Within minutes the bicycles were masters of the field. Their numbers were so great and their presence so dangerously disruptive that the flow of traffic had been forced to slow, then stop completely, the way barred by impenetrable picket lines of bikes. Dozens of policemen were falling upon the square but as soon as one cycle was moved on, another took its place. So what were they supposed to do? Arrest several hundred bikes?

A young cyclist drew alongside Goodfellowe. 'Shove it up their exhausts!' his fellow biker greeted him, clapping him painfully on the shoulder.

Goodfellowe was inclined to agree, but only up to a point. After all, the good citizens of the rural constituency of Marshwood relied on cars for everything, including delivering his majority on voting day. There were two sides to this one and such moral dilemmas were best considered at leisure, not while rushing to make the Division Bell. He dismounted and attempted to press on through a warcry of car horns, whistles and increasingly angry noises of complaint.

In front of him a uniformed inspector was shouting into his personal radio, demanding that reinforcements be winkled out of the police canteen at Charing Cross, while nearby a Sky TV news crew had arrived just in time to witness a cyclist moaning in the gutter after being knocked from her bike by a confused motorist. Around the base of the column a group of protesters were unfurling a banner half the length of a football pitch: 'Save Our Streets!'

Bedlam.

It took Goodfellowe several minutes to force his way to the south side of the square. He was now directly beneath the superb equestrian statue of King Charles, one of the few to have survived the Civil War. The hapless monarch gazed down Whitehall towards the site of his scaffold, around which the crowd had watched in silent disbelief as the head had been struck off at the fourth cervical vertebra with a single clean blow. Goodfellowe glanced at his watch – he was late, very late, if he missed the vote he doubted that the Whips would be as merciful – but with a final heave of his handlebars he found that salvation was at hand. The police, reinforced and now regrouping, were throwing barriers across the top of Whitehall to prevent the demonstrators descending on Downing Street itself. Beyond the cordon lay the Houses of Parliament, the way to which was entirely clear.

'And where d'you think you're going, Sunny Jim?'

'Let me through, please, Constable. I'm a Member of Parliament and I've got a vote to catch.' Anxiety and lack of time made him sound pompous.

It riled the policeman. The constable inspected the figure clad in luminous yellow helmet and baggy trousers that had appeared before him, then stood his ground. 'Piss off before I nick you for obstruction.'

'Don't be offensive.'

'Piss off – sir. Will that do you?'

'Look, I've got a vote in the House of Commons in less than ten minutes. Let me pass. I insist!' Goodfellowe reached out and shook the metal barrier that stood between them.

'Don't get violent or I'll . . .'

'Violence? Is that what you want? Because that's what you'll get when I report this to Chief Superintendent Ainsworth.'

The mention of his superior's name gave the constable pause both for thought and for a little anxiety. 'You really an MP?' he demanded, sucking a broken front tooth. 'Where's your ID then?'

'My ID?' Goodfellowe began slapping his pockets in frustration. 'I'm not carrying it. I rarely carry it.'

'No ID, only cycle clips? Then they're not going to let you into the House of Commons, are they?'

'They all know me there, for God's sake. Let me through!'

By this time a number of other cyclists, genuine demonstrators, had drawn up to witness the confrontation and to heckle Goodfellowe on, demanding not only that he be let through but that they all be let through. Goodfellowe groaned.

'Look, Constable . . . 169OW. You prevent me from getting through and you'll be in breach of the Sessional Order of the House of Commons.

Can't remember the exact quote, but something about the police ensuring that no obstruction be allowed to hinder the passage of Members to the House on pain of being inflicted with all sorts of cruel and unusual punishments. You'll not only be on the Chief Super's doorstep first thing tomorrow but also find your way into the pages of *Hansard*. Ainsworth'll boil your balls for his breakfast. The rest of you'll go for mince. You've got . . .' – Goodfellowe glanced despairingly at his watch; he wasn't going to make it – 'about ten seconds to make up your mind or end up on the back shelf of your old mum's fridge.'

The constable hesitated. If he let one through the others might follow and he'd have caused a cavalry charge down Whitehall. On the other hand, whoever this man was, he clearly knew Ainsworth and his appetites. God, if only he'd joined the *gendarmerie* he could have beaten the crap out of them all and no questions asked. The constable tossed the consequences back and forth, weighing his doubts against the merits of his manhood, until eventually he relented. 'The rest of you get back,' he shouted at the demonstrators, 'just this one's getting through.'

It took more agonizing moments of delay before they complied, the barrier was dragged back, with a muttered apology from the policeman for any mis-understanding, and Goodfellowe was allowed to pass.

As he remounted his bike and began pedalling furiously, he could hear Big Ben striking in the distance, tolling for the bodies to be brought in for counting. Already he was sweating and he'd feel like a dish rag when he arrived. He had only a few more

63

minutes before the doors of the voting lobbies would be locked. He took a huge breath to fill his lungs with oxygen. His legs ached with the effort and suddenly he felt very middle-aged. Time was running out for Goodfellowe, in all sorts of ways. There was still so much he wanted to do, to achieve, but he knew he could do none of it left out in the cold on a bicycle. There was also the matter of Elizabeth. How was he going to hang on to someone as classy as that if all he could offer her was the back of a bloody tandem? As he raced past the Red Lion, he knew that the time had come for him to move on in his life. The bicycle clips had to go.

Goodfellowe cast a despairing, angry look over his shoulder at the confusion he had just left behind. To his surprise he thought he caught sight of Sam, almost buried in the crowd on the other side of the barrier. But no, it couldn't be. His daughter was in her first year at London University, she'd be busy right now with lectures or essays or something, not out causing mayhem. No, it couldn't be, wouldn't be Sam. Anyway, he didn't have time to stop.

Now he was on the long sprint towards Parliament, putting his back into it, the noise of battle fading. As he pedalled he reflected; how easy it had been for a relatively small number of people armed with nothing more than a little initiative to overwhelm a modern city, to clog the arteries and bring the heart of a great metropolis to the point of seizure. The Cold War military blocs had amassed their arsenals of nuclear-tipped missiles along with chemical and biological agents, weapons that they could launch from land and sea and air and even from space. Vast military machines constructed at huge and often crippling expense. When all they'd needed was a few bicycle pumps.

Goodfellowe chuckled in relief. Thank God the Soviets hadn't been plugged in to Sky News.

'Tom!' A high, almost musical note, a sound of welcome.

Then: 'Oh, Tom.' Softer, deeper. About six feet deep. 'By my mother's beard, I really don't know what to do with you. An angel in hobnail boots, if ever I saw one. Never know whether you're coming into my office to bring me good news or give me a bloody good kicking.'

The Chief Whip waved him onto the single leather sofa and, without prompting, handed him a tumbler of whisky. 'First you ask to see me. Then miss a bloody vote so I have to have you dragged in here by the cods anyway.'

Eddie Rankin sank wearily into the sofa beside Goodfellowe. The Chief was a Border Scot whose family over generations had seen all sides of the question as armies had tramped their way north and south across his country. His family had fought on all sides, too. Resilience and reticence were woven into the Rankin genes, which made him an ideal Whip. So unlike Battersby.

Goodfellowe had arrived at the House, panting after his dash down Whitehall, his collar askew, his hair like a nesting site for sparrows. He'd missed the vote. Battersby had been waiting for him. Wearing yellow socks. *Yellow*, for Christ's sake.

'Amazing what rubbish floats past if you sit by the river long enough,' the Whip had weighed in. He was a little drunk, his tongue slow, and he was having trouble with the words, like some badly dubbed film.

'Damn it, Battersby. I bust a gut trying to get here. Not my fault.'

'Too busy shagging the waitress, were we? You gotta be careful, Tom, or the News of the Screws is gonna find out about that little arrangement of yours. Fact is, think I can guarantee it.'

'You should be studied by ornithologists,' Goodfellowe had countered. 'As living proof of an old Chinese proverb.'

'What Chinese proverb?' the Whip had responded cautiously.

'That everything which craps on you isn't necessarily a bird.'

Battersby's eyes narrowed. He was supposed to be in charge of this, yet somehow Goodfellowe always put him on the defensive. Still, he had one weapon in his locker. Time to produce it. 'It's not me you have to worry about, my old deary. The Chief wants to see you. Bit of a command performance, I'm afraid.'

'Don't worry. I had already made an appointment with him,' Goodfellowe had smiled generously, leaving Battersby in confusion, which wasn't all that difficult once one had progressed beyond counting to ten.

The Chief Whip was a different breed. Subtle. Even

a friend, so far as politics allow. 'You see, Tom, we've known each other so many years. I watched you when you were a Minister. Thought you were the one, perhaps the only one of our generation, who had the ability to make it to the top. Seriously I did. Yet now you can't even make it to a bloody vote.' His fingers drummed impatiently on the arm of the sofa. They were delicate, almost feminine fingers, carefully manicured, the mark of a man who had once played the classical guitar with the Scottish National Orchestra, fingers that could pick the conscience from a backbencher's pocket without him ever knowing.

'Not my fault, Eddie,' Goodfellowe responded. 'Not this time, at least. Got caught up in a demonstration at Trafalgar Square.'

'Tom, just listen to yourself. Missed a vote because you got caught up in a mob demonstrating against your own Government? What do you think this is? A kindergarten class?' The colour drained from Rankin's voice. Goodfellowe was going to have to earn his whisky the hard way. 'You've spent the last couple of years being about as much help as a nun in a knocking shop. We've been patient, sympathetic. Hell, after you lost your son, and Elinor cracked up . . .' He paused in sorrow. The ancient leather of the sofa creaked as he leaned forward to refill their glasses. 'You know as well as anybody that we're not all prehistoric like Battersby. But we all have to move on, Tom. I'm running a parliamentary party, not a dog pound.'

'Aren't we allowed the occasional bark?'

'I haven't got time to waste on rounding up stray mongrels,' Rankin retorted. 'In your case, some would argue that it was better simply to have you put down. Including, so I've heard, some in your own constituency party.'

So, the ripples on the Marshwood pond had reached as far as the Chief Whip's lair. Goodfellowe ran his finger around the rim of his glass. An average blend, not a single malt. Unmistakable evidence that this was serious rather than social.

'Look at it from my point of view, Tom. If you were standing in my socks, what would you be saying?'

Goodfellowe stifled a sarcastic response – this wasn't the moment for cheap lines – and gazed around the panelled room with its dark window and conspiratorial atmosphere. On Rankin's desk lay a small pile of folders. Personnel files. Files from the safe, the armoury where the Whips stored most of their weapons, those little secrets and shames that were committed to paper and locked away, to be brought out and brandished whenever one of the dogs started barking. (No computer files here, too easy to copy, only the handwritten daily notes torn from the Whips' Book, along with a few press cuttings and unpaid invoices. Perhaps even a couple of charge sheets, too.)

There were some secrets that even the Whips were unwilling to commit to paper, matters so sensitive they were confined only to that collective memory that bound together the brotherhood. Such as the whereabouts of the Foreign Secretary's first wife, whom he had inconveniently forgotten to divorce before marrying the second. Her bank account number, too, although a slip of paper recorded details of the regular payments. There was also the identity of the MP's daughter who fed her drug habit by prostitution and by playing the Stock Market with exceptional good fortune following her occasional visits to a Junior Minister for Industry. Nestling alongside the other secrets was the identity of the Whip, one of their own, who'd had a heart attack in his room, tied to his chair with underwear around his ankles. Women's underwear. No need for a paper record. They would for ever remember him as Little Miss Naughty, baby pink, extra large. For a moment Goodfellowe wondered whether Rankin had been running through his own file, and what might be in it.

'If, as you say, I were standing in your socks, Eddie,' he responded, picking up the Chief Whip's challenge, 'I would say here was a mongrel of some talent. Awkward sometimes, to be sure. The sort of dog who waits until you've built the kennel around him, driven home the last nail, then jumps over the bloody gate. But a dog who's looking for a new . . .' – he took a deep breath while he hunted for the right word – 'adventure.'

'Adventure? I prefer the quiet life. No surprises.' Yet curiosity drew him on. 'What sort of adventure?'

'One that doesn't require me to cycle in the rain around Westminster and get caught up in the crowd.'

'You want money?'

'No, you Scottish *teuchter*!' His voice rang unnaturally jocular in his own ear, too loud, trying too hard. He sipped his whisky, finding it difficult to plead. 'I want to be back with the team, Eddie. It's a tough game in this place and I'm tired of trying to score goals all on my own.'

'This is a new Goodfellowe,' the Whip responded wryly. 'Why the sudden change?'

'I've got new interests, new friends . . .'

'I'd heard.'

'New enthusiasms,' Goodfellowe continued, now certain that Rankin had undoubtedly reviewed his file, and that Elizabeth was on it.

'You want back on the inside of the tent?'

'It would be more comfortable than staying on the outside. For you, too. I'm so messy when I put my back into it.'

'So you want in. And you thought the best way to impress me was to balls-up a simple vote?'

'Think positive. Get me off my bike, Eddie, and you rob an old rebel of his excuse.'

They held each other's gaze, testing.

'You pick your moments, Tom,' Rankin eventually responded. His tone was considered, contemplative. Not dismissive. 'The tom-toms are beginning to beat from Downing Street. Testing the tune of an early reshuffle. One or two braves to be burnt at the stake, so rumour has it. Somebody will need to take their place.'

'I'd like it to be me.' There, he'd said it. No ambiguity, ambition to the fore. It felt good, like favourite shoes.

'Ah, the appetite returns!'

'Put it down to menopausal vanity. An insane desire for a higher profile. Before I have to start dying my hair.'

70

'And suddenly you've become enamoured of our beloved leader?' There was no hiding the sceptical note. Rankin was a musician, he could recognize a duff score.

'You know me better than that, Eddie. Y'know Brother Bendall better than that, too. One day there'll be a great shaking of the ground and he'll get buried beneath an avalanche of his own bullshit. But while History makes up her mind as to when the burial will be, I can be helpful. I *want* to be helpful.'

'And some might say he needs all the help he can get,' Rankin responded, so softly that it wouldn't carry as far as the walls.

'Will you put my name forward?'

'It's my duty, now you've offered.'

'But will you recommend it?'

The Chief Whip took a slug of whisky. 'Recommend you? Bit like recommending jumping as a cure for vertigo. Who knows? You're such an awkward sod, Goodfellowe . . .'

The McDonnell Douglas MD-82 banked gently over the sea as it positioned itself for a final approach to the airport at Odessa. The sight that greeted her through the cabin window was remarkable and Elizabeth hoped it would prove to be something of an omen.

Through the window of the Austrian Air flight she could see a fleet of aircraft set out beside the runway, a testament to the might of the infant and independent republic of Ukraine. Bombers, transports, fighter planes, helicopters, MIGs, Tupolevs,

71

Yaks and Sukhois, all ranged in straight rows like the tentacles of a great war machine ready to form a guard of honour.

'Our air force,' the male passenger in the seat beside her indicated. 'Big bloody air force,' he added. Yuri's English was not good and was very guttural, like an engine running on its last drop of oil, but somehow throughout the afternoon flight from Vienna he had managed to make his meanings entirely transparent to his unaccompanied companion. She had already turned down his repeated invitation to dinner.

As they taxied past the aircraft on the ground he returned to his theme, jabbing his finger for emphasis. 'Air force in mothballs. Big bloody moths, eh?' A laugh originated from somewhere near his large intestine. 'But no bloody balls!'

She could see what he meant. The aircraft that at a distance had looked so imposing at closer quarters revealed nothing but disaster. The place was an aeronautical knacker's yard. There were old military planes with engines stripped, their sides still covered with Soviet stigmata, single-seater fighters shorn of their canopies and propped up on concrete slabs, helicopters with some rotors missing, the others sagging in surrender. Passenger planes, too. One huge hurry-before-they-rot-and-rust clearance sale. You could buy anything here, she'd been told, even buy a navy to match if you took a trip to Sebastopol, and for a price that was always right. An omen, indeed, she hoped.

She had heard about the wine from a Ukrainian customer who had come to dine at The Kremlin after

72

delivering his son to his Wiltshire public school. The wine was not his personal business, that at least she had managed to gather from his fragmentary command of the language, although what his business was remained something of a mystery. When she had enquired, he frowned in concentration, hunting for elusive English words, then picked up an imaginary weapon in both hands and, with a juddering motion, sprayed the restaurant with bullets. 'Ah, a soldier,' she had deduced. He shook his head. 'A policeman, then?' He scowled in contempt, at which point she had let the matter rest. A man with access to weaponry and sufficient hard currency to send his son to English public school was not someone she wanted to press too hard. Anyway, he left a substantial tip along with a mysterious reference to wine. There was a specific mention of the Tsars, and mutterings about a lost cellar.

A few days later she received a warbling international phone call from someone who called himself Vladimir Houdoliy and whose English was, thankfully, exceptional, although delivered with intonation that was entirely American. His mastery of metaphor also left something to be desired. He introduced himself as a man who 'has a lot of experience tucked away beneath my belt,' which left her crippled for days. He apologized for the intrusion, called her Madam Proprietor, and explained his purpose.

He spoke in colourful tones, so engaging to Elizabeth on a day of leaden London skies, of his homeland and of a magnificent palace that overlooked the sea. A place of dreams, he said, somewhere on the coast of the Black Sea, a former summer residence much favoured by the last Tsar and Tsaritsa and equipped, in their time, most magnificently. Vast floors of the coolest Italian marble. French chandeliers that outshone diamonds. Statuary that would have graced Florence, fountains whose waters tumbled like a constant peal of bells, and beneath it all, dark and secure, an extensive wine cellar whose contents were the pride of the owner of the palace – Vladimir's grandfather.

In those ancient times when riot and unrest had rushed towards revolution, Vladimir's grandfather had grown increasingly concerned. The Bolsheviks showed such little respect for palaces let alone for French chandeliers, and no respect at all for cellars, particularly those holding the Tsar and Tsaritsa. So he had shipped out the statues, turned off the fountains, draped sacking around the chandeliers, even allowed peasants to sleep in the stables. He also decided to brick up the wine cellar in the hope that he could liberate it at a later time.

That time had never come. Grandfather had been put to the purge, the palace had been stripped of its marble and then nationalized. Lenin had promised to turn it into a sanatorium, but instead it became a munitions factory and, after a period in World War II when it had been occupied by the Germans, it had been used as a mental asylum. No one had bothered with the cellar, its secrets preserved behind crumbling brick and in faded family legend.

Yet, thank God and Gorbachev, the New Revolution had changed all that. Vladimir had been able to reclaim his inheritance and was planning to restore life to the crumbling palace by transforming it into a headquarters building for a Western company. A great opportunity for him – except for the problem of his cash flow. The chaos in those wretched currency markets, you understand? So would Elizabeth be interested in some rather fine wines? Mostly reds, of course, fortified, from the Crimea, plus a wide range of local spirits. All Russian imperial, pre-1917 vintage? At prices in hard currency that would do them both a favour?

Timing is everything in a woman's life and Vladimir Houdoliy found his timing was all but perfect. Elizabeth needed Vladimir, or someone just like him. Recession had begun to nibble at Westminster's sense of well-being and takings at The Kremlin were down. Not desperate, but down. There was a black hole emerging in her accounts and her bank manager, although appropriately primed with an excellent lunch and one of Elizabeth's most daringly cut dresses, had proved unsympathetic. He had accepted a large Remy then whined throughout the refill about the slim margins and poor security of the restaurant trade. Wanker.

Elizabeth was resolved. A little fun needed to be put back into the business, and a few cases of good Tsarist vintages at the right price might prove a very considerable source of amusement.

Houdoliy turned out to be fun, too. Tall, sixty-something, with a sea of silvery waves for hair, he greeted her at the terminal with a chauffeur-driven Audi and a look of gentle mischief in his grandfatherly eyes. There was also a bouquet of yellow roses. 'For a beautiful and most welcome guest,' the card announced.

They had driven along the gentle tree-lined boulevards of Odessa with its pastel-painted mansions, once clearly a graceful mercantile capital, now desperately wrinkled at its many edges. 'But safe!' Vladimir had emphasized. 'At night, the most dangerous things on our streets are the potholes.'

'Why so safe?' she had enquired.

'Because our local mafia requires all muggers to be off the streets by sunset,' he had exclaimed, before clasping her hand and bursting into laughter. She noticed he had smooth hands, not at all leathery like some men of his age.

He made her most welcome. He had booked her into the Shevchenko, a floating hotel moored in the harbour that had been converted from an old passenger ferry. Its rooms were small but comfortable, although the main attraction for most visitors seemed to be the much larger bar. That night he took her to The Valday, a restaurant that stood at the very top of the Potemkin Steps. The exterior was inconspicuous but it was beautifully decorated inside and offered the most absorbing dishes of fish, both fresh and smoked. There was also black and orange caviare by the forkful, a little vodka and a remarkably good local sparkling wine. Modern Ukrainian wines had a poor reputation but by heavens they were getting better – although nothing like the pre-1917 vintages, of course, Vladimir had insisted forcefully.

She discovered that for herself the following afternoon. The palace was a short drive along the coast, at a point where the cliffs swooped down to the great sand beaches of Odessa Bay to play tag with the sea. A place of princes, exactly as he had described, although not as large as she had imagined, brooding, with a cracked whitewashed portico. Outside in the grounds there was nothing but a toppled sundial and a few empty plinths, crumbling like long-forgotten graves in gardens that had been tended by nothing but a few grazing cattle for more than half a century. Inside, the palace was guarded by echoes that swirled around columns and scurried across floors that had been stripped of their marble and patched with bad cement. And deep within, behind a new steel door, he led her to the cellars, rows of musty underground enclaves that smelled of old souls where the bottles were laid out like corpses.

Oh, but what a confusion of wines! Dessert wines that had been protected by their high sugar and alcohol contents, some of which were still improving. Heavy ports, red and white Muscats, Tokays. Many of the wines were from Massandra, the bottles bearing the double-headed eagle that marked them as once belonging to the Tsar himself. Like a magician, Vladimir would produce yet another surprise, stroking away the layers of dust and encrustation with the tenderness of a young lover to reveal still more wonders. An 1896 Prince Golitzin Lacrima Christi. An Alupka White Port. A Muscat in a bulbous bottle with a huge royal seal on its shoulder, made for the Tsar in the very year they had dragged him from his throne.

They sat at an old wooden table stained the colour of dried blood from the lees, and in the candlelight Vladimir subjected her to a series of temptations, first with a wine from the Crimea, then a bottle from further along the coast. They tasted wine after wine, nine in all, mostly reds but with two darkly sweet whites and a brandy. Not all of them had worn as well as Vladimir, but they inspired in spite of that, simply because of their history. From the shadows of the wall an icon of a gilded Madonna smiled contentedly, while Vladimir entertained Elizabeth with more stories of his family, of the palace, and of the purge that had emptied it of his grandfather's family.

'He was killed in this cellar by the NKVD,' Vladimir explains, with a hint of pride. 'Stood up against the same wall he had built to hide this wine and shot. On the very day they murdered the Tsar and Tsaritsa. This is more than wine, this is the blood of my country.'

'You must find it difficult to part with.'

He nods, a short bow of his head as though submitting to God. 'Of course. But necessary in order to restore the palace. Sadly, our bank managers are less trusting than yours.'

Which must put them in the Crippen league, she muses. Money has been mentioned. It is time to begin. 'I suppose you'll be expecting a good price for the wines?'

He holds his head to one side, as though considering the matter for the first time. 'A good price, yes. But not a great price. I need to sell some of the wine quickly. Direct, not through an agent. They're all mafia! They would charge a huge commission on the wine they sold, then steal the rest as soon as they knew of its whereabouts. No, by selling direct to you we can both gain.'

'So . . . how much?'

'Ah, Elizabeth. You are young. You are beautiful. And you are impatient!' He chuckles as though scolding a granddaughter, but his smile is anything but grandfatherly. He is a man of refined tastes, in both wine and women. 'Before we discuss business, let us try one last wine. Not a great vintage but a young Ukrainian wine. A Cagur. A little sweet. Like port. But strong and honest. Like our friendship!'

It is as he has promised, clean, honest, brimming with the taste of blackcurrant. This bottle they drink, not taste, as they sit across the flickering flame of the candle and he quotes the prices he expects. For the Tokay, twenty thousand hryvna a case. Which is fair. For the Madeira, nearly thirty. But it is too dense, she protests, like ink. It is like a woman's virtue, he replies, you will get double for it in London.

She laughs, returns his stare, which in the candle-light suggests more than simply business. He is exceptionally good-looking for his age, his frame elegant and self-disciplined. Undoubtedly experienced. To her surprise she wonders what he is like in bed. She's never been to bed with a man over sixty.

'You are wondering, perhaps, what an old man like me is doing with such longing for a beautiful woman like you, Elizabeth?' he enquires with startling insight. 'Have no cares,' he laughs. 'Before we are even halfway through this bottle I shall probably not even be able to stand.'

Suddenly she feels elated. For as they discuss the wines she might buy and she struggles with the mental arithmetic of conversion, it's as though a great weight has been lifted from her. She will take twenty cases. Average cost quoted by Vladimir of £2,600. She will sell half the cases at auction through Sotheby's for what she estimates will be double the price paid. Which will leave her with another ten cases absolutely free, and available for sale at an even larger mark-up at The Kremlin. With only a little luck she might clear £75,000 on this deal, enough to sort out all her own cash-flow problems. Next time that undersized, illegitimate and copulatory bank manager of hers can pay for his own lunch.

'Vladimir, I like this place. I like this wine.' Without wanting to admit it, she likes him too. 'I think we have a deal.'

'Magnificent! So tonight we shall have a little party, you and I. But first, a toast. To beauty.'

Vladimir drains the last of his wine and with an agile flourish throws the empty glass against the cellar wall. Elizabeth, giggling and a little intoxicated from the alcohol and excitement, does the same.

Vladimir leans across and kisses her, in celebration, and not like a granddaughter. He feels warm, smells good, masculine. She notices he isn't having the slightest trouble standing.

FOUR

Mary Wetherell climbed out of her taxi in front of the Army & Navy Club, wondering what dinner might hold in store for her. You could never tell with Amadeus. Bit of a mad bugger, was the Colonel.

He'd been one of her course instructors at Sandhurst and even at forty he'd been able to flay most of them around the cross-country course. A warrior, not just a soldier. He wasn't the type who fitted neatly into the little boxes so favoured by the planners and their flow charts. Instead Amadeus adopted an idiosyncratic and almost detached approach to authority which inspired as much enthusiasm from the junior ranks as it raised eyebrows amongst the apple polishers. He would make a point of wearing his camouflage trousers so crumpled, for instance, that they might have been taken from the back of a teenager's closet. They were battle fatigues, he explained, they weren't intended to be covered in spray starch but in mud and unpleasant bits of anatomy, preferably some-one else's.

There was also the leg of lamb. It had been served up as an excuse for dinner, a joint so gruesome and gristle-bound that it probably contravened several provisions of the Geneva Convention. Amadeus hadn't just complained, he had acted. On the spot and in full view of the entire Sandhurst mess hall, he had convened a field court martial at which the carcass had been accused, tried and summarily condemned, whereupon amidst much cheering and ribaldry it had been taken to the firing range, propped against a sandbag and repeatedly shot. 'And when we've run out of carcasses we'll start on the cooks,' he had announced. Standards in the mess hall improved rapidly after that.

No, dinner with the Colonel was never likely to be dull.

That wasn't the only reason she had accepted the invitation. It had arrived on a day of purple clouds over Exmoor that melted with the dawn, when the rains drummed interminably upon her patience and the rivers of slurry hadn't stopped until they reached the Bristol Channel. It got her to thinking, which was bad. She hadn't been out of the valley in two months, had trouble remembering when she had last seen anything as exciting as a traffic light. She was spending more time than ever on distractions. On the Internet, on solitary walks. Away from her husband.

They'd had a row when she said she was going to London, a silly, pointless grumbling match, and endless, too. Had he sensed what she sensed, that it was all going wretchedly wrong for them? That this wasn't simply an invitation to London but an excuse to run away? He didn't regard himself as her jailer, but she knew it would hurt him if she went. Trouble was, things had got to the point where it would do more harm to stay. She needed to breathe once more, to stretch her wings. To fly away.

'Glad you've come. You can add a bit of class to this bunch,' Amadeus offered as he made the introductions to the other two dinner guests in the bar. 'This excuse for illegitimacy is Captain Andrew McKenzie, late of the Royal Engineers. Met him in Bosnia when he was with 33 EOD, dragging out a Scimitar crew that had run themselves into the middle of a minefield. He's completely mad. The other one comes from a much longer line of bastards – may I present Major the Honourable Freddie Payne? Grenadier Guards, which was formerly commanded by his father. Known as the Great Payne amongst his colleagues in the regiment, for some reason . . .'

As they exchanged greetings, Mary found her instincts immediately abraded and sensitized. The Army & Navy Club was an unambiguously male bastion, she felt out of place here, and it seemed as though she were watching them all from a distance. She felt uneasy about Freddie Payne from the moment he opened his over-confident mouth. Too much bloody nose, a class thing. Yet there was hunger in his eyes and, she thought, a glint of fear. Like a man who every day has to cross a tightrope just to live, knowing that one day he must surely fall. The air of confidence was a mask as carefully constructed as his expensively capped teeth.

Her feminine instincts played an entirely different game with the other guest, McKenzie, a Highland Scot by upbringing and accent. He was quieter, more intense, not so much withdrawn as watching. On watch, even. He was softly spoken but his sharp blue eyes never rested, as though searching a Highland river for salmon. She could smell the animal in him. She was both shocked and amused to discover herself looking for his wedding ring; she was still more amused to discover there wasn't one. For a moment, Exmoor seemed very far away. So was Cambodia, from where McKenzie had recently returned after several months' defusing land mines.

'Why d'you do it, Andy? After all, there's damn all money in it,' Amadeus probed.

'Perhaps I simply like making things go bang.'

'Bloody dangerous work.'

'Even more bloody dangerous if the work's no' done.'

'Trouble with you, Andy, you are the most dangerous kind of soldier,' Amadeus concluded. 'Not only a rifle and a sackful of explosive, but principles as well.'

'Little wonder there was no place for me in the modern Army,' the engineer replied softly. He gave a perfunctory smile to take the cutting edge off his comment, but Mary noticed the humour failed to reach as far as his eyes. She also noted that Amadeus had spoken in the present tense, like a man who couldn't let go.

Payne had arrived at the club by an entirely different route. Amadeus had met him during a tour of duty in Northern Ireland which, according to every other unit in the Army, was one of the few postings where Guardsmen did active duty with anything other than pink gins and pussy. Payne's speciality had been reconnaissance, tracking bandits through the rough terrain of the border country and into the bad-arse areas of Belfast and Derry. Seeing without being seen. Not a soft posting, for had he been caught his ultimate fate was undeniable. A bullet in the back of the head. The only matter left to argument was what they would have done to him before putting him out of his agony. The choices ranged from a portable Black & Decker drill through the kneecaps to a sledgehammer applied with vigour to both his feet. Either way you weren't going to walk to your funeral.

Payne had seen Amadeus's letter while in a crowded commuter train on his way to his job in a Mayfair gallery. He had stood – he'd had no choice on that front, for even if he'd fainted he would have been kept upright by the press of bodies around him – and melted with self-recognition as he had read it, particularly the line about 'a greater humiliation than surrender'.

He understood humiliation. On a daily basis. For Payne had married both well and badly. Well, because of his wife's connections, the daughter of a former Governor of Bermuda whom he had met when serving as the Governor's ADC; badly, appallingly badly, because she had turned out to be such a genetically untameable shrew. Her ceaseless harassment had been tolerable while Payne remained an officer in the Guards, their lifestyle maintained by regular subsidies from his father which covered mess bills, polo ponies, skiing in Villars and two spoilt daughters. Yet nothing lasts for ever. His father had fallen into that black hole of financial despair called Lloyd's and, seeing no respite, had blasted his cares away with both barrels of a shotgun. A Purdey. Tortoiseshell stock, beautiful balance. A family heirloom, later to be sold along with all the rest. 'The simple dignity of being shot', in the words of Amadeus's letter. 'Nothing but spite and selfishness', according to his wife, who regardless of Lloyd's expected her comforts and connections to be maintained, may blisters abound in her crotch.

Payne couldn't break away. There were times, dark times, when he understood how his father must have felt. He knew he had no grand intellect, that's why he'd failed the Staff College exams. Twice. There were times when blowing out even a half-brain seemed like a reasonable option, if only to annoy his wife. But here, at least, in the Army & Navy Club, he felt safe, with his wife out of sight and hearing on that dark side of the moon they call Crawley. He felt revived, almost like old times, glad he had written to Amadeus.

The Colonel led them upstairs to the dining room, where they were seated in a quiet corner overlooking St James's Square. On all sides towered portraits of great men.

'How about a toast? To the heroes of our nation,' Amadeus offered.

'England expects?' the Scot muttered.

'Expects too damned much nowadays,' Payne responded. 'Lay down your life. Then pay for your own fucking funeral. Bit like marriage.'

With that, the game began.

*　　*　　*

87

As the *hors d'oeuvres* arrived, they began to compete with each other. During the first bottle they fought to prove how the British Army was still the best in the world; during the second they began to acknowledge that, arguably, this was no longer the case. Their best battles were behind them. By the time the third had been ordered, the game had focused on finding ever more vivid means of expressing their contempt for the politicians who had broken faith with them and with so many of their colleagues. The fourth bottle made it clear how much they thought it still mattered to them.

'Know what those useless sons-of-Soviets are up to? Flogging everything – enriched uranium, any sort of surface-to-air stuff, even full-scale C&B armouries. It's a nightmare . . . I know a private collector who bought a T-60 tank last month. Arranged it on the Internet. They even offered him high-explosive squash-heads for the bloody thing, just imagine . . . That pond life we have for a Foreign Secretary whines on about an era of peace. Doesn't he know there are at least three active war zones less than a couple of hours' flying time from London . . . Don't bother flying. Fuck, come home with me. Hell of a lot closer than Chechnya. Warfare every damned day . . . D'ya ken, there are more ter- rorist groups out on the streets of Europe now than there were when they bulldozed the Berlin Wall . . . Hey, more means of delivery, too. Not just missiles but suitcase bombs, toxins . . . How long would it take to wipe out half of London Underground, d'you reckon? Probably got time to do it before the cheese course. Come to think of it, great idea, getting wiped out. Before those bastards in the Inland Revenue do it for me. How about another bottle?'

'And when you've finished ordering it, Peter, shall we stop playing with ourselves and get you to tell us what the devil we're all doing here?'

'Ah, Mary, always the direct one. Tell me, how is your former Commanding Officer? Still crawling around on his hands and knees looking for the pieces of his tooth?'

'I sincerely hope so.' For a moment memories tugged at the corners of her mouth. 'But enough of the diversionary tactics, Peter. Cough. What are we celebrating?'

'Celebrating? Not quite the word I would use.' Amadeus's tone grew pensive, almost sad. 'Met a man the other day, my old RSM. You know the type – would take a raw recruit at breakfast, scare the shit out of him by lunch and by supper have him ripping tanks apart with his teeth. One of the most remarkable men I ever had the honour of serving with. Or getting legless with, come to that. Saved my life once. Mount Longdon. That's when I swore I would always be there for him.' He paused. 'Know where he lives now? On the street. Swapped his uniform for an old dog blanket. Nearly killed himself rushing to pick up one of my cigarette butts.' He rolled his glass between his palms but didn't drink. 'I felt ashamed. To the bottom of my being. I said to myself – this shouldn't be. I owe him. And all the others like him.'

'So you write a letter to the bloody newspaper saying so, and the Minister tells you to go fuck yourself,' Payne interjected, a shade too forcefully. Amadeus studied him carefully, suspecting that the Guardsman had had a drink or two before he'd arrived at the club.

'What you say is true. I wanted an apology from the Minister. Some sign of remorse. It would have helped. Only words, I know, but words are important in a matter of honour. And this *is* a matter of honour. But the Minister wouldn't have it, insisted on telling me and every other man and woman connected with the armed forces to . . . How did you so eloquently put it, Freddie?'

'To go fuck ourselves.'

'Precisely. So unnecessary, I thought. Not a gentleman, our Mr Earwick.' For a moment it appeared as though he had finished while he attacked his rump steak until the blood ran around his plate.

'So what are you going to do about it?'

'Mary, what gives you the idea that I plan to do anything about it?'

'Because I remember Swanleigh.'

'Swanleigh?'

'The cadet who fell asleep in one of the classes you were instructing at Sandhurst.'

'Aaahh . . .'

'You had him stripped and thrown into the river. That's you all over, Peter. You don't take crap lying down.'

'But I was so soft,' Amadeus protested.

'Soft? You had his feet tied!'

'I left his hands free.'

'It was the middle of bloody February. There was ice on the river . . .'

'Was there?' He sounded almost distracted. 'Splendid. I bet the dopey bastard never fell asleep in class again. Or on patrol, either.'

Mary laughed. Her laughter was like a call from a distant mountain, noises from a time past. Suddenly she realized how much she was enjoying her day – the invigorating chaos of London, the adventure of meeting new people, even someone like Payne, the excitement of discussing something other than warble fly and infected udders around the dinner table. She was engaged in life once more. She'd almost forgotten what it was like. Suddenly, she dreaded going back.

McKenzie took up the challenge. 'So what are ye going to do, Peter? Grab Earwig and douse him in the river, too?'

'What would be the point, Andy?'

'To encourage him to more vigilance. To change his mind, perhaps.'

'Assuming he has a mind to change.'

'Then what about the unadulterated pleasure of revenge? That'd be enough for some.'

Amadeus pushed aside his glass of wine, which had scarcely been touched. It was as though he were making room on the table cloth in front of him for a plan of battle. 'I think we need more than that. Much more. We need to move the Government. To change their mind.' Gently, almost tenderly, he smoothed out the creases in the linen. 'Or have it changed for them.'

'What, bloody revolution?'

'No, not revolution. Perhaps more along the lines of a little encouragement. A gentle prod in the right direction. I think they need reminding that the world can still be full of misfortune.'

'Tell us 'bout it,' Payne muttered, heavy tongued, as he refilled his own glass.

'That's why I invited you all here for dinner. To see whether any of you might be interested in . . . a matter of honour.' He returned to the phrase once again, like a call to arms. Or an alibi, perhaps.

He gazed around the table. All three of his guests returned his stare, even Payne, through eyes that were turning to glass.

'It would require a little risk. And perhaps more than a little time. Here in London, Mary,' he added, addressing her directly.

'Not a problem. I'm not going back to Exmoor.' Her words startled her. The words were entirely unexpected; she hadn't known until this moment. Yet it seemed so obvious.

'But what is it that four of us can do?' McKenzie pressed.

'Look at yourselves. All of you specialists. The finest the British Army can produce. Communications. Reconnaissance. Munitions. One lunatic Paratrooper. Expertise and madness – the sort of talents that ought to scare the hell out of anyone with a little imagination. And what could we do?' He looked slowly around the table, staring once more into their eyes, testing them. 'Why, practically anything we damn well wanted!'

He began to beat his fists upon the table, as though beating a drum, until the cutlery rattled and the glasses sang. And, one by one, the others joined him, a war party, until the noise became so loud that it echoed around the large dining hall.

The waiter turned and slowly shook his head. He might have known it. Ah, Colonel Amadeus. Bit of a mad bugger, that one. Or so he'd heard.

Goodfellowe's pager stirred. He uttered something rude and not at all profound. The wretched thing made him feel like a criminal, allowed to roam only on condition that he was electronically tagged. For tuppence he'd have thrown the thing in the Thames, but for ambition he now kept it with him, and switched on.

The small screen lit up and began to flash a sickly green.

'UNLESS YOUR AREA WHIP ADVISES YOU OTHERWISE YOU ARE NOW ON A ONE-LINE WHIP.'

Simon says stand up. Simon says stand down. Turn around. Go jump . . .

Was it any different when he'd been a Minister? Had high office given him any more control over his life? Control over others, certainly, but his own life? He tried to remember, but couldn't. It all seemed so long ago, wrapped up with the death of his son Stevie, and he'd spent much of the intervening years trying to block it all out – as his wife Elinor had done, to such terrifying effect.

Goodfellowe rebuked himself; he should stop being churlish. A One-Line Whip meant he didn't have to bother. It was good news. An evening off. And his thoughts turned to Elizabeth, away in the Ukraine. Half seven in London, two hours later in Odessa. Should be back at her hotel by now.

So he rang, but there was no reply. Nor when he tried again half an hour later.

He hated the feeling of emptiness that struck him when she was away, the insecurity that bit into his humour at times like this. Was it that he felt inadequate? Or didn't trust her? Or was it that he didn't trust himself? The more he struggled with the questions, the more he realized he wasn't likely to enjoy any of the answers, so he stopped. He tele-phoned Sam instead.

In the years since the death of Stevie and during the misery of his wife's final and irreversible mental decline, Samantha had often been his only hold on happiness, the rock on which he had managed to rebuild his shattered life. She was now eighteen, studying the history of art at London University, and had digs less than two miles from his own apartment, yet he hadn't seen her in almost a month. His fault. Things always seemed his fault. Time to do something about it.

But life somehow never quite fell into place for Goodfellowe.

'No, don't come round, Dad,' she insisted when he called. 'I'm meeting a friend in half an hour. At the coffee shop. But . . .' – a sudden decision – 'come and join us. He'd love to meet you.'

Whoever 'he' was.

Goodfellowe made it there five minutes early and commandeered a table with a good view of the window. They arrived holding hands. 'Dad, meet Darren. And so forth.' She waved the two together.

Darren's hand was firm, his eye steady, his hair neatly trimmed, indeed everything that one might expect of a graduate student at the Business School, as Darren turned out to be. He was amusing, ambitious, evidently a young man of the world. Holding hands with his daughter. Touching. Brushing against her. Being almost proprietorial.

Goodfellowe decided he'd have to be adult about that. Trouble was, he wasn't always very good at the 'grown-up' thing when it came to his daughter. Every time she produced a new boyfriend it was always the same, that initial feeling of panic and distress. Like sitting in the dentist's chair watching the needle approach, knowing it was likely to hurt.

'It's been too long, Sam,' he smiled, extracting the teabag from his mug. There was nowhere to put the dripping mess. That's how they made tea in a coffee shop.

'S'pose it has,' she offered, trying to bend her youthful mind around the elusive concept of Time. 'Almost like when I was younger. You remember? Those years when I only ever saw you on television?'

It wasn't *intended* to make him feel guilty. She succeeded nonetheless.

'Not quite the same, I dare say.' He made a fuss over his hot tea, as though his lips were burning rather than his cheeks. 'But since we're discussing seeing each other at a distance, did I catch sight of you the other day? At Trafalgar Square?'

She beamed. 'Sensational, wasn't it?'

'Bloody inconvenient. But I got your point.'

'You should have joined in, Dad.'

'I did. No choice. But for what it's worth, I agree, something has to be done.' He bit into a croissant, the pleasure of which was considerably devalued by the avalanche of flakes that was sent tumbling down his chest.

'That's not quite what I expected to hear from a politician, Mr Goodfellowe,' Darren interjected.

'My party bosses frequently tell me that I'm not what they expect from a politician,' he responded, picking crumbs from his tie.

'I don't understand . . . You agree something ought to be done. Everybody seems to agree. So why doesn't it happen?'

Goodfellowe rubbed the motif on his tie, wondering whether it was a stain or the design. 'Because I am a humble backbencher. Parliamentary pond life. If I speak sense no one will hear it above the noise of the rabble. If I shout loud enough for anyone to take notice I simply make myself part of the rabble.' Damn. Stain. 'Anyway, it's all very well setting yourself up as Robin Hood, rushing around trying to right all those wrongs, but I can tell you it gets damp and very cold out there on your own in the forest.'

'You're saying parliamentary politics are pointless?'

'No, not at all. But if you really want to make things happen – as you put it – you need to have your hands on some of the levers. Be a Minister.'

'So it's being a backbencher that is pointless?' Darren pressed, before realizing the unintended slight. 'Oh, I'm sorry, Mr Goodfellowe . . .'

Goodfellowe laughed, wondering how Darren managed to keep his tie so straight. Did he use a different knot? Somewhere he'd read there were seventeen different ways of doing it. 'Call me Tom. And, no, being a backbencher isn't entirely pointless. It only seems that way at times.' Most of the bloody time, actually, but he didn't want to take honesty too far. Might scare the children.

'But I thought you rather enjoyed being Robin Hood,' Sam joined in. 'You know . . . the independence. The free life. Getting out among the serfs.'

'Sure, but . . . It's one of the things I wanted to chat with you about, darling daughter. Get your view. Of course I enjoy playing Robin Hood. It's just that at times – perhaps too many times – you feel about as much use as a fly on a windscreen. That's why I'm thinking of becoming – *trying* to become, at least – a Minister once more.'

'You? A Minister?' Sam sounded startled.

'Bit like you at Trafalgar Square the other day. In fact, just like that. You know, wanting to make a difference.'

'You want to become a Minister?' The question was repeated, very slowly, the breath rattling hoarsely in her throat, with every syllable emphasized as

97

though the words were being constructed from first principles.

'Yes.'

'I can't believe you.'

'Why?'

'You want to join the most bankrupt Government since . . .'

'The economy's a mess, sure, but . . .'

'I'm not talking money,' she bit back, her voice raised. 'Whatever happened to principle? To all those promises that Bendall conned us with at the last election? About education? About the environment? About the future?' She was trembling, her half-drunk cappuccino spilling into the saucer. 'I thought you cared about all that. And now you want to climb into bed with those sleazeballs?'

'It's precisely because I care that I want to help. Make changes. Push the system along from the inside.' He had been taken aback and was grasping for suitable words to explain. 'A wise old Tibetan once said that a single drop of rain upon the desert . . .'

'Dad, this isn't sodding Tibet,' she butted in, shoving her way past his words. 'You're selling out.'

'I'm not. Be reasonable, for God's sake. There has to be a bit of give and take.'

'What – like last time?' There were tears brimming in her eyes, now they were tumbling down her cheeks. 'Haven't we given enough? Mummy? Stevie . . . ?' She could say no more, choking back the pain, scrabbling for a tissue from the bottom of her bag.

Goodfellowe found himself utterly lost in the midst of this sudden blizzard. Hadn't he given enough, too?

What was he supposed to do, give up his ambition, his desire? Turn his back on the new life he had embarked upon, with its influence and its authority? And with Elizabeth? Simply because the Prime Minister had the scruples of a timeshare salesman?

'Sorry, Darren,' he apologized for the family scene. 'Politics are all about passion.'

'I agree.' His voice had remarkable authority for his years. 'That's why I voted for Bendall. He talked about all the things I feel so passionately for.' He shrugged. Broad shoulders, athletic. 'But perhaps I'm naïve. I agree with Sam. Above all politics should be about principle. And for Bendall to take a stand on principle is about as likely as Scunthorpe hosting the next Olympics.'

'That's a little harsh . . '

'A very flexible man, is our Prime Minister. He promised us the earth at the last election. Trouble is, we're still waiting for it. Bit like a drunk in the bar who promises to buy a round but always has to borrow the money to do it. Well, if he won't pay, he'll just have to be forced to pay. And if that means screwing up Trafalgar Square and every other part of London, so be it. Nothing personal, you understand, Mr Goodfellowe.'

'Hang on, I thought you were in business studies,' Goodfellowe offered breathlessly.

'I am. I'm also chair of the university Environmental Alliance. That's how Sam and I met.'

'Well, I suppose it's all very wonderful being young and able to ride two horses at once. Business. Environmentalism. But, sadly, life forces us to make choices – yes, even to make compromises. Just like politics.' He knew it was patronizing crap a millisecond after it'd left his mouth.

'I don't see why. One day I want to run a major corporation. Where better to be if you're passionate about the future of the planet? Or are you still locked in that time warp where all environmentalists wander around in dreadlocks and live in some sweaty tunnel beneath a motorway?'

'Somehow I feel I'm the one who's just been digging himself a hole.' He looked across at Sam, moved his hand towards her. 'I need help. Should I send for a shovel?' It was meant to lighten the moment, a peace offering. She threw back a look of bloodshot betrayal.

Once again Goodfellowe's life had turned into a battlefield upon which the two halves of his being, family and politics, were waging war. Stevie had drowned while Goodfellowe was attending to his red boxes. Too busy to play dad. No one's fault, really, just one of those bloody unfair things. No one had said anything, but Goodfellowe knew that Sam, his wife, everyone, blamed him. He knew that beyond any doubt because he, too, blamed himself. So a family at war, a war that was undeclared but never forgotten. It was the reason why he had resigned as a Minister in the first place, from a sense of guilt and also a sense of duty to his wife and to Sam, to find the space in which he could sort himself out. Yet now his life had become more complicated than ever, with Sam on one side, Elizabeth on the other. Damn.

Sam left without saying goodbye, one arm wrapped in proprietorial fashion around Darren's waist, the other wiping an eye. Her parting words were little more than an accusation. 'Daddy, you've changed.'

Had he? Was his mind already shuttered? Had he already fallen into Ministerial mode? He was clambering back over the wall, but did this mean he would have to leave Sam behind? She was pleading with him to stop, while Elizabeth, and all the other things he wanted for himself, were pushing him onward. Torn to pieces by the two women he loved most in the world.

He got back to his apartment around ten, and telephoned Elizabeth once more. He wasn't checking up, merely wanted to say goodnight.

Still no reply.

It took Amadeus three days and nights to find him.

He was all but unrecognizable in the lamplight beneath the covering of cardboard. The face was blackened more effectively than any camouflage stick could manage, because the dust never stopped swirling at gutter level.

Amadeus squatted beside him in the foul-smelling doorway, squeezing him aside to make room, silencing the storm of protest by producing a full pack of cigarettes.

'So, Albert Andrew, I was sort of wondering.'

'Won'ring what?' Scully snarled, in between hungry draws on the first cigarette. 'Sir,' he added as the nicotine began to calm him. Old habits.

'Whether you've had enough of sitting on your arse in shop doorways. Bumming drinks and cigarette ends. Smelling like a field latrine.'

'Wha' the fuck's it gotta do wi' you?'

'Oh, Skulls,' Amadeus scolded. Of course it had to do with him. 'I've got something of a proposition. See if you want to get back into the business.'

'Business?' The eyes were darting in agitation around the alleyway as though he feared someone was about to pounce and steal his precious cigarettes. He didn't seem to want to look at Amadeus.

'Red Devil business.'

'No such bleedin' business any more. They don't fuckin' want me. An' I've got a busted fucking foot.'

'*I* want you, Skulls. You were the best soldier who ever served with me. You see, me and a few pals, we've got a little skirmish planned. We want your help.'

The red-blown eyes steadied, lost their look of a wild ferret, and considered. Somebody wanted him again. It had been such a long time since anybody had wanted him.

'Fuck you, Co'nel.'

Slowly a hand extended from beneath the dirty blanket. Scully pushed a cigarette towards Amadeus. A peace offering.

'No thanks, RSM. Given it up all of a sudden. Got better things to do.'

Scully's lips were cracked and sore, but working hard now to rub a little precision back into his speech. 'You think I'm up to it?'

102

'After a wash and a good breakfast, sure. Can you give up the booze?'

'Booze? You think I'm a drunk? Wha' do you reckon I'm trying to do, fucking kill meself?'

'No, I want you to leave that to me.'

Slowly, in the manner of an elderly dog, Scully began to shake himself. Layers of blanket and bad times began to fall from him until he was standing, almost erect in spite of his foot.

'Breakfast, eh? It's a deal. Dunno about the fucking bath, though.'

'Wouldn't you like to know what it is I want you to do?'

'Don't nced to. Not if it's you askin', Colonel.'

A silence. Then, softly: 'Thanks, Skulls.'

Scully began to scratch himself with considerable vigour. 'Only one question, sir.'

'Give it.'

'Which way's the fucking canteen?'

Now there are five.

Amadeus, the leader.

Scully, the loyal disciple.

McKenzie, the man of principle, who is drinking in a pub in Victoria with others he's met earlier that evening at a lecture sponsored by Amnesty. For him it's the principle of the thing, coupled with the adventure.

Then there is Payne, a man of confusion. A man who knows fear all too well. He is also drinking, heavily, in his club on St James's. Indeed, Freddie

Payne is drunk. He has been gambling heavily, at backgammon. Losing. He hasn't the funds with him to pay his debts, in fact he doesn't have the money anywhere, so he leaves an IOU. Payment within two weeks. Such things are acceptable, amongst gentlemen, so long as the debt is honoured. For Freddie Payne, life always seems to be a matter of honour. And a burden.

Mary Wetherell is at home. Or what passes as home. A room in a desperately undistinguished boarding house behind Shepherd's Bush. She sits in the dark, listening to the thunder of traffic past her window, hoping it will drown out the ringing of her mobile phone. The display informs her that the caller is her husband. She doesn't answer.

He rings twice more that evening, until she switches the phone off. Only then does she let go of her tears.

FIVE

'Welcome home, darling.' No sooner had he said it than Goodfellowe realized his good humour was probably a terrible idea. Elizabeth was looking at him as if he were a rabbit in her vegetable patch. He could feel the stems of the roses he was carrying beginning to buckle in his hand.

'Not your fault, poppet,' she muttered before disappearing into her little office at the rear of the restaurant. He pursued her.

'What's not my fault?'

She picked up a large sheaf of papers from amongst the clutter that covered her desk, then threw it back down again in disgust. 'I've just had a cancellation. Ten for tonight. We might as well rename this place the Marie Celeste.' Her maximum cover was only fifty; the missing ten would take a hefty bite out of her week's work.

'Can't you start charging a cancellation fee?'

'And make sure they never book in the first place?' Clearly she wasn't in the mood for masculine logic. This wasn't to be a problem-solving session, she simply wanted an audience, someone to share with, and perhaps to shout at.

'Then this,' she continued, throwing a letter at him

from the very top of the pile. From a Mr Sandman of Shepherd's Bush Green. 'The lease is up for renewal and the bastards want to shove the rent up another fifty per cent. In the middle of a bloody recession!'

It hadn't been the triumphant return from Odessa she had expected. The rent rise would cost her sixty thousand, practically the entire profit she would make on the wine. She was back to square one.

'Sorry, darling,' she offered in remorse, at last catching sight of the roses. She placed her arms around him and held him tight.

'Yeah, me too.' He had missed her more than he could have thought, a feeling made all the more intense by the difficulty in telephoning. He had come to The Kremlin intending to tell her so, with roses to show her that she was the most important thing in his life and that he couldn't imagine living without her, but it was the wrong time. The bloody landlord had got there first.

'It's just that we're coming up to the end of the financial year and business always goes quiet around then. Cash flow's going to be tough. And my house is the guarantee for the overdraft.'

'Surely you're not suggesting that the restaurant might . . .' He didn't want to complete the thought; even so, it stuck there like cold goose fat. 'What will you do?'

'Maybe I'll pull in some of the hotel concierges for a free dinner. See if they'll push some of the tourist trade our way. If not, I'll have to let one of the chefs go.' Or maybe sell off all the wine at auction. She needed the money up front.

She began sorting through the bottles in the wine rack beside her desk, feeling better now that she had indulged her outburst. 'It's either that or marry a rich peer,' she joked. She held a bottle up to inspect the label. 'Fancy being my bit on the side?'

He had arrived with emotions like a tightly wound spring. He, too, needed the chance to unburden himself, but he wasn't going to get it, not today. Discussion of her finances reminded him how irrelevant he was to a huge part of her life. He was not a provider, merely an observer. In the circumstances her humour fell flat.

'Drink, Tom?' she asked, searching beneath the clutter for a corkscrew.

'Not right now. Only wanted to pop over to say . . . to make sure you got back safely. Busy back at the House,' he lied. 'See you later.'

Damn. The moment had gone, lost its varnish, been rubbed down to the bare wood.

Lunch at the members' table of Payne's club had been simple. Faggots. Little balls of god-knows-what covered in a dark gravy and washed down with a carafe of excellent club claret, followed by a large cognac to settle the stomach, and another just for the hell of it.

No, let's be honest, not just for the hell of it. Because he *needed* it. That morning he'd lost the sale he'd been working on for weeks, and his commission with it. The week before he'd told Charlie, the owner of the gallery in King Street, that the sale had been made, that it was only a matter of tidying up the paperwork. An excuse to get an advance on the commission. Now he'd have to go back and face Charlie. Fuck it. He damned the slick-haired little bastard from Kyoto who'd run out on the deal even more quickly than his granddad had scarpered out of Singapore. Couldn't trust the Nips. Not then. Not now. *'Not my fault, Charlie old chap, truly, but you know what these bloody heathens are like . . .'* To console himself he had another cognac. Maybe something would turn up.

It did, even before he'd made it out of the club. In the cloakroom, while he was still struggling to get his arm into the sleeve of his raincoat. In the shape of Jamie Cairncross.

'Freddie, allow me to assist you.'

'Jamie! Ah, thanks . . .'

'Looking well, Freddie, good to see it. Thought you might've been ailing or something.' The slightest pause. 'Hadn't seen you around for a couple of weeks.'

'No, I'm . . .'

'Not seen you since our little game, in fact. Enjoyed it. Must do it again some time.'

'Sure . . .'

'Chance to get your own back.'

'Yeah.' Payne was still struggling with his coat. His companion's efforts to assist seemed to have achieved nothing but to entangle Payne still further, as though his hands had been tied behind his back, denying him any chance of escape.

'But in the meantime, my old mucker, there's the matter of that IOU of yours. Due yesterday.'

'Oh really? Shag my old nanny, really? Lost track of the date.'

'And eight thousand quid's a bit thick to go overdue. You know? Bad form.'

'Good God, Jamie, you don't think . . . ?' With a savage effort Payne at last wrenched himself free from his companion's embrace and turned to face him. 'Look, tell you what. Let me give you lunch here this time next week. Take the afternoon off and we'll make a real go of it. Sort it out then. Double or nothing if you like.'

'No, no thanks, Freddie. Just the eight thousand'll do.'

'Grand, whatever you like. This time next week, then. Dashing just now, got a deal to do with a little Nip from Nagasaki or wherever. You know how they don't like to be kept waiting. So I'll see you next week?'

And he was outside, stumbling into the street, the afternoon rain sneaking its way into the soles of his hand-stitched shoes that were long overdue for repair.

Oh, shit. Shit. *Shit. Shit. Shit.*

Ramsay MacDonald, the first Labour Prime Minister, once bought a painting by one Samuel Scott that for many years hung in the inner hallway of Number Ten. The painting is dated 1755 and features a view of Horse Guards beyond the walled garden of Downing Street. It also features two men urinating up against the wall, although whether they are politicians, or simply members of the public expressing their point of view about politicians, is unclear.

The aspect featured in the painting remains largely unchanged to this day. The wall still stands around the garden, affording Downing Street a measure of security, although much less effective against modern forms of protest. In 1991 the IRA fired mortar bombs from the back of a lorry parked outside the Ministry of Defence. The bombs passed over Downing Street and fell into the garden, only narrowly failing to kill the Prime Minister, John Major, and a large number of his Cabinet. Walls, no matter how high, would not have been enough. Today, security in this area is afforded largely by vigilance – and dozens of security cameras covering every point of access.

The layers of protection overlap like the skin of a vast onion. Inside Downing Street the doormen oversee a large bank of screens linked to the closed-circuit cameras. The doormen are also responsible for monitoring the control panels of the alarm systems that are attached to the doors and windows throughout the building. Even the great black front door is nowadays made of blastproof metal and has detector systems around and even underneath it, designed to ensure that no one with hostile intent can pass undetected – unless, of course, he is carrying a Ministerial red box.

Outside, there is a cat's cradle of security services. Downing Street itself and the environs of the neighbouring Foreign Office are patrolled by armed policemen of the Diplomatic Protection Group, while Special Branch takes care of the personal security of the

Prime Minister as he enters and leaves. Everything in front of the wrought-iron gates guarding Downing Street is the responsibility of the Metropolitan Police, while to the rear runs a claret-coloured road dividing the Government area from the lush acres of St James's Park, which is monitored by the Royal Parks Constabulary. If that were not enough, Bronwyn the cat can often be found keeping watch over the comings and goings in the street from her post on the air-conditioning duct beside the front door. DPG, SB, the Met, RPC, an entire menagerie. More than enough security, you would have thought.

Or, perhaps, too much.

General Karl von Clausewitz, the nineteenth-century military strategist, wrote the famed treatise entitled *On War* in which he described the quality of boldness as 'the noblest of virtues, the true steel which gives the weapon its edge and brilliancy'. It is a standard text at Sandhurst.

So when, towards evening, a water contractor's van began travelling slowly down the claret-coloured road, in full view of anyone who cared to look from any of a thousand windows overlooking the park, no one's suspicion was unduly roused. Not the DPG, the Parks Police, Special Branch, certainly not those monitoring the security screens within Downing Street over their mugs of tea. None of those whose balls were going to be hammered mercilessly into the ground the following day had any reason for misgiving. After all, a telephone call had been made to the Parks Police that afternoon, supported by an immediate fax of confirmation, explaining a slight loss of water pressure in the area and a requirement to investigate.

Which is where too much security can fall apart. For the claret-coloured road was frontier land, marking in somewhat uncertain fashion where the responsibilities of the Parks Police, the DPG and the Met rubbed up against and overlapped each other. The road itself was clearly the responsibility of the Parks Police – but who was supposed to be responsible for the manhole cover in the pavement alongside?

As a matter of course, a Vehicle Identification Mark verification was run on the van when it arrived, and in the normal course of events the VIM check should have revealed that the vehicle had been stolen a few days beforehand in North London. But the registration plates had been changed to duplicate those of a genuine and unstolen van. The computer said it was kosher.

In the back of the van had been the papers that provided the letterhead used on the fax. All the details of the letterhead were genuine, except for the contact telephone number, which had been altered after it had been scanned into Mary's computer. Not that anyone from the Parks Police checked. After all, they'd already had a telephone call and a piece of paper. Their backsides were covered. Until the morning.

So when the van arrived at the back of Downing Street and a small awning was erected around the manhole cover, no one raised the alarm. The scene was overlooked by no fewer than five security cameras, and one of the workmen went out of his way to chat with a duty policeman and show him a copy of the fax. He had a pronounced limp. Not the material from which top-line terrorists are carved.

Nothing was being hidden. All four workmen wore brilliantly luminescent yellow work jackets that would have been impossible to miss even at midnight, let alone at a time of day just before the street lamps were lit. Not exactly broad daylight, but neither was it the dead of night. And the rear doors of the van were wide open, revealing the usual paraphernalia of utility workmen. The Prime Minister was unlikely to be under undue threat from a flying shovel.

Thirty-one thousand kilomctres of mains water pipes run beneath London, through which two thousand two hundred million litres of water flow every day. Relatively little of this was used in Downing Street since only four people actually lived there, the Chancellor and his wife in Number 11, and the Right Honourable and Mrs Jonathan Bendall in the next-door premises. On the night in question, as anyone who rcad a newspaper would know, the Walrus and wife were away in Washington DC while Mr and Mrs Bendall were attending a formal dinner and not likely to get back until almost midnight. Downing Street was practically empty, with only a handful of civil servants left manning the bunker. Their demands on the water supply were light, a few cups of tea, the occasional flushing loo.

No one even noticed the slight interruption of the water supply.

*　　*　　*

They located the square-pin valve about three feet down, beneath a sheet of polystyrene that protected it from frost. McKenzie had done this all dozens of times before. In Kosovo one of the Sappers' many duties had been to reinvent the water supply. The others – Amadeus, Scully, Payne – also understood. They'd manned the Green Goddesses during the firemen's strikes. They knew water. Simple stuff.

A six-inch main ran directly from the valve in the direction of Downing Street. It was old, constructed of cast iron rather than modern blue polyethylene, but not as old as many in the area. This section of piping had been replaced in the early 1960s when Downing Street had been largely rebuilt after they'd discovered that the original developer, George Downing, had been a wholesale cheat – 'a perfidious rogue and a most ungrateful villain', as Pepys had described him. Not only had Downing cheated the axe during the Civil War by constantly changing loyalties, he had also cheated the taxpayers by building his famous street without proper foundations. The staircase sagged, the walls bowed and upper floors bent. So the Prime Minister Harold Macmillan had moved out while the structural engineers moved in. Downing Street had been completely refurbished. Safe as houses.

It was as McKenzie was positioning himself above the valve to begin his work that he thought someone was shooting at him. A ringing sound, so sharp it made his heart shudder. But there was no impact, no pain, in the end nothing more than a rueful Scully.

He'd dropped the heavy metal valve key from the back of the van and it had bounced angrily off the pavement, its complaints echoing back across Horse Guards. Scully scratched his broad chin in apology. None of the watchers seemed alarmed. McKenzie got back to work.

The valve key was retrieved and slipped into place, locating over the square-pin spindle of the valve. A couple of turns and the water would die, but it wasn't yet time. First they put a repair sleeve in position around the main, like a bandage to heal a wound, but for the moment it was left loose. Once the sleeve was in place they began to twist the valve key until the flow of water died. Then came the hole. Drilled to the size of a two-pound coin, through the cast-iron pipe and into the main. Normally with ten atmospheres of pressure behind it the pierced main would have sent a fountain of water gushing forty feet in the air, but with the valve turned off it did nothing more than dribble miserably.

It took only seconds to stuff the pellets – fifty of them – through the hole and into the main, a few seconds more to slide the sleeve over the wound and bind it tight. Then the valve was released. From the main they could hear the gentle hiss of water flowing once more under pressure. Mission complete. Downing Street was back on stream. It had been without water for little more than two minutes.

Within twenty minutes of arriving, the water van had left. Darkness had now fallen and the rattle of traffic along the claret-coloured road had subsided.

A pelican called from the park as it settled down for the night.

Samuel Scott, reborn, would have recognized the scene instantly. In two and a half centuries, only the boldness with which protesters pissed up against the wall had changed.

It was, by consensus throughout the country, an outrage.

The second person in the country to discover this outrage was none other than the Prime Minister himself. At 6.45 a.m., with the gentle sigh of a blade being inserted between his ribs, a large manila envelope had been pushed beneath his bedroom door. It was the draft of the speech he was due to make the following afternoon to bankers and industrialists in the City. An important speech, and a first draft. A draft heavy on rhetoric and utterly impenetrable to detailed financial analysis. So a good draft.

For a few moments Bendall tried to fight the intrusion, refusing to stir, allowing his weariness to wash over him, hoping for sleep. But he hadn't slept properly for months. Perils of the trade.

There was another reason why he resisted opening his eyes. How he hated this bedroom, stuck under the eaves of Downing Street with its low ceilings and floral overload. His wife had no eye for simplicity, no sense of order, so every corner was crammed with ideas plundered from different pages of the catalogue. Frills, flowers, frump, a cross between Laura Ashley and Peter Jones-on-the-run. Tentatively he prised open one eye. Directly above him, from the canopy above the kitsch four-poster bed, a large red rose stared at him like some hungry triffid. He groaned. Time to rise.

He was sitting in his dressing gown with his second cup of black coffee, two sugars, checking the draft, when the commotion occurred. His pen was poised above a proposed sound bite rendered, he had to admit, with considerable skill by his speechwriters. It was an appeal to the Dunkirk spirit, rousing national passions amongst tabloid editors and, by implication, suggesting that it was the City and its unpatriotic money men who were in large measure respon-sible for this latest crisis. But he hesitated. Hadn't he, when he was Leader of the Opposition, said something very rude about 'the sickening sight of a Prime Minister trying to embrace the Dunkirk spirit in the way a common drunk reaches for a lamppost'? He was debating the memory spans of most political journalists when his concentration was shattered by what appeared in the room before him.

In the doorway leading from the bathroom stood his wife. She was naked. Her navel was heaving. It was an awesome navel, a route map of the march of time, a detailed historical record of childbirth, sur-gery, charity teas and, ultimately, lack of resolution. It was also the colour of a stagnant pond. As was the rest of her.

She stood like some demented and melting Tele-tubby, her whole body streaming with garishly coloured rivulets, shampoo suds in her eyes, her hair hanging limply like the tattered rigging of a sinking ship. A tide of glistening green slime was spreading on the carpet around her feet.

And she was screaming her head off.

'OK, let's get on with it. Before we start on the detail, let's get a feel for the mood of the Parliamentary Party. Chief Whip?' Bendall turned to Eddie Rankin, seated at the end of the Cabinet table. Bendall preferred formality at Cabinet, particularly emergency meetings such as this one. He'd hated all the Tom-Dick-and-Harriet first name nonsense favoured by his predecessor. Cabinet wasn't about bonding, it was about beating the system – and beating Ministers – into some sort of identifiable shape. Nothing personal, it was simply business. Use their Christian names instead of departmental titles and it gave them nothing to hide behind, made all defeats a personal slight. It started feuds, extended rancour, and there was no need to cause unnecessary personal antagonism, not when the farmyard of political life was already awash with enough of the necessary kind.

Rankin chewed his cheek. 'Well, Prime Minister, let me start by saying it's not all bad news. The attack was clearly aimed at you personally and it's done wonders for your own ratings. Nothing like it for getting the troops to rally round.'

Bendall raised an eyebrow and a wry smile, the first of the day. 'I shall begin to think you might have organized it yourself.'

'If I'd thought of it, I might have done. But there may be trouble ahead. The lads want to know why it was so easy to mess with the water supply of the most sensitive piece of real estate in the country. There are worries they may be targets, too. They're refusing to water their whisky. There's a danger of our majority getting swept away on a flood of neat alcohol.'

Rankin was an indispensable tool for the Prime Minister. He was calm, cool, with a gentle sense of humour that helped to defuse many difficult situations, but this was a no-win meeting, there were bound to be casualties along the way. Bendall was not to be deterred.

'Before we all find ourselves drinking in the Last Chance Saloon, perhaps we can catch the bastards concerned. What about it, Home Secretary?'

Noel Hope, the Home Secretary, had carried two great burdens throughout his political life. The first was the middle name bestowed upon him by his dull-witted parents.

His middle name was Osmond.

N.O. Hope.

An unfortunate label to be stuck with. One of God's little gifts to political rivals and graffiti artists. His majority was regularly three thousand less than it ought to be, simply because throughout every campaign the opposition were utterly merciless. They simply took the piss out of him.

Thanks, Dad.

The second burden was less apparent but struck still deeper. At Oxford, he and Jonathan Bendall had been contemporaries. The best and the brightest. And it was Hope who initially had shown the greater intellectual and sporting prowess. It was Hope who would gain both the better degree, and the football blue. But they also vied for something far more intimate, the presidency of the Union, and over the three years of head-to-head encounters in the debating chamber it was Bendall who, through rhetorical flair and a compelling meanness of wit, won every encounter. Every damned one.

Something was missing in Hope, those sinews of steel that drag a man through hardship and out the other side. It left him as Bendall's silent whipping boy, both of them knowing that he hadn't that necessary quality ever to take Bendall's place, other than by the most happy of accidents. So Hope's career in Cabinet had on the one hand been spent in dread of once more being turned on by Bendall, and on the other in silent prayer that the bus with the Prime Minister's name on it might be waiting just around the next corner.

'First, Prime Minister, let me start by offering a measure of reassurance,' Hope began, sounding considerably more confident than he felt. His briefing on this was absurdly thin. 'Forensics at Aldermaston have already established that the substance used in the attack was nothing worse than food dye. Not in the least harmful. I'm sure your wife will make a complete and rapid recovery, Prime Minister.'

So much he knew. It wasn't the food dye that had sent her off to hospital under sedation, although the shock had been unpleasant enough. No, what had pushed his wife to the very edge was the fact that, as she stood in the middle of their bedroom, wobbling, screaming and completely vulnerable, the door had burst open and in had charged McGivens, a personal protection officer, brandishing a Glock 9mm and pointing it in her direction. This had sent her into hysterics.

This was to prove unwise, for as her screaming redoubled a second and yet a third protection officer burst upon the scene, at which point Mrs Bendall had taken the only sensible course of action available to her and fainted. It was rumoured that McGivens, too, had required treatment for shock.

'Food dye? That reassures you? Then how easily you are comforted, Home Secretary. They could have put any damned thing into the system. Why, even a truth serum. Think of it. The consequences could have been devastating.'

Bendall smiled, performing, fighting woes with wit, and around the table they all responded dutifully, very British, until he sliced through the humour.

'It could have been anything! The most monstrous substance known to man. Typhus. Anthrax. You talk of reassurance and God knows I've tried, Home Secretary. I've looked at it every way I can, but I'm damned if I can find a single shred of reassurance in any of this. My wife could be dead. *I* could be dead. The whole of our system of government paralysed.'

Hope now knew he was on trial. 'I believe we are all very conscious of the potential seriousness of what has happened, Prime Minister. I think I speak for all your friends around this table in expressing our relief and joy that it did not turn out to be more serious.'

His friends around this table? Bendall had few true friends, and none in this room. His leadership qualities had been based not on intimacy but in no small part on his campaigning abilities, constructed around a richly decorated voice that expressed things, even nothing, with exceptional eloquence. His phrases were well seasoned, capable of turning the dullest of statements into a worthwhile sound bite. But the words were merely tools, and while they were being employed the eyes remained expressionless. It was said that the closer you got to Bendall, the less you understood him, although, it had to be admitted, such things were never said very loudly, and not while you still had ambition.

Hope cleared his throat. 'Sadly, there is little the food dye can tell us about the perpetrators since it is readily obtainable and won't be easy to trace. What we do know is that the action was carried out in little more than twenty minutes last evening by four men using a stolen water contractor's van. It seems they temporarily interrupted the water supply and introduced the dye into the system.'

'Slowly,' Bendall instructed, holding his hand up like a traffic policeman. 'Pass that by me once more. A van was parked right outside Downing Street? Poisoning the water? And no one checked?'

'Indeed they did, Prime Minister,' Hope responded forcefully, making the best of his meagre defences. 'A vehicle identification check was carried out by a member of the Diplomatic Protection Group.' Then, somewhat less positively: 'However, although the van was stolen, it was apparently using false plates. The computer in Swansea gave it a clean bill of health.'

'Ah, so it was the computer's fault. Now I understand.' His expression was so stiff it might have been chiselled. The eyes were arctic.

Hope retreated to his second line of defence. 'A telephone call was made to the Parks Police to say that there was a pressure problem, the water mains would have to be checked. Confirmation was faxed through. While the work was being undertaken, a Parks Police constable engaged one of the men in conversation . . .'

'Conversation, good. Never let it be said that the British bobby lacks courtesy. Didn't anyone think to offer them a cup of tea or a guided tour?'

Hope cleared his throat once more. This was just like Oxford. He could feel the heat rising beneath his collar, his head dropped and his eyes danced around his briefing paper like a condemned man invited to inspect the noose. He needed an escape route. He didn't like what he was going to do next, but the ditches along the road to survival are filled with one's friends.

'Sadly, the Royal Parks Constabulary is not the responsibility of the Home Office.' A brief shuffle of papers. 'It falls under the auspices of the Department of Culture, Media and Sport.'

It was as though Hercule Poirot had turned round in the sitting room and pointed an accusing finger at his own maiden aunt. All eyes swivelled upon the hapless Secretary of State for Culture, a sensitive individual whose idea of mayhem amounted to nothing more than raising entrance fees for museums and attending an occasional meeting of the Arts Council. He was way out of his depth, and looked as if he might drown beneath the ripples on the brown baize tablecloth. The Home Secretary sat back in his seat, the mark of Judas on his moist brow.

'Ah, this is a cultural matter. I should have guessed.' Bendall's tone suggested for all the world that he might be chiding himself for being so pedestrian. 'And what light can you shine upon us?'

'Very little, I'm afraid,' the Culture Secretary stuttered. 'I . . . I was at the theatre last night.' His office hadn't even realized he was in the frame until two hours ago.

'But your policemen, at least, were on duty. Even chatted to them while they were playing games with my plumbing. So what did they look like?'

'It was dark. They all wore hats,' the Culture Secretary offered, barely above a whisper.

'It was dark. They all – wore hats,' Bendall repeated doggedly, in case the gods had missed this admission while they were drawing up the Bill of Execution, but he didn't bother to pursue either the point or the man. It would be like burning the wings off a beetle, enjoyable only if you were an extreme sadist or exceptionally bored. Instead, he turned once more to Hope. 'Let's try the surveillance cameras. I assume you're willing to take responsibility for those, Home Secretary. Some of them, at least?'

Hope undertook an instant diversionary tactic.

'Colleagues may remember, Prime Minister, that security expenditure has been cut in three successive Budgets. Maintenance and upgrading of these systems are woefully behind what I would have desired and, indeed, recommended in my Budget submissions.' It wasn't a particularly adept attempt to shuffle off the blame elsewhere, but dancing on coals is never elegant. Across the table, the Chancellor bristled in indignation.

'We are having the images computer-enhanced,' Hope continued, 'but . . .' – he drew himself in – 'as the Culture Secretary said, it was getting dark. The police are not optimistic.'

'Somebody – I think it was George Bernard Shaw – once wrote that to do nothing at all is the most difficult thing in the world. Yet your security forces appear to have achieved it, Home Secretary. I congratulate you.'

'Actually, it was Oscar Wilde . . .'

Silence. The silence that prevails in the moments before the trapdoor falls. Faces turned in sorrow towards Hope, the man who had chosen to contradict Bendall in his present mood. A small slip, perhaps, but when you are standing above a trapdoor . . . Then suddenly Bendall laughed. 'You're probably right. Bloody Wilde. You're probably right. And I don't mind being told I'm wrong. Why, as Prime Minister I shall fight to your death for your right to say so.'

And everyone around the table joined in the humour, even those more practised observers who had noticed Bendall's deliberate twisting of the aphorism, and with it, Hope's neck.

Hope. His lifelong colleague and rival. A man so desperately removed from reality that he had chosen this of all moments to try and score a debating point. Just like Oxford. Like a dog eating its own vomit. But soon the feast would be over. The time had come to elevate Hope to that great Cabinet table in the sky. Another Banquo. Another eternal enemy. Another risk. Bendall felt the collar of Macbeth weigh heavily on him and getting tighter all the time. There would come a point, there always came a point, where his Administration could no longer be presented as a vine in need of pruning but would be seen as a gangrenous carcass with no prospect of revival. It happened to them all, Thatcher, Major, Blair. In the long run they were all victims, it was only a matter of time. But how much time? Oh, if only he had a little oracle to guide him, yet all he had was focus groups. So he would go on cutting and slashing in order to save himself, because in the end that's what all Prime Ministers did. Sacrifice others in order to save themselves. He had no alternative – and, as he would explain patiently to the political editors, in this case no choice. The public demanded a Home Secretary who was constructed of altogether sterner stuff, one who was more capable of kicking hell out of the European Court, and even a few illegal immigrants, if he could get away with it. Someone skilled in the black arts of propaganda and punishment.

Someone just like young Earwig.

SIX

Goodfellowe is doodling at his desk. He can't concentrate. Every moment of his day, from the time he leaves his front door in the heart of Chinatown until he cycles wearily back, is filled with problems. Other people's problems, which crowd in upon him. There never seems time enough for his own.

Yet at the end of the day, when the door of his tiny apartment thumps shut behind him, his life suddenly seems full of empty spaces. The private loneliness behind the public smile.

It's why the presence of Elizabeth in his life has become so important. She fills so many of those empty spaces within him. She is a class act, it rubs off on him, and gives him the sort of sexual self-esteem that is important in a man approaching fifty and who still has ambition. Sexual self-esteem is vital in the chaotic world of Westminster. The lust that enables a man to seduce and satisfy a woman often walks hand in hand with the desire to seduce an entire nation, and so it is with Goodfellowe. Elizabeth gives him the strength to climb Ministerial mountains, although the daily mountain of constituency correspondence is another matter entirely.

Goodfellowe's heart sinks as an elegantly crafted

pair of legs enters his House of Commons office supporting a pile of letters that look as though they could fill a dozen waste bins, and eventually almost certainly will. Somewhere behind it all lurks Mickey Ross, his secretary. It has been said that those elegant legs have got her off more speeding tickets than possession of a Chief Constable's warrant card, although when she wants, which is frequently, they prove even more effective at getting her into a little trouble.

'Morning, bwana.' Her usual tone, as if she doesn't give a stuff about anything. She does, of course, but hates to admit it. Tough East End upbringing. Rules of survival not decreed by the Marquess of Queensberry.

'And what has my favourite native wench brought me today?'

The pile of correspondence wobbles. 'The good news or the bad news?'

'Get on with it.'

'OK, so here's one from the Typing and Terrorism Brigade. Local section.' A letter flutters like a flag of surrender.

'The officer workers' union? What do they want this time?'

'Your undying support in a case of industrial injury. It appears that one of their merry widows yawned so hard at work that she dislocated her jaw. Now they want compensation on the grounds that the job was so jaw-twistingly boring it amounted to a health hazard.'

'You are kidding, of course.'

An ornate eyebrow arches in rebuke. Goodfellowe groans.

'So what's the good news?'

'The really good news – this will really nibble your nuts – is that the employer in this appalling case of industrial abuse is none other than the Marshwood branch of the National Farmers' Union.'

Goodfellowe's groans reach a higher pitch of intensity. His local brotherhoods, Mafia and Masons, knocking six bells out of each other, with him in the middle like a carcass stretched between two stampeding horses.

The mountain of letters approaches. An avalanche is about to bury him.

'Anything else?' It's a plea. Go easy on me. Go away, even. But, as usual, it's Have-A-Go-At-Goodfellowe Day.

'The usual birthday letters to eighteen-year-olds. Declaring your undying interest in their lifestyles and personal futures now they have the vote.' The tone leaves no doubt as to her comprehensive disbelief.

'I was young once,' he protests in his own defence.

'Listening to Barry Manilow does not make you young.'

More correspondence appears.

'Then there are begging letters to be signed to your Patrons Club, a letter to your bank manager inviting him to lunch . . .'

'Overdrawn again?' he mumbles.

It has become their habit, at times of more than usual financial embarrassment, to invite the bank manager to lunch in the House where he can be subjected to their combined persuasive abilities. In Goodfellowe's case, this means producing a Minister who will join them for a drink. In Mickey's case, it means wearing a blouse several degrees beyond modesty. However, the bank manager is now used to this treatment, forcing Goodfellowe to employ the firepower of ever more senior statesmen, and Mickey to discover ever more intricate ways of revealing her qualities. Soon one of them is going to run out of cover.

'And Trevor called.' The sigh on her lips implies more than the average weight of problems.

Trevor Fairbanks is the treasurer of Goodfellowe's constituency party. In that position he is the rock on which many of Goodfellowe's political fortunes are built. His is perhaps the least popular job in the executive, without the glamour of the chair or the rhetoric of the political committee, which explains why he has held on to the position for almost a decade. No one else wants it.

Yet it is a position of hidden strength, for whatever goes on within the constituency party, from planning election campaigns to replacing a typewriter ribbon or a jar of coffee, requires money. So Trevor knows everything that's going on. Usually before it happens.

Local politics can be far more predatory and personalized than at Westminster. In the constant game of one-upmanship that infects Marshwood, Trevor Fairbanks is a steadfast friend of Tom Goodfellowe, a one-man watchtower at the heart of the constituency from where he can spot forest fires even as they are lit, while Goodfellowe has his back turned in Parliament. He is Goodfellowe's Praetorian Guard. He also has a bad heart.

'He's been to see the doctor.' At last Mickey places the pile of letters in front of him, where they peer over the edge of his desk, threatening to jump.

'What's he want? Another holiday?' Goodfellowe growls distractedly, scrabbling amidst the paper.

'You're not going to like this, Tom, but his doctor insists. Immediate retirement.'

'What, not even a little gentle politics?'

'Especially no politics.'

He is suddenly alert. He seems to have aged five years in a moment. 'Oh, damn the gods. You know what that means?'

'What does it mean?'

The air escapes from him as if it were his last. 'Beryl. That's what it means. Bloody Beryl.'

The letter arrived at Downing Street as the Cabinet was meeting in their emergency session. It was handed to one of the constables on duty at the gate by a motorcycle messenger. The messenger had no face, only a helmet.

Paperwork pollutes all aspects of Westminster. It is the debris that clogs the system and causes the gutters of delay and discontent to overflow. If Goodfellowe believed he had a problem with paper, it was as nothing compared with the tide of correspondence that pours forth every day like a mudslide and all but overwhelms the Prime Minister's correspondence secretaries. Forget all you may have imagined about the glories of Downing Street, for at best it is a pleasant if poorly planned Restoration townhouse, yet on most days for those inside it bears a far closer resemblance to a Victorian sweatshop. Much of the sweating is done in the correspondence unit, located in the basement, where temperatures and language are known to resemble the boiler room of the *Titanic* at full speed.

All letters are routinely screened for explosives (and, it has to be said, for still more personally offensive content). If they pass this first examination, they are then subjected to a series of further tests to determine how they will be handled, and onto which pile they will be placed, for there are several piles.

The first pile is reserved for letters requiring instant action – correspondence from friends of the Prime Minister, or those he might like to have as friends. A second pile, less urgent, is passed to other parts of the Government machine for draft replies, which are generated in large part by computer.

A third, much larger, pile is set aside for complaints. To the beleaguered members of the Prime Minister's correspondence unit it often seems that every Englishman's father was a shop steward and his mother a fishwife, while the Scots rarely seem to have had any parents at all. Such letters never even get close to the Prime Minister, although all will receive replies. Eventually.

Yet another pile is reserved for letters categorized as being written by eccentrics, often devoted but quite dotty people who will wait eagerly and for weeks for their reply, signed by some minor placeling at Downing Street, which they will frame and display on the mantelshelf alongside their late husbands' ashes.

For the correspondence secretaries there is no resting place.

Amadeus's letter arrived on a day that was neither more nor less frantic than any other, which meant that his letter was one of nearly a thousand. He had taken great care with its drafting, seeking to explain, entirely anonymously, why he and the others had done what they had done, and once again demanding an apology on behalf of all former servicemen and women. He had taken great care to hide his identity. The paper and the envelope had been purchased at the Sloane Square branch of WH Smith, and handled only with gloves. The envelope was self-sealing and had required no stamp, so no trace of saliva was available for DNA testing. The letter had also been prepared in his bursar's office rather than at home. The dot-matrix printer at the school was from a major manufacturer and on the point of being junked, which would make any prospect of tracing the physical source of the letter all the more impossible.

Which is where Amadeus made his mistake and began to sow the seeds of exquisite confusion. For Amadeus's problem with letters was lifelong and intense. A dyslexic. Word-blind. From his earliest years he had struggled with the art of reading and writing, his brain turning into a kaleidoscope of confusion every time a letter of the alphabet knocked at its door. To Amadeus, the whole world was an impossible anagram. Like sieving treacle. And through this sieve 'b's became 'd's, 'j's turned into 'g's and 'f's into 't's. The words on the paper in front of him often bore only passing acquaintance with those he carried in his mind. As a boy he had written to a maiden aunt thanking her for the tuck money she had sent, and in return had received a sound thrashing. He had been regarded as a difficult child.

In many ways, it had been the making of him – as it had other word-blind people, like Leonardo da Vinci, Thomas Edison, Nelson Rockefeller. At school he'd had to push himself harder than the rest, finding new ways of attacking a problem. Lateral thinking and a formidable memory, qualities that had marked him out at Sandhurst, had become his means of avoiding the minefield of words. His talents lay in the practicalities of warfare, not in its paperwork, which is why he had become a Paratrooper. Completing the *Times* crossword hadn't been a prerequisite for jumping out of a Hercules at 600 feet with a hundred pounds of equipment hooked to his chest, knowing that in thirty seconds he might be dead or broken. His word blindness was also, perhaps, why he knew he would never become a general, and instead had become a leader.

Not that he could avoid paperwork entirely. He'd always wanted to command, but he couldn't command a Para battalion without going through Staff College first. It was perhaps the greatest battle he'd ever fought. He'd survived only through stubbornness and pride and the spell-check programme on his word processor, and later there was always someone else, an adjutant or secretary or even reluctant wife, to help the spell-check programme make the right choice between laughing and fucking and ducking. But, late at night in his bursar's office, there was no one to help him compose his letter to the Prime Minister. So he took exaggerated care, reading and rereading it until his mind had become an impenetrable jungle. The spell-check programme sanctioned the letter. Twice.

Yet dyslexia is a strange affliction. It can wax and wane like the moon, but without its predictability. And, according to some, the problem can be magnified at times of unusual stress. In any event, despite the great care Amadeus had taken, and notwithstanding the support of spell-check, the letter that was opened by the harassed secretary in the correspondence unit began: *'Dear Pry Minister, Yew are . . .'*

Almost a thousand letters a day. Every day. Which requires the correspondence unit to process more than one hundred letters an hour. Two every minute. On average, one every thirty seconds.

Amadeus's letter didn't get its thirty seconds. Wiping her brow from the heat of the boiler room, the correspondence secretary let forth a small moan of frustration as she read. Then she threw Amadeus's letter straight onto the pile marked with a large hand-written label: 'NUTTERS'.

Thoughts of Beryl left Goodfellowe ominously distracted as he set foot inside the Members' Lobby.

Her family name was Hailstone, as was her effect.

Enough hair lacquer to spark an environmental alert and buttocks so abundant they might have required separate passports. Distinguishing features? How much time do you have? Her dress sense would have better been put to designing tablecloths. Yet she could hardly be described as flippant. She was the chair of the constituency party in Marshwood – in effect, Goodfellowe's employer – and she had about as much time for him as she might have for a request for oral sex from Saddam Hussein.

Oh, but politics would be impossible without structures such as Beryl. She was indefatigable, unbending and, when necessary – which in constituency politics was frequently – utterly unreasonable. She drove others to the limits of exhaustion and beyond, which meant that when the crucial decisions were made, she was there to make them almost by herself, other more reasonable mortals having long since returned to their families. For Beryl had no family. She was a spinster of the parish, 'married to Marshwood', as she would declaim. Had she been a man she would have made a formidable Member of Parliament, and had she arrived on the scene twenty years later there would have been some politically correct quota that would have insisted she be so. But as it was, Beryl was out of time, a victim of male insecurity – 'the Little Willy Syndrome', as she called it – and in Beryl's eyes, Goodfellowe was the shrimpiest of them all. The man who now occupied her rightful place in the nation's council. Who five years ago had irresponsibly thrown away his Ministerial office and with it Marshwood's short-cut to the inside track.

And the man who, several years before that, had rebuffed her passions.

It shouldn't have been a moment for resistance. The occasion was an executive committee meeting, shortly before Trevor Fairbanks appeared on the scene. Beryl had swept all before her, all because of the drains.

Local politics is often about drains, and those at the Marshwood constituency office had always smelled a bit. Then they had become stubbornly blocked. A plumber was called, who had summoned a surveyor, who announced that the drains were overflowing because the foundations had decided to take an extensive and extremely expensive holiday. They weren't where they should be. The cost of their relocation would inevitably be crippling. Even by the standards of local politics the plight of the Marshwood party was dire, but all agreed afterwards, Beryl had been magnificent.

Estimates for the remedial work had been obtained and the executive committee had gathered in the mood of missionaries facing the pot. Faith can only stretch so far. There was no money, and a repair and restitution order had arrived that morning from the Environmental Health Officer giving them a month to fix it. Had anyone any ideas?

Beryl was the most junior member of the committee, invited because they needed a woman . . . well, even in these modern times, somebody still has to make the tea. Yet three weeks after they had first met she had stood before them, her blouse heaving as though filled with ferrets, and she had produced Mr Gupta. Mr Gupta proved to be their salvation, a local businessman with a cautious smile and a pinkish wart on the end of his nose who craved three things: his secretary, planning permission for a site he owned near the by-pass, and an invitation to Downing Street. He suspected that achieving the latter would assist him greatly in obtaining the planning consent which, once granted, would enable him to elevate his secretary to the position of office manager and *en passant* to leverage himself into her bed.

Not that the executive committee of the local Marshwood party was able to peer into the dark convolutions that marked Mr Gupta's soul. All the members knew was that the man wanted to be helpful, and how much more did they need? So Goodfellowe had arranged the invitation to Downing Street, a reception for several hundred, nothing of great import, but enough to guarantee Mr Gupta a photograph alongside Bendall's predecessor and wife and sufficient, during the course of the following week, for Gupta to underwrite the local party's overdraft with an interest-free loan.

Beryl was triumphant. And rampant. As the other members of the committee drifted into the night, exhausted from their repeated rounds of commendation for her efforts, Goodfellowe had discovered himself with Beryl in the tiny kitchen of their sinking office. She was clearing up the biscuit crumbs and emptying tea slops into a galvanized bucket. He, too, had wanted to express some form of admiration for her efforts but had always found words with Beryl difficult, so instead he had placed a congratulatory hand upon her shoulder.

This had caused her to turn and face him. In the confined space, and with Beryl built like a medieval siege machine, he had suddenly found himself trapped. It must have been like this at Stalingrad. There was crimson in her cheek and a weird, acquisitive glint in her eye. Before he knew it, he was under direct assault, those lips advancing and closing in on him like a sea fog.

It was not that he had rejected her that caused her passion to turn into undying enmity, it was more the manner of his rejection. The fact that he had retreated so instinctively, a look of abject terror twisted across his face, his innermost feelings laid bare. Revealing the things he truly felt about, and for, Beryl. The sort of emotion that no man should declare. There was no time for the diplomacy of muttered condolences or passing excuses about his wife, nothing that might help reestablish their precoital relations, nothing but an upturned galvanized bucket, a banging door and a car disappearing hastily into the night.

Every time Goodfellowe looked out of his window thereafter, the siege machine was waiting, looming darkly on his doorstep, ready to exploit any weakness in his defence. Their relationship had degenerated into warfare, during which Trevor had been his staunchest ally. Now Trevor was gone. Goodfellowe was on his own, and the rumblings about deselection that had surfaced before the last election would sound like drums of war before the next.

So Goodfellowe was distracted as he crossed the Members' Lobby on his way to take a seat in the Chamber. So distracted, in fact, he even signed the Early Day Motion that someone thrust in front of him. Early Day Motions are parliamentary billboards on which backbenchers scribble their names to protest about something, or someone. If there were enough names to show genuine grievance, the Speaker might even allow them a debate, but more frequently EDMs amounted to little more than graffiti. Jimmy's a Wanker, Tessa's a Slag, Down With Fat Cats. That level of sophistication.

This particular Motion implored the House 'to take note of the recent call by the Shadow Chancellor of the Exchequer for increased subsidies to the textile industry', while drawing attention 'with surprise and disapproval to the fact that the Right Honourable Gentleman habitually wears nothing but Italian suits'. In truth the EDM had stuff-all to do with the plight of beleaguered weavers and dyers, and everything to do with the fact that for the past twenty-three years the Shadow Chancellor had enjoyed the comforts of an Italian mistress. And let no one forget it! Tommy's a Double-Dealing Dog! A Wop Shagger!! The Motion was about as subtle as a can of spray paint.

Normally Goodfellowe would have passed by on the other side and would not have been tempted, let alone inhaled. But he was distracted. So he signed.

Added his name to the parliamentary scribble. Anyway, he wanted to become a team player once more; he had to begin to show a little willing.

Goodfellowe was forced to push his way through, jostling to find a seat in the busy Chamber as Members gathered for Prime Minister's Question Time. They sat in long and rowdy rows, in the manner of crows crowded along a telephone line waiting for roadkill. Over many years Question Time had proved a more profound test of Prime Ministerial mettle than most of the nation's leaders cared for. Macmillan, for instance, had been a true professional, acting his way through his premiership with the aplomb of a seasoned performer at the Old Vic, but before entering upon the stage for Question Time even SuperMac had been overtaken by anxiety. On occasion his aides had found him bent over a sink, throwing up.

Now, thanks to live television and the blow-by-blow coverage it gave to this hugely devalued occasion, the entire country could throw up.

Before he'd even started, Bendall had made trouble for himself. Members were distressed by the attack on the water supply, not because they cared particularly about the circumstances of Bendall but because it amounted to an attack on the heart of government, an attack on them all. Hell, this wasn't just a matter of water but an incitement to terrorists and germ warriors everywhere. It was one of those occasions when their concern was genuine and to meet their concern Bendall should have granted them a full parliamentary statement, an open and frank exchange, but his instincts were otherwise. He considered the time he spent in the House of Commons as wasted and he'd become accustomed to ducking and diving rather than delivering. Anyway, he had so little to say, knew so little of the real reasons behind the attack, so he covered his ignorance in insult and evasion. From their perches, the crows began to squawk their displeasure.

'When will he make sure our water is safe?'

It was a simple enough question. Too bloody simple. He hadn't a clue about what he was going to do, except pass the buck.

First he laid down a smokescreen. He used words like 'deprecate' and 'wanton act of violence', he adopted a tone that was selfless and a pose that was statesmanlike, but being noble wasn't enough. So, 'I have instructed the Home Secretary to mount an immediate inquiry . . .' – in other words, let me make one thing perfectly clear, folks. *Any shortcomings in security are the responsibility of Bloody Hopeless.*

'But what about the water?' a plaintive voice insisted from somewhere across the Chamber.

'The specific issue of water quality is a matter for OFWAT, the water regulator . . .'

What are they going to do, then?

'As I have just explained, that is a matter primarily for the independent regulator . . .' *How the hell do I know? OFWAT is independent. I don't control them.*

So how much?

How much what?

How much is it going to cost to make the water safe enough to put in the whisky?

'These are early days . . .' *I've got no damned idea. But whatever it costs. What else can I say? Would someone ask me a different question? How about the upcoming summit meetings, for instance? Anything but bloody water!*

Oh, but damn the Papacy and all its wicked works, if London is to get better water, doesn't the same apply to those most loyal citizens of Ulster, too?

Bendall's shoulders almost sagged. 'The Honourable Gentleman has made an interesting point . . .' – *Well . . . I suppose so, with reluctance, yes.*

The whole country, in fact?

Yes.

So how much is all that going to cost, then?

'Allow me to repeat what I said to the House a moment ago . . .' – *I'll spell it out to those who are simply too thick or too inattentive to have got it first time around. Whatever. It. Costs.*

You could almost hear the thunder of lobby correspondents' hooves as they rushed to instruct their brokers to sell water shares. Water companies operated down deep holes. And that's precisely where their business was heading.

The House was in fractious mood. The Prime Minister had rubbed against them like sandpaper. A feeling hung throughout the Chamber that he must bear *some* responsibility for the situation. After all, it had been his bloody bathtub.

It was at this point that the Father of the House rose from the Opposition benches. Sir Bramble was the longest-serving Member of Parliament who, although well into his eighties, still carried a sardonic smile and a chestful of medals for gallantry from ancient wars fought in his youth. He also possessed wandering hands, if secretarial gossip was to be believed, or perhaps it was only a rumour that he himself propagated. In any event his hands were now well in evidence, grasping his lapels as he turned in the direction of the Despatch Box and the early evening news.

'Is the Prime Minister aware that we on this side of the House applaud his determination to ensure the security of the country's water supplies? Even if in the circumstances it appears a trifle belated . . .' The firm angle of his mouth implied that this was no more than a ranging shot. He was simply gauging distance. 'But wouldn't he accept that there is one way above all he can ensure such security? That's not to put a rocket up the Home Secretary, as much as I wish him well in his endeavours. It's certainly not to cast shareholders of the water companies into penury. The only way he can deliver on his promise is to apprehend the villains. Who are these wretches? What does he know about 'em? When's he going to catch 'em? Eh?'

Sir Bramble was an old duffer but it was an excellent point. A growl of enthusiasm rippled out from those around him until it had infected the entire House. Bendall stood isolated, a mariner facing the storm.

'The entire country will understand, indeed Britain expects, that this Government will not cease in its efforts . . .'

More heckling. They knew he was bluffing. 'Answer the question! Who are they? What does he know?' The Opposition benches became agitated, like a sea hurling itself against a foundering ship as Order Papers were waved in protest. Bendall gripped the Despatch Box with both hands, determined that he was not to be swept from his position.

'Does the Opposition want to listen? The country is listening. And watching their efforts to score cheap points from a matter of great national concern. They're pathetic!'

He pointed at the baying ranks opposite. Behind him his own side were at last rallying to the cause.

'That isn't an Opposition,' Bendall continued, jabbing his finger across the Chamber as though trying to gouge out their eyes, 'it's nothing more than a rabble!'

The tempest struck and for many moments the noise became intolerable, making it impossible for him to be heard. He'd won his respite. It took several moments of considerable parliamentary indignity before the storm had subsided sufficiently to allow the Leader of the Opposition, Oliver Creech, to take his place at the Despatch Box.

'Isn't it clear,' Creech began, loading every word 'and clear beyond any question, that the Prime Minister has lost control? He's lost control of the economy, and quite obviously of his colleagues . . .' – Government backbenchers bayed like imbeciles, and Creech paused extravagantly to allow them to make the point for him – 'but isn't it clear above all that he has now lost control of the country? It's bad enough that he's put Britain on the breadline, now he can't even guarantee us *water*!'

The sound bite had been delivered, tomorrow's

headlines guaranteed. Above their heads the Sirens in the press gallery were composing frantically while below them the ship of state seemed all but dis-masted.

But Bendall hadn't stood at the helm for four years without learning to master his fear.

'I am a fortunate man, Mr Speaker . . .' – *Hang in there, guys, I'm not finished yet.* 'The entire country can now see this Opposition for what it is. A gathering of hypocrites – hypocrites who will sink even to embracing environmental terrorism in order to score cheap points.' He waved his arms theatrically, his cufflinks glinting in the lights. His forelock had fallen across his face and a blue messianic glint appeared in his eye, a look much practised by Bendall in private and held in reserve for just such a time. Now his voice deepened, more vibrato, booming across the Chamber without need of amplification. 'Over recent months in their increasingly desperate quest to find some group who will support them they have backed every strike. Supported every abuse. Climbed into bed with the eco-hooligans and wreckers, those who have strangled our streets, blockaded our power stations, undermined our motorways. They shout about water, yet they lie on their backs for those yobs who want to cut off the power supplies to pensioners.'

It was nonsense, of course, but the noise it gen-erated would ensure that Creech would have to share the headlines in the morning. And time for one last salvo.

'They pretend their politics are green but these

aren't green politics, these are the politics – and the politicians – who would turn this country back into a medieval swamp!'

Behind him, carefully positioned in a stunning red suit to catch the eye of the television cameras, one of Bendall's enthusiastic altar girls tried to stifle a moan of animal desire and almost swooned in delight at this outburst of Prime Ministerial passion. She'd not felt this way since she'd been invited on an RAF orientation course where they had squeezed her into a gravity suit that seemed to fondle every feminine part of her, before she had discovered it could be still more intimately explosive when pulling six Gs in a Tornado. For a few moments the colours swam before her eyes, but she recovered sufficiently to cross her legs and take a mental note of the precise time for her diaries. Parliamentary history was being made, and she was making it. The first politician to have a full-flushed orgasm upon these hallowed leather benches. At least while the House was sitting.

Those who make it to their feet in the Chamber place themselves in the hands of hazard, for no sooner do they start speaking than they discover that the green carpet they are standing on has turned to sand.

Sometimes they are able to make an impression in the parliamentary sands that will endure, some mark that will linger after them for their children and grandchildren to admire. More often, however, the footprints are washed away with the evening tide. And sometimes politicians discover they've stepped into quicksand that is just about to swallow them whole.

Goodfellowe knew all this. He'd seen it all before, yet still he ventured out. He'd been watching the proceedings with wry amusement, detached from the mayhem. It had been a first-class parliamentary cockfight, it would take days for the sand to soak up all that blood. The purists would object, of course, insist that it did nothing but bring Parliament into disrepute, but Goodfellowe had never found much that was pure about politics. However, he was still deeply distracted. The shadow of Beryl was enough to cast a pall across the finest of spectacles. He had only half a mind on the action, hadn't thought the thing through, and was as surprised as anyone to find himself on his feet, wanting to join the fray, for reasons that he himself didn't fully understand. Something was buzzing around in the back of his mind about the sensible environmentalists, and the need to distinguish between the Swampies and the Sams. There was a difference, wasn't there? The Swampies didn't give a stuff about the law, while in Sam's case . . .

Suddenly he was back on his bike. In Trafalgar Square. Confused. But it was too late.

'Is the Prime Minister aware that I wholeheartedly applaud his caution in matters relating to security? Will he allow me to draw him a little further? He has implied that the attack on Downing Street was carried out by some environmental group. Eco-hooligans, I think was the phrase he used . . .'

Several other more lurid phrases were offered by

those around him, which, although heard clearly throughout the entire Chamber, would fail to be recorded in *Hansard*.

Goodfellowe continued. 'Can the Prime Minister tell us why he thinks this attack was an environmental protest?'

It was not only meant to protect Sam but was also intended to be helpful – in Goodfellowe's view, the Prime Minister could only gain by being a little more explicit, and solemn, about the matter. It was an invitation to regain the high ground. However, in his distraction Goodfellowe had failed to comprehend one crucial factor. Bendall didn't want the high ground. When it came down to it, he hadn't a single shred of evidence that this mess was the responsibility of green-freaks, but it was a reasonable assumption and he desperately needed a scapegoat. Anyway, it was all good rhetoric, and admitting he had no bloody idea wasn't going to get him anywhere.

'I'm perplexed,' Bendall began his reply, his brow wrinkled, his eyes dismissive, as though inspecting cold porridge. 'Has my Honourable Friend been sitting elsewhere for the last half hour? I thought I'd made things really rather plain. The reason I suspect it is the work of eco-hooligans is simple. It's not pensioners and nurses who are trying to close down our power stations. It's not motorists digging tunnels beneath our motorways. It's certainly not commuters and shopkeepers bringing London grinding to a halt by staging protests at every corner. And in case he hadn't already figured it out for himself, I can assure him it wasn't me or my wife who decided to turn our bathroom into an environmental war zone.'

Goodfellowe was being made to feel like an alien life form, a visitor from another galaxy which had somehow blundered onto earth.

'To be brutally frank,' Bendall continued, 'if the Honourable Member for Marshwood truly wants to be helpful, he'd do far better by bringing round some bath scourer. Then he could really help us clean up. Eh?'

Bendall was in no mood to take prisoners. Two places down from the Prime Minister, the Chief Whip turned in his seat to cast a look of scorn at Goodfellowe. The lips parted to form a silent but unmistakable word.

'Idiot.'

SEVEN

A day of broken skies and clouds like sheets of crumpled kitchen towel. Mary's mood precisely matched the weather. She sat along with the others on top of an open-deck sightseeing bus as it crawled along Regent Street, doing battle with the traffic. Condensation clung to the plastic seats and there was the constant vague tang of diesel fuel in the air. Around them sat a scattering of Japanese tourists. An unlikely meeting place, perhaps, but good for security. Amadeus had reasoned that the surroundings would make anyone trying to observe them stand out 'like crap in a bowl of custard', and the constant rumble of London made it impossible for them to be overheard.

The bus continued to pass slowly in front of the fine Nash buildings that lined the crescent of Regent Street, and Mary's eyes snagged upon those of a man sitting at a first-floor window. He had the sort of sad, distant-world expression that suggested he might be thinking of jumping, but for the fact that the window was, after all, only on the first floor and constructed of plate glass. Behind him the wine bar, of which he was almost certainly the proprietor, stood empty. His eyes seemed exhausted but, as he caught Mary's glance, he offered her a small wave with plump fingers. Yet the smile was forced. He raised his eyes to heaven, perhaps in hope of discovering salvation, but found only used kitchen towels, and the smile died. Another soon-to-be victim of the downturn.

On the seats around Mary, the morning newspapers were caught by the breeze and began to flap in imitation of dying swans. Their contents were all the same. Water. Suddenly she and the others were famous, or at least notorious. The front pages were filled with Bendall's condemnation of them as hooligans and eco-terrorists. **'PM Slams Eco-Yobs.' 'Bendall Batters Swampies.'** And so forth.

Perhaps, deep inside, Amadeus and his band had hoped that one blow would be enough, that their opponent would acknowledge his error and immediately submit. But Clausewitz had known better. War is never an isolated act, he had written. Victory never comes gift-wrapped. Instead of offering the apology they had demanded, Bendall had piled insult upon indignity, and made it even worse.

'So?'

Payne put the question they all carried in their frowns.

'Fine bunch of crotchkickers we turned out to be. Given Brother Bendall a better press than he's had for months. Look at it all.' The Guardsman picked up the pink pages of his *Financial Times*. 'Still, could've been worse. Hell, we could be the water companies.' He adjusted his rimless reading glasses and seemed almost to smile. 'Getting hammered, they are.'

'But not quite the target we had in mind,' McKenzie added impatiently, failing to see the humour.

'And what really stinks' – Scully threw his edition of the *Express* contemptuously to one side – 'is all this horseshit about us being hooligans and terrorists. I know Bendall's a lying bastard, but why's he lying about us?'

Amadeus examined Scully. How much better he looked for a few days' fodder. Hair neatly trimmed, hiding the streaks of grey, and standing several inches taller in his new clothes. Almost the man Amadeus once knew.

'I sent him a letter, Skulls. Hand delivered. Made it clear enough that this was a military operation, and what we were about. But . . .' A moment's silence, a slow, defiant shake of the head. 'Who knows what goes on in his warped mind?'

'Perhaps that's it. Mind games,' Payne offered.

'What is?'

'What Bendall's doing. Calling us names. Insulting us.' He waved at the newspapers. 'He's playing mind games. He knows it's a military operation that could only have been planned by officers . . .' Payne paused for thought, too late, followed by a moment of drowning as he remembered the presence of Scully. 'Officers . . . and senior NCOs,' Payne added hurriedly, trying to extricate himself. He shouldn't have bothered. 'Anyway, Bendall knows that the last thing we would want is to be thrown in the same barrel as sodding Swampies. So he wants to demean us. To provoke us so seriously that either we walk away in disgust . . .'

'Nail my balls to the top of Big Ben first,' Scully snapped.

'. . . or we show our hand a little too obviously. He hasn't the slightest idea who we are, so he's goading us. Trying to flush us out into the open.'

'But why should he encourage us to do more?' Mary pressed, clearly unconvinced.

'Why the hell not?' Payne retorted. 'We've probably just handed him an extra five points in the opinion polls. At this rate he'd be happy to keep us in business until Christmas. As far as he's concerned, yesterday *was* Christmas.' He paused, sucking at his lower lip. 'Which may be one good reason for pulling out now. While we're still . . .'

'Ahead?'

'Alive. Actually I was thinking "alive".'

McKenzie sniffed, a gesture that might have been an indication of the damp atmosphere rather than of disdain, but only if you didn't know the man. 'Is that what ye want? To pull down our colours?'

'We have to consider that option, Andy. Decide what the hell we're doing here.'

'Getting our own back. Getting the Government to change its mind.'

'And what have we achieved? Made bloody Bendall all the stronger.' Payne wrinkled his nose in disgust. The aroma of roasting coffee from somewhere at street level surrounded them for a few tantalizing moments, before it was swamped by the stench of diesel and drying paint. 'Face it, this is a fuck-up.'

The Engineer's cheeks flushed, as though Payne had slapped him. 'So you do want away, then?'

There was the slightest pause before Payne responded,

a hesitation that spoke all too loudly. 'What I want to know is what the hell we're supposed to do next.'

It was clear that things had changed between them, between them all, and inevitably their eyes began to settle upon Amadeus. He offered no reply, seemed distracted.

'Peter?' McKenzie pressed. First names. No ranks, not in public. Use a military rank in a pub in South Armagh and your life expectancy might be measured in minutes.

When at last Amadeus responded, softly, he seemed not to want to join in their concerns, almost as if he wanted to escape entirely from the problem. 'I was never much of a reader, Andy. How about you?'

The Scotsman seemed startled. 'Why, *Penthouse*, *Hustler*. On a quiet evening maybe a few bomb-disposal manuals . . .'

'What about Livy? Ever read him at the Academy?'

'No' exactly from cover to cover.'

'It's coming back to me. I seem to remember you spent most of your spare time chasing the commandant's daughters. Although, if I recollect properly, neither of 'em ran too far.'

McKenzie's tongue passed briefly across his lips as he tasted sweet memories, but he wasn't to be deflected. It was a characteristic of his, refusing to be deflected from his target, even while under heavy fire. That's why he'd been mentioned in despatches in Bosnia. Twice. 'I believe we were discussing your chum Livy.'

'So we were. Roman historian. Worth struggling

with. He wrote about Hannibal. You remember? The guy who wanted to take his elephants on tour to Italy?'

'Seem to remember one o' the commandant's daughters made a wee mention o' the matter. Said I looked like Hannibal in my uniform, and reminded her of an elephant when I took it off.'

'Must've had something to do with your wrinkled arse,' Mary suggested, attempting to sound disdainful, but McKenzie simply smiled.

'Hannibal wanted to invade Italy,' Amadeus continued, 'but couldn't figure out how – until he had a dream. Now the dream told him to march his elephants over the Alps. Most people thought this wasn't so much a dream as an extended nightmare, but Hannibal had something of the Para in him.'

'He was clinically mad, you mean?'

'I was thinking more stubborn. Bloody stubborn. There was something else, too, because the dream also told him that, once he'd started, he could never stop. That he mustn't even look back. But, as I said, he was a Para . . .'

'Too thick to understand an order, let alone obey it.'

'Obstinate. Unable to resist temptation and a challenge. So he turned to look behind him and saw this huge set of teeth ready to swallow him.'

'Must remind you of your nights with the general's daughters, Andy,' Mary tried again.

'Some o' them, maybe,' McKenzie replied, staring directly into her eyes. Inside he was laughing at her. And why not? If you played with bombs, when every day you risked having your brains blown out through your backside, you were entitled to laugh a little. 'But since it's clear that my brains are located in an entirely different part of my anatomy to the rest o' you, could someone give me just the smallest wee hint where the hell Livy enters into all this?'

'Something to do with not stopping, I guess,' Scully offered.

'Correct. Yesterday was only Day One. We daren't look back, not now. Not unless my balls are to join yours dangling from Big Ben.'

'None of us were trained to run, Peter,' McKenzie added, almost as a challenge to them all.

Payne spoke next, his tone no longer aggressive. 'So the next step is . . . what?'

Before Amadeus could answer, any further attempt at conversation was drowned by an eruption of protest from all sides. While they had been talking, the bus had been inching forward ever more slowly, like a boat rowing through thick weed, until any trace of progress had disappeared and it had come to a full stop. It could advance no further, yet neither could it retreat, and it was blocking one of the main escape routes from Piccadilly Circus. Exasperated drivers in other vehicles began to push forward, trying to squeeze round the obstruction, but every yard they gained succeeded only in strangling the other escape routes until everything began to choke. The Circus was dying, and the horns of a hundred vehicles wailed in dismay.

'This is Hell!' Payne barked, resentful.

'No, no,' Amadeus roared above the clamour, suddenly exhilarated. His eyes had grown several watts brighter as they cast around the scenes of disorder. 'Can't you see? This is like Hannibal's dream! London is talking to us.'

'And telling us what?'

'That we should give Mr Bendall precisely what he wants.'

'Which is?'

'An opportunity to get to know us a damn sight better.'

He drew them into a huddle around him, and as they bent their heads he began gesticulating forcefully, one hand chopping repeatedly across the palm of the other as he made his points. It was several minutes before Amadeus straightened his back. The Circus was still blocked, the chaos continuing to grow. A few feet away, the statue of Eros rose disdainfully above it all.

'By the time we're finished with Mr Bendall, he'll wish he had wings to fly away,' Amadeus concluded.

'Balls of lead, too,' Scully added.

'Are we all agreed, then?' He looked around at faces filled with renewed expectation. 'Good. Let's go round up an elephant.'

They prepare to depart. Payne picks up his copy of the *Financial Times* and heads for the stairs. When he reaches them he pauses, glancing back at Mary. 'Fancy a spot of lunch? Terrific little Italian bistro just around the corner. Superb linguini . . .'

'Sorry, can't,' she replies in a flat tone. His gaze is a little too obvious. Something instinctive, feminine, tells her she doesn't much like him. Anyway, she's already agreed to have lunch with McKenzie.

Payne shrugs, his smile suggesting it's a matter of considerable indifference to him, and disappears.

They make their way off the bus, one by one, Scully the last to leave with Amadeus. The RSM scratches away at a stubborn tuft of grey stubble that has survived beneath his left ear. Perhaps he isn't yet back into the routine of shaving every morning. Or perhaps nowadays he simply misses little pieces of the picture.

'You look troubled, Andrew.'

The scratching stops abruptly. 'Can't help thinking about bloody Hannibal, sir.'

'What about bloody Hannibal?'

Furrows stretch across Scully's brow. 'You know, after the elephants and the Alps. Didn't they end up kebabbing the bastard?'

Following his encounter the previous day with the Prime Ministerial lash, it might have been understandable if Goodfellowe had felt a little sorry for himself. He didn't. He was surprised to discover that he saw it not so much as a humiliation as a rite of passage, like some Tuareg initiation ritual designed to summon up the blood before setting out on a lion hunt or mounting a raid on the slaver caravans. The scars were necessary, even welcome, because they would remind him. No more wandering distractedly into the Chamber with only half a mind on the game, no more flippant gestures aimed at Ministers in the guise of 'being helpful', no more succumbing to the temptation to throw bricks into the pond for the simple pleasure of watching everyone getting soaked. He wished once more to be part of the tribe, to come in from the shadows and share the warmth of the campfire. He couldn't achieve this by force of arms, he had to be invited, so he was decided. Whatever it took.

However, much to his discomfort, this was not the line taken by Sam when she telephoned him early at his apartment. He was preparing his diet herbs, a broth of strange substances that smelt so foul it was little wonder it persuaded the appetite to run away and hide.

'I just had to call, Daddy. You were wonderful. Standing up for us like that. Darren and I – he's really become your biggest fan – we thought you were magnificent. We saw it on the late night news and I'm so sorry about what I said the other day.' The words tumbled out breathlessly and from the heart. 'Say you'll forgive me.'

She was under a considerable misapprehension, of course, but Goodfellowe was in no mood to enlighten her. What she had seen and heard was not Goodfellowe doing battle in defence of his environmental principles but the Prime Minister attacking him for what Bendall, and now Sam, assumed them to be. His new-found hero status was much exaggerated. Still, better a live, tick-infested sheep than a slab of frozen lamb.

'You're beautiful and I'm glad you called.' He stirred the sense-numbing herbal gruel that bubbled in the pot in front of him. The steam curled up slowly, in a mood of malevolence, as though it were looking for someone to strangle.

'You do forgive me, don't you?'

The steam swirled closer to him, settling on his exposed skin and making the hair on his forearm prickle. He wondered whether the concoction was also a depilatory if applied externally. Or maybe they'd just given him the wrong bag of herbs.

'Course I do, silly.' He laughed, then hesitated. 'Er, for what?'

'For ever suggesting that you were . . .' The words melted in embarrassment.

'The shiny bit on Jonathan Bendall's trousers?' He laughed again. 'I really must send you a Dictionary of Insults. Your horizons need broadening.'

'Oh, Daddy,' she blurted.

He paused to take maximum advantage of her discomfort, squeezing the last drop of credit for his case. 'I still want to be a Minister, Sam. You must realize that. Work from the inside.' He swirled the spoon around the bubbling liquid, sending a fresh fog of vapours onto the attack. They caught his throat, he could say no more.

'I know I can trust you.'

He wasn't going to argue, for soon he would need all her support, and then some. For walking hand-in-hand with ambition went desire. His desire was simple. Elizabeth. To lie between her legs so long that she would begin to tremble and cry for him to

161

stop, then to march to the House and do the same to the Opposition. These things he wanted. Together. He wanted once again to be a Minister, and once more to be married.

To Elizabeth.

Which meant setting aside poor, innocent, mind-broken Elinor, and for that he would need all the love and forgiveness Sam could possibly give him.

He felt dampness on his cheek. Damned steam.

When it came to matters of the media, Jonathan Bendall was a wholehearted disciple of the Art of Anticipation. He knew that of all the conflicts made by man, that between Prime Minister and Political Journalist was the most difficult to avoid. Almost a law of the jungle, ordained by the gods of wrath. You cannot have both harmony and two people in the same room who think they know all the answers. So in order to delay the inevitable onset of verbal violence, Bendall often indulged in anticipation.

Which is otherwise known as keeping the bastards waiting.

It was Bendall's firmly held view that the Fourth Estate was populated by two kinds of creature. The first were those exotic birds who nested on top of the many ivory columns that had been erected around the estate. These 'columnist' birds were unlike the other creatures of the colony, for they were never forced to forage for themselves. Their food was laid on for them, usually in vast quantities, in return for which they were supposed to act as lookouts for the estate, to give advance warning of impending peril or inescapable doom. However, bred into their genes was a fundamental flaw, for these were birds of exceptionally colourful plumage and typically would spend their days (and particularly their feeding times) preening themselves and competing to adopt ever more outlandish poses. So involved would they become in their own vanities that frequently they would neglect their duties, burying their heads so deep within their feathers that most of them, in truth, could hear nothing but the lunch bell and would have missed the arrival of Armageddon. At the very last moment they would be overcome by panic and would attempt to justify themselves by squawking in the most outrageous fashion. As a result, no one paid them the slightest attention.

The other creatures of the Estate all had an unmistakably canine quality. Some developed into intrepid hunters who would patiently and courageously track down their quarry, no matter what its size. Others proved to be excellent guard dogs, even managing on occasion to rouse the attentions of the columnist birds on their lofty perches. But the majority, it must be said, were scavengers, animals who hunted in packs and preyed on the weak, the sort of creatures who spent much of their time with their noses firmly stuck up each other's arse. They had not a single redeeming quality, but such were their numbers that they were feared, for they brought terror to public servants and piled torment upon princes. They could even reduce princesses to tears. Anyone was potential quarry, except their own. Some base instinct manifested itself within the pack and drew them to the vulnerable which, once bloodied, would be attacked time and again until it had been torn to pieces.

This was where the Art of Anticipation came into its own. Bendall knew that the sight of food can throw dogs into a feeding frenzy, a raw, primitive call of the wild that has no limits and allows no mercy, yet in *anticipation* of that food, a dog will slaver and come quickly to heel. So it was Bendall's custom to keep the media in a state of constant anticipation, telling them what they were going to get, and when. In the meantime he would watch them sit up and drool. (He also relied heavily on the principle of idleness, which states that most dogs will eat almost anything so long as they don't have to go looking for it.)

Out of this grew the idea for what came to be known, in the first instance, as the Surf Summit.

It seemed inspired. Bendall would travel or 'surf' around Europe, meeting separately with seven other heads of government in a single day – a day that would, in the portentous words of the press briefing, 'shake up the politics of indifference and kick-start the European economies out of recession.' Well, up to a point, Lord Copper. That sort of schedule allowed for no more than forty minutes for each meeting, barely enough time for handshakes and photo-calls. But if modern statesmanship was all about imagery, then those images would be superb. A politician on the move, shoving aside apathy through sheer force of character, his thinning hair tussling in the wind as he ran down stairs, stepped off trains and planes and waved to the carefully prepared camera positions. Look up, young man, look up! And let the whole world follow your gaze, lest they see the nature of what it is you're standing in . . .

So the Surf Summit was born, although one early problem emerged. The French President was recuperating from a reported illness at his holiday home near Porto-Vecchio in Corsica. It seemed so much better for his health than Paris, where the streets were plagued with violent protests by impoverished farmers and over-indulged students. He had no intention of returning anywhere near the French capital until either the barricades had been swept from the streets or his hapless Prime Minister swept from office, he didn't much care which. Yet either eventuality was likely to take some considerable while, and in the meantime the emphasis was on caution – and clean hands. In the circumstances, illness seemed a far better option. The most he would agree to was a video link-up, but at least it was pictures. It would suffice.

Preparations were made, then remade, and at last the day had arrived. As a confident new sun crept across the rooftops of Whitehall and set fire to the gilding on top of the Victoria Tower, Bendall's private secretary checked the schedule one final time. It had been honed by experts and polished by repeated examination until it shone.

At eight a.m., with breakfast television and radio drawing their largest audiences, Bendall would greet the Irish Prime Minister on the steps of Downing Street. The press communiqué had been agreed well in advance; they only had to sign. They would even have time to discuss the merits of remarriage, a shared interest.

At a quarter to nine Bendall would make the three-minute ride in armoured convoy to Leicester Square where, after a walkabout of precisely ninety seconds, he and the assembled press corps would occupy one of the picture halls of the Moviemax cinema, at which point Monsieur le President would appear many times life size on the screen behind him. Stunning. (It was mere coincidence, of course, that the Moviemax was owned by a close friend of Bendall, who was also a considerable contributor to party funds and soon to be included very publicly in the Honours List. Much less publicly, he would then be touched for a contribution to match the size of the enormous publicity he was pulling from the summit. But that was for the future.)

For today, Bendall would hurry out of the cinema, coat tails flying, to be greeted by a crowd of well-wishers. It was certain that the crowd would consist of well-wishers since every single one of them had been hand-picked and shipped in by party headquarters. Nothing was to be left to chance.

He knew where the cameras would be positioned. He knew which part of the future to gaze at, forty-five degrees, no higher, otherwise his neck would begin to look scraggy, then, with a theatrical sweep of his arm, he would leave them all behind as he made the six-minute dash to the international terminal at Waterloo, where he would be met by the Swedish Prime Minister, Kristen Svensson. A railway station in south London might seem an unlikely location for an Anglo-Swedish summit but there was no time for Bendall to get to Stockholm. Anyway, the Swede was delighted to cooperate. She and Bendall had always hit it off, their public relationship full of clinches and clutches to the point that some suggested it could only be built on a private and much more intimate relationship. Disgraceful suggestion, of course, but it gave him instant sex appeal, made him a real lad, while she'd made it onto the front cover of *Private Eye* almost as often as Prince Edward.

So, after more synchronized smiling it would be a quick wave through the window of the Eurostar on its way to Brussels. And still only ten-fifteen!

At least, that's what the schedule called for, but as any old soldier will tell you, it's the best-laid plans that roll over and take the duvet with them.

Amadeus could not know precisely when Bendall would be surfing around London, or which route he would take. There are, for instance, seven entrances into Leicester Square and a dozen near-direct routes to it from Downing Street. However, the Art of Anticipation had required that the summit story be sold and resold countless times before it took place. Inevitably, and in spite of security considerations, the individual parts of the programme had begun to float into view like pieces of an iceberg fragmenting in the thaw. It was enough.

Amadeus had chosen Trafalgar Square in part because it was a celebration of a great British military triumph. He felt good about great British military triumphs, and felt nothing but contempt for those who kept apologizing for the past. OK, so it was inevitable that the British flag couldn't fly for ever above an empire that had spanned half the globe, but why were the British required to get down on their knees every time it was lowered? Take Nelson. No, not Mandela, our one. There was some half-brained modern theory being peddled that he wasn't blind, that he'd simply put on the eyepatch in an attempt to screw a bigger pension from the Admiralty. Critics! Bed-wetters and pillow-biters, the lot. Nelson, by contrast, even with one arm and a dodgy squint, had still been able to blow the French navy to smithereens, even while maintaining a firm grip on Emma Hamilton. A real man.

In those days they had valued their heroes. They'd given Nelson one of London's greatest squares, complete with fountains, ceremonial lions, statues of bootless kings, and even for many years the capital's tiniest police station (in its south-east corner, hollowed out within one of the lamp pillars).

Oh, but times change. Amadeus wondered what the modern world might erect for him. Never a statue. A gallows, maybe.

Trafalgar Square is more than a mere celebration of victory, it is also the heart that pumps life through the entire traffic system of central London. From it radiate the great arteries of Pall Mall, Regent Street, Charing Cross Road, the Strand, Northumberland Avenue, Whitehall itself, and that avenue of plane trees called the Mall which points like an arrow directly at Buckingham Palace. The beating of this vast heart is controlled by a complicated system of traffic lights, in effect an enormous electronic pacemaker which keeps London alive. The controls for the pacemaker are located on an island in the square, at the point where it is joined by Northumberland Avenue, just beneath where King Charles gazes down Whitehall from his horse. The controls are enclosed in five metal-clad boxes, about four feet high, arranged in a neat row.

From Northumberland Avenue these boxes look like five skittles standing at the end of a gigantic bowling alley. At least, they do if you're trying to blow away Trafalgar Square.

Modern man is sometimes his own worst enemy, too clever by half. He builds cities that grow ever more sophisticated – and as a result, more vulnerable. Systems become interdependent and interlocking – what in fashionable terminology is known as 'joined-up living'. It has one huge fault. It looks pretty, but spit across the right terminal and all the lights go out, all the telephones go haywire and you can't even play the Lottery.

Trafalgar Square is so easy to blow away. Sam and her friends had done precisely that, for a while, with nothing more malicious than a couple of hundred bicycle pumps. The same effect could have been achieved with far fewer hands, simply by forcing open the control boxes to the traffic lights – they are not substantial – and short-circuiting the wires or disabling the power supply. A cigarette lighter held across the wires to melt the insulation, then a quick twist to bring the bared wires together, perhaps. But there were five boxes, and timing was everything.

In the wide open spaces of Trafalgar Square there was no cover, nothing to hide behind, nothing to distract the watching eyes. It had to be achieved as quickly as possible.

So they chose the bowling alley approach, straight up Northumberland Avenue, with a bright yellow JCB earth mover as the bowling ball.

'Hannibal report ready, over.'

Hannibal. Mary's idea. Seems to sum it up rather well. A JCB for an elephant.

'Hannibal ready, over.'

The JCB is approaching, queuing patiently in the traffic, Amadeus at the wheel, dressed in luminous workman's jacket. Mary is on lookout, mounted on a Suzuki motorcycle, loitering inconspicuously by the central pavement of the Square. She is wearing a helmet, he a hard hat, both have goggles. No chance of being recognized, no matter how many times the CCTV video will be replayed. They also wear short-range walkie-talkies. Forty pounds off the shelf from Tandy's, and modified in under five minutes by Mary to provide a secure frequency. Nothing complicated, a screwdriver job.

The lights change, the heart pumps, the traffic flows. The red buses and delivery trucks and taxis edge forward, all doing their own thing. No one pays much attention to the lemon-coloured JCB in their midst, nudging alongside them, coughing a small cloud of half-burnt fuel.

She takes a last look round, and a deep, lung-stretching breath. Keep the voice down, don't let the anxiety show. Then: 'Stand by – Stand by – Stand by! Hannibal is go!'

'We are go,' Amadeus breathes into his lapel mike. With a slip of the clutch, the earth-mover skips forward.

At the same moment Scully and Payne, a few hundred yards away in Piccadilly Circus, are levering open the first of three control boxes. The doors to the boxes have been loosened under cover of darkness and swirling crowds the night before, and now it's the task of only moments to complete the job with a crowbar. They, too, are hidden beneath hard hats and protective jackets. Those who bother to take any notice assume they are official workmen, perhaps cleaning off the thick layers of fly postings.

Amadeus has lowered the mechanical grab while waiting at the traffic lights. He now has a battering ram. A bit like cleaning up in Bosnia.

He'd been leading a convoy of ambulances and food trucks, trying to get through to the isolated communities of Muslims near Srebrenica that were being slowly sliced to pieces by the Serbs. Or had they been Croats? Couldn't remember any more. What he did remember was the burning barricade of trams and old tractors they'd managed to drag across the narrow highway. Everything covered in thick, foul-tasting smoke that scoured the throat. Sniper fire ringing off the metalwork of the Warrior. They'd already got his corporal, a 7.62mm bullet through his groin that meant, as the surgeons told him later, he'd never need a vasectomy. Hell, but wasn't that the price of humanitarian aid? The convoy had to get through. So the Muslims, or Croats, or Serbs, could live to fight another day.

The JCB slows fractionally as it approaches the kerb. *Don't hit it too hard, you'll lose control.* A taxi horn blares in protest as the JCB swerves to get into position – *Move! I'm bigger than you are, and in even more of a hurry . . .* – but there is little danger of a collision. Everyone knows that JCBs are driven by mad Irish Micks. You keep your distance. Amadeus moves on. The slightest hesitation – *Abort? Abort? Abort?* – as the JCB clambers up the kerb. A dab of the clutch. A shove on the accelerator. Another belch of diesel smoke.

Other vehicles are beginning to slow now. A twitch on the wheel – *Almost . . . !* – and Amadeus is lined up exactly as he wants.

The first box is dead centre, the grab at precisely the right height. Like a knife about to hack through a soft-boiled egg.

They are forced to choose a different approach to screw up the lights at Piccadilly Circus. The control boxes are scattered at different points around the Circus, and mostly tucked away behind metal crowd control barriers. Impossible to eliminate quickly with a JCB. This one has to be a hand job. So it's a quick drenching of the internal wiring with battery acid, then a sprint across the road to the next.

Not all the control points are going to be taken out, they have decided, three will be enough. For if Trafalgar Square is the heart of London's traffic, Piccadilly Circus is its prostate, and chaos spreads like cancer.

The first box in the Square goes down with a cry of strangled metal and a whoop of joy. In the fraction of a second before the power cable snaps, the wiring suffers a violent short-circuit and throws up a cloud of acrid smoke. But already this box has clattered into the next. They are, after all, designed to crumple on impact in the event of an accident. One after the other the skittles topple, their cries of complaint growing ever more fierce as the grab slices into them and they fall beneath the wheels. At the fourth box, Amadeus is forced to back up a couple of feet in order to regain momentum. Then it's gone, and the fifth, too.

Trafalgar Square has lost its central nervous system, and London its heart.

Mrs Annabelle Whapshot from Wandsworth was able to tell the police first-hand some of what followed. She'd been making her way to Selfridges in Oxford

Street before going for lunch with friends at Le Palais du Jardin in Covent Garden. Normally she would have taken the Underground, but she had begun to suspect her husband, an advertising executive, of having an affair with his secretary. As a result she had resolved upon a little shopping therapy. No way would she get all those parcels onto the Tube, so she'd taken the car and was driving around Trafalgar Square oblivious to the confusion that was already beginning to erupt when, as she later related in the colourful style of a former amateur dramatist, it seemed as though an enormous yellow dragon had jumped out in front of her, coming to an abrupt halt, blocking the road, belching smoke and fire, like something out of an episode of Power Rangers (an effect greatly enhanced by a disembowelled power cable that was smouldering fiercely beneath one of the JCB's wheels).

At this point a taxi rammed into the back of Mrs Whapshot's car causing extensive damage, a fact that gave her relatively little annoyance since the car was her husband's, his favourite Porsche Boxter. She'd been trying to find the courage to trash it for weeks.

Mrs Whapshot's description of what happened next was fragmentary, since she was suffering from the effects of minor whiplash and was able to add very little to what the police could determine from the surveillance cameras. She told them that the man who suddenly appeared in front of her was wrapped up like the invisible man. She could tell nothing more of him behind the goggles, scarf and hard hat, except that he was smiling at her. She suspected he might have crystal blue eyes but, as she freely admitted to the police inspector, that may have been only feminine instinct and a little wishful thinking. At this point a motorcycle appeared, onto which he jumped and rapidly disappeared, but not before he had offered her the crispest of military salutes. Not an American salute, like John Wayne, all soft and sloppy, but crisp, longest-way-up, shortest-route-down, entirely British. Like Alec Guinness in that film about the bridge. And all less than fifty seconds since he had entered the Square.

An ambitious stone's throw away, beneath the shadow of Eros's wings, a similar story was being enacted. The CCTV surveillance was more intensive here, a consequence of the long history of vandalism inflicted upon the famous statue, but their greater number did nothing to improve the quality. They saw little more than two men, identities smothered in hats and dark glasses, running like hares between the control boxes. An average of eight seconds in front of each.

Then off into Glasshouse Street, which leads directly into the heart of Soho, with its maze of alleyways. From time to time it seems as if the whole of London hides within Soho's clubs and clip joints and exotic watering holes. It's a place to hide an army, let alone two men.

Payne and McKenzie disappeared down Glasshouse Street and into the warren of back doubles that lay beyond, laughing even as they ran. They were followed at a discreet distance by the slow-footed Scully who, like Mary, had been acting as lookout astride another motorcycle.

It was over for them, although for Bendall, the affair was just beginning.

Pity poor Bendall.

The Prime Minister emerged from the Moviemax just as Amadeus and his JCB were bouncing into Trafalgar Square. He didn't know it yet, but already his day was shot to hell.

When Amadeus slammed on the brakes of the JCB and ripped out the ignition, he also ripped out the heart of the capital. In the minutes that followed, paralysis began to spread and overwhelm its other parts. Major traffic intersections slowed, stiffened, then died. Oxford Circus. Hyde Park Corner. Tottenham Court Road. Frustrated traffic wardens were soon raising their hands in surrender. As the paralysis reached the Aldwych and Parliament Square, it turned south and crossed the river. Soon Waterloo surrendered. The Swedish Prime Minister might as well have been waiting for Godot.

It didn't take long before Bendall knew something was amiss. There were two routes to Waterloo from Leicester Square, one across Waterloo Bridge, the other across the bridge at Westminster. His Special Branch officer McGivens – poor, much abused McGivens – had chosen to use Westminster Bridge since this route offered more avenues of escape, more alternatives in case of slow traffic. But the traffic hadn't slowed, it had rolled over and died. As the car tried to skirt Trafalgar Square they discovered that *rigor mortis* had set in. Even though McGivens had jumped out and was hammering on the windows of the cars that pressed in on either side, he only succeeded in carving a path a few feet further into the graveyard. And they could no longer turn back.

For five minutes the car didn't budge. The schedule allowed for a maximum delay of twenty. Bendall sat behind the inch-thick windows of the armoured Daimler and fretted.

Another five minutes passed.

Then he shouted at McGivens.

At this point, defying all McGivens's frantic pro-testations, he jumped out of the car to see for himself. Hoping to clear a path, like Moses. It made no differ-ence, of course. Not even standing in the middle of Trafalgar Square, waving his arms in all directions and screaming his head off made any difference. He could have all the alternative routes in the world, but nothing was going to move, not anywhere, not for hours.

Bendall might have taken the Underground to Waterloo, but as Trafalgar Square began to die all nearby stations were closed as a routine security precaution. He might even have walked; it would have taken him no more than forty minutes. Some of the day might have been saved. Perhaps the Swedish Prime Minister might have been persuaded to accompany him on the Eurostar to Brussels, enabling them to make up a little of the lost time, even to start satisfying rumours that they had joined the Chunnel Club. But as soon as Bendall was out of the car he realized the news cameras that should have been capturing his triumph were, instead, recording his humiliation. By noon the whole world would be pissing on his day.

The Art of Anticipation only works if you can deliver what you have so lavishly promised. And he couldn't.

So he didn't walk to Waterloo. Instead he stomped the four hundred yards back home to Downing Street.

EIGHT

During her relatively short life Mary Wetherell had been forced to surmount many obstacles. Her father, the lack of education, her dismissal from the Army and, more recently, her marriage. A story that was not the stuff of heroism, simply of survival. She'd always followed an uncomplicated code in dealing with these circumstances. Never look back. Fight the next war, not the last.

Of the many names on her long list of confrontations, Colonel Abel Gittings was in no way the most significant. OK, so he had screwed up her career and with it her life-plan, he had humiliated her and been at least partly responsible for the vulnerability that pushed her into a disastrous marriage. If she thought about it, he'd been the cause of much of the misery in her recent life. Yet she tried not to think about it. She'd been able, by and large, to put him behind her. Exmoor was a long way from Blandford, and in her world of fractured emotions she'd decided not to waste any more time on Gittings. Out of sight, out of mind.

Trouble was, she was no longer in Exmoor. She was in London. She had spent much of the last few days on reconnaissance in and around Whitehall.

And in the very middle of Whitehall stood the vast milk-white Portland stone edifice of the Ministry of Defence, within which was located a Planning Staff and on which, on secondment, was Gittings.

She hadn't wanted it to happen, had tried to ignore it. She didn't even like to think of his name, usually referring to him only as the 'Black Bastard', but his proximity had begun to prey upon her mind. Memories – and pain – began to seep back. The worm began to turn once more. Up to that point she'd had a job in hand and she would allow nothing to distract her from that, but now it was over. She and the others had dumped the gear and the bikes at various points around Soho, out of sight of any CCTV cameras, and wandered into the day, unrecognized and untouched. They'd agreed to meet later for dinner at the Army & Navy Club, and in the meantime went their own ways – Amadeus to the sauna, Payne to his club, McKenzie to God-knows-where. They all found their own separate ways of dealing with their anxiety and dispersing the adrenaline.

Wherever her clothes touched her skin, Mary found herself damp with that strange mixture of fear and exhilaration she so missed from her days in the Army. It was no use going back to that claustrophobic room in the boarding house with its nagging phone, anything but that. The day was bright and inviting, with a cooling breeze, so she took a river boat – one of the few modes of transport still functioning in central London – to Kew Gardens, where she sat and ate apples with her back against the bole of a giant cedar and listened to the sound of its branches whispering to the breeze. For a while it was as though she had been transported to a different planet, far from the shadows of her life, and by late afternoon she felt thoroughly refreshed. On the return journey she stood in the prow of the boat, the wind on her cheeks and tugging at her hair. She imagined she hadn't a care in the world.

Then the boat drew in to dock at Charing Cross. Alongside the Ministry of Defence. And Gittings.

He was like a rash across her body, creeping up on her, and the more she thought about it, the more her skin crawled. Without any clear idea of what she was doing, she found herself loitering opposite one of the two main entrances to the Ministry, waiting.

Scratching. Burning.

Like a moth around a flame.

She watched as in growing numbers the MOD staff scattered down the steps beneath the towering limestone columns and headed off into what remained of the day. No idle bantering tonight, no suggestions of a casual drink in the Duke of Clarence or the club. This evening every man, woman and transvestite in the place had only one purpose, that of getting back home. The battle ahead was guaranteed to be a nightmare.

Somehow it had all become very personal for Mary. Bendall was their target, but she had never met him. Yet she had met Gittings, had felt his hands all over her, molesting, abusing her, and suddenly she wanted to make sure he suffered, too, and to suffer more, much more, than most. If she could screw up the whole of central London, how much easier must it be to screw up just one wretched and unsuspecting excuse for a man?

She wanted to hurt him. Compensation for some of the hurt he had caused her. Retribution. How she would find her revenge she was not yet certain, but the lure of his presence nearby became irresistible. She couldn't draw herself away. She waited, and watched, for nearly two hours as staff descended the steps and went on their way.

The Black Bastard was not among them.

Yet he was there. She *knew* he was there, she could feel it.

The following morning she telephoned the Ministry of Defence and asked for Colonel Abel Gittings. The switchboard put her through to an extension where a woman answered the phone. Mary asked for Gittings once again, and in turn was asked who was calling. He was there all right. She rang off.

That afternoon she loitered beside a bus stop in Parliament Street from where she could see the other, south-facing entrance to the MoD.

So many things might have happened to alter what took place next. He might have worked late, been lost in the crowd, or even been away on a course, but Creation is full of those unplanned and seemingly insignificant turning points that nudge a life from its path and send it hurtling down an embankment.

There he was, striding from the entrance. A touch greyer, in a civilian pin-striped suit, a briefcase rather than a swagger stick swinging from his grip, but unmistakably Gittings. The sight of him inflamed her. She didn't understand what she was doing; she only knew that it was right. Like a moth singeing its wings.

He set off at parade pace. Mary followed.

Every part of her relationship with him had been the cause of disaster for her, yet still she was drawn. It seemed so easy. He appeared to be enjoying the exercise and at times she was forced to scamper to keep pace. He didn't look back. Mary was able to pursue him all the way to Pimlico, a brisk twenty minutes, to a stucco-fronted building on St George's Square that had been converted into small apartments and *pieds-à-terre*, ideal for men like Gittings who worked in town and only saw their wives at weekends. He didn't always sleep there. Over the next few evenings Mary found herself watching from across the square, and following. She rejected any suggestion of obsession, telling herself that it was more fun than either idleness or television soaps, particularly when her pursuit led her across the river to a small terraced house in Clapham where he spent two of the next three nights in the company of a considerably younger and ridiculously unsuitable woman.

Like any moth, Mary thought she had found the gates of Heaven.

Bendall was examining his belly in the bath. Last time he'd looked there'd been some sort of muscle tone, a pressure beneath the skin that spoke of vigour rather than institutional dining and the third Scotch.

Now the belly button had disappeared, had become nothing more than a void, an interstellar wormhole into which many of his manly dreams had been dragged and disappeared. It spoke not so much of fleeting youth but youth that had already disappeared around the corner and scarpered.

He had arrived back at Downing Street, over-heated with humiliation, and had brushed aside all the entreaties of his private secretaries in his dash for the bathroom. He needed to cool down, hide. But he couldn't hide from his belly. It told him that the image he had so carefully crafted, the appeal of freshness and vitality that had swept him to power, was way past its sell-by date. Trade Descriptions time.

He would have to move on. Run on his record rather than his sex appeal. Unless, of course, he could reinvigorate the rumours about him and Kristen Svensson, but for that they would need to meet, and smile. Which brought him back to his morning. Fuck it. Then the telephone rang.

'I said I wasn't to be disturbed.'

'Except in emergencies, Prime Minister. You said except in emergencies,' the private secretary insisted. He had a slight lisp, which already made the conversation ridiculous.

'So where's the fire?'

'Beneath the Bundeskanzler. He's on the phone personally. I believe the translation runs roughly along the lines of "Wherever are you, old chap, and don't you know how much I had to set aside to accommodate your photocall?" Although nowhere near so polite.'

184

'What the devil . . . ?'

'Remember, Prime Minister, there's a European Council meeting in a couple of weeks. Difficult agenda. He wants a huge rebate for Germany and I believe is now in the process of reminding you that you owe him. It was my judgement that the longer we kept him waiting, the larger would be the bill. I know you're in the bath but . . .'

'So was Dr Crippen's wife.'

'Indeed, Prime Minister.'

So Bendall had wallowed. In further humiliation. In impotence. In waters that were proving increasingly turbid. And tepid.

When, at last, he had dragged himself out and was standing dripping on the bath mat, the phone had rung yet again. There were no harsh words on this occasion. He had simply listened intently for several minutes with nothing more than the odd grunt of acknowledgement until the bath mat was soaked and he had begun to shiver.

Then: 'Why does it always start in my bloody bathroom?'

'We are still gathering information. From the CCTVs. Eyewitnesses. Early days yet, but I am hopeful.' He doesn't sound it. The *Evening Standard* is already running a front page with a simple banner headline. **'HOPELESS!'**

'What makes you so?'

'So what, Prime Minister?'

'Hopeful.'

The Home Secretary clears his throat, a sound of a chainsaw engine that refuses to fire, and heads for his brief. 'As a result of the . . .' – he searches for the appropriate words. He is considering something like 'earlier outrage' or 'initial incident' when the Prime Minister helps him out.

'First fiasco. As a result of the first fiasco. What?'

Hope clears his throat more forcefully, it still doesn't fire, and embarks once again upon a voyage that he already knows will lead him into dangerously uncharted waters.

'As a result, we identified all the likely targets amongst the environmentalists. Those we considered both capable and sufficiently motivated. There are, I must admit frankly, a disarming number, but we have many of them under observation.' He gazes around the Cabinet Room. Less crowded than usual. The Cabinet has been summoned into emergency session at less than three hours' notice and several of its members are out of London. The Foreign Secretary is still in Brussels, waiting for the arrival of the Prime Minister and the Surf Summit. 'As a result we will be able to eliminate a large number of them from our enquiries. The net closes in.'

'You can eliminate the whole damned lot.'

'I beg your pardon, Prime Minister?'

'Eliminate the damned lot. Your net's so full of holes it couldn't catch a fart.'

The metaphor is senseless, of course, and deliberately crude. The Cabinet Secretary stops taking notes and busies herself studying Bendall's reflection in Gladstone's silver inkwell. It makes him seem as if

186

he has but one enormously distended eye. A Cyclops. Across the table the Home Secretary's back goes stiff. The sweat is gathering beneath the forelock.

'I understand you've been caused grievous embarrassment, Prime Minister, but nevertheless . . .'

'You understand less than a bull who's lost his bollocks!'

Bendall's palm smacks down on the table. The Cabinet Secretary's pen wobbles indecisively once more. Hope has no idea what to say, so remains silent. Awesomely pale. And no one else volunteers to help him out.

Now Bendall's voice is lower. But not softer. There is no other sound in the room apart from the ticking of the clock on the mantle. They all strain to hear, like sentries listening for the click of a safety catch in the night.

'They are not environmentalists.'

'But . . .'

'You have been wasting our time, Home Secretary. The people behind these outrages are not environmentalists, they are former Army officers. Can you advise us how many of them might be involved?'

Hope's lower jaw drops, but he does not speak. Indeed, he is incapable of speech.

'Ten? A hundred, maybe?' Bendall presses.

Hope scans his briefing document like a shipwrecked sailor scans the horizon.

'Maybe take an informed guess, even? How many, who they are?'

A strangled whisper. 'I have no information, Prime Minister.'

'No clue. That about sums it up, doesn't it? We've got a load of renegade boot shiners rampaging all over bloody London. And you don't have a clue.'

'I . . . I scarcely know what to say.'

Bendall stretches back in his chair, as though to maximize the distance between himself and his hapless colleague. 'There is nothing to say, Home Secretary. I think the Cabinet will understand if you wish to leave the room. While you write your letter of resignation.'

'What . . . now?'

Hope feels his chair pulling back from beneath him; it seems to have a mind of its own. He can't move a muscle, yet finds himself being swept towards the door.

He is almost there. His hand is on the polished brass door knob. He steadies himself, turns. All eyes are on him. Even the clock seems to have stopped ticking.

'How do you know? How do you know it's military? Not environmental?' An edge of stubbornness. After all, he's got a right to know. He's the one who's drowning.

It is a moment that reveals the animal instincts of the Prime Minister. The instincts that require an animal to gorge upon a carcass without moderation, just in case tomorrow there are no carcasses left.

'That's privileged information. And you no longer have the privilege.'

It is also calculated. For no one else is likely to ask the same question and risk the same fate. No one else needs to know about the other telephone call that came while he stood examining his sagging belly in the bathroom mirror. A call taken by the Downing Street switchboard in the basement by the Tudor tennis court, from a public phone box out of sight of any cameras. A call in a voice disguised so heavily that although the computers had captured every syllable it would be a work of genius to decipher anything other than that it was male, reasonably educated and probably verging on middle age – although the caller was willing to admit to all that anyway by identifying himself as the author of a letter sent earlier to Downing Street. A letter that in the last two hours has been rescued from the compost section of the Garden Room. A letter that Special Branch's initial conclusion indicates has been written in some form of code or deliberate jumble to disguise the identity of the writer.

A writer who demands an apology, and a change to Government policy.

Bendall decides he'll go halfway. The bastards'll get a change, all right.

Enough of No-Hopers. Now they are going to get what they bloody well deserve.

Earwick.

'Beryl says to notify you that there's going to be an extraordinary meeting of the Executive.' Marshwood's part-time constituency secretary sounded unusually formal. 'To appoint a new treasurer. But she says it's a formality. No need for you to come.'

A formality meant only one thing. Beryl was

planning to appoint her candidate without any argument or opposition. Wanted one of her own, not another Trevor.

'I'd like to attend. When is it?'

'This Wednesday evening.'

Goodfellowe groaned. All but impossible. There was bound to be a vote. Beryl knew it. Deliberate.

'I'll be there.'

'Oh,' the secretary responded, surprised. This wasn't what she'd been led to expect. 'I'll tell Miss Hailstone you're coming then, shall I?'

'Thank Beryl for me. And tell her I'll be there.'

Bloody Beryl.

They found themselves together in the old ground-floor toilet just outside the Cabinet Room. The Chief Whip was relieving himself, a most necessary undertaking after a meeting such as that, when the Prime Minister walked in.

'So what do you think, Eddie?' the Prime Minister growled as he stepped alongside Rankin.

'As a man or as a politician?'

Bendall turned and stared, inspected Rankin up and down, as though he could scarcely believe what he was hearing, or seeing. Enough to disturb any man when he's urinating.

'What I think, Jonathan, is that you should make sure the media are properly briefed. Before Noel gets out there and muddies the water, and starts giving the impression he walked away as a matter of principle, or even stormed out in passion. There's a limit to what we'll be able to say about a security matter. Don't want to give him a head start.' God, how he was looking forward to washing his hands after this one.

'Good advice, Eddie. Yes, very sound.' The words were fulsome, yet Bendall seemed utterly unmoved.

'Do you want me to warn the press secretary, then? Get him moving?'

'I'd rather you didn't disturb him right now. He's over at the lobby. Explaining why No-Hope had to go. How I was forced to part with the services of a lifelong friend. We go back such a long way together, you know.'

'He's briefing the press already?'

'Has been ever since Cabinet began.'

'You knew . . . ?'

'As you said, Eddie, didn't want to give Noel a head start.'

Rankin looked down, trying to hide his ragged emotions. It seemed to him that he had shrunk and somehow felt less of a man. Sometimes he hated this job.

'Something had to give, Eddie. There's got to be more than just sitting around waiting for the next humiliation.'

'You sound worried.'

'Be a fool not to be. It's all very well getting Noel to carry the can, but how long before they come knocking on my door? After all, it was my bathroom, my bloody summit. In this job you either control events or you run before them, and at the moment . . .' – a slight pause, an uncharacteristic insight into insecurity – 'I don't control even my own bath tap. Don't care for that, Eddie, don't care for that one bit. So it can't be just the one, you know, not just Noel. Others'll have to go. Destiny calls, and for some sooner than others. We need new blood. New ideas.' Bendall flushed the urinal, as though dispensing with a great misfortune. 'Got any ideas?'

Rankin began soaping his hands. 'You will already have decided who's going to replace Noel.'

'Earwig. I was thinking young Earwig.'

Rankin paused, and picked up the soap once more, as though he had discovered an unusually stubborn stain. 'Then . . .' He hesitated. The most difficult part of his job. Get it wrong, offer a few impossible names, and he'd go down with them. 'Not one of us,' they'd explain, as they flushed him away alongside the rest. 'I think you should go for a balance. Youth. Plus experience.'

'What sort of experience?'

Rankin made a dash for the towel to give himself a further moment for consideration. He didn't fully understand his own logic. Was he about to say this because he thought it right? Or because he thought they deserved each other?

'Goodfellowe.'

'What? A Burke and Hare job? Rob the graveyard?'

'He was one of the best. Once. And he wants back in.'

'So do Maggie Thatcher and Joseph Stalin.'

'But – and remember this – Tom was the only one in the entire country to question whether it was environmentalists behind the attacks.'

'Made a bloody fool of himself in the process.'

'No, Jonathan, *you* made a bloody fool of him. There's a difference, you know.'

'S'pose there is.' He sounded as if he'd been offered a compliment. 'Suppose he was right, too. Just got his timing wrong.' Bendall inspected his hair in the mirror, redistributing the sparse fringe around the brow. 'Man of Conscience. Hmm, could be a useful reinforcement, add a little principle to proceedings. At least until the next round of spending cuts.'

'Call him in. Talk with him. Make up your own mind.' Get out from underneath this absurd suggestion. Shove it back into Bendall's lap.

The Prime Minister was already heading for the door. 'Right. Call him in. Let's have a drink.'

Rankin noticed that Bendall hadn't washed his hands. Come to think of it, he never washed his hands. 'When?' Rankin called after him.

'Wednesday evening.'

Elizabeth was distracted. She was not at her best when she was distracted.

She was the sort of woman who fought hard to ensure her life ran along a path she controlled and was, so far as was possible, emotionally risk-free. For all her beauty and wit, there was a deep well of insecurity that even those closest to her had trouble fathoming. To most people she was an object of envy – she had beauty, charm, her independence, a delightful wisteria-covered Kensington mews house, and the restaurant. Oh, and Goodfellowe, although few people regarded him as the most obvious of her attributes. Politicians were two a penny around beautiful women.

Yet to see the glittering exterior was not to understand Elizabeth. Not even Elizabeth entirely understood Elizabeth, or, if she did, there were dark corners she preferred to avoid. So her wit and acid humour had been developed to help her survive, to cover up vulnerability. To keep people out, not to involve them. Her relationships had been plentiful, her love-making passionate and often unpredictable. On the prow of a cruise ship, for example, with a complete stranger, as she had leaned forward over the rail to embrace the star-filled Caribbean sky, also on the bonnet of a boyfriend's brand new Ferrari as it was parked outside The Belvedere in Holland Park. She'd forgotten to take off her shoes, made an awful mess of the coachwork. Orgasms in heels can do that for a girl. And for a Ferrari.

He didn't complain. She knew he'd keep that car until the wheels fell off, would never part with his memories of her, or the dent in the bonnet. He'd never abandon her, not like that bloody boy when she was fourteen.

Yet for all her experience and experiences, she still found it so difficult to share. She kept men hungry, like Penelope at her loom, fed their desires but not their souls, and in the end it always told. The one man she had been determined to trust, her husband, had grown frustrated and eventually had gone. Not entirely anyone's fault. Circumstance. She'd been five months pregnant, there had been a car crash in which he'd been driving. She lost the baby, and her ability to have more babies, and along with it for a while had died something inside her that allowed her to trust and to share with men.

Until she had met Goodfellowe. He was wounded, too. Both damaged goods. Something they could share.

She loved Goodfellowe, but he was a man and so carried with him a little of the baggage of every man she had ever known. She wanted to love him more, and perhaps one day she might, but in the meantime she could find solace in her restaurant, something to which she could commit herself completely. It was a relationship she could control.

Or so she had thought. But these were difficult times, times of cash-flow problems and cancellations.

Salvation was at hand, of course, in the form of twenty-two crates of the finest Tsarist vintages, for which she had signed a contract in both English and Russian, lodging copies with the customs, taxation and foreign trade authorities in Odessa, and had then transferred the US dollar equivalent of almost seventy thousand pounds into an account at the People's Bank of Odessa in the name of Vladimir Houdoliy, frozen until such time as a certificate of export for the specified goods had been presented.

Vladimir Houdoliy had become a man of great significance in her life. Perhaps too significant, for ever since the money had left her account and found its way to Odessa, it seemed to have disappeared into a hole in the ground.

Now there was no answer from Vladimir's phone, no matter how many times she rang.

'Come in, come in . . . er, Tom.' Bendall seemed to be struggling for the name. 'Whisky?'

Without waiting for a reply the Prime Minister nodded to Eddie Rankin, who busied himself at the small drinks cabinet. Goodfellowe had intended to decline, had he been given an option. He was way behind on his diet this week. Had been all month.

They were in Bendall's study on the first floor of Downing Street with three large sash windows that offered a fine view of the silver birch in the garden and the park beyond. The windows had a faint green tinge, on account of the inch-thick glass that was blastproof and tested on the Royal Engineers' proving range at Chatham, a legacy of the IRA mortar attack that had left the garden and most of the windows looking like a bad day on the Somme. Not that the reinforced windows offered complete protection. They were so heavy they had to be opened and closed with huge winding handles, and were now far more robust than the ancient brick walls into which they were bolted. In the event of another explosion, they'd probably fall into the room in one huge piece, reducing everyone inside to specimens on a microscope slide. Not so much immunity, simply a different path to immortality.

Goodfellowe hadn't been in this inner sanctum before. It had the unmistakable feel of a boy's den – cracked leather chairs and sofas, yards of book-shelves, disrupted piles of papers on floor and desks, the lingering smell of beeswax and alcohol. At the far end of the room, much to Goodfellowe's astonishment, stood a Sixties jukebox, switched on and ready to go, and on the wall above it a huge oil painting by some modernist that had been borrowed from the Tate.

'So,' Bendall began after they had seated themselves, examining his cufflink as though he had nothing better to do. 'You were bloody rude at Question Time the other day.'

'Was I, Prime Minister? If so, it was unintentional. Anyway, you were far bloody ruder.'

Suddenly Goodfellowe had won all of the Prime Minister's attention. 'True. But that's what I'm paid for.'

'Ah, I'd wondered about that.'

Bendall considered this backbencher, this strange creature who appeared to be in neither awe nor fear. 'You know, when I first got into Cabinet, they said that you were the one to look out for. The man who would most likely make it. Here, in Downing Street. Perhaps even beat me to it.'

'Then they got it wrong. Whoever "they" were.'

'God, I thought you were going to come out with something crass. Like "the best man won".'

'I long ago stopped thinking of myself as even a good man, let alone the best man.' It neatly ducked the matter of his opinion of Bendall.

'But you got it right, didn't you? At Question Time. You knew they weren't eco-freaks. How? How did you know that?'

Goodfellowe gently swirled the whisky around his

tumbler, savouring the hints of peat. Lots of peat, and seaweed. From one of the islands.

'You don't want to know, Jonathan.'

'I certainly do.'

'Believe me, you don't.'

'I insist. Dammit, this is a matter of national security. I could have you dragged to the Tower and tortured for such information.'

Goodfellowe sighed. An image of Sam and Darren appeared before his eyes, their faces earnest, their arguments giving no quarter.

'Very well, if I must. I knew they couldn't be environmentalists because . . . well, because these guys were making fun of you. Mocking you. And it's a time-hardened fact that environmentalists have no sense of humour.'

Rankin, from his sentry post by the black-and-white marble fireplace, quietly choked.

'Just instinct?' Bendall pressed.

'And experience.'

There followed a long silence while Bendall looked out of the window, for all the world as though he'd suddenly become fascinated by the branches of the silver birch. As the silence lengthened, Goodfellowe came to the conclusion that he'd blown it. He began chastising himself. Dammit, couldn't he simply be pleasant to the bastard for just a few minutes?

Bendall turned back towards him, the eyes cool, not trying to impress. 'You don't bother with the niceties, do you, Tom? Still, I shouldn't worry 'bout that. I'm never short of a few arse-lickers, am I, Eddie? But instinct and experience? They're about

198

as rare in these parts as a whore's charity. I need them. Maybe I need you.'

Goodfellowe gave no reply, contenting himself with a large slug of whisky to calm the tautness that had grown inside.

'Let me put my cards on the table, Tom. There's a reshuffle coming up. If you want, you'll be part of it.'

The slightest pause, then, slowly: 'I want.'

'But first I'd like your help and ideas on these attacks. We know they're former soldiers, but that doesn't help us much. Something like forty thousand've left the armed forces in the last five years, it's still like searching for a bedbug in a brothel. And no knowing what they'll do next. So we've raised the level of security, called together COBRA' – he offered the acronym of the national security committee that held its meetings in the Cabinet Office briefing room – 'and I want you on it as my special adviser.'

'He'll have to sign the Official Secrets Act,' Rankin advised.

'Not necessary, already done it,' Goodfellowe contradicted. 'When I was Foreign Office Minister. The obligations of the Official Secrets Act last until you die. Sometimes longer, I'm told.'

Suddenly Bendall was on his feet, with Goodfellowe struggling to follow.

'Don't cross me, Tom. Don't get like all the rest. Stay with me, and you'll find me a good friend. Hell, you might even make it here after all. When they finally get me.'

*   *   *

'That was a little bit of history.'

'At last, I'm a footnote.'

'Maybe more than a footnote, Tom. A whole chapter even. Perhaps the entire bloody book.'

'What bloody book?'

Goodfellowe and the Chief Whip were in Parliament Street, walking briskly, a little breathless, floating on adrenaline.

'Try Lear. Like the mad king, handing on his empire.'

'What the hell's that supposed to mean, Eddie? Stop being so bloody opaque. You sound like a prison letter trying to wriggle its way past the censors.'

'I'm a Chief Whip, for God's sake. You're not supposed to understand me, just do as I say.'

They paused at a pedestrian crossing.

'Try being human for a change. Give me a clue.'

'Should've worked it out for yourself already. About Jonathan.'

The electronic man turned green in their favour. Goodfellowe wondered how long it would be before traffic lights were accused of being sexist.

'What about Jonathan?'

'He's not long for this world, some might say. Not me, you understand. But then I'm only a loyal Chief Whip. No opinions of my own.'

'Hell, I've only just got there. And you're saying the party's practically over?'

'Not yet. But soon, maybe.'

'You bursting my balloon already?'

'No, quite the opposite. Imagine. You in Cabinet a year or so. Mr Clean. Mr Fresh. Mr Not Responsible

For All This Lousy Mess. Unlike all the others. It could be you sending out invitations to your own party.'

'You mean . . .'

'Yes. As Prime Minister. Let's face it, more ridiculous things have happened.'

They had come to an abrupt halt in the entrance to New Palace Yard. A taxi hooted impatiently.

'My own party? It'll never happen. Beryl will get to me first and tread on every balloon in sight.'

'Beryl?'

'My constituency chair-monster. I'm supposed to be at an Executive meeting right now. They're appointing a new treasurer. While they're at it I think she's also organizing my lynching party.'

'Don't worry about Beryl. I'll give her a call. Can't be too specific, not yet, but I'll give her some prattle about you being the Prime Minister's right-hand man and his gratitude to her for sparing you this evening. Mutter about greater things to come. She'll be wringing out her knickers by the time I've finished with her.'

'I doubt it. You haven't seen her knickers. Only a guy rope short of a Millennium Dome.'

'You've forgotten, haven't you, Tom?'

'Forgotten what?'

A duty policeman nodded in recognition as they passed into the Palace precincts.

'Power's what it's all about. An aphrodisiac. Use it. Enjoy it!'

NINE

Afternoon sex is one of the few entrenched traditions in the House of Commons that has refused to die with the times. They haven't yet set up a working party to 'modernize' it; and probably they never will. To die for, those moments of gratification squeezed between lunch and the time the good and the great wend their way to the Tea Room.

Elizabeth arches her back to make herself more comfortable and to spread Goodfellowe's now-relaxed weight. He is still on top of her, and inside her, and distinctly damp. He has been extraordinarily vigorous, as though being whipped, driven on, which in turn has driven her on, and on. A good one, even a great one.

She begins to tremble. Deep inside something's moving, rushing remorselessly through her and taking no prisoners. She has no effective way of expressing what she is feeling, so she begins to cry.

He is alarmed. 'What's wrong?'

'Oh, bloody men,' she gasps. 'You'll never understand.'

'Understand what?'

She shakes her head, closes her eyes, bites deep into her lip to stifle the sobbing and let the sensation take her.

When it's over, reluctantly she opens her eyes. He is still staring at her from five inches above, trickling perspiration, a blob of it wobbling on the end of his nose. So much for romance. He is frowning with concern.

'Don't worry, hunk.' She plants an enormous kiss of gratitude on his mouth. 'Only aftershocks.'

He raises himself a little, their moist bodies part. Cooling air rushes in and tickles her breasts. She moans once more.

'Not fair on a girl, Goodfellowe. I come home for a couple of hours' rest before the evening onslaught, you rush in like a shipwrecked sailor and leave me feeling like I won't be able to walk for a week. What pills are you popping?'

'Not bad for an ancient mariner, eh?' He feels masculine, almost smug.

She arches her back again, stretching the vertebrae to pull out the creases. He's still firm, still not moved from her. She tries to draw back, to examine him, burrowing into the pillow, her instincts quivering.

'Something's happened, hasn't it?' It's part question, part accusation. He still looks smug.

'Not supposed to tell you. They'll cut my balls off if I tell you.'

She reaches down for him. 'Something comes to mind. Like why worry what might go on in the bush tomorrow when at this very moment a bird's already got your balls in her hands. Come on, cough. Your secret's safe with me.'

'Promise?'

She squeezed just enough to make her point. 'It's called COBRA.'

The Cabinet Office Briefing Room. COBRA. (The 'A' is there simply to give the acronym a bit of bite.) A modest room-within-a-room that lurks behind the Victorian façade of the Cabinet Office in Whitehall.

COBRA is a world of ancient and modern. You approach it through a lovingly restored Tudor brick tunnel that was once part of the old Palace of Whitehall. Half-close your eyes and you can almost catch the cussing of Good King Harry as he chases the ball around his tennis court, but no sooner have you walked on just a few paces, through the door that is both soundproof and blastproof, than you realize that you have been propelled into the digital age.

The rectangular table that dominates the room has space for twenty people, each with his or her own touch-sensitive computer screen. Functionaries and support staff sit at chairs that are pushed back against the wall; they follow proceedings on a large master screen that hangs on one end wall. At the opposite end of the room are two small offices in which wait other support staff, communications staff in one, the appropriate security service in the other. The security service concerned is often the SAS, for this is the grubby end of government.

COBRA deals with matters of security. Secret matters, sometimes unpleasant matters. The sort of things that get zipped up in body bags and don't travel well with either pink broadsheets or screaming-blue tabloids. The sort of things that hide deep within the folds of the Official Secrets Act. Frequently the room is used for 'hypotheticals', rehearsals against the day when their worst fears become reality, like an attack on the Channel Tunnel, or the kidnap of a Cabinet Minister's daughter. Or New Labour selling itself to Rupert Murdoch.

But no one had foreseen this one.

Goodfellowe had arrived through the front door of the Cabinet Office, leaping like a salmon up the few steps – he'd rather hoped to find a posse of photographers waiting to capture this historic moment so that he could smile knowingly and tease them with a terse 'No comment!', but the only onlooker was a one-footed pigeon perched precariously on the grimy windowsill.

Many of the others attending had walked through the back way, from Downing Street. It was a collection of allsorts, with Secretaries of State for Foreign & Commonwealth Affairs, for Defence, for the Environment, Transport and the Regions – without his private secretary, who was having a termination that morning, but with his deputy, the Minister for London, who rumour had it was the cause of the private secretary's concern. Also in attendance was the creepy Permanent Under-Secretary with the pallid skin and drooping right eye, and the Director-General of MI5. The Commissioner of Police was there, too, encrusted in braid.

Oh, and Earwick.

He'd arrived in the company of the Prime Minister, hovering so close that he looked like a tailor taking a fitting. Earwick's appointment as Home Secretary had been announced only the night before, rather more rushed than had been planned but in time to steal the headlines on the evening news away from the midwives' pay talks. They'd collapsed. So, according to the midwives' leaders, had the health service. A time for desperate measures. So they had brought forward the announcement of Earwick's appointment. The soot of midnight oil was smudged beneath his eyes, yet the eyes themselves still burned bright, fuelled with ambition.

Even though the Prime Minister had taken the chair, Earwick was allowed to lead the discussions. Goodfellowe wondered why. The attacks were good news for the Government and had boosted its popularity as the British public instinctively rallied round. There was glory to be had here, a commodity as precious around Westminster as a good meal on a motorway, so why share it? Perhaps the Prime Minister sensed the situation was not yet under control, that the unexpected might yet happen. He was being cautious.

'I'm grateful, Prime Minister, for this opportunity to address colleagues on the current situation. In the hours since my appointment I've spent the time reviewing progress on this matter. Let us be frank. It's been a disappointment. In all honesty up to this point we've made practically no progress whatsoever . . .'

Ouch. Goodfellowe winced. One in the guts for Hope. Kicking a man once he's down is never the most attractive of activities. On the other hand, it is so much easier.

'However, I'm delighted that we now have real

206

developments to report. Thanks largely to the efforts of the Prime Minister's office' – a nod in Bendall's direction – 'I can confirm that these outrages are the work of a group of disgruntled former military officers. They've made contact twice now, by both letter and telephone.' An animated stare around the table. 'I hope I don't have to emphasize that this aspect of the operation is to be regarded as strictly confidential. No public announcement at this stage about the military connection.'

'If I may interrupt through the chair?' It was the Walrus, without raising his head. Earwick had thought he'd been snoozing.

Bendall nodded his approval.

'Why not?' demanded the Walrus.

'Why not what?'

'Why not let the public know? Gain their assistance in the hunt?' His head was still down, as though he didn't want to look up to Earwick. As though he were determined that he would never look up to Earwick.

Earwick paused, steepled his fingers, debating whether to embrace the old fool or to throttle him. Throttle him for preference, but that would have to be left for another time. 'There are two main reasons for silence, at least at this stage. We don't wish to alarm the public unnecessarily. The IRA and animal libbers are one thing, the prospect of our own highly trained professionals quite another. It could prove most disturbing, particularly to editors with overactive imaginations – as I'm sure the Chancellor of the Exchequer with all his experience will understand . . .'

'And the second reason?' the Walrus demanded, interrupting the flow of grease.

'To put it bluntly, because we haven't got the faintest idea who these people are. They don't fall onto any of our traditional lists of extremists and activists. We've no idea at this stage even how many, let alone who. It's a bit like searching for snowflakes in Siberia.'

'So what do you propose to do?'

'Be vigilant! They've hit water, transport. Who knows what next? So I have raised the state of alert on all government buildings and asked the Commissioner to draft as many police officers as possible onto the streets, to make their presence more obvious. I've also cancelled all leave in SO-13, the police armed response unit.'

'You think lives may be at risk?'

'We are dealing with military hoodlums. They may be unstable. Worse than terrorists. I'm not going to be the one who has to stand up in Parliament after some appalling tragedy and say that I wasn't prepared. I have also told the security services that I'll authorize electronic surveillance and phone taps under any reasonable circumstance. We can't afford to lack the necessary courage. As of now London is on a twenty-four-hour alert.'

'Sounds a little like short cuts.'

'Let me put it this way. I intend that we should deal with these renegades sooner rather than later. They've put themselves outside the law, and if we have to go to the very edges of the law ourselves in order to defeat them, I can live with that. It's results that count. And – let me phrase this carefully – all the opinion-poll evidence suggests that the people expect us to act decisively. To defend their interests. Hell, we have to trust the people.'

'But not tell them what they are up against.'

'If the voters' – a slip of the tongue; he'd meant to say 'people' but for some reason he seemed to be thinking of elections – 'thought there was a bunch of little Hitlers wandering around the streets of London intent on mayhem, there would be chaos. And unnecessary fear. The economy would lose billions. So first things first. What the public wants to know above all is that their security is safe in our hands. When we know who we're dealing with, then we can decide what information to give out, but what they need to know in the meantime is that their Government is ready to act. So whatever it takes, gentlemen. Whatever it takes.'

'I take it that no one has any objections?' Bendall instructed.

Goodfellowe swallowed. He had all sorts of objections, particularly and very personally to Earwick. A loathsome object but, according to the Prime Minister, a very necessary individual. Within a few short minutes of his first appearance as Home Secretary he'd defiled the grave of his predecessor, shoved his head so far up the Chancellor's backside that it wouldn't appear until next Budget Day, and had threatened action that was unprincipled and – who knows? – maybe verging on the unlawful, threatening an armed response to those who so far had done no more than bring Trafalgar Square grinding to a halt. That was no more than Sam had done. What was Earwig going to do next time she waved her bicycle pump around? Shoot her?

Objections? Sure he had objections, but he also had his back against the wall. Quite literally. He hadn't been invited to sit at the table along with the big boys, merely to sit in attendance. To the rear. On the seats reserved for officials and advisers. His role was to listen and to learn. If he behaved himself, maybe later he would move up to the top table.

But it couldn't be much later. Goodfellowe had gone past the stage when he had his whole life before him. A good chunk of it was already well behind him or hanging around his waistline. What had Churchill said? It was a line Goodfellowe often used in speeches, one he could always rely upon for a ripple of laughter and applause. Churchill and Lady Astor, entering the Guildhall in the City of London, side by side. 'Look around you, Winston,' she had demanded caustically, 'you could fill half of the Guildhall with all the brandy you've drunk in your life.' The Old Man had looked around the great hall through weary eyes and replied: 'Ah, yes. So much more still to do. And so little time to do it.'

Damn it, Goodfellowe couldn't deny it any longer. He was middle-aged, stuck in a world that placed an ever heavier premium on youth. But you are only as young as you feel, and he didn't feel middle-aged, not with Elizabeth beneath him.

He choked off his misgivings. Time to be not only middle-aged, but also grown up. This was his route back. Back to office. Back to happiness. Back to helping make little bits of history, like COBRA. Back to making a difference, for others. Back to youth, even. Recapturing the many things he'd lost since last he had buried his attentions in a Ministerial red box, and Stevie had drowned.

Give and take. Compromise. A team player. As though he were playing on a football squad, accepting the need to pass the ball, helping others score goals, not battling on his own any more.

So much better than shouting angrily from the touchline, wasn't it?

Although he'd better watch out for the professional foul.

When first they had gathered, they had done so as a matter of honour. Now the conspirators met in a mood of anger. Anger becomes conspiracy, and they now knew that *conspirators* were what they were. Earwick had left them in no doubt of the fact during his statement to the House.

'A conspiracy not just against the elected government,' he had thundered, 'but against the people, and our capital city. *A conspiracy against democracy itself.*'

The time of mischief when they had worn toy helmets and played games with the Bendalls' loo seemed to be from another age.

Earwick had attacked. He had abused.

'These are not people of principle but parasites, Mr Speaker. Men of malice. Nothing less than wreckers . . .'

Earwick had distorted.

'. . . whose objective is to inflict misery and chaos upon thousands of innocent Londoners.'

He had gone on to belittle them.

'We are dealing here with a conspiracy of spite . . . extremists whose overriding objective is as simple as it is selfish – to create chaos and confusion. Bully boys who target the innocent for their own narrow ends.'

Then he had impugned their honour.

'These are extremists, nothing less. They may claim to be working in the public interest but, in truth, they are working in no one's interest other than their own . . .'

And finally he had threatened.

'Lawlessness cannot be allowed to rule our streets, Mr Speaker. Lives are at risk in these attacks. By polluting our water supplies, by disrupting emergency services – our ambulances and our firemen, not to mention the police – they attack the people themselves. And so I feel entitled, indeed duty bound, to use every means at our disposal to protect the public and prevent further outrages. While the House will understand if I do not give full details of the security measures I am implementing, let me give the assurance that they will be rigorous and comprehensive . . .'

The threat was left vague, but vivid. There were mad dogs roaming the capital. The implication was clear. Like mad dogs, they would have to be put down.

*   *   *

'Seems we may have upset Mr Earwick. Pity. Such a nice man.'

'A true gentleman.'

'Ferret turd, more like.'

'Upgraded security everywhere.'

'You're right. All too bloody obvious. Trafalgar Square. The Circus. Outside Parliament and at Hyde Park Corner. All over the shop. Mr Earwick seems not to trust us.'

'They were checking the rubbish bins every twenty minutes outside Harrods. Dammit all, they think we're fucking bombers.'

'I *am* a fucking bomber,' McKenzie insisted.

'Then we are done for!'

Half jest, half in deadly earnest.

'So what do we do? It's sort of a point of no return. Could get messy from here on in. Anybody want out?'

Amadeus had to pose the question. The matter had changed, grown beyond what any of them had envisaged. No longer could this be a simple matter of apology; Earwick had made that abundantly clear. It had become a battle of wills, of implacable positions and inflexible egos. War is never simply an affair of violence but of achieving a set of objectives, and now those objectives had shifted. Bendall wouldn't change, so . . . So he had to be changed. Overwhelmed. Forced to climb down in the face of adversity, before they themselves were caught and overwhelmed. It was one or the other. The risks, of course, were mighty, but in a matter of honour the burden of doing nothing far outweighed the perils of failure.

The others also understood this. They had been naïve to believe there could be any sort of victory through simply muddying the Prime Ministerial waters, but this was a very different kind of foe from any they had previously fought. Yet in facing adversity, each of them had found opportunity.

For Scully it was the opportunity to rebuild himself and, in his different way, for Payne to rebuild himself too, and renew his fortunes. They barely considered the risks. Amadeus had given them both something to cling to, and drowning men don't ask too many questions.

McKenzie saw it as a matter of principle. Bendall was both preacher and poacher and McKenzie, as a Highlander, had been bred to distrust both. He thought Bendall the worst of his kind, a man who would sacrifice any principle or position for his own advantage. That made him no different from any of the petty warlords who had scattered land mines and left a trail of shattered lives across so many innocent communities. In McKenzie's eyes, it scarcely mattered that Bendall hadn't started any wars; he hadn't done a damned thing to prevent any either. He'd even slashed the British contribution to the land-mine clearance programme in Cambodia. Typically, the cut had been announced by means of a Written Answer put out on a Friday in late July, as if it were just some other parliamentary game. That same day the Scot had watched a seven-year-old girl and her small brother walk hand-in-hand into a rice field near Kompong. They were searching for butterflies. After the explosion he'd found himself covered in UFCs. Unidentifiable Fragments of Child.

Mary's motivations were both simpler and yet immensely more complicated. For her, this wasn't just a battle against Bendall but against all those men throughout her life who had stripped her of everything – her childhood, her hopes, her career, her value as a woman. Bendall symbolized that bloody male arrogance that had torn her life to shreds time and again. Now she had the chance to fight back. It involved risk, of course, but there was always a price to pay, and it was nothing compared to the price she had paid repeatedly at the hands of people like Bendall. And Gittings. Both of whom were now so close at hand, and so vulnerable. When she thought of Gittings, the question of giving up never entered her head.

Amadeus's question hung in the air. Mary was the first to respond.

'What, throw in my hand and go back to mastitis and mud?'

'And just when I was beginning to ha' fun? Hell, no.'

'You too, Skulls?'

The RSM seemed to stretch his battered body, to grow taller. He was standing on one foot, his right boot no longer touching the ground. 'When the other bastard starts to squeal, usually means you got 'im by the balls. Not the time to stop squeezing, if you ask me.'

Payne was nodding in agreement.

'Which seems to leave us with only one wee question.'

'What's that, Andy?'

'Where do we squeeze 'em next?'

For the next two and a half hours, over burgers and beer, Amadeus explained in meticulous and carefully prepared detail how they were going to make Bendall squirm, then scream, then cough up his guts.

And how, by and by, they were going to bring themselves to the edge of disaster.

TEN

Goodfellowe had slept fitfully and risen with a nervous stomach. The full English breakfast he had prescribed for himself at Mr Chou's hadn't helped, either. It blew his diet, made him flatulent and only increased his feeling of unease. Anyway, his old friend Chou, a near-neighbour on Gerrard Street, couldn't cook a full English to save his last remaining gold tooth. How on earth did he scramble eggs so that they actually bounced, not only off the plate but inside the stomach? Goodfellowe knew from the first mouthful that it was an awful idea but all the while Chou had stood over him, beaming and hopping from foot to foot like a nervous parent, forcing Goodfellowe to eat out of politeness. And to suffer.

Yet as the day grew older, Goodfellowe began to realize that his problems weren't dietary. By late afternoon he found himself in the Chamber, occupying a place at the far end from the Speaker's Chair and on the very highest bench, which gave him a view over the entire leather-shod assembly. For all its faults it was to him still a fine place, a place of beauty and awesome history, at times a place of wisdom yet at other moments a place of masterly confusion and indecision, stalked by ghosts and by greatness and by fools. To be part of this place had always been his dream, but as he watched the proceedings he began to realize that it wasn't enough.

For what was gripping him inside was not indigestion but ambition. The Chief Whip's words had kept returning to him, that one day, this Chamber could be *his* Chamber.

It was a reckless desire, of course, but not impossible. All Prime Ministers are ultimately put to the sword, and what would happen when the mob came to kick down Bendall's door? What if . . . What *if* it came down to a choice between him and, say, Earwick and Vertue? *Il Buono, il Brutto, il Cattivo*. To stand any chance in such a contest would require commitment and endless endeavour, not all of it wholesome. Spending more time around the corridors and in the well-polished corners, embracing lobby correspondents, gossiping, whispering in their ears, following the whisper with his tongue. Ugly business, but you couldn't work your way to the top by leaving the place strewn with virgins.

The bike would have to go, of course. Yet on second thoughts he might be able to make the bike a selling point. Not so much a rusting piece of scrap as a symbol of sincerity and independence. Like Harold Wilson's pipe, or Ronald Reagan's jelly beans. The Pedalling Premier! Trouble was, all his grand visions of sincerity and independence were contradicted by what was taking place in the Chamber directly in front of him. Earwick was posturing at the Despatch Box like a brawler propping up the bar, throwing threats in every direction. So what if the Prime Minister had been made to look ridiculous? That's what politics were about, but Earwick was making it sound like the onset of the French Revolution. Goodfellowe couldn't shake from his mind the thought that the whole thing was faintly absurd.

In the quieter corners of Westminster he found others who, out of earshot of the Whips, admitted to having enjoyed the spectacle of Bendall drowning in front of the Surf Summit cameras, who thought that those responsible deserved not so much a guillotine as an award for comic entertainment. Sure, they had stuffed up the centre of London, but so had the Mayor and the Minister for Transport on a daily basis. Was Earwick going to throw them in a tumbrel, too? There was fine sport to be had in mocking Earwick – but for the moment the sport was pursued only gently, for Earwick was Today's Man. Best not call his bluff, they argued. Wait until tomorrow.

A drowning Prime Minister. A Home Secretary who was one wheel short of an undercarriage. This was the team Goodfellowe had signed up with. No wonder he felt such a sense of unease.

He tried to work it out during the hour he spent in the Tea Room, but couldn't. So he followed that with a serious session out on the Terrace and a button-straining dinner in the Members' Dining Room, after which there was yet another session on the Terrace before the final vote.

It was at this point he began to realize there was a fundamental flaw in his plans to claim his place in the history books as the Pedalling Prime Minister. For no matter how hard he struggled and concentrated and swore, he found it was impossible for him to ride his bloody bike. Not when he was completely legless.

'We could always wait for one who's grown up. More your age, perhaps.'

'Do something useful for a change, Freddie. Turn into a lamppost or get in another round.'

Mary rocked back on her uneven stool and squirmed. She didn't like this place, the Ring o' Bells, a smoke-and-soiled-varnish pub that was hidden down a little passage off Camden High Street. It had nothing to recommend it, other than the location. Even the beer was foul. It had too much head and tasted of Rotherhithe, and reminded Mary of her father. For almost an hour she'd been sitting at a sticky-topped table, exchanging stilted conversation with Payne, and waiting – for what, she wasn't entirely sure, but as it drew closer to six their patience was rewarded. The pub had begun to fill with drinkers, a good number of whom were employees from the Telecoms Technical and Engineering Centre located less than a hundred yards down the road. They worked in an environment designed for computers with air conditioning that was bone dry, which all helped build up a scorching thirst by the end of the day. The Ring o' Bells was the nearest watering hole.

She watched the young man for twenty minutes. He seemed a likely prospect. His conversation identified him as a Telecoms software engineer, while his bright yellow socks featuring Butt-Head on one ankle and Beavis on the other suggested the lack of any woman in his life.

'Christ, he's even got an anorak,' Payne sniggered.

'Be a good boy and go play with yourself, Freddie,' she whispered, rising to her feet.

Anorak Man had gone to the bar to refill his glass and she squeezed in beside him, close enough to demand his attention and for him to feel her presence through the sleeve of his jacket. Startled, he turned, and his eyes began to flicker in embarrassment, dancing across her chest like a ride of the Valkyries until, with an act of willpower that made his jaw crack, at last he found her face.

'Hi,' he croaked while his mind raced through any number of memory banks in search of something appropriate to say. 'Er, can I buy you a drink?'

'I was just getting one in for my friend.'

'Oh, sorry,' he apologized, diving into his glass as if an Old Bailey jury had just pronounced him guilty of multiple molestation.

'No problem,' Mary reassured. She paused before adding: 'He's going in a minute.'

Anorak Man brightened, sensing a reprieve.

'You could always buy me a drink when he's gone . . .'

Ten minutes later they were sitting side by side, elbows propped on the sticky-top table, within twenty they were into the world of geeks and gigabytes, and it took only another couple of pints before he was laying in front of her all the wondrous possibilities of cyber communities and 3-D graphic accelerators. Mary had been fortunate in her choice. Anorak Man turned out to be Roy, whose fascination with computer programming was matched only by his passion for science fiction films and photography. A creature, if not of the night, then certainly of many darkened rooms – and of Chingford, where he had a modest flat to which she was soon invited after expressing an innocent interest in learning how to go active on the Internet.

Payne was waiting for them outside the pub as they left. He'd spent three tours tracking active service units through the rat runs of Ulster. He smiled. Following a flapping anorak was going to be as simple as sin.

Above all else, Elizabeth was a practical woman. She had sat all afternoon and well into the evening in her small and windowless office at The Kremlin, waiting for an asteroid to strike and relieve her of any responsibility for sorting out her problems, but after the sun had set and the sky turned to darkness there was still no sign of any ball of fire hurtling from the heavens, so she had done what any practical woman would do in the circumstances.

She panicked.

Ignoring the fact that the restaurant had less than a fifty per cent cover that evening – and what did a few hundred pounds matter when she was in the steam bath for tens of thousands? – she opened a bottle of Irish Cream and got drunk.

She hated Irish Cream, that sickeningly sweet confection of coffee and Irish alcoholic ineptitude, but in the first place she simply wanted to get drunk and in the second, she felt she needed a little punishment. Punishment for the past and the present, and perhaps for what she might yet do. She also drank it because it cheered her up – an inconsistent attitude, perhaps, but why should a practical woman bother with consistency? The Irish Cream cheered her because it reminded her of a time when she was younger and had a refined taste for adventure, and of an evening spent in the company of a hotel mini-bar liberally stocked with the stuff. There had also been a young companion. Couldn't remember his name, but it was never going to be a long-term relationship, not with a teenage backpacker from Palo Alto.

Nor, it appeared, with Vladimir Houdoliy.

There was some small consolation in the fact that at least the uncertainty had been stripped away. She had at last heard from Vladimir that morning, not directly but *via* the People's Bank of Odessa. A Mr V. Voroshilov of the bank's legal department had written on paper so thin it was almost transparent to inform her that she could have neither the wine nor her money. The ownership of the wine, it seemed, was the subject of a vigorous dispute between Mr Houdoliy, the local community council for the city of Odessa (who regarded the wine as some sort of treasure trove) and the administrator of the health board (who had run the palace as a mental home for more than two decades). So convoluted had the wrangle become that there was even talk of an elderly Romanov putting in a claim on the basis that the bottles with the double-headed eagle had undoubt-edly been stolen from the Tsar's personal cellars at Massandra.

Since ownership of the wine was in question, it could not be released. Moreover, since her money had been deposited in legal payment for the wine, that could not be released either, until the Ukrainian justice system had decided who was the legitimate owner of the wine, and who was due the money. Mr Voroshilov regretted, but she would understand that the bank's hands were tied, and since the dispute covered property rights that went back into the mists of time, he could give no indication as to how long the legal fog might take to dissipate. Indeed, he could give nothing but his most sincere regrets.

'May your mistress be diseased and your wife for-ever vengeful, Mr Voroshilov,' she mumbled, raising her glass in toast.

It made her feel a little better, the cursing and the bottle, but it still didn't wipe away the fact that she was now the dollar equivalent of seventy thousand pounds in a hole.

So what was a practical girl to do? She'd already done the panicking bit and was now bored with the indulgence. She didn't do tears and smashing of fragile china, not without an audience at least. Which left only friends. A Rolodex of names and telephone numbers stood on her desk, a brief history of her entire time. The contacts, entanglements and adventures of her adult life, the good and also the bad. Once she had kept shoeboxes full of mementoes – letters, cards, trinkets, the menu of an enchanting dinner or the keepsake of an enchanted night. An odd cufflink. A pressed rose. Memories that were tied up in her boxes and under her control, to be brought out and relished, then locked away before they could cause any complications – until her sad, insecure husband had found them and, in a hail of accusation during one of their final tumultuous rows, had burned the lot. But not the Rolodex and its contact numbers. Almost casually she flicked her way through, turning it in the manner of a lottery wheel, dancing from one memory to another and relying on fortune to dictate what number might come up next.

Suddenly it had stopped and was screaming at her. A name from the past. *That* name. A name that could make light of her current problems with one swish of his Mont Blanc pen. Oh, but a name that would undoubtedly make for new problems. A business proposition, that's all it would be, she argued with herself. So what if it entailed taking a few risks? Her whole life was at stake and it's what any practical woman would do.

Then she thought about the risks and argued with herself some more. It took another glass of Irish Cream before she was finally convinced. Only then did she pick up the phone.

The apartment in Chingford was pretty much as Mary had expected, untainted by any trace of feminine influence. Abandoned laundry had spread across the furniture like a rainforest intent on reclaiming lost lands. The spider plant propped on the windowsill had already shrivelled in fright.

Geek City.

But twenty-three-year-old kids weren't notoriously tidy – for twenty-three years was what Roy admitted to being, and a kid is what Mary (at some damage to her own sense of eternal youth) regarded him as. He had a self-deprecating sense of humour and, beneath the anorak and unironed T-shirt, a lean and muscular body. There were weights lurking in a corner, running shoes by the door. He scurried around clearing up cereal bowls and magazines. Soon she could hear him scrabbling in his bathroom cabinet. He emerged reeking of aftershave.

She couldn't resist a wry smile of amusement. He made her feel almost matronly.

'Used too much, haven't I?' he confessed, melting a little in misery. He proceeded to cover his confusion by rushing round the room and removing several drying shirts from the backs of chairs. 'Bet you wouldn't know it, but I'm not used to bringing women back here.'

Her smile turned to laughter, and soon he was laughing, too.

'Sorry, I was forgetting. We came here to discuss computers. Seem to have this habit of making a complete fool of myself.'

She placed a hand on his shoulder. 'You're no fool, Roy. That's why I'm here, remember?'

It was a lie, as uncomplicated as it was unfair. She intended to make a complete fool of him.

'Let's go for it. I'll log on.'

'How about ordering a takeaway first? I'm famished.' Her eyes sparkled with mischief. 'We may be here some time. I'm a very slow learner.'

It was while he was in the kitchen ordering a Red Fort Special with extra popadoms and don't-forget-the-mint-yoghurt-sauce that she set to work. From her bag she withdrew what seemed like a telephone wall box, plastic, standard white. Next she unplugged the cable that led from Roy's modem to its telephone point on the wall, and in between the two inserted her own small box before reconnecting the modem. The operation lasted no longer than a sparrow's breath and her device added less than two centimetres to the depth of the telephone point. It was almost indistinguishable from the original and was securely hidden behind the usual chaos of wires and connections that wrapped themselves around each other behind his terminal. In a thousand nights, Roy would never notice.

Anyway, as he logged on, he was in a state of deep distraction. Distracted by Mary, by her proximity, and most of all by the fact that, as he switched his attention from the onion bhaji to the lamb pasanda, Mary swivelled the mouse and appeared to stumble into the twilight world of soft-porn news groups that began to smother the screen in lurid images.

'Does this . . . ? Do they . . . ? Can they really . . . ? Wow, now I see why you spend so much time with your keyboard,' she chided gently.

He didn't respond, uncertain where this was leading, finding it easier to hide inside his can of Tartan.

'You like this sort of stuff, Roy?'

'Er . . . Don't most guys?'

'Some girls, too. Although most of this seems . . .' she rolled the mouse around in slow, gentle circles – 'a little tame?'

He took another swig from his can. Maybe he was on to a good thing here. 'I can do much better than that.'

'Can you?' she said, goading him with innocence.

There are standard protocols for the design of computer networks that are supposed to ensure that the systems are secure. Available only to the authorized. Which means no illicit access, no getting caught with your bits in the wrong bundle.

Yet like many other things in the world of computers, these protocols are a piece of virtual reality. In other words, they don't really exist. For in spite of these protocols there is an equally standard tradition that every software engineer tasked with designing those security systems always leaves a back door, his or her own private entrance into the Forbidden Garden, which allows it to be accessed twenty-four hours a day from wherever he or she chooses. It's a form of intellectual copyright, a claim of ownership over the system they themselves have developed.

It is also a form of larceny, for once you have access to hardware that far exceeds the capabilities of anything you might have tucked away in the spare bedroom at home, there's an almost irresistible temptation to expropriate a portion of it, to store within its vast memory banks a few thousand megabytes of your own. It's much like taking the corporate Ferrari for an illicit spin while the boss's back is turned. As a result, buried deep within the root directories of almost every substantial corporate mainframe computer are caches of private contraband, usually high-resolution images of photographs and video clips that gobble up far too much memory to be accommodated on domestic PCs.

It took no more than twenty seconds for Roy to access the Telecoms computer with its vast store of information, which included a library of tawdry pictures that the Telecoms software engineers, in the manner of software engineers everywhere, had accumulated. With a flurry of mouse strokes Roy put on display his formidable computer skills and, alongside them, his considerably less formidable sense of taste.

As he dialled the access numbers, and then the passwords, the digital data recorder she had installed across the telephone point tracked it all. The DDR copied everything, all the numbers and notations that made up the entry codes to the Forbidden Garden. It was some little while later, as Roy was excusing himself in order to straighten his duvet and arrange a little mood music on his radio alarm, that she unplugged the DDR and stuffed it back in her bag. Telecoms' back door was left swinging open. Poor sap would never know.

Mission accomplished. Objective achieved and all in under two hours. Soon she would be back in the car where Freddie Payne was waiting, securing her escape route.

Freddie Payne. With his irritating smirk and molesting eyes. Dribbling all the way back with asinine comments about nerds and nookie. 'Did the anorak put up much of a struggle, dear?' Sneering. Demeaning her.

He was a lot like Gittings.

She disliked Freddie. She wanted to spend as little time in his company as possible. Didn't give a damn about him freezing his balls off in the car; in fact, she positively approved of the idea.

Roy had returned from the bedroom. He'd changed out of work clothes into a wash-tight T-shirt and Levi's and showed none of the wearied sinews and frayed ardour that clung to her husband. The eyes were bright, hopeful, not threatening or taking advantage – hell, she was the one taking advantage. As her own eyes wandered from brow to biceps, and inescapably to butt, she discovered something wonderfully spontaneous about all that fresh muscle and raw hope, something so very different from what she had known.

She thought of Payne lingering outside, wriggling in discomfort, and she smiled. Catching the moment, Roy smiled, too. Poor dear. His thoughts were entirely elsewhere.

Bless him. He had so much to learn.

'Sorry, Freddie. Tutorial lasted longer than I expected,' she offered in excuse as she climbed into the car. 'And turn the heat on, will you? Christ, it's freezing in here.'

He sulked all the way back.

*　　*　　*

In Goodfellowe's humble opinion, it had been altogether one of his finer inspirations.

Because of his absence from the emergency meeting of the executive committee he had not been able to prevent Beryl from appointing a new treasurer-elect but Goodfellowe could, at least, oil the slippery downward path that awaits the unwary who enter upon the world of politics.

It was not the new treasurer's fault that his name was Rodney. The name had presumably been appended long before anyone realized he had a slight speech impediment which turned all his Rs to ruination. Poor Wodney. Neither could he be blamed for the fact that he had a face that appeared not yet fully formed, even in his late twenties, with an Adam's apple that worked overtime as if he'd just swallowed a sparrow.

In fact, he had just enjoyed cold cherry soup, one of The Kremlin's most popular *hors d'oeuvres*, a middle-European pleasure he had shared with Goodfellowe and Beryl. Relations between Goodfellowe and Beryl had now changed, becoming indisputably less venomous from the moment Rankin had telephoned the chair-monster to inform her of her Member's new significance in public life. 'A quiet role. Behind the scenes for the moment. But in the Prime Minister's view he's one of the favoured few. Going places. Hold on to him.'

So Goodfellowe had invited Beryl and her new protégé to dinner at The Kremlin, where he got everything at discount, in an attempt to reestablish some form of diplomatic relations. An innocent invitation. Yet opportunities in politics are there to be grasped rather than to be studied, and if the gesture had begun as a token of good faith it was not to last, for as the evening wore on, the pouring of oil on troubled waters had been accompanied by copious quantities of alcohol, from which arose a significant opportunity. At first Goodfellowe had poured to drown his own discomfort, then for his own enjoyment, but soon he had begun to exploit the advantage of playing on home turf and had corralled a steady stream of other Members to linger at their table for a glass of wine while they sang his praises and fussed over his guests. Beryl's initial response to the adulation and alcohol was to flush gently from the top of her breasts, following which she stiffened and took a little more time over everything, but the flush on Rodney went straight to his cheeks. He wasn't used to so much excitement and attention. Or to being out of bed after ten.

The flush on both of them increased when, after dessert, the Chief Whip himself approached to insist that they join him in a glass of dessert vodka.

'My name's Wodney,' the treasurer-elect introduced himself, holding on to Rankin's hand as a countryman clings to tradition. He only let go in order to join in a fresh round of toasts.

'One more?' Rankin enquired. 'On me?'

'I think we may have had enough,' Beryl responded, trying to recover a dignity she felt she had somehow mislaid. The red tide had swum high up her bosom and was about to attack her throat.

'But no, let me,' blurted Rodney. 'Excuse me for butting in, Bewyl, but this is a ware tweat.'

'A what?' enquired Goodfellowe, quietly choking.

Rodney struggled to repeat himself.

'Yes, I think we've had enough,' Beryl repeated, more stiffly.

'I insist. Tweasuwer's turn.'

'Treasurer-*elect*,' Beryl enunciated with feeling, as though to emphasize that elections, even the rigged ones, don't always turn out as expected.

But her pause for precision proved fatal, for even as she was reminding him that his position had yet to be confirmed at the AGM, he was already waving his hand to attract the attention of Olga, the Filipino waitress whose real name was Maribelle. 'Another wound!' he barked.

A pause. 'Another what, sir?'

'Another wound. Of dwinks!'

'We will have just one more. *And only one more*,' Beryl insisted, seeming a little breathless. 'That's if you'd care for one, Mr Rankin?'

'Delighted. Fine. You know, I'm grateful, Miss Hailstone, or may I call you Beryl? Not just for the hospitality, but your unswerving support for Tom here. Can't tell you how much the Prime Minister appreciates it. May I recommend the Armagnac?'

Goodfellowe sat back, almost a spectator in this little game, and as far as games go, Rodney was playing a blinder. As soon as the crystal balloons of Armagnac had arrived, he raised his glass in salute. 'What shall we toast?'

'Why, to Tom,' Rankin responded. 'A fine parlia-mentarian. And the power behind the throne.'

All glasses were raised. Beryl sipped at hers as though to dull the pain. Rankin downed his in one in order to get on with it, but Rodney had suddenly begun to look with a fixed gaze into his glass as though he'd found a goldfish swimming in it. His eyes were moving round and round the rim as if looking for a beginning and an end.

'To Tom!' Rankin insisted.

And Rodney threw his head back and followed suit by downing the Armagnac in a single draught.

Then his head fell forward. 'Excuse me, where's the . . . ?' He wanted to use the term 'rest room', but knew it was beyond him, and was unsure whether such words as 'loo' or 'lavatory' were correct in polite Westminster company, or at least in front of Beryl. His courage failed him, as did his sense of occasion.

'Oh, God. I think something has disagweed with me. Excuse me, Bewyl. Tom. And 'specially you, Mr Wank . . .'

'You're excused!' Beryl cried in desperation.

He rose unsteadily to his feet. He seemed to have left his colour at table level. His face was now like molten wax, held too close to a flame. He dipped for-ward, sending the small flower vase spilling upon the cloth, then he lurched back, so far that Goodfellowe had to prevent his chair from crashing to the ground. With limbs that extended in the manner of an early robot, Rodney made his uncertain way towards the back of the restaurant.

They watched him go in silence until, with a final rush, the door banged shut behind him.

'Not one for the vicissitudes of Westminster, I fear,' Rankin offered sympathetically.

'Nor for the long road back to Marshwood,' Beryl added in a tone devoid of any trace of sympathy. 'The bloody man was driving.' The red tide had turned into angry hives which camped upon every part of her exposed flesh.

'He'll recover.'

'Somehow I very much doubt it,' Beryl spat.

They watched as Beryl hustled her fallen idol out of the restaurant. She didn't want to lay hands on him, not in public, but his progress was like that of any rake, wandering from side to side, so she was forced to dance around him and nudge him forward as though she were rustling cattle.

'Thanks, Eddie. You were bloody magnificent.'

'No problem, Tom.' His stomach groaned softly inside. 'Did it work?'

'Wodney's got about as much chance of making it to the AGM as you have of making Pope.'

'The black arts survive.'

'And flourish. I owe you a drink.'

'Look forward to it.' He offered a soft belch, a sigh of relief. 'But not tonight, eh?'

Not twenty minutes after the Chief Whip had departed to practise the black arts in other corners of his

235

kingdom, the pager at Goodfellowe's belt began to rattle.

His world glowed green. Good news. He was back on a One-Line Whip, which meant that the realm would survive without his presence in the Chamber until the morning. He scrabbled to switch off the pager as though it were a nuclear accident waiting to happen, anxious to allow no opportunity for those Simple Simons in the Whips' Office to change their minds and snatch away his evening once again. He had other things planned.

Elizabeth was in her office. She had seemed pre-occupied all evening, had been for days, in fact, but he thought he knew how to bring a smile back to her face. He'd been pondering upon it for some time, and the more he pondered the more it all became clear. Paris.

He didn't have the money, of course, never did, but one of his constituents had died and left him two thousand from her considerable fortune (the rest went to the cats). Yes, it happens. It would pay off the overdraft and leave just about enough. He needed a new refrigerator and a new bike, but what the hell? He could squeeze a trip to Paris from it. After all, it wasn't every day you asked a woman to marry you.

It had been nigh on a quarter of a century since he'd been to Paris, but the memory refused to fade. Of an endless weekend, spent walking hand-in-hand with a woman he loved (but would later forget), happy to lose themselves in the perfumed streets, to let chance take them. For a few days they had owned it all, the parks, the boulevards, that wonderful cherry-and-garlic smell of Paris in the spring. The bars on the Champs-Elysées had their own atmosphere, of Bogart and Sartre and strangers in love but with too little time. It had been Saturday, and after nightfall they'd wandered along the banks of the Seine, the sounds of life dancing across the muddy waters, until they had come upon Notre Dame. During the day the cathedral seemed a dark and oppressive place to the deeply agnostic Goodfellowe, a place of witches and spells and soot, yet by night it was transformed into a place of hope and dreams. Flickering candlelight reflected off brass, incense filled his head while the organ announced salvation and the choir reached out to lift the congregation's souls as it had done for a thousand years. It was one of those moments that left its mark on Goodfellowe's mind for reasons he couldn't entirely explain. Thereafter, even in his bleakest moments, he would remember those bent women in their shawls clinging stubbornly to their rosaries and their hopes, memories of faith that would help him cling equally stubbornly to those things in which he believed.

To Goodfellowe, Paris continues to mean hope. And love. Which means Elizabeth.

So now he is perching expectantly on the corner of her tiny desk. 'Hey, I'm excused. No parade tonight.'

Elizabeth appears determinedly unimpressed.

'Thought I might hang around. Until you're finished. Share a drink, maybe? There's something I want to ask you.'

237

A frown flickers across her brow. He needs a different tactic.

'Second thoughts, maybe I'll see if I can score with the blonde sitting over there by the mirror.'

A pause. Still no response.

'Obviously, Elizabeth, I'm doing something wrong. Am I sitting on your winning Lottery ticket or what?'

'If you were I'd be feeding you through the mincer right now.'

'That bad?'

When she looks up, the answer is in her eyes. Not just distracted, despairing. Not wanting to face Goodfellowe, not wanting him to be there. Still a hostage in a cellar by the Black Sea.

'Anything I can do?'

The question seems to deflate her even further. No, he can't help and what's worse, she realizes with a flush of guilt that she's never even thought he might. She feels a little ashamed. 'The wine deal's gone wrong. Very wrong. I can't get either the wine or my money back and I desperately need an early night, Tom. Do you mind?'

'Of course I do,' he responds, then pauses, hoping she might change her mind. 'Nothing I can do?' he asks again.

'No.'

'Fine. I'll see you, then.'

'Thanks.'

He is almost out of the door when she remembers. 'Oh, I'm sorry, poppet, what was that thing you wanted to ask me?'

'No matter.' Another pause. 'It can wait.'

He leaves, to think of Paris and his Paradise post-poned, while Elizabeth can think only of Odessa.

ELEVEN

Amadeus had taken to running, long jogs through the City at night when the traffic had gone and taken most of its fumes with it. He couldn't think in the rabbit hutch that his wife insisted they call home, even when she wasn't there, which was frequently. He needed space, time to figure it all out, wanting to squeeze away the last effect of those cigarettes and get himself honed for what he knew lay ahead. The Barbican where they lived might have been convenient for his wife's shopping and social life, but to Amadeus it was worse than useless, the farthest point from any green field of almost any spot in London. He wished he were back on the mountainside of Longdon, and yearned for an enemy that could be fought with rifle and bayonet.

He was clear that matters had escalated beyond his control. What had started as a skirmish had grown into all-out confrontation. It happens, things slip in war. They had begun in search of an apology but apologies only counted in matters of honour and they'd been disastrously naïve to believe they might have found any shred of honour in Bendall. So now the stakes had to be raised. There was no middle way, no subtle means of getting this Government to change its policies. The Government itself had to be changed.

The logic was compelling, inexorable. Bendall had to go.

The consequence was equally inescapable.

Treason.

It was something they couldn't admit to, of course, not out in the open. For a soldier to seek the downfall of an elected Prime Minister was an offence so inexcusable that it would force Bendall's most implacable opponents to rally to his defence. Even the BBC would have to behave itself. It would make the bastard all but impregnable. No, a direct attack was impossible. Instead, Bendall would have to be worn down, undermined, humiliated and hounded until his position had crumbled and he crept out of Downing Street, or was dragged out by envious colleagues.

Somehow treason had become their duty.

This evening Amadeus had run as far as Regent's Park trying to clear his mind, struggling to understand the process by which he had started as a loyal officer and ended up a revolutionary. He still wasn't entirely clear by the time he had got back to the Barbican and headed for his apartment on the thirtieth floor. He used the stairs.

As he opened his door, the first thing he saw was the answering machine blinking at him. He punched the button. A message from a Sergeant Harris at Wood Street police station. Amadeus didn't know a Sergeant Harris, or why he should be calling, but the policeman said it was important. Amadeus was to call back any time up to midnight. Or Sergeant Harris would call again in the morning.

Oh, bugger.

The sun had not yet risen, yet already the Telecoms Chairman was standing at his desk, tieless, unshaven, agitated. A copy of the morning newspaper trembled in his outstretched hand.

'**WHIPPED!**' it screamed. '**Bendall Humiliated As Government Loses Vital Budget Vote**.'

The front page recounted the dramatic events of the previous evening when, amidst scenes of great frenzy, the Government had been brought to its knees by the failure of dozens of its own backbenchers to vote for a vital financial measure. Yet this was neither insolence nor insurrection; to put no finer point on it, they had simply been nobbled. Only ten minutes before the vote their pagers had vibrated into action and called them off. Go home, the message had encouraged, go sleep or go play or whatever it is you do when the Whips are no longer watching – but go!

It had been a hoax, of course. The Whips had realized that immediately and had made desperate efforts to correct it, only to discover that the telephone number assigned to their paging system was inexplicably and constantly engaged, as if someone was deliberately sabotaging it. So they had called the operator, who had explained that she was powerless to interfere, so they had shouted at her, but the more they had shouted the more she had insisted that there was nothing she could do, and would they please stop using such language. It was, she explained with commendable patience, a number that had been issued with a special security coding and under no circumstances could be interfered with. After all, someone might try to use it irresponsibly . . .

By the time the Whips had battered their way through female intransigence, it was too late. Many Government supporters had been thrown into chaos, milling about in uncertainty like rustled cattle, while others simply trudged home, blissfully unaware, pagers switched off, as did Goodfellowe. Despite numerous and increasingly desperate points of order the vote had been taken. And the Government had lost.

'How could this happen? How *could* it happen?' the Telecoms Chairman asked yet again. Since his arrival at the office it had seemed his only form of expression. He was in a state of considerable turmoil, having been woken at two by the Prime Minister. A personal call. Usually a pleasure, for they had been room-mates at university and remained close. It was one of the reasons he'd been given the job as chairman, to use his connections to smooth the path of controversial licence applications and to blunt the edge of government competition policy. He wasn't supposed to get hysterical phone calls in the middle of the night from a Prime Minister threatening to reintroduce transportation to the colonies especially for him.

Over the following three hours, the problem had grown worse. He couldn't raise his personal assistant, and so had incredible trouble raising anyone else.

He'd even had trouble getting into the building when he arrived unshaven with eyes like blood drops in the snow – and without his security pass. He was chairman of the company, for pity's sake, he didn't need a pass! But the night security staff, at least those who spoke English, were having none of it. No pass, no come in. It was the only part of Telecoms security that seemed to be working that night.

'The sodding Government loses some sodding vote, all because some sod sods up our sodding pager system. And what I want to know is – *which sod's responsible?*'

In fact, Bendall had made it crystal clear, in one of the more coherent portions of his telephone conversation, who he deemed to be responsible. The Chairman was responsible. Unless, that is, he could find some other copulative colon to take the blame, and quickly.

The Chairman faced one of his staff. Just one. Sod it, even after all the redundancies he still had more than a hundred thousand on his payroll, and yet all he could find at this hour of the morning was one miserable wretch. An audience of one was not much to share his humiliation, but at least it was an audience. He needed someone to shout at. He stood behind his desk, shaking the newspaper as if to emphasize his point, although in truth it was simply his hand that was shaking.

For a while, the young man standing before him listened in silence to the outpourings of anger until he decided that he was on the brink of one of those moments in which careers suddenly changed paths, where they might be destroyed. Or perhaps made. He was a gambler. So he jumped.

'It was the Opposition.'

'What? What sodding opposition?' the Chairman demanded. 'Anyway, who the sodding hell are you?'

'Hadcock. Tim Hadcock, sir,' the young man introduced himself once more. He was a junior member of the Policy and Presentation staff, not yet into his thirty-somethings, corporate lowlife, yet because of the bizarre accidents that litter a man's life he was confronted at this moment by opportunity. It was a pity, of course, that his director had been forced to commute by rail from Surrey ever since he'd lost his licence and wouldn't be arriving for at least another hour, but Hadcock was nothing if not resourceful and had no intention of hanging around waiting for one of life's accidents. Neither had his Chairman.

'Explain yourself!'

'Well, sir, I've talked to the Director of Engineering – he's hoping to be here shortly – and he is adamant it couldn't have been an accident. And the Director of Security – I got hold of him at a conference in Rio de Janeiro – insists that our internal systems are practically impregnable, both physically and technically.'

'So?'

'So it means that the breach in security didn't come from us. More than likely it came from the other end. From Westminster.'

'What? What are you suggesting, Badcock? That I tell the Prime Minister it's his fault?'

'Well, I don't suppose for a moment that the Government Whips sent out the message. So it must have been someone else at Westminster. Someone with an interest in making a laughing stock of the Government. Someone who's familiar with Whips and pagers, who might have had the opportunity of activating the system. Someone whose presence around the House late at night would be entirely acceptable.'

'You mean . . . ?'

'Someone with both the motive and the means, sir.'

'Such as . . . ?'

'Someone in the Opposition!'

The Chairman's lips began moving as though silently rehearsing a plea. He experimented for a few moments, tried again, then shook his head in defeat. 'What evidence do you have for this allegation?'

'Not a shred.'

'So how do you know it's the sodding Opposition?'

'I don't, sir. But if you'll forgive me . . .' The young man hesitated. He was about to make that career choice. He was not a Director. Not an Assistant Director. Not even an Assistant to the Assistant. He had so little to lose. 'I thought the purpose of the exercise wasn't so much a matter of proof as one of . . . well, of presentation. We know it wasn't us. So we need to put someone else in the frame. To take the pressure off us – off *you*, sir. And since we're unlikely ever to find out who was responsible, someone else will do. Anyone else, actually.'

The Chairman's lips were moving once more, practising, following as Spatchcock – wasn't that his name? – set out his case that it *could* have been the Opposition. It was the sort of explanation the Government would willingly embrace. No direct accusation, of course, just a whisper or two in a friendly journalist's ear. Unattributable sources, that sort of thing. Or perhaps an allegation from the back benches under the cloak of parliamentary privilege, get everyone running around trying to identify some sort of dirty tricks squad. Press'd love that.

'And there's that new licence application for digital TV around the corner on which we'll need the Government's help, sir,' the Chairman heard the young man remind him. 'We really need to get this one off our plate.'

The Chairman was now sitting. He had had his head in his hands, contemplating.

'Security's certain it couldn't have been our fault?'

'Almost certain.'

'Almost . . . ?' Outside his window the sun was creeping above the horizon. Dawn. The time of scaffolds and executions.

'There is always a *theoretical* possibility it was down to us, sir.'

The Chairman moaned softly.

'You really want to be hanged for a theory, sir?' A pause. 'Go for the Opposition. It's what the Government wants to hear, isn't it? Bury your doubts, go for what's certain.'

The Chairman raised his eyes. 'What did you say your name was?'

'Hadcock, sir. Tim Hadcock.'

The Chairman's shoulders seemed slowly to discard

the steel pins that had been keeping them taut and painfully hunched. 'Tell me, young Haddock. Are you by any chance free for lunch?'

The five of them are crowded into an anonymous hotel room. It's an unlikely location for war. Wilting roses on the wallpaper, cigarette burns on the bedside table, cheap foam sofas, that sort of thing. A place that caters for package tourists, where no one will remember their faces. But they'll remember what the five have come here to do.

Amadeus's stomach is a whirlpool of adrenaline and unease, the same feeling he used to get standing in the door of a Hercules with the PJI screaming instructions at him. The man is screaming because the wind is whipping past at a hundred and twenty knots, turning their lungs to ice and beating like a hammer upon their ears. Amadeus has an SA80 rifle hooked to his chest, along with his container and a bergen that is stuffed with ammunition and food and clothing. The red is on and he's about to jump into total darkness.

He knows that's the point where it can all begin to go wrong. You can prepare only so far. There's always the unexpected, things that get out of control. Little things. Like Mary, who decided to try out her new toy on the Whips' paging system without consulting him first. And Skulls's leg, which, now he is sober and sentient, is hurting like hell. Then there is Freddie Payne and his mood swings. Nervous one day, morose the next, followed by outbursts of arrogance and sometimes all three in quick succession.

There's also the interview Amadeus has agreed to have in the morning with Sergeant Harris, and he still doesn't know what the fuck that's all about, although if the good sergeant only wants to talk to him rather than drag him off by the balls then Amadeus knows he's still ahead of the game. Just.

Yes, there's always the unexpected, the sudden shift of the slipstream that can spin you round until you've no bloody idea which way you're facing, only that you're heading down. Knowing that in thirty seconds you might be dead. Or worse, broken.

Thirty seconds is about as long as Mary says it will take.

For this is Mary's piece tonight, inspired with almost comic irony by that halfwit Earwick. Bloody fool didn't know when to stop posing. He'd been showing the news cameras around his new empire of the Home Office, that curious mixture of reprieves and repression that glowers like a decaying white elephant beside St James's Park. It'd only been an establishing shot for the evening news, the sort of thing where politicians are shown walking stiffly up the stairs or browsing self-consciously through a briefing paper trying to pretend they are speed readers. Those who have no clue whatsoever might be seen plucking some book from the library shelf, presumably as evidence of their intellectual curiosity, then destroying the effect by flicking through the pages backwards. Earwick was wise to all this; he wanted to display himself as a Thoroughly Modern Minister, every part a man of the new Millennium, revved up and switched on. So he had seated himself at his computer terminal and logged on. Not that you could see the screen or the password he had entered to access his e-mail, but his two fingers had wandered across his keyboard 'like slugs across a leaf of lettuce,' as Mary had described it later.

There are few surprises in the passwords used by laymen. Many consist of the word itself. PASSWORD. People can be so gloriously unimaginative. But Earwig could never be commonplace, he was a man of theatrical flourishes, his password had to be both personal and significant. He had chosen HOMO.MAN. An obvious signature for a Home Secretary, although perhaps open to misinterpretation if it fell into the wrong hands. Which it wasn't supposed to.

But it had.

Mary had spotted Earwick on the early evening news, taped the replay an hour later and enlarged the image of the keyboard section on her own laptop so that by nine she had everything she needed to know. The following day she had e-mailed his office at the House of Commons, purporting to be a journalist for a provincial newspaper and asking for full biographical details, which she received by return from his parliamentary researcher. The enthusiastic researcher had included everything from his master's love of dogs – *a King Charles spaniel named Jessie . . .* – to his abiding commitment to the elderly, the High Church and the family, although from the details provided it appeared that Earwig didn't have a family. What the researcher failed to realize is that in replying by e-mail to Mary he was also supplying her with the encrypted techy scribble that accompanied all e-mails and that included clusters of information such as Earwig's Server Name, his Return Path, and even his User Name.

So now Mary is sitting in the hotel room with the drooping flowers, in front of her laptop, which is plugged into the telephone line. She also has in front of her a copy of the *Sun*, open at the letters page. She is about to go to war, on Earwick and on Bendall, and to achieve that she intends to go to war on the whole of London. What follows may be incomprehensible to anyone over fifty, just as it is clearer than Shakespeare's English to most teenagers.

She opens up a window for her modem and dials **9** for an outside line.

The cursor on the screen is panting like a greyhound in the slips. So she taps in the number of Earwig's e-mail server at the House of Commons. The hound is off and running. It soon returns, bearing with it a prize – the command **LOGIN**.

She types in his **User Name**, presses **Return**.

Then she enters the difficult bit, Earwig's **Password**. *HOMO.MAN*.

Presses **Return** once again. She's in.

She creates a new file called **Forward**, and instructs it to copy everything to another address. Not just any other address, mind you, but the editor@the-sun.co.uk. (This address involves a dash of guesswork, based on details included on the newspaper's letter page, but when her greyhound doesn't come back with its tail between its legs she knows it's OK. She smiles. She's there.)

Then she hits the **Control** and **D** keys simultaneously, a combination that instantly logs her off the system, neatly and quickly so as not to alert any system administrators at the House of Commons. No one knows she's been there.

It's done. A fraction more than thirty seconds, and an effect that will last a lifetime.

The rest of her evening's work on the laptop takes longer. She is completely engrossed, ignoring the distractions around her. Her concentration is total, as if she is under hostile fire, triangulating the position of an enemy mobile communications HQ that is on the move and directing the enemy's own fire upon her. She knows there is only one winner in this sort of game. The screen is becoming hypnotic; at one point she is forced to leave her work and wander into the bathroom to splash water on her face. It's a squalid little room. She ignores the tang of bleach and the mess of men.

As he watches her work, Amadeus feels equally engrossed, but for entirely different reasons. He knows they have now jumped, are out in the slipstream, winds of fate and all that. Nothing to do but wait and pray a little. He wipes the palms of his hand along the sharp creases of his trousers. The others sit around distractedly. Scully is watching television with the sound on mute, McKenzie is browsing through the bible left by the Gideons in the bedside drawer. Beside the door where he is standing lookout, Freddie Payne crushes a can in his hand.

Tonight, in a hotel room filled with drooping flowers and the smell of anxious men, they have gone to war. Many lives are about to be irreversibly changed, and some ended. Soon Amadeus will have blood on his hands.

Mickey scurried into the Central Lobby through the morning crowds of sightseers and plaintiffs that had already begun to gather. Although she had never met him, she thought she recognized her man instantly. Tall, lean, hair a little longer than was customary in the military but neatly trimmed and swept back, a cleft on his chin that looked as deep as a duelling scar. He was no longer young but in altogether better decorative order than most men of his age. Disturbing slate green eyes, though, eyes that had seen too much.

'Colonel Amadeus?'

Amadeus turned from where he had been examining the almost overpowering mosaic of the ceiling and began to inspect her. His eyes seemed to take everything in; she found it disturbing, but also sensual.

'I'm Mickey Ross, Tom's secretary.' She held out her hand. It disappeared inside his own. 'This place is like a kitchen at Christmas right now. Somebody screwed up the vote last night and everyone's running around like chickens with their feathers on fire.' She was about to take him by the sleeve and guide him to a quieter corner but changed her mind – somehow he didn't seem like the sort of man you took by the sleeve, let alone pushed around. 'So Tom's had to disappear, rush off for a meeting with the PM.'

Amadeus's eyes arched in surprise. 'Now isn't that a pity.'

'He was so looking forward to that drink with you, believe me. And he'd like a rain check, if you'd be willing.' She wouldn't mind a rain check either, come to that. He had an unmistakable muscular intensity. Built for stamina, this one. Anyway, the man deserved more than a polite brush off. The drink had been arranged at Goodfellowe's request, it seemed rude simply to cast him back into the street without a proper explanation. 'I'm not sure whether I'm supposed to tell you this, but seeing as you're in – were in – the military, and an old friend, I know you'll understand.' Now she did take his sleeve. 'The Prime Minister's put Tom on a special Downing Street committee to deal with all the recent attacks.'

'I had no idea.'

'After last night, well, it's all hit the fan again and Tom's been summoned. Orders, orders. I'm sure you'll understand. He's so very sorry. He was really keen to catch up with you.'

'So was I. But if I'd known how important he'd become to the Prime Minister I truly wouldn't have bothered him.'

The irony, inevitably, went beyond her. 'Tom is full of apologies. He insisted that I rearrange the date and take you for a cup of coffee in the Strangers' canteen – not elegant, I'm afraid, but the coffee's wet. Then I can throw you out with a better conscience.'

'That . . .' – he hesitated, weighing up the invitation – 'would be very kind, Miss Ross. I'd enjoy a coffee. Dry as a bone, in fact. But I wonder if I can ask you for a small favour in addition?'

'Anything.'

'I'm supposed to be meeting a Sergeant Harris at Wood Street police station in a little while and the traffic is the very devil. It'll probably make me . . .' – he glanced at his watch, calculating – 'a little late. Would you telephone him? Tell him I've been delayed at the House of Commons visiting my old friend Tom Goodfellowe, and that he's got time to issue a few more parking tickets before I get there.' *And, while you're doing that, Mickey Ross, you can begin giving me the cover I'm going to need. Glorious cover, as a friend of the friend of the Prime Minister himself.*

The police officer had been quite explicit on the phone. He apologized for bothering Amadeus, but they were making enquiries into the attack on Trafalgar Square and other matters. Apparently there had been suggestions it might have had something to do with former military people, and as a matter of routine they'd been asked to look at all recently retired officers. Routine, did he say? There were hundreds of them, thousands, the sergeant wearily admitted. 'And after your letter to the *Telegraph*, sir . . .' Amadeus had assured the sergeant that he quite understood. 'Simply a matter of eliminating as many people as possible from our enquiries, Colonel. Just routine. A little chat, at your convenience.'

They were getting closer. But not that close. The military grapevine had already told Amadeus he was no more than one amongst thousands, many hundreds of whom at some time or another had bitched and bawled about higher authority. No, it shouldn't be a problem, so long as he played a straight bat. Hell, with the use of Tom Goodfellowe's name, he might even score a few runs while he was about it.

Amadeus smiled. 'You make the phone call, Miss Ross, I'll queue for the coffee.'

The precise constitutional grounds for summoning a fresh meeting of COBRA were open to question, but as the Prime Minister had pointed out, since Britain didn't have a written constitution the question – and any questioners – could go hang. He'd left the Cabinet Secretary debating with the Lord Chancellor whether making fools of the Government Whips threatened the end of civilization while he, Bendall, got on with the matter in hand.

There had been an unfortunate turn of events to encourage his impatience – unfortunate, that is, for Bendall and his hopes of containing the situation, for Amadeus had grown weary of sending letters that remained unread and unreported, and so, prompted by Sergeant Harris's phone call, he had decided on a change of tactics. Sergeant Harris had explicitly requested that Amadeus keep the matter confidential. Instead, Amadeus telephoned the editor of the *Telegraph*. The public had a right to know. There were no mad environmentalists here, no army of Swampies. No fanatics, no Fascists, no Freemasons, neither Ayatollahs nor Iraqis, and not a bloody Marxist or Leninist amongst them, Amadeus had explained. Nothing more than a group of retired and disgruntled but very British army officers. The editor had, at first, struggled to contain his surprise.

'You're saying you were responsible for the attacks? The water? Trafalgar Square?'

'The pager system too.'

'But why?'

'To show that this Government has lied when it says it can defend the country. We're simply proving it can't even defend itself.'

'So you're not eco-warriors as the Prime Minister claims.'

'Bendall's lied about that, too. He knows we're military. He's putting the squeeze on all retired officers even as we speak.'

'What's your next step?'

'You don't seriously expect –'

'But you're going to carry on?'

'Of course. We have a duty.'

'Like Oliver Cromwell?'

'We're retired, not antiques.'

'Sergeant Bilko, then?'

'British, we're British. Not Bilko. More like – I don't know. Beaky? That's it. More like Captain Beaky,' Amadeus had mused, citing a comic song based upon a band of woodland animals who had set out to deal with an evil snake named Hissing Sid. It had been an extraordinary hit back in the early Eighties.

'It's coming back to me . . . *The bravest animals in the land are Captain Beaky and his band . . .*" Isn't that it?'

Amadeus had laughed, then hung up.

Conscious of his public duty, the editor had called the Prime Minister to tell him what had happened. The Prime Minister had thanked him profusely and indicated that in view of the great sensitivity of the matter he felt sure the editor wouldn't be publishing. The editor had replied that the Government had been weaving such a web of nonsense it was in serious danger of throttling itself, so he was going to do the Government a considerable favour and publish the lot.

The Prime Minister had begun to shout. Something about issuing D-Notices on grounds of national security, to which the editor had suggested that if hacking into the Whips' paging system was so life-threatening the Prime Minister shouldn't be encouraging his bully boys to lay the blame at the doorstep of the Opposition.

At that point the Prime Minister had almost choked. He recovered sufficiently to insist that the editor cooperate fully with the ongoing police investigation. The editor had assured him that he would withhold nothing. In fact, he was going to publish everything he knew in his newspaper, and he would be happy to send a copy round to New Scotland Yard.

This was the moment when the Prime Minister lost touch with his sense of humour and suggested he was going to 'do' the editor personally. The editor enquired whether the Prime Minister had ever heard about freedom of the press and then, like Amadeus, had put the phone down. Faced with an outbreak of insurrection on the news stands, the Prime Minister had decided to summon the unscheduled meeting of COBRA.

Goodfellowe found himself able to listen to the ensuing discussions with only half a mind. He sat fiddling with his watch strap, distracted by the telephone call he'd had the previous night from Sam. It had been an unsettling conversation. She'd asked for money, eight hundred pounds for a summer trip to Florence in order to pursue her university course in the history of art. It was unsettling in two respects. In the first place, Sam wouldn't normally have asked for money, since she knew all too well the financial desert on which his tent was pitched. She demanded his loyalty, not his wallet, so it was clear to him without the need for elaboration that this trip to Italy was important to her. In the second place, it forced him to make a difficult choice. Normally, her request would have caused him few problems because he had no money, so the answer must be no. Yet life was no longer quite that simple. Thanks to the small bequest from his constituent, for the first time in three years he was receiving bank statements printed in black. It wasn't so straightforward saying no any more. He had the money, but it was earmarked for his trip to Paris with Elizabeth. Now Sam was calling upon it. He could split his affections, but not his finances. Elizabeth or Sam, which was it to be? It was a dilemma he found unusually discomforting. He'd lost sleep, didn't want to decide. This was giving him more grief than when he was broke. Somehow he found poverty so much simpler.

Suddenly he brightened. He was a fool. Why did he need to worry about his wallet when he had in his pocket a promise that he was soon to be kicked up to the Cabinet? That was worth money, hard cash, and a considerable amount of it, about another sixty thousand above his backbencher's salary. Come to think of it, more than he'd ever earned in his life. He'd soon be able to afford both Paris and Florence and a hell of a lot more beside, just as soon as the Prime Minister had seen off these irritating Army types.

However, he had to admit that today wasn't proving to be one of the better days in the campaign. True to its editor's promise, the morning's *Telegraph* had shouted from the top of its front page that the Government had been caught in a lie. Bendall had stretched the truth so tight that the elastic had burst. He wasn't fighting eco-freaks but former soldiers, Britain's best and bravest, and suddenly the morality of the situation was no longer so simple. Slowly but perceptibly, the sands on which the pillars of public opinion rest had begun to shift. What yesterday had been termed 'outrages' were now referred to simply as 'attacks', and Bendall was seen to be fighting not so much for freedom as for himself. The conspirators had an identity, too. 'Captain Beaky' was excellent headline fodder and there wasn't a single newspaper in the land who could resist it.

It all sounded a shade too comic, almost comfortable. So the Prime Minister grew ever more impatient and Earwick sought the opinions of others – a sure sign he was in difficulties and wanting to spread the responsibility, although he had come to one solid conclusion, that whoever else might be included in the ranks of the enemy, the editor of the *Telegraph* was going to be right up there on the list. Earwick told COBRA so in terms that were remarkably colourful for a Home Secretary. At the point where he suggested that the editor was a national menace and they should bug all his phones, the Police Commissioner went puce. There'd be hell to pay if they were caught bugging an editor. So what? Couldn't they bug a bloody telephone without getting caught? What had the capital's police force come to?

The discussion was beginning to get undignified and more than a little unconstitutional when it was interrupted by a commotion from the door. A dishevelled figure burst in, pursued by a protesting security guard who continued in a state of considerable agitation until the Prime Minister waved him away. After all, it wasn't every day that the Downing Street press secretary kicked down his door looking as though he'd run all the way from Hyde Park pursued by a pack of Chelsea supporters. It had to be more than a bad set of inflation figures. It was.

'They've stuffed up the phones,' the press secretary, Arnold Jumpers, almost choked. He was experiencing considerable difficulty coordinating his need to take in great gulps of air with his need to speak. 'Everything in central London. All the 0207 numbers. It's chaos out there.'

'They've cut off our phones?' Earwick gasped, incredulous.

'Oh, more than that, Home Secretary, much more than that.' Bendall let out a slow moan of understanding. 'They've just cut off our balls.'

In fact, Bendall had it wrong. They had cut off no one's telephones. The press secretary's descrip-

261

tion had been the more accurate one, if technically a little obscure. The telephones had simply been 'stuffed up'.

All around the centre of London, whenever an 0207 number was dialled, the telephone system chose at least one random digit. The result – constant wrong numbers. From eleven o'clock that morning London had begun to buzz like a nest of dyspeptic hornets. Pick up a phone and the only thing you'd get for sure was chaos.

It was an adaptation of a hacker software program originating in Texas that Mary had pulled from the Internet and that had played the crucial role in a scam inflicted upon one of the more popular TV evangelists during his annual fund-raising drive. As followers phoned to make their credit-card pledges, every second call had been diverted to a different number where their pledge was taken by computer and transmitted to a different bank account. It couldn't last, of course, not for more than a few days, but by the time the authorities had caught up with the operation both the perpetrator and the profit, running into several millions, had been lodged out of harm's way in the Cayman Islands.

The matter hadn't been allowed to rest there. Under pressure from the evangelist who explained that he believed in an eye for an eye and brimstone heaped upon the bitch who had cheated him, the police had proceeded to arrest the perpetrator's husband on a flimsy charge of conspiracy, hoping to lure the wife out of hiding. Instead, out of spite, she had shoved the software on the Internet, making it freely available to everyone and anyone. Ouch. The American telephone companies had been forced to move quickly in order to ensure that Elijah, as the software programme was called, could never be resurrected, but it seemed that their British counterparts had been far less agile. It had taken Mary many days and most of her nights to adapt the Elijah programme, but at the end of it she had been able to talk to the computer that ran the Telecoms regional management centre responsible for central London and persuade it to divert calls, not to a specific number, but simply at random. Anywhere would do, so long as it was wrong. Of course, in normal circumstances such problems would have been overridden by the central network management centre at Oswestry, but these weren't normal circumstances. Mary had fixed Oswestry too.

As COBRA broke up in confusion the capital's streets began to echo with the sound of numbers dialled and redialled in vain. Truly essential services on freephone numbers – police, ambulance, fire, gas leaks and so forth – weren't affected, and Mary had spent a full afternoon of painstaking programming to ensure that all hospitals, doctors' surgeries and other medical facilities listed in the Yellow Pages were passed over by the plague. Yet in a modern city, communications are as important as water, more important than roads. Cut off from its communications, a modern city begins slowly to die. And with it begins to die the authority of those who govern it.

TWELVE

If there was any humour to be found in any of this chaos, it sailed far above the head of Arnold Jumpers, the Prime Minister's press spokesman, upon whose shoulders had fallen the responsibility for mounting the first line of defence. Since there was little point in denying the situation was anything other than a calamity, he had decided upon a diversionary attack and accordingly had prepared a draft statement which blamed the mess not only on the conspirators but also the telephone company, the *Daily Telegraph* and even the Government's political opponents, accusing them of multiple if ill-defined crimes. There seemed little other option. It was all very well the Prime Minister ordering him into the breach once more, but in order to fill it he would need to round up as many bodies as he could find, and no one else had any sensible advice to offer. They were all too busy shouting down telephones at strangers.

He had shown his draft to the Prime Minister, who pierced him with a look that Jumpers suspected might have been tinged with gin. 'Bring me some answers, Arnold,' Bendall had barked, 'then maybe I'll take some questions. Until then, you do it!'

So Jumpers had called together the lobby correspondents. He had tried to summon them by telephone but he was merely mortal, not a miracle
worker, and feeling more mortal by the moment. The
Government Telephone Network which embraced
official Westminster was not part of the 0207 fiasco
but in this hour of adversity had come to resemble an
overloaded refugee convoy and was going nowhere.
Jumpers had been reduced to sending a runner off
to the Houses of Parliament to bring the journalists
hotfoot to Downing Street.

They had, indeed, arrived hotfoot, gathering outside the basement entrance to the press lobby at the
appointed time, but the door remained firmly closed.
Jumpers kept them waiting – they assumed out of
arrogance or an attempt to show them that he was
master in his own kingdom, but in truth because he
was making last-minute alterations to his draft in a
state of rising panic. So the members of the lobby sat
on the low wall outside the basement door, beside
which some joker had placed the rat traps that were
supposed to keep Downing Street free of vermin, and
they had smoked and speculated and grown impatient.
And waited some more. Finally the door had creaked
open and a breathless junior press secretary had offered
mumbled apologies before ushering them in.

The press briefing room itself was claustrophobic,
decorated in battleship grey and provided with inadequate services and small windows set high in one
end wall. It was a little like a prison. In Jumpers's
opinion it was precisely what they deserved.

'Morning, Woolly,' the *Telegraph*'s correspondent called across as the official press spokesman entered the room. 'What's the line today, then?'

How he hated his nickname. How he hated the correspondent and the newspaper, and what it had done to him.

Being the press spokesman at Downing Street is a little like being a lump of prime meat on a butcher's bench. So long as it's there on the bench, in pristine condition, the passing dogs will gaze upon it with a mixture of reticence and respect, but should it fall into the gutter both reticence and respect are immediately cast aside and the dogs compete to tear it to pieces. Jumpers had thrown himself into the gutter with his lies about the attacks; now the teeth were bared and he would be shown no more mercy than a string of yesterday's sausages.

'Good morning,' he began, trying to affect a pretence of normality. He clutched the sides of his podium for comfort. The podium was new, something he'd introduced to give briefings a greater air of formality, make it seem a little like the White House. It also gave him something to hide behind. 'Nothing on the record at the moment, if you don't mind. Nothing for direct quotation. Only background.'

'Why's that, Woolly?'

'Because we don't yet know . . .' – he had to struggle to avoid saying 'what the bloody hell's going on' and instead retreated to 'the full circumstances of this situation.'

'Hasn't stopped you before.'

Jumpers licked his dry lips and softly muttered

a phrase he'd seen spray-painted onto a wall in Kilburn. 'No one should underestimate the seriousness of this situation. This is nothing less than an attempt to cripple life in London. You'll have seen the impact on the Stock Exchange . . .'

'Falling like a nun's knickers on bath night,' someone cracked.

Jumpers ignored it. 'Business has all but ground to a halt. But you'll appreciate it goes much deeper than that.'

'I hear there may be rumblings on some of the inner-city estates. Rumours about barricades going up. Gangs of youths steaming through the high street. That true, Woolly?'

Jumpers had no idea, it was all happening too fast for him to stay abreast. 'What I can confirm is that it will be ordinary people who will suffer most from this outrage. Think what is likely to happen after dark. Remember that many burglar alarms and security systems use an 0207 number, a number that is no longer of any use. We are talking here about a potential catastrophe . . .'

'Talking of potential catastrophes, Woolly,' – there was an ill-concealed snigger from several of those in the room – 'who are we blaming today? That is, assuming we can dispense with the nonsense that this is an attack by the paramilitary wing of the World Wildlife Fund?'

Jumpers felt his chance had come. He glanced down at his briefing paper with its list of accused in order to refresh both his memory and his morale, yet before he could begin he was interrupted yet again. It was that turd from the *Telegraph* once more.

'You know who's going to get the blame, don't you, Woolly? Even if they find that Captain Beaky has robbed a bank and screwed his sister. You know who they're going to blame?'

Jumpers paused. He had the feeling of something cruel and canine brushing up against his leg. The pack was about to pounce. 'What do you mean?'

'They're going to blame you, Woolly. Not you personally, of course; they don't know who you are. But your boss. Hissing Sid. The Prime Minister. That's who they'll go for.'

From a distance, across the rooftops and chimneys of Whitehall, came the sound of Big Ben striking the hour. One o'clock. Feeding time.

'That's absurd . . .'

'You see, your boss, Mr Bendall, has been fiddling with the truth. To put no finer point on it, he lied. Now, we know our lords and masters like to mess about with the truth at times, but what we don't expect is for them to get caught quite so blatantly. Trousers down, arse in the air and everything on full public display. So they're going to kick his butt and say that if he hadn't lied, this might not have happened. That's what they'll say.' At least, that's what his newspaper was going to say and, as Jumpers knew, sometimes the public are so easily led. It was the moment for him to step in, to take control of the situation.

'Let's be clear about this. What we are facing is nothing less than a full-scale terrorist situation. It's electronic terrorism. Not even the IRA was able to bring London grinding to a halt like this. No avenue is going to remain unexplored and no stone unturned in our efforts to stamp down on these outrages.' It was going better now; they were all busy scribbling down his clichés. You couldn't have too many clichés, not in his job. Get them stuffed into the first four paragraphs of any news report and his job was almost done. But this one needed something more. It needed someone to blame . . .

'So we have ordered Telecoms to work flat out until they have isolated the fault and corrected their computer, regardless of the expense. We are going to ensure that they have their systems back on line at the earliest possible moment. Then we can start discussions as to how they managed to let something like this happen and to see if there are any grounds for compensation . . .' Good, very good. Blame clearly implied without any direct attribution. Time for the personal touch. His Master's Voice.

'The Prime Minister doesn't underestimate the seriousness of this situation. He's working on it right now in the Cabinet Room. Let's not beat about the bush. Phrases like "Goering" and "Luftwaffe" spring to mind. It's worse in many respects, because the Luftwaffe only hit a small proportion of buildings not the whole capital and – SWEET MARY AND JOSEPH WILL YOU SWITCH OFF THAT BLOODY PHONE!'

Jumpers almost lost it. Ever since he had started his counterattack that bitch-in-heat from the Press Association had been fiddling with her earpiece and her mobile phone, distracting him, not listening to him, and he'd just about had enough.

'No it's not,' she responded without a trace of remorse.

'No it's not *what*?' Arnold bit back.

'No, it's not worse than the Luftwaffe,' she replied, one hand on her earpiece and the other held high to still Jumpers's agitation. 'They're playing with you, Arnold. The phones are back on. At the stroke of one, my office is telling me. The computer corrected itself and . . . the land lines are now working.' She paused to examine the press spokesman. 'Why, Arnold, you should be happy. It's all over.'

The Press Secretary knew it wasn't all over. Something was going on at the level of his trouser leg. Maybe the dogs weren't pulling him apart, not for the moment at least, but something unpleasant was happening nonetheless. He had the distinct impression he was being pissed on.

The dismay felt by Arnold Jumpers crept from Downing Street through the streets and alleyways of Westminster like a Dickensian fog until it reached as far as The Kremlin. The day had started badly for Elizabeth. She had been forced to sack two of her staff, an under-chef and a waiter. It was time for cutbacks, even though she knew she was cutting back on the things that made The Kremlin special. Needs must. Then the fog of chaos closed in until it had all but cut off The Kremlin and wiped out the lunchtime bookings. Her profit margin for the entire week lost at a single stroke. At this rate she knew she would be closed in weeks unless something turned up.

*   *   *

'So how far would you go?'

At this point, Goodfellowe is still lying on top of her. One day, maybe, she'll get some feeling back in her legs.

'How far what?' he replies. 'What are we talking about here? Group sex? Chandeliers?'

'No, you fool. At least, not right this minute. I'm talking about things like your job. Mr Squeaky Clean gets hold of the Ministerial inkpot once more. Doesn't that mean you have to get your hands dirty?'

'Does politics have to be a dirty game?'

'The more relevant question is whether it can ever be clean. Tell me you didn't lie for your country when you were Foreign Minister.'

'That was different. That's called diplomacy.'

'And you expect me to believe you when you tell me you've suddenly fallen in love with your Prime Minister and all his works?'

'That bit's called collective Ministerial responsibility.'

She wriggles and hooks her legs behind his, pulling him into her, her tongue exploring his ear. He emits a low groan that sounds like a protest, but isn't.

'Tell me, Goodfellowe, would you screw for your country, too?'

'How could I refuse, if she looked like you?'

She takes the sides of his head in both hands and forces it up from her body so that she is looking directly into his eyes. 'Seriously. Say there were . . . I don't know, say a female journalist. Drop-dead gorgeous, legs up to heaven. And she had something – apart from the bloody obvious – that you wanted.'

'Like what?'

'Something vital. Some piece of information, some pillow talk that was essential. Or perhaps she had a story on you, or a close friend, that you wanted to bury beneath the bedsheets. Would you do it?'

'Does a one-legged duck swim in circles?'

'Depends how aroused he is.'

'How should I express it? To lay down one's life for one's country is a noble thing, but to lay down one's virtue seems to have altogether more amusing possibilities.'

He's laughing but she's not joining in. Something's troubling her.

'What's up, Elizabeth?'

'No, nothing. Nothing except . . . You can be such a black-and-white person at times, yet the world is so full of grey. Sometimes you have to do things you don't particularly want to do. Like the lying and cheating, even worse things. How do you live with that?'

He has caught her solemn mood, digs into a former life. 'Do you remember when it all turned nasty in Ghana? First there was the coup, then a counter-coup. CNN had a field day. Ministers being strapped to oil barrels on the beach and machine-gunned, left for the crabs. That was when I was Foreign Minister and I gave the order for all our diplomats to get out. But our ambassador telephoned. He spoke to me personally. Asked for permission to stay on in post.

There were too many British aid workers around the place, he argued, he didn't want to desert them. He *wanted* to stay.'

Then a silence. Goodfellowe's memories seem to be weighing him down.

'So?'

'So I agreed. I could hear the gunfire in the background even as we were speaking, but . . . I agreed. He stayed. He got most of the aid workers out, saved dozens of lives. And a week later they strung up his body from a lamppost. We both knew the risks, it goes with the job. He knew the risk was of dying, I knew the risk was of having to live with his death. Sure, sometimes you have to lie, to cheat, even to sacrifice a man's life. Occasions when almost anything can be justified.'

'So what makes it right, or wrong?'

'What makes a deed good or bad, I suppose, depends not so much on the deed itself, but on your motivation for doing it.'

'Even sleeping with the devil?'

'What, Bendall? If I climb into bed with him, it's only because there's no other way. Doesn't make me a slut.'

She remains very silent, seems troubled. He wonders if he's disappointed her, let himself down. She can be so difficult to read.

'Not wrong am I? Gone too far?'

She buries her head in her pillow. 'No, my love. I don't think you have. Not if you don't.'

She doesn't want him to see the tears that have gathered at the corners of her eyes. He thinks this conversation is all about him. Poor, blind fool. It's not about him, it's about her. And about wine and the restaurant and ghosts from her past, and not relying ever again on any one man, even a man like Goodfellowe. And not entirely trusting herself, which is why she can't bring herself to place her trust in him, even though she loves him, which makes it all so much more complicated. Bloody men.

He lies on top of her, content, oblivious. He doesn't realize his world is on the brink of falling to pieces.

London lay prostrate and in confusion. Like a man kicked in the groin or a woman who has lost her handbag, for a while the world no longer made sense. An entire city had been left gasping, disorientated, yet the causes of despair for some are viewed by others as opportunities, and Earwick was nothing if not an opportunist. The failure of the phones had played havoc with his diary for the day, causing all sorts of duties to be rearranged or cancelled. It soon became clear that a hole had appeared in his diary some time after three in the afternoon. Gaps in the schedule of a Secretary of State are as rare and as richly prized as pearls, and he resisted all the entreaties of his private secretary to spend the rest of the afternoon going through his backlog of correspondence and preparing for his five-o'clock meeting with his security advisers. Earwick looked out of his window in Queen Anne's Gate and found not fog but brilliant sunshine. He braced his shoulders and issued a decree that he would spend an hour at home, studying papers without disruption. And without his private secretary.

A red box was hurriedly stuffed with appropriate briefing material and Her Majesty's Secretary of State for Home Affairs quit his office promptly at three. But not before he had sat down at his desk and sent a personal e-mail.

Brett Eatwell, the new-ish and straight-ish editor of the *Sun*, didn't envy the lot of politicians. Why should he? He pulled a salary three times that of the Prime Minister, plus bonuses and an unlimited expense account, he could call his staff bitches and bastards without being threatened with a law suit, and his private life was never, but never, going to be the stuff of gossip in any newspaper column. He occupied that position of respect which ensured that when he changed his mind and stood his views on their head, it wasn't called a U-turn or a retreat but simply a matter of editorial independence.

At this precise moment he was engaged in a particularly delicate exercise of editorial independence. Eatwell sat in his office in Wapping, sleeves rolled up and pondering the future of the Government. Up to this point he had been a reasonably consistent supporter. Bendall was a greaseball, of course, but a little grease was always necessary to oil the wheels of the presses. Better a Prime Minister up your bum than on your back. Indeed, so assiduous had the Prime Minister been that on the news desk they usually referred to him as Bendover. When he had called

Eatwell to congratulate him on his birthday, the editor had played the phone call over the newsroom intercom, accompanied by extravagant and exceedingly childish hand gestures that he had first practised at public school.

But Jonathan Bendall was beginning to be a pain. He had brought London grinding to a halt, which on the day in question had made Eatwell's proprietor late for his lunch. Now he had cut off all the bloody telephones. Politicians needed to be lucky, and Bendall's luck was beginning to look as though it had spent the night on a park bench. Perhaps it was time to drop him. Eatwell was contemplating a choice of headlines which varied from **'Kicked In The Bendalls!'** to **'Telef***ed!'** when he became aware of the cartoon platinum blonde on his screen. She was an icon developed by his software department to guide him through the electronic maze of his computer system, and at this point she was opening and closing her legs. This told him that he had received an e-mail message.

Eatwell was not normally an excitable man. It was not his custom to become agitated, rather it was his pleasure to agitate others, and particularly his reporters, until they had squeezed the last traces of life from a story. But this little one was going to see him through to his dotage.

The first anyone else knew of this was when they heard a scream coming from his office that made his secretary think he'd been setting light to his farts again – another habit from public school. She rushed in, concerned, only to be told she was a knickerless little scrubber. She was unable to obtain any further sense from him and so she summoned the news editor.

The rest, as they say, is history.

Mickey was always stylish. Today's style appeared to be a dress that was one size too small and heels that were more like traffic hazards than shoes. Goodfellowe, by contrast, had arrived sporting a charcoal grey suit he had bought with a little of the proceeds from the bequest of his constituent. His first new suit in a couple of years. He paused at the entrance to his office to allow her to admire it.

'Got a funeral?' she enquired, without raising her eyes from her work.

Suddenly Goodfellowe realized how little he had seen of his secretary in recent days, and how much he missed her. She brought a sense of irreverence to everything, never allowing him to take matters – particularly himself – too seriously. It was the type of loyalty he needed right now. Goodfellowe had spent a sleepless night wrestling with self-doubt. His life had changed so much in recent weeks – haggling with Prime Ministers and Chief Whips, scooped up in the struggle to save the nation. If power corrupts, proximity to power distracts, and much of the fun seemed to have been squeezed out of his life.

Most distracting of all was the dilemma he faced about Elizabeth and Sam. Was it to be Paris? Or Florence? It was a silly and spurious debate, he knew, for a Ministerial salary would sort everything out for him, but somehow he felt he was losing control, becoming beholden once more. He didn't want Jonathan Bendall to sort out his life for him, he wanted to be able to do that for himself. Yet the two women he loved most in the world were pulling him in opposite directions. He owed Sam everything, but surely there should be room in his life for ambition. And for Elizabeth. Somehow the two women he loved seemed to be drifting into different camps and he didn't want to decide, couldn't decide. Paris or Florence.

Obstacles, nothing but bloody obstacles. As he walked towards his desk, a metal wastepaper bin blocked his path, as there always seemed to be something in his path. It was time to change that. Or change the bin, at least. He gave a small hop, drew his leg back and let fly. The bin hurtled the full length of his office and hit the wall with a satisfying clatter.

'What did you do that for?'

'Needed the practice. Haven't kicked anything in ages. Or anyone, come to that.'

'Like that, is it? Sounds like woman trouble. Or money.'

'Both.'

'Sam? Or Elizabeth?'

'Both.'

Mickey studied Goodfellowe as though measuring him for a straitjacket, then rose from her desk and walked over to the battered bin. She rescued it, examined it for signs of fatal bruising, then walked back across the office in order to place it upright in front of him.

'Go ahead, be my guest.'

This time he sent it flying into the door.

'Why does everything come down to money?' he demanded, feeling better for his exertions.

'Sex or money. Everything comes down to sex or money,' she corrected, before returning to her work, sucking the end of a pencil with which she had been drafting a reply in the margin of a letter. It was from a constituent, Mrs Godsell. Mrs Godsell was complaining about the warble fly. She often wrote to complain, and would write again if she hadn't got a reply within a week. There was always something that concerned her – one week the disappearing habitat of the long-eared bat, the next the destruction of the ozone layer from the methane of French cattle which, according to her, was particularly pernicious. Opinionated and impatient, was our Mrs Godsell. Yet at every election she was the first in line to volunteer to stick stamps and lick envelopes in one of the Marshwood committee rooms, so Mickey always took care to ensure she got a rapid and personalized response. Some day she might even let Goodfellowe see one.

She looked up, distracted. 'It's the reason Justin and I split up,' she mused.

'What, sex?'

'No, idiot. That was great. You think I'd get myself engaged to a choirboy? It was the money.'

'I thought he had plenty of it.' Goodfellowe stepped forward tentatively, knowing he was on marshy emotional ground. It was the first time in more than a year that Mickey had disinterred the remains of her former fiancé. 'Didn't he do something in the City?'

'A market maker. With a tan, a jacuzzi and a tight butt. And a mother who lived north of Manchester. Or was it Middlesbrough? Anyway, it was enough she hated travelling. Yes, plenty of money, too. And very sensible about it, he was. That was the problem. I remember he wanted to buy me a very sensible and tasteful engagement ring, while I . . . you see, I wanted something really huge and vulgar. Hell, if I'm going to wear it, I want people to know about it. Until my arm aches.'

'You're kidding. Aren't you?'

She smiled sweetly.

'Maybe you should consider counselling,' he ventured.

'On the grounds that I'm grasping? Or on the grounds that even though I'm grasping I've still somehow ended up working for you?'

Goodfellowe pressed on. 'So why *did* you break up with him?'

'Oh, hell . . .' As the memories revived, her careful marginal notes grew into absentminded doodles. Mrs Godsell became covered in extravagant bundles of flowers. 'Because I wasn't ready for him. He was a really nice boy, thought I was perfect. But you know me, I still felt in need of a second opinion. Several of them, in fact. The wedding ceremony would have turned into a fiasco. I wouldn't have got the odd one or two standing up to object, I'd have got a full-scale Mexican wave. It wasn't going to work, would have hurt him even more if I'd stayed.'

'No regrets, then?'

'None at the time, I was too young. But now . . . ?' Suddenly the point of the pencil snapped, sending a fragment of lead spitting across the desk like a missile headed for Serbia. 'I suppose I've changed. Dunno if it's maturity, but it's certainly older. Nowadays when I go into a hotel on the arm of a forty-year-old man, the receptionists don't snigger anymore. That hurts.'

His face creased. She had this extraordinary ability to raise him from the deepest of despairs.

'It's serious, Goodfellowe. I may have to dip into my face-lift fund sooner than I expected.'

'A stitch in time . . .'

'Saves a lot of tears. And a lot of money.'

She returned her attention to Mrs Godsell while he retrieved the battered remains of the waste bin and placed it distractedly on top of his desk like a hunting trophy. 'I wonder if you're right.'

'About what?'

'About Captain Beaky being in it for the money?'

'I said that?'

'It's a thought, at least. Possibly an inspired one. You really can be quite brilliant at times.'

She was beginning to lose track of this one. 'What thought?' she asked, enunciating both words carefully as though addressing a foreigner.

'That Beaky or whatever he's called might be in it for the money.'

'What money?'

'Good question. The water companies lost a small fortune as a result of the attack on Bendall's bath-

281

room. Someone loses, someone gains. The money didn't simply get flushed away. I've got this funny feeling that telephone shares are being murdered, too, right this minute.'

'Beaky's in it just for the money?'

'You really think so? You could be right. In which case, maybe we should do some digging. You know, you were right not to get married. You're far too good for Justin. There are brains buried somewhere inside that delectable body of yours.'

'You're patronizing me, which is always a sign you're up to something. Where's all this leading?'

'It's simply that I think you're right. That it's worth trying to find out if anyone *has* made a killing on the shares.'

'Isn't that sort of share-dealing information confidential? You'd need someone in the City for that.'

'Yes, I suppose we would.' A slight pause, like a missed heartbeat. 'What did you say Justin does?'

She sat bolt upright. 'Goodfellowe, you devious bastard. You can go jump in the Thames along with your bloody shares. I am *not* going to meet up with Justin. Hear me? *Not*. Nor am I going to telephone him, smile at him, beg him for favours, use him, fondle him for old time's sake or . . . or anything else. Absolutely not. Understand? Get that into your scheming head. *No Way*.'

'Sure, Mickey.'

A pencil came spinning through the air. Goodfellowe ducked.

*   *   *

She found him in a watering hole nicknamed the Essex in Exile in one of those little alleyways off Bow Lane, barely a stone's throw with a good shoulder from his office. It was the usual Thursday-night crush, young blood and brash money sandwiched between the uncertainty of short-term employment contracts or no employment contracts at all. On the ground floor the drinkers were sweating in spite of the air conditioning, while in the basement, where the toilets had been turned into a makeshift coke hole, the young customers were way beyond discomfort. The bar itself was soulless, all brushed stainless steel and blue glass; the waitresses appeared to be constructed of much the same unforgiving materials. They'd probably squeeze more from the customers after the bar had closed than ever they did serving drinks and designer sandwiches, it was that type of bar. Everything was for sale here.

He was leaning on a bar stool, his tie loosened, his Italian jacket sagging.

'Hi, J.'

A startled glance. A pause. Then: 'Shit.' Uttered more in resignation than hostility.

'If you don't want me here you can throw me out.'

'Get my own back, you mean?'

She ignored it. 'You still making markets?'

'You still shagging in shifts?'

She couldn't ignore that, and flushed.

He ran his hand through his thick highlighted hair. 'Sorry. Shit. Hell. Shit. Have a drink. Old time's sake.'

'On one condition,' she instructed, sensing he was beginning to lose the battle with that part of him which wanted to pour the entire contents of the ice bucket over her. 'That you let me ask you a favour. For old time's sake.'

'You've got bigger balls than an elephant, know that? Shit!' he offered yet one more time. He had never been very good at expressing his feelings – well, you rarely needed to, driving a Porsche. Already she knew she had been right, it would never have lasted. Still it hurt.

'Deal?'

'Southern Comfort with ice and orange,' he snapped at the girl behind the bar before returning his attentions to Mickey. 'You still drink that shit?' She could see in his eyes that he'd already had too much. Perhaps it was a good thing, his resistance was low.

'I want to ask you a favour, J. About shares.'

'What shares?'

'I want to know if anyone made a killing out of the water fiasco the other day.'

'Dunno.'

'But you could find out.'

'Naughty, naughty. Chinese walls, and all that.'

She glanced extravagantly around the bar before touching an immaculately manicured nail to his third shirt button. 'I see only glass walls, J. No Chinese walls here.'

He stared at her, trying to look ferocious, but couldn't hold it. 'You sure know how to pick your time and place. But then you always did.' Another swig to wash away the memories. 'There's only a handful of guys making a market in water shares, 'n' it's a small old world. One of them's that fat twister in the corner over there auditioning for the part of village drunk. Hey, Rosenstein,' he called out, waving to attract the attention of a man who was draped over the end of the bar. 'Rosie, come 'ere.'

Rosenstein raised his head, took in Mickey and did as he was bidden, squeezing his early-obese frame through the throng. 'Charmed,' he said, looking deep and drunken into Mickey's eyes.

'Trust me, you wouldn't be,' Justin replied.

'Trust you? I suppose I could always give it a try.'

'Look, Rosie, cut through the shit and tell me. Did you get raped when the water shares fell out of bed the other day?'

'Me, raped? Didn't even come close. No, not me.' Rosenstein's alcoholic eyes gazed once more into Mickey's but couldn't focus properly, so drifted slowly down to her chest, where they roamed, then rested. 'Got a little tickle, though.'

'Which means what, exactly?' Mickey asked.

'Which means we may be halfway there, darling,' the former love of her life replied.

THIRTEEN

The meeting of COBRA had started badly, and was about to get worse. The Cabinet Secretary had begun by reporting on the findings of TAG, the Threat Assessment Group made up of representatives from the security services. The findings didn't put it in so many words, but the scribble on the Prime Minister's blotter summed it up succinctly.

No bloody clue.

Water. Transport. The Government's paging system. Telephones. What next?

The TAG team had sat long and deliberated, but they had so little on which to base any solid conclusion. All they knew was that the Government, not so many years ago, had spent several small fortunes honing the abilities of the conspirators to find imaginative ways of bringing cities like Moscow and Baghdad grinding to a halt. So what chance had London? The TAG team found itself plagiarizing its own earlier work, suggesting that the conspirators might copy the IRA who had mounted an attack on London's electricity substations, or food terrorists who had poisoned supermarket supplies, or the lone mad blackmailer who had threatened to flood the London Underground. No one could be sure what might happen next, they had so little to go on. All they knew was that unlike either the IRA, the food terrorists or the mad blackmailer, these conspirators had succeeded in remaining entirely undetected. What was even worse to Bendall's mind, their identification with humorous cartoon characters was beginning to stick in the public consciousness. 'Beaky' made for neat, sharp headlines, and that bloody record was being played on the radio again. Even the BBC was at it. As long as they stuck to making fools of the Government, there was a distinct danger of the conspirators gaining cult status.

When Goodfellowe slipped into his seat in COBRA a full ten minutes after everyone else, failing miserably in his attempt to do so unobtrusively, Bendall was not amused. The Prime Minister felt isolated and in need of an opportunity to show he was still in charge of proceedings. In short, he needed a victim, and latecomers always provide an ideal target. It was possible that Goodfellowe had an excuse, of course. Perhaps his bike had a puncture or he'd lost his bus ticket, but whatever the reason it wasn't going to be enough. Bendall decided he was going to make an example of Goodfellowe.

Maybe it was going to be a bit like World War I, Bendall thought. Perhaps this one wasn't going to be over by Christmas, either. With every passing day the mood of his security advisers was becoming more bleak and their explanations less digestible. They'd be talking about the long haul and heavy pounding next. He needed fresh impetus, to introduce a little terror to stiffen the backbone, and for that he needed a bloody sacrifice. Stir up a little fear, inflict a little violence. To encourage the others. Yes, Goodfellowe would do, and do nicely.

The Police Commissioner was in the middle of giving his report in which he was ticking off a long list of completed actions and proposed new initiatives when Bendall interrupted.

'Yes, yes, yes, Commissioner, but perhaps we can all save time if I direct you to one simple question. What hard evidence have you managed to find?'

The Commissioner studied the nail on his thumb. 'We have to accept that it's early days yet, Prime Minister, and –'

'Anyone?' Bendall interrupted once more, testily. 'Security services? SIS? What's your budget this year – more than a billion? What do you do with it, apart from buying curtains and restocking the drinks cabinet, eh? And what about you boys at Defence? Or GCHQ?' He glanced around the table at each in turn.

Silence.

'I've given you everything. Anything you asked for. We've got bills for overtime running into millions, we've raised security on every public building in the country, we've interviewed thousands of suspects, done wiretaps, a bit of burglary too, and for all I know we're coshing the Roman Catholic Cardinal to see if he's heard anything in the confessional. I've got the Attorney General on my back telling me we've pushed things to the very limit of the law, but it's what you asked for so I gave it to you. And what have I got in return . . . ?'

More silence, broken only by the rustling of grown men trying to shrink.

Suddenly Bendall's fists banged down on the table, sending the papers scattering like grouse in August. 'Give me strength. Doesn't anyone in this room have a clue?'

Much more silence. Very serious silence. Then a sound, innocuous, almost apologetic, of Goodfellowe clearing his throat. It had an effect similar to the rivet of a submarine popping at the bottom of the Marianas Trench. Without further effort, he had everyone's attention.

'Prime Minister, I'd like to apologize for being a little late . . .'

Inside, Bendall smiled grimly. The turkey had walked into the abattoir.

'. . . but it was the matter of a few phone enquiries which I think might help our discussions.'

'Help is a rare commodity around this table.'

'Since we can't establish their identities and we have little clue as to their intentions, I've been wondering about something else. Their motives. Now, on the surface they claim to be military men with an agenda which is almost political –'

'Excruciatingly bloody political when it's aimed at me.'

'Well, precisely. But I've been considering the possibility there might be another motive.'

'Such as?'

'Money.'

'What – ransom? Blackmail?'

'More in the line of a killing on the Stock Exchange.

There would be a lot of money to be made out of water and telephone shares if you knew that the attacks were about to take place. And who would know that – other than the attackers themselves?'

Chairs were being pushed back from the briefing table and necks twisted round as everyone strained to get a good sight of Goodfellowe.

'So I made enquiries of a market maker in water shares – there's only a handful of them.'

'What about telephone shares?' Bendall interrupted yet again.

'A huge market, too many market makers there for me to check on my own. But water's almost pocket-sized by comparison. So I asked if anyone had enjoyed a little windfall.' He paused to enjoy the effect before continuing. 'One investor did, indeed, seem to have a remarkable stroke of luck. He took out some put options only two days before the attack on Downing Street. Betting that the shares would crash.'

Oh, but he had 'em now. None of them dared breathe. He kept them waiting. Eventually the Prime Minister, softly but very insistently, prompted him.

'And . . . ?'

'He walked off with about three hundred thousand. And because of the timeframe involved, he didn't have to put up a single penny himself. A very astute man. Reasonably restrained, too. Three hundred thousand's not a lot in this context. He could've made millions.'

'Then why didn't he?'

'Maybe he thought that would be a little too obvious. Or, more likely, because no one would have accepted such an enormous gamble from him. It seems he's not a regular investor on the Stock Exchange. The put option was placed through a small broker near Cheapside, a one-room operation above Boots the Chemists, would you believe? We're not talking high finance here, Prime Minister.'

Justin had been awesome. Having squeezed the name of the broker-above-Boots from the rat-arsed Rosenstein, he had then seduced the broker with a tale about how he himself was going to start making a market in water shares. Brokers know only one tactic for dealing with a market maker, that of adopting a position of complete and unrestrained wantonness. The fellow had crawled all over him with offers of drinks and dinner followed by an extended evening of lap dancing. The confidential details of one very lucky small investor seemed so trivial in comparison with their new-found friendship, particularly after the first couple of bottles. The Chinese walls that secured secrecy in the City had been undermined and toppled by the constant pounding of a tide of alcohol and greed. By the early hours of the following morning an exhausted Justin had been left in the condition of a sailor who had only narrowly survived a shipwreck, and not for the first time Goodfellowe wondered what it must be like to be pussy-whipped by Mickey.

Now Bendall was gesturing vigorously in Goodfellowe's direction. 'Tom, what are you doing sitting in the corner? Come and sit by me. So that they can all see.'

'Them' and 'us' already, Goodfellowe noted.

'So, let me get this straight, Tom. This man, a complete stranger to the stock market, places a bet that water shares will take a pounding. And he does this less than forty-eight hours before the attack on my bathroom?'

'Exactly.'

'And walks off with . . .'

'Three hundred thousand. Give or take a little loose change.'

'And does this remarkably astute investor have a name?'

'Oh yes, Prime Minister. He has a name. It's Payne. The Honourable Freddie Payne, to be precise. It appears that before he became a player on the Stock Exchange he was a Major in the Guards. The Grenadiers. We kicked him out two years ago.'

Bendall is shouting.

'No! No, I will not have it! Enough!'

'But, Prime Minister,' the Commissioner tries for one last time. He's showing courage, everyone else has given up. 'If Payne is our man, he must have accomplices. Let us give him a little rope. Let him lead us to the others.'

'And give you the slip? Run rings around you? Like he's been doing ever since this whole fiasco started? Not any more!' Bendall rises from his chair to indicate the meeting is about to be adjourned. 'I want him picked up within the hour, and I want him broken. I've lost count of the times I've had to stand up in Parliament and defend you against accusations of police brutality, so now I want you to start living up to your reputation. Squeeze the bastard, squeeze him dry. I want him, then I want the rest of 'em. I want action, not argument.' *And if I sound strident, almost desperate, it's because that's precisely what I am. A Prime Minister who can't safeguard his own capital city will soon be no Prime Minister at all. The authority and awe that come with this office have been leaking away like water through a ruptured dyke, but now I have something – someone – to throw into the breach. So I want the entire ungrateful world to know that we've got one of them, that these creatures aren't a bunch of quaint comic characters but instead are grasping bastards who have been lining their own pockets, and I want them to know all this because it will tell every single one of them that I, Jonathan Bendall, am back in business. Understand?*

'And Tom? Good work. I'm glad there's someone I can count on.'

There is a general shuffling of papers, and glances of envy tinged with relief are cast in the direction of Goodfellowe. Slowly, stiffly, they depart.

No one seems to have noticed how very, very quiet Earwick has been.

It has been a day of triumph, to be followed – or so Goodfellowe hopes – by a night of conquest.

But Elizabeth has cried off. Short-staffed at the restaurant, she says, she will have to fill in. One of those things.

When he telephones to say goodnight, she isn't

293

there. Hasn't been there all evening, according to Maribelle.

Perhaps she has changed her plans, or wanted a quiet night on her own, to worry. A silly white lie. One of *those* things. Unnecessary, he thinks.

That night his bed feels unusually cold.

The following morning brimmed with optimism, but Bendall wasn't to get the headlines he wanted.

Neither was Earwick.

'DIPWICK!' screamed the *Sun*, straining to cram the huge typeface onto its front page. The rest of the media tumbled in its wake like lemmings over a cliff, although some preferred not to dwell on the more graphic details.

Earwick's House of Commons researcher, he of the e-mail, was called Ernest. Ernest was like many parliamentary researchers, youthful, bright-eyed, exceptionally eager. He was unusual although not unique in that he was also deeply and, in the eyes of many, beautifully black, which had caused the *Sun* to ensure that his image on the front page was in colour, since monochrome photos tend to wash out the features on black faces.

editor@the-sun.co.uk still had no idea by what mixture of alchemy or electronic artistry he was getting copies of the Home Secretary's e-mail messages flashed onto his screen, but through frantic hours of analysis Brett Eatwell and his staff had resolved that these messages were indisputably genuine. These included the communications about his forthcoming speech to the annual general meeting of the Lancashire Women's Institute, the reminder for Ernest to pick up his shirts from the laundry in Horseferry Road, and the request for Ernest to *check local newspaper archives – make absolutely certain, no messing on this one,*' that the Fred Whittles who had just been appointed to the Opposition Front Bench as Spokesman for Home Affairs and apple pie and other worthy sorts of thing was the one and the same Fred Whittles who, according to shadowy Home Office sources, had been sentenced to community service for a minor assault on a policeman outside a Bristol nightclub. It had been the occasion of his eighteenth birthday.

Trouble was, there was also the e-mail that Earwick had sent on the afternoon the telephones had run amuck, an unfortunate e-mail by any standards, in which he had requested that Ernest get his *beautiful black bum over to my place in twenty'*. The full text now occupied a considerable part of the front page. What space remained was devoted to a photograph. Under a caption describing it as 'the moment of madness', it showed Ernest entering the front door of the Home Secretary's stucco-fronted house in Pimlico. It was a rather fuzzy picture, since the hastily summoned photographer had arrived only seconds before Ernest himself and scarcely had time to take off his lens cap. The photograph on page five, however, was much sharper, showing Ernest leaving fifty-five minutes later, with the ghostlike face of Earwick staring after him from behind the curtains. (There was also more material on pages four, five, six, seven, twelve and

thirteen, with further sensational revelations promised in the next day's edition.)

Little wonder he'd found it difficult to concentrate
during COBRA.

It isn't, of course, a crime to be a homosexual and
to conduct one's relationships in private, even if you
are Home Secretary, but if you are to escape without embarrassment from such relationships then you
have to choose partners less brittle than Ernest, who
had cracked and blubbed at the first sign of a reporter,
and then agreed to hand over his story, illustrated
with original copies of handwritten letters, photographs and excruciatingly personal memorabilia, in
return for twenty thousand pounds and a club-class
ticket to Florida.

Did the nation care that the third most powerful man in government, behind the security of his
own front door, went by the sobriquet of Lady
Lydia? That he bought his underwear from Agent
Provocateur in darkest Soho and mailed his undevel-
oped films for processing to a photographic shop in
Chelmsford which advertised its confidential services
in the classified pages of *Boyz* magazine? Or that
last New Year he had thrown a dinner party by
candlelight at his hideaway in France during which
the ever-artistic Ernest had played the piano wearing
nothing but a chorister's ruff? None of this was
necessarily life-threatening in a modern and liberated
country, given a little careful media management, but
what rearranged all the furniture and finally threw it
overboard were the notes in which Earwick compared
Ernest's manhood to the size of the Prime Minister's

ego, suggesting it was over-inflated and forever on display.

Stupid, of course, to have written in those terms, but middle-aged men under the influence of alcohol and pink poppers tend to do such silly things.

Later that morning the Home Secretary's private secretary telephoned with his apologies, but Mr Earwick would be unable to attend Cabinet. He was too busy writing his letter of resignation.

Outside Number Ten, the gaggle of correspondents gathered before television cameras and tried to extract comments from those arriving for the meeting of the Cabinet, but failed. They didn't get any smiles, either. However, a consensus did emerge amongst the waiting media. It was their unanimous view that, with two Home Secretaries down inside a month, Bendall's administration seemed suddenly to have the sense of direction of a supermarket trolley.

At the Cabinet meeting the Lord Chancellor insisted on delivering a statement. He was an old personal friend of the Prime Minister, well intentioned but with two considerable defects. He was incredibly dour – 'the personality of a computer screen with the screensaver switched off,' as one columnist had put it. He also possessed even less imagination than a screensaver, a characteristic which, up to now, had protected him from the many vagaries of politics. But his friend was hurting. He wanted to help. So he had hijacked proceedings by insisting on delivering a statement – 'on behalf of all your colleagues and friends around this table, Prime Minister' – that was unusually extravagant in support of Bendall and extolled the many virtuous qualities of his leadership in these troubled times. 'We wish you to know that without either reservation or hesitation, Prime Minister, we support you one hundred per cent.'

The rest of his colleagues banged the table in a show of unanimity.

Fuck, but the guy was in trouble.

Dipwick's curt letter of resignation was reported in full in every newspaper.

Amadeus cut it out, smoothed the creases and placed it in his file alongside Dipwick's letter to the *Telegraph*. The one that had started it all. All that crap about feather beds. The one that said: *'The truth of the matter is simple. The nation's security remains safe in this Government's hands.'* Except, of course, when those hands were straying.

He placed it back in the drawer of his desk, which closed with the gentle sigh of a knife being replaced in its sheath. One down, one still to go.

They hadn't been able to pick up Freddie Payne easily. Sod's law. His wife had taken the children away to her mother's so he'd grasped the opportunity to stay over in London at his club in St James's. He'd invited Jamie Cairncross to dinner, paid him the eight thousand he was owed – *'splendid*, never doubted you for a moment, my dear fellow' – and then settled down over several large tumblers of Highland Park to play a little backgammon, during which he'd doubled up with the brashness of Zorba on his saint's day and promptly won two thousand of it back. Just when he didn't need it. And when, over a late breakfast the following morning, he'd heard of Dipwick's discomfort, he'd decided to take the day off. A minor celebration was in order. Buy some new ties, perhaps sacrifice a few virgins. The gods were playing on his side once more.

Or so he thought.

After another indulgent night, he had arrived at the gallery the following morning with cobwebs in his eyes and a tongue that had the tactile qualities of Velcro. He'd assumed the three men in raincoats were viewers of the new exhibition, but they weren't. They were police officers. He was arrested as soon as he walked in, directly in front of the new white-on-white sand thing by Stephane Graff. He hadn't even had time to take off his brand-new overcoat.

The moment they put their hands on his shoulder, Freddie Payne knew that his life had changed completely and for ever. There was no going back now, not to the way things had been, to that period of his life when his father was alive, to the years when he had served well and loyally in the cause of his country. Least of all could he go back to that short but elegant time when his wife had been in love with him, and he had loved her. He should have realized this much sooner. Perhaps he had been fighting too hard inside himself to hang on to what he had lost, looking back, clinging to the wreckage rather than rebuilding. Now he had no choice. There was no going back to the way things were, not when he was handcuffed to a police inspector in the back of a speeding police car filled with the sound of its wailing siren.

The sweat was beginning to trickle onto the fold of his new collar, his wrists were already sore and in the car mirror he could see a face that belonged to someone else, a face that was hollowed and aged with eyes shot through with red flecks of fear. A familiar face, but not his own face. It seemed to be the face of his father. That was the moment Freddie Payne realized he hated himself.

As he looked at the angry eyes staring out at him from the mirror, they seemed suddenly to grow huge and fill his mind, boring into those hiding places he had built inside himself and confronting all the excuses he had made for failure. He had worshipped his father, tried to emulate him in everything he had done – joining the Guards, but never making it to command the regiment. Facing the dangers of active service in Northern Ireland, because that's what his father would have wanted, but never winning the Military Cross. Why, he had even learned to abuse women in imitation of his father, learned how to lose money, too, although he had done both of these with considerably less finesse than the General. He had tried to live his life in his father's footsteps, yet just when Freddie had needed him most the old bastard had blown his brains out. Taken the easy option, left the field of battle and run away, leaving Freddie to face the mess on his own.

It seemed to Freddie that he had spent the years

since then in an impossible struggle, trying to continue to love his father even while he had learned to loathe him, blaming his father for everything, using him as the excuse of last resort. It was all the old man's fault, or so he pretended. Now, sitting in the back of the police car as it jumped the lights on the way to the top security cells at Paddington Green, Freddie Payne reckoned he had about ten minutes in which to grow up.

He had little idea why they had picked him up or what they knew, but many things were already certain. His wife would leave him, that was inevitable, taking their two daughters with her. They were spoilt brats anyway, took after their mother. The job at the gallery was history, too; Charlie would never forgive him for the embarrassment. The bank manager would also get in on the act and bring a complete stop to his stumbling line of credit. That part of the equation gave him cause to smile. He had made the best part of eight hundred thousand on the water and telephone deals and almost none of it had found its way into that unimaginative idiot's hands. Payne had opened a new account, in Switzerland, where neither his wife nor his bank manager could get at it; maybe they'd never find it, maybe it would still be there for him when he got out. Something to look forward to.

His wife, his bank, most of all his father, they'd all let him down, but not as much as he'd let himself down. Throughout his adult life only one thing had always been there for him, constant and unquestioning. The Army. Until the bloody politicians had got at it. The Army was the one thing he'd always been able to rely on, and in turn it had always been able to rely on him. It was the only thing in his life he had ever got right.

As the car swept in behind the reinforced steel gates of Paddington Green, Payne knew what he had to do.

'He's done what?' Bendall didn't try to hide his exasperation.

'Remained silent. He refuses to give us anything but his name, rank and serial number,' the Police Commissioner sighed, not sure what he might say that would mollify the Prime Minister. There had to be more to life than being used as a doormat.

Police work had become so intensely political. You entered the service with some vaguely formed idea about fighting for justice but instead, as you rose through the ranks, you found yourself distracted by the fight for budgets, for press coverage, for breathing space from the onslaught of pressure groups and politicians. You never won, it was always a rearguard action, until you ended up disillusioned and simply fighting for something to retire to.

The Commissioner of the Metropolitan Police, Peter Jevons, had played the game with skill. Throughout his career he had always kept on the move, taking care not to get bogged down in unnecessary confrontations with either the media or his political masters, making sure he never gave the impression of being stale. A career wrapped in clingfilm, they had said, out on show but untouched, although now he was seated behind the Commissioner's desk with nowhere else to run there was the suspicion that his reputation was beginning to moulder slowly at its edges. Yet a safe pair of hands, they'd always said that of him. That's why he had decided to bring the news of Payne's arrest personally to the Prime Minister, not because he wanted praise, but because he expected trouble. His instincts were entirely accurate.

The interview in the Downing Street study had started civilly enough. Faced with the possibility of several more days' revelations in the *Sun* about his colleagues' dipped wicks, Bendall knew he was in desperate need of a diversionary tactic. The tide was beginning to run ferociously against him; if he couldn't turn it, perhaps he could at least redirect it before it succeeded in surrounding him completely.

'This is the moment to hand the media another story, wouldn't you agree, Commissioner?' Bendall had suggested, drawing on a cigarette. He only ever smoked in private, and only when under pressure. Bad for the image, to be seen smoking, so he never did so in public and never allowed any photographs of himself with a cigarette. Bit like Hitler and his reading glasses, thought Jevons. 'So we'll call a press conference this afternoon. To announce the latest developments.'

'Developments, Prime Minister?' the policeman's face had crumpled into creases of concern.

'That I have taken personal charge of this investigation. Hands on. I'll not tolerate any further failures. And neither will the public.' He had disappeared for a moment behind a grey-blue haze before reappearing, his eyes agitated, dancing around the room in search of a resting place. 'I'll be able to announce the bloody man's arrest and reveal that they're no better than common thieves, in it for the money. I want no doubt left in the voters' minds that these people want nothing less than to hold London to ransom.'

'That may be, but I would advise strongly against a press conference so soon.'

'Why, for heaven's sake? It's the only decent spin we've had in weeks.'

'Because the matter is still spinning. It's not yet under control.'

'He's locked up in top security at Paddington Green. How much more control do you need?'

It was at this point that Jevons had told him about Payne's stubborn silence. Nothing but name, rank and serial number. And there was more, Bendall's equanimity was about to undergo a further assault.

'That's not our only problem, Prime Minister.'

'What?'

'Unless we find some hard evidence – and so far we haven't – we're going to have the devil of a time making any charges stick.'

'Several hundred grand in his pocket and you say you've got no evidence?'

'It's all circumstantial. Completely circumstantial. We may have to let him go.'

'He's not the only one who can be let go, you just remember that, Commissioner,' Bendall spat.

Jevons flushed. 'Am I to take that as a threat?'

Bendall didn't answer immediately but stubbed out his cigarette – only half finished – before straight away lighting another. Then, through the smoke: 'Of course not. Just a reminder that there are all sorts of potential outcomes to this one. For both of us. We need to nail these bastards.'

'I can't guarantee a charge. We may have to let him go. We have power to hold him for thirty-six hours, no longer.'

'For God's sake, have you no imagination?' Bendall exploded. 'Can't you think of some other charge? His kind often have exotic tastes. With traces of it in their pockets, so I'm told.'

'You're suggesting we plant evidence on him?'

Bendall's lips twisted in frustration. His words, when they came, were slow and very precise. 'I would never suggest anything like that, Commissioner.'

'Of course not.'

'So use the Terrorism Act. Then you've got him for days, not hours.'

'Terrorism? This isn't the IRA.'

'No, it's worse!' Bendall was straining forward in his chair, like a condemned man who had just received the first tickle of eternity. 'This isn't a game we're playing here, it's a premeditated assault against millions. The entire capital. Striking at the heart of the whole damned country.'

'Forgive me for pointing it out, but your opponents might suggest you're confusing the interests of the country with the interests of your Government.'

'Dammit, these people are a national menace! They've already disrupted London far more seriously than the IRA ever did. That makes them terrorists in my book, terrorists under the law, too, and I'll find a dozen different law officers who'll back me up on this.'

'I don't doubt it.'

'So you hold him under the Terrorism Act and you sweat him. You understand?'

This time it was the Commissioner's turn to consider carefully before replying. 'I'd be grateful for your instructions on this matter in writing. It helps to have things in proper order, don't you think?'

'In writing, you want it in writing? No problem. In fact I insist we handle this thing, as you put it, in proper order. Which brings me to another development I want to announce this afternoon.' Bendall moved over to the window from where, through the inch-thick glass, he could gaze across the garden of Number Ten. The tubs were full of flowers in bloom and the silver birch was casting a long shadow over a lawn. He obliterated the scene in cigarette smoke. 'What do you think they planned to do with the money?'

Jevons paused before replying, uncertain in which new direction they were heading. 'I can do nothing but speculate. Why, almost anything . . .'

Bendall swung to face him. 'Almost anything, you say?'

'Of course.'

'Reminds me a little of the IRA, you know. All those bank robberies. Extortion rackets. They used the money to buy their arms and explosives. D'you think it's possible that's what we have here?'

'Anything's a *possibility*.'

'Bombings? Assassinations perhaps? An attempt to cripple London as it's never been hit before?'

The policeman held up his hand as though to stop a wayward driver. 'You're going too fast for me, Prime Minister. It needn't be anything like that.'

'We're dealing with highly trained officers, and the one we've got locked up has years of experience in Northern Ireland.'

'Even so, bombings and assassinations are far too –'

'It's what the latest TAG assessments are going to suggest is an option.'

'My own Deputy Commissioner is on the TAG team, Prime Minister. I wasn't aware that they were predicting full-scale war.'

'It's because they haven't thought of it. Yet.' A smile died almost before it had appeared. 'But they will by the time of the press conference this afternoon.'

'I can't say I care for this.'

'And I don't care for the fact that you're getting nowhere with these bloody people!' Suddenly Bendall was shouting, seemingly so exasperated by the other man's reticence that he was on the point of losing control. 'Christ, I'm not asking you to prove the Virgin Mary was on the game, I'm only asking you to protect the elected Government. We're being slaughtered on every front page. That's what you should care about. Because things are going to change, you hear me? No more holding back, not any longer. From now on we're taking the gloves off and we're going to screw these bastards!' Bendall was shaking so forcibly that he turned his back to give himself a moment in which to gather himself.

Jevons examined the lines of the well-cut suit, and concluded he was watching an act. First the bullying, now the anger. Bendall wanted something. When at last the Prime Minister spoke again the mood had changed and he spoke as if for the public record.

'I would be failing in my duty if I didn't share with the people the dangers they might face from these renegades. They need to know that their Government is doing everything within its power to prevent further attacks on their capital city. I expect your full support in that.'

The Commissioner lowered his head, but the contempt in his eyes had already betrayed him. The Prime Minister began wandering around the room, apparently aimlessly, as though looking for something he had lost. He knew he had already lost the Commissioner.

'We'll have to raise the level of security on everything. Public buildings, public people. Gives you a hell of a lot of contingencies to cover, doesn't it, Peter?'

First names? Friends? Jevons's alarm grew. He swivelled in his chair to keep Bendall in his sights. The Prime Minister was now at the far end of the study, standing beside his jukebox.

'We have one of the most experienced police forces in the world, Prime Minister –'

'Yes, of course. But can you cope?'

'Are you doubting –'

'Simply wondering. The force has come under great strain in recent years. You've got fewer men and fewer resources than you had, yet now we're faced with something quite exceptional, something no one foresaw.'

'I've warned repeatedly about the damaging effects of the cutbacks.'

'Yes, I take the point.'

'Why, we've met – what? – twice in the last eighteen months in this very room. Meetings I demanded in order to protest at –'

'Let's not dwell on it, Peter. We both know that Chancellors get it wrong more often than not. But it seems to me we're here to deal with the present situation, not rake over old coals. I come back to my point. Can you cope?'

'With difficulty. With very great difficulty, in fact. And I refuse to be held responsible if –'

'I need your full support in this matter, Peter. Nothing less is acceptable.'

'What, with all this talk of terrorism? TAG assessments? A security blanket thrown across London? Simply to save the reputation of you and your –'

'OK. You win.'

A short pause for bewilderment. 'Win what?'

Suddenly music came blaring out from the jukebox, something horrid and thumping from the Seventies. Bendall was drawing closer to Jevons in order to make himself heard.

'You win your argument. Your logic, it's irresistible,' Bendall began, squatting informally on the arm of the Chesterfield next to the Commissioner. The noise forced him to bend close to the Commissioner's ear to make himself heard. 'Seems to me I've no choice other than to accept that the cutbacks have gone too far, and that as a result you might be considering your position. I respect that. A Commissioner who resigns on a matter of principle.'

'I wasn't aware that I had mentioned resignation!'

'And I don't think I'd mentioned the fact that in the light of the present situation it's my intention to ensure that the damage done to the police budgets in recent years will be repaired. In full. That's my promise to you.'

The Commissioner nodded stiffly, uncertain whether he had heard correctly above the din.

'I want the TAG assessments acted upon, Peter. No holds barred on this one. And if it means extra resources . . .'

'I can't conjure up additional policemen out of thin air, Prime Minister.'

'And there we have it, the nub of the whole matter. You're going to need some help.'

At last Jevons thought he had caught up with where this one was going. This was a guns and butter conversation. He'd just been offered the butter, and now . . .

'Public Order Act, Peter. Military Aid for the Civil Power.'

'You mean the Army.'

'Discreetly, of course. As low profile as possible. But you need it, and frankly I need it, too. To show that these guys are nothing less than extremists. Fighting their own.'

'The Army on the streets of London? For PR purposes?'

'It's a PR war we're fighting, Peter, and we're losing

it. The stakes don't come any higher than this, for either of us. There's a war going on in this city and there'll be no sympathy for those who come second. I'm not going to lose this one, I'm going to fight it with everything I've got.'

'But the Army . . . ?'

'I would understand if you feel obliged to resign. That would be a pity. Not what I want, you understand. Awkward timing for you, handing over to someone new just at the point when the police are about to be handed massive new resources. Chucking in the towel just when you're about to win the fight.'

Bendall, seated on the arm of the sofa, was hovering above the Commissioner's head, crowding him. And squeezing the constitution. For under the Military Aid to the Civil Power provisions, responsibility lay firmly in the hands of the Police Commissioner to write to the Home Office requesting the support of the armed forces. The law was clear, Bendall needed the Commissioner's consent if the Army was to be involved. And yet nothing was clear. If Jevons refused and resigned, Bendall would simply make sure his replacement did anything that was required. If Jevons didn't resign but fought his corner and refused to summon the Army, the blame for any further outrages would fall like rocks upon his shoulders. They would drag him off in disgrace. And yet, if he did what Bendall asked, the capital's police force would be showered with gifts throughout the next fiscal, indeed right up to his retirement. The coppers' copper, they would call him, the Commissioner who took care of his own. Bendall had made it so easy for him, and at the same time so impossible. He couldn't quite work out whether he was being blackmailed or bribed.

He sat there, twisting his signet ring until, eventually, he let forth an extended sigh. He desperately wanted to get out of this room. 'I'll sign an appropriate request as soon as I get back to my office, Prime Minister.'

'Not necessary. I think you'll find my private secretary has a draft waiting downstairs in the Cabinet Room.'

Jevons rose wearily to his feet, his eyes glazed, unfocused, like a man not wishing to catch sight of his own reflection. 'I hope you will understand if I don't attend your press conference this afternoon, Prime Minister. I feel very slightly violated.'

He left the room, not bothering with the pleasantries of farewell.

As soon as the door had closed, Bendall crossed the room to turn off the music. He hated the mindless head-banging crap, but it had its uses. The taping system he had set up to record the conversations in his office would one day provide a unique historic archive, a record to be studied by future generations, the mortar that would cement his place in the memories of the nation.

But there would always be some conversations he wouldn't wish to have analysed too closely, even at the risk of having those future generations question his obscure and apparently appalling taste in music.

What the hell. When he retired he'd get a new concert hall on the South Bank named after him. That should do the trick.

FOURTEEN

The phone seemed to baffle them. Everything else at the meeting of COBRA that followed on the heels of Payne's arrest had gone well. No more prevarication and indecision, the Army was coming and Bendall felt back in control.

But they couldn't explain the mobile phone. It had been in Payne's possession when they arrested him and, in spite of an exhaustive search of his home and workplace that had left both in disarray, there was as yet no other substantive evidence. It was a pay-as-you-go model, bought across the counter for cash along with fifty pounds' worth of call vouchers. No contract, no credit-card slip, nothing to trace, and both Payne's distraught wife and furious work colleagues confirmed that he had taken to carrying it with him at all times. Charlie at the gallery, with his empire strangled in the blue-and-white bunting of crime scene tape, had made several lurid suggestions as to what might be done with the phone, but the police decided that this would not help their investigation. They needed Freddie Payne intact, at least for the time being.

The curious thing about the phone was that it had never been used. No call had been made from it, neither had any been received. Yet it was switched on and fully charged even when they arrested him.

No one had an explanation, but it did nothing to diminish the fresh sense of enthusiasm that permeated the COBRA meeting. One suspect had been arrested, the level of security raised significantly, there was a new impetus and a triumphal press conference to come – at which Bendall would choose his words carefully, of course, while Jumpers would stir it up behind the scenes. And if the media chose to speculate that Freddie Payne and his associates were involved in bombs and blackmail and extortion, that would be nothing less than the prerogative of a free and imaginative press. Dipwick was yesterday's news. Everyone seemed content.

Except for Tom Goodfellowe.

As the meeting of COBRA broke up and the Prime Minister looked beyond the throng of officials and acolytes that surrounded him, the brow of Goodfellowe stood out like a fly struggling in thick custard.

'Problems, Tom?'

'No. No problems. Not really. Just . . . thoughts.'

'Share them. Walk with me.'

So Goodfellowe had accompanied Bendall on the short walk back to Downing Street. Their path took them through Cockpit Passage which connected the Cabinet Office to Number Ten, where their footsteps echoed back from ancient brickwork of the old Tudor palace that had once stood on this spot. Beyond the mullioned window lay the remnants of King Harry's old tennis courts, while in the dark vestibule that brought them back into Number Ten they were greeted by the unsmiling bust of Oliver Cromwell, who had chopped off the head of one of Henry's inheritors, the ill-fated Charles. Westminster had always been a place of swings and roundabouts. And scaffolds.

'It's the phone,' Goodfellowe began as a private secretary produced an electronic swipe card to allow them back into the Prime Ministerial lair. 'I've been trying to figure out why it was never used.'

'And?'

'It was all powered up. So I think it must have been used. Probably frequently, and certainly regularly. To keep in contact.'

'But no calls were ever logged . . .'

'Because the calls were never answered. Perhaps only three or four rings, then cancelled. No record, no trace.'

'Why?'

'Security. A safety signal. To tell whoever was at the other end that everything was OK.'

'But it's not OK, is it? Not for Freddie Payne.'

'That may not be such good news, either.'

'You trying to spoil my day?'

'If the phone was used as I think, then the others knew within a couple of hours that Payne had been arrested.'

'Damn.'

'Even if Payne begins to sing like the proverbial canary and leads us straight back to the aviary, we'll find –'

'Nothing but a pile of guano.'

'Precisely.'

'They made arrangements.'

'They're still one step ahead of us.'

They had reached the main staircase of Number Ten with its winding banister and collection of portraits of previous Prime Ministers that stretched back to the time of Robert Walpole, regarded as the first modern Prime Minister. He'd been condemned for corruption and kicked out of office. Most of his successors had been kicked out of office, too, over nearly three centuries. None of them ever seemed to know when their time was up. 'Events, dear boy, events' always got them in the end. The thought encouraged Goodfellowe to make a mental note, a promise to himself, that if he ever got to stand where Bendall was standing, he would do things differently. He would instruct Sam to tell him when that moment to leave the scene had come. Goodfellowe would go timely into the night, not stay and haunt the place like a vampire. Yes, that's what he'd do. If he ever got the chance.

'But I don't understand, Tom. Why on earth didn't you suggest this to COBRA?'

'Because if I'm right –'

'Which I suspect you are.'

'Then some of those at COBRA would be saying . . .' He hesitated.

'Come on, Tom, cough.'

'Well, they'd be saying that we shouldn't have pulled him in so quickly. That we should've had him followed. As they suggested.'

'That I made a complete bollocks of it?'

Goodfellowe chose not to contradict.

From his position on the first step of the staircase, Bendall studied his helper. 'You use your honesty a bit like a flame thrower at times, Tom. It's one of your most attractive faults.'

Goodfellowe merely shrugged.

'Doesn't matter. We're ready for the bastards.' Bendall was bounding up the stairs now, taking them two at a time, shouting over his shoulder. 'By tomorrow the country will understand that we live in a world that's still bloody dangerous. Full of evil people trying to take advantage of us. That we've got to be prepared.'

'Somehow I think that's precisely the point Beaky has been trying to put across,' Goodfellowe muttered – but not loud enough for the disappearing Bendall to hear.

Swinging his dead left leg, Scully kicked the blossom that had blown from the cherry trees in Battersea Park and been left piled high by the swirling wind. It scattered around him like unseasonal snowflakes.

'What the bloody hell went wrong, Colonel?'

'No idea, Skulls.'

'They on to us?'

'On to Freddie, that's for sure.'

'Shite.'

Scully bent to rub his leg. The others slowed, wishing neither to stop nor to leave him behind, knowing that either would embarrass him. His leg was getting worse. It was one of those days when wherever they looked they could see nothing but obstacles. Even the heavens joined in, clouds scudding overhead like pebbles being skimmed across grey water. The group fell into silence for several minutes.

'It was Freddie. Must've been Freddie, something he did,' Mary eventually insisted, wrapping her coat more firmly around her in the fading light. 'It *had* to be Freddie's fault, or they would've picked us all up.'

'Picked me up, at least,' Amadeus corrected. He had ensured that none of them knew how to contact the others, save for himself. A cut-off system, designed for disaster, for moments like this. 'Look, if they come knocking on my door, don't any of you hang around. You each do what you think is necessary. You know I won't talk.'

'Seems Freddie hasn't either,' Mary added with almost reluctant respect.

The rain had arrived. They scrambled for shelter in the lee of a refreshment kiosk that had already closed for the day. Scully brought up the rear.

'Poor Freddie. One soldier down,' McKenzie reflected.

'And another Home Secretary down,' Amadeus insisted. 'By any measure we're still well ahead. Oh, and revenge is sweet! Dipwick was the one who started all this. Now he's gone.'

'And Bendall has taken over,' Mary reminded him.

'Put himself right in the firing line.'

'This is getting very personal, Peter.'

'Yeah. Ain't it just.'

Battersea Power Station stands on the south bank of the River Thames less than two miles upstream from the Houses of Parliament. Its brooding presence dominates that part of London, its stark, almost brutal industrial architecture exciting passion and prejudice in equal degrees. Like it, loathe it, the one thing you cannot possibly do is ignore it. To some it is like an immense alien spaceship that has come to earth and died, its four huge white brick chimneys reaching out desperately towards the stars; to others it provides all too earthly evidence that Man has completely lost his sense of proportion. Yet for all its aesthetic aggression, the power station has been more victim than aggressor. Since it opened in 1934 it has been the target of repeated attack – first by Goering's Luftwaffe, then by subsidence into the underlying London clay, more devastatingly by environmentalists who claimed that the half-million tons of coal it burned every year were polluting the air from Essex all the way to the Urals. Finally it came under attack by developers who ripped out its soul along with every ounce of scrap machinery in their attempts to turn it into a theme park.

Yet ugliness on such a massive scale also entices. To the surprise of many tourists and astonishment of most Englishmen, the power station was embraced by the heritage lobby. It had, after all, been designed by Sir Giles Gilbert Scott who also gave the nation its beloved red telephone boxes. The building was listed as an architectural treasure, Grade Two, which meant it must be preserved. But for what? In Florida the site would probably have been sold at immense profit to the Disney Corporation, in Barcelona or Berlin perhaps they might have commissioned some young artist to wrap it in cellophane, while in Paris they would have scratched their heads and wondered who on earth allowed the bloody thing to be built in the first place. But in London they simply held their breaths and grew red in the face. No one would decide, and the forty-acre site was turned into a battleground on which warfare raged between conservationists, developers, planners and local pressure groups. The result was twenty years of deadlock and depredation that had left it roofless, gutted, its immense and filthy red-brick walls surmounting a bare industrial wasteland, home for nothing but memories.

Apart, that is, from the occasional film crew who used this brutal backcloth for any number of productions, McKellen's *Richard III* being by far the most memorable.

Thus far.

The most recent aspiring producer and location manager to turn up at the site were named Donnie and Mike. They were a little vague about the project they had in mind. They were also, in the opinion of Sammy McManus, the site supervisor, a rather odd couple, heavily into sunglasses and hats. They also both had thick designer stubble which served to hide the contours of their faces, but over the years he had grown used to the odd couples who floated around the film industry.

Sammy had enjoyed taking them around the site. It got lonely here on his own when the wind was blowing, with nothing to distract him but a garden of straggling geraniums, Oprah Winfrey and a small library of well-thumbed books centred around Shakespeare and Trollope (both Anthony and Joanna). Anyway, Oprah was putting on weight again.

So they had walked and smoked and talked about Charlton Athletic, about Sammy's forthcoming holiday, and the local residents' groups who couldn't make up their minds whether they wanted the site to be a wonderland or a wasteland, and McKellen's awesome pyrotechnics that had brought half of the fire crews in London rushing to the scene to extinguish a five-hundred-year-old fire.

'So, Sammy, what's with all the scaffolding around the chimneys?'

'We're just checking their stability. Routine structural check. Normally we do it with infrared scanners but the local planners want to have a look-see for themselves. If one of those bastards fell down it'd sound like Krakatoa. Won't put you off, will it?'

'Depends. How long's it going to be like that?'

'Couple of weeks, maybe. No more.'

'I think that should be fine, don't you, Mike?'

'Sure. Sure, Donnie. I think that'll be just fine.'

Success is its own deceiver. And, for a few days, Bendall found success knocking at his door. Londoners' characteristic spirit of defiance in the face of adversity came forth and greeted the changes they saw around them with understanding and a measure of reluctant acquiescence.

It was the little things that some found most aggravating, like the disappearance of waste bins from many public places, and particularly from those corners near major Government buildings where the bins hadn't been swept away in the earlier campaigns against the IRA. So London grew a little grubbier, and also a little slower. Many of the major routes through the City of London had been blocked to control access during that same IRA bombing campaign, and now that experience was translated to the City of Westminster. Parliament Square ground to a complete halt as plastic barriers filled with sand were manoeuvred into position. When the Square reopened, traffic could pass the House of Commons only by means of a single file and two separate chicanes. No would-be terrorist was going to make a quick getaway from this part of London, and in the circumstances it seemed a relatively minor inconvenience that no one else was going to make a quick getaway either. Londoners took it in their behobbled stride.

Indeed, there were some distinct advantages. The very obvious presence of armed policemen at major traffic intersections ensured an unusual degree of etiquette from motorists. Yellow boxes remained unblocked, no one ran a traffic light, even cyclists dug deep into their memory banks for ancient recollections of the Highway Code. Rush hour traffic actually moved. And if a few Londoners were disturbed by the presence of the Armoured Personnel Carriers tucked away behind Admiralty Arch, less than ten seconds from Trafalgar Square, they were in a minority. Most treated them as nothing more than a tourist attraction.

*   *   *

The next contact, when it came, consisted of another brief telephone call to the editor of the *Telegraph*. The security services who were monitoring the call timed it at less than twenty-two seconds and traced it to a little-used callbox in rural Hertfordshire. Inevitably the callbox was deserted by the time the local constabulary had arrived, and forensics produced nothing beyond the suggestion that it had been used sometime in the last four days for the purposes of unprotected sex and the rolling of a joint. Even the voice analysis told them nothing they didn't already know, that the caller was probably in his forties and reasonably well educated – the conversation was too fragmentary to get a reliable regional trace, although it did suggest that he was under a measurable degree of strain.

'This is tomorrow's headline.'

'Good evening, Beaky. Is it OK to call you Beaky?'

'Call me what you bloody well like so long as you shut up and listen.'

'Sorry.'

'This thing hasn't finished yet.'

'There's more?'

'Within the week.'

'What are we talking about here? More disruption in the streets, or are we talking more personal attacks like Earwick?'

'Oh, no, we're aiming higher than that. Much higher.'

Then the line had gone dead.

Higher? Higher than what? Than the streets? Than Earwick? What the hell did it mean? Were they going to disrupt air traffic, for God's sake? Or had they set their sights higher than the Home Secretary? But who was there, apart from the Prime Minister? Or – no, surely not her . . .

It was extraordinary misfortune that such questions should have been hanging in the air when, later that night, a mud-spattered Range Rover had been sighted driving well above the speed limit and heading along the B976, the lonely road west of Aberdeen that hugs the River Dee in the general direction of Balmoral. It was further cruel luck that the Vehicle Identification Mark check that was called for by a police constable at Glen Tanar showed that the vehicle belonged to a certain Colonel Charles Julius Anthony Forsdyke. Retired. Formerly of the Grenadier Guards, and one-time Commanding Officer of none other than Freddie Payne.

This was an unhappy coincidence for the Colonel, for the police check also showed that he appeared on two further lists. The first, which ran into tens of thousands, had been prepared by the Ministry of Defence and covered all known former military associates of Payne's. Forsdyke figured on this list, inevitably and also prominently. The greater difficulty was that he also appeared on a second, much shorter, list that had been cobbled together in a hurry by Special Branch. This contained the names of anyone with a connection to the armed forces who was also suspected of being a critic of the Government. Not that there was any suspicion about Forsdyke. His views of the Government were unambiguous and had been delivered at a charity dinner less than two weeks previously within earshot of a Minister of State from the Foreign and Commonwealth Office. Forsdyke had used the occasion to refer to the Prime Minister as 'Jonathan Bugger-All' and to the Government as 'containing more shits than a convenience in Calcutta'.

Perhaps Forsdyke had had too much to drink, or perhaps the Minister of State had too little sense of humour for the occasion, but in any event it meant that the Colonel's name was on both lists. While inclusion on either rendered you a suspect, inclusion on both classified you as a major security risk.

Now this major security risk was heading for Balmoral.

Had he got a little further along the B976 he would, perhaps, have been dealt with by officers of the Royal Protection Squad, but the VIM check had been called in by a local panda car, and once the computers had declared that Forsdyke was in every respect a prime suspect, the response had been instantaneous.

Stop. Detain, if necessary. Detain if unsure. Take no chances, not on this one, laddie. On pain of banishment to one of the outer isles, do not let him pass within a million miles of Balmoral.

Reinforcements were already on their way when Forsdyke's Range Rover was pulled over by the patrol car.

'Evening, sir. I see we're in a wee bit of a hurry.'

'Good. So you'll not be detaining me any longer.'

'What, late for dinner with the Queen, are we?'

325

'Matter of fact, I am.'

'May I trouble you for your licence?'

'No.'

'Why is that then?'

'Because I haven't got it.'

'I see.'

'I very much doubt if you do. Look, I really am in a hurry, so why don't you jump on that little radio thingy of yours and –'

'Would you mind stepping out of the car, sir?'

'I bloody well would.'

'Step out of the car.'

'Haven't you got something more important to do?'

'Like what?'

'Like suggesting to your parents they might get married?'

'Step out of the car. *Please*.'

'Why?'

'Because I'm placing you under arrest.'

'Don't be a little squit. On what charge?'

'Fer being a shite. *And fer tekin' the piss out of the polis*.'

It wasn't entirely the constable's fault. It was the problem with using raw data, the type that finds its way onto computer lists hurriedly thrown together by the security services. In many respects raw data resembles raw sewage. It's all fine after it's been treated, but until then . . .

It was only later, much later, after they had hemmed him in with their panda cars, their blue lights turning the countryside into a scene from *Independence Day*, and carted him off to the cells at Aberdeen, that they discovered the awful truth. He *was* late for dinner with Her Majesty.

They had arrested the Queen's second cousin.

FIFTEEN

The Prussian strategist Clausewitz defined war as being the pursuit of politics by other means. Fortunately for the great man's clarity of thought, he was not well acquainted with the system of politics we call democracy, which makes the pursuit of anything that requires consistent application fiendishly difficult and the pursuit of modern warfare almost impossible. For war in the new millennium is not a matter of personal sacrifice but of smart bombs deployed at great distances with battlefields that look as if they have been designed by Nintendo. Nowadays, when it comes to war, we're all far too busy to bother with the mucky bits.

So, as the Government began to take further precautions in response to the escalating but ill-defined threat, London's sense of humour began to fade. While the authorities were desperately trying to locate back-up generators and mobile electricity substations, Londoners were with equal desperation searching for somewhere to park. Substantial swathes of central London had been declared a 'no park' zone and Londoners fought and fumed for every inch of available kerb space. Ill-tempered queues developed outside carparks, in spite of the fact that the car-parking companies had doubled their tariffs overnight. Meanwhile vehicle-clamping contractors issued urgent pleas for additional temporary staff. It did nothing to help the capital's sense of humour that the sequencing of traffic lights at many important junctions had been changed, slowing down the traffic still further in an attempt to assist the police observation squads who were now armed with video cameras and recording everything that moved, if it moved.

Insult was added to the overall sense of injury by the dramatic increase in helicopter traffic above the rooftops of London. Horse Guards Parade and the parade ground at Wellington Barracks were turned into temporary helipads as Ministers, on the advice of the security services, took to the skies to avoid becoming sitting targets in stationary traffic. This was nothing more than a sensible precaution in official eyes, but to most Londoners stuck in that stationary traffic it was simply another example of politicians taking the piss.

The helicopters were joined in the skies above the capital by an airship. Until the previous week it had been doing service as a mobile advertising blimp but it was now hurriedly requisitioned and fitted out with infrared and other surveillance kit, along with an emergency war-room communications facility – just in case. Its presence above the rooftops rapidly became as unpopular as that of the Army reinforcements who had been drafted in with instructions to make their presence painfully obvious. No longer were they tourist attractions, they couldn't be. Most of the tourists had been frightened off. Those travellers who did brave the journey into the no-man's-land of London found, as they emerged from the tunnel leading out of Heathrow Airport, that the APCs of the previous weeks had been replaced by Scimitar tanks.

The game was afoot, the stakes had been raised, but most ordinary people had no wish to join in. Sure, the plotters had been a pain and had themselves brought London grinding to a halt, but only for a couple of hours. It had all been over by lunchtime. Now the Government was doing it every day of the week.

It seemed to the average Londoner that the plotters could at least claim to have a sense of humour, while all the Government had to offer was a blimp that droned above their heads day and night, like a mosquito in the bedroom. It was rapidly christened the Wimp Blimp.

What was more, while the common man suffered in the cause, where had the politicians gone? Buggered off in their helicopters, every one of them, or so it seemed.

Soon bumper stickers began to sprout on cars throughout London. Their message was simple and heartfelt.

'Bring Back Beaky!'

Gibraltar Barracks is a military complex of low red-brick buildings and green fields just off the M3 motorway. It is the headquarters of 3RSME Regiment, the Royal Engineers training outfit. Gibraltar Barracks is where soldiers gather for ten weeks of basic training in the mysteries of how to make things go bang.

The Crown and Cushion pub, six hundred yards down the road, is where they gather once those mysteries have been unravelled. The pub's Meade Hall to the rear is particularly popular. It has high vaulted ceilings and walls littered with ancient agricultural instruments, and it was in the Meade Hall that McKenzie had agreed to meet a freckle-faced young man named Kenny Evans. Evans stood out in any company. He had inherited from his Celtic father a shock of hair that looked more like an upturned bowl of carrot scrapings, while those who knew him well recognized him as a master in the handling of PE4. Plastic explosive. He had also been one of McKenzie's corporals: 32 Engineer Regiment

They were lucky. The pub was crowded – much of the bar had been taken over for the birthday celebration of a sales rep in bathroom accessories from nearby Camberley – but they managed to find an unoccupied booth and settled in.

'Guinness and a whisky chaser, I seem to remember, Kenny.'

'Thanks, Andy.' Evans took possession of the proffered glasses. 'Don't often get the chance of a chaser in these hard times.'

'They giving you grief?'

'Like you wouldn't believe.'

'Och, I suspect I might . . .'

'No, Andy, you wouldn't. It's got worse than ever.' Evans's lilting Welsh pronunciation seemed to add pathos to his words. 'It's not an army any more;

they've turned it into play school. Everything crawling with civilians. Even the security guards at the camp. You remember O'Shea?'

'Corporal O'Shea?'

'Not any longer he's not. Comes back late the other week and starts getting grief from one of the civvy security guards. The guard barely seems to understand a word of the English language, so O'Shea uses some traditional English on him and tells him to go fuck himself, so he does. Next thing you know he's been busted down to sapper.'

'It's a sadly changing world.'

'*Iechyd da*, my friend. And so it is. You know, we just finished an exercise, joint ops with an Italian regiment. Cooks or something, so they were. Our European cousins are camped up in a wood on Salisbury Plain, and we're supposed to take the position from 'em. What a bloody waste of time. Everything's been scraped back so far that the British Army rattles when it walks and those brain surgeons in Logistics hadn't even given us enough blanks to scare the bloody crows, let alone put the wind up Eyetie cooks. So what were we supposed to do, blow kisses at 'em? Anyhow, we get ourselves all kitted up, ready for the off, like, then the bloody truck arrives. The driver's civvy, right, and says he's been held up in traffic and he's already over his legal hours. So what does he do? Goes and takes his break. Right then and there, that's what! In the middle of the bloody war!' He ran a hand through his hair in an attempt to bring some semblance of order to it, but it proved to be another wasted exercise. 'You know, Andy, next

332

time they send us into battle they'll probably give us bus tickets. Bugger it. Looks like my round. Last one seems to have disappeared in rather a hurry.'

So they sat and drank, and reminisced about their time in Bosnia, building camps for the refugees, repairing bridges, opening routes that had been blocked first by one side then another, and all the while ducking bullets as they tried to dig the country out of the mess it had got itself into. Perhaps they might have been due some gratitude instead of bullets, but no one in Bosnia seemed to give a damn, apart from the children. And once CNN had moved elsewhere, to Kosovo and Chechnya and East Timor and Dagestan, no one back home seemed to give a damn either. They couldn't even show you where it was on a map.

'Anyway, Andy, you said on the phone you wanted a favour. It's yours, my friend.' Evans drained the last of his dark drink and watched the remnants of its sticky head drain slowly back into the bottom of the glass. 'So what's up?'

'I'm away up to Scotland in a couple o' weeks, Kenny. My father's sixtieth. Big family reunion on the estate. Thought I might arrange a wee fireworks display in his honour.'

'You'd like a little PE4.'

'There's an old milking shed, a real eyesore he's been itching to get rid o' for ages, and a few old trees. Thought I'd bring in a couple o' ancient cars, too, just for the pyrotechnics. That kind o' thing.'

'How much you want?'

'A couple of cases. Three if you can manage.'

Evans sucked his teeth. 'That gives me a bit of a problem, Andy.'

It wasn't the request for PE4 that bothered him. Amongst engineers a case of explosive is no more significant than a case of Diet Coke, there's always some lying around somewhere. Neither was it the purpose for which the explosive was wanted – if you've trusted a man with your life, as Evans had trusted McKenzie time and again in Bosnia, you take many other things on trust, too. Siphoning a couple of cases out of the system was simpler than liberating sweets from Sainsbury's. It was the responsibility of the officer in charge of the range day to sign for all munitions used on exercises, but it was Corporal Evans who provided the manifest. The officer would have no more interest in checking the number of cases on that manifest than he would have in counting the sparrows in an orchard.

It was a little light larceny, no worse than using the office photocopier for your tax returns. But Kenny Evans had other problems. 'You see, Andy, I've promised to take the kids to the new Spielberg film tomorrow evening, so I couldn't possibly let you have a couple of cases then. Earliest would be the night after. Will that do?'

The drilling crew arrived promptly at seven a.m. at the security gate to the Battersea Power Station in Kirtling Street. They needed an early start.

'Gotta be finished by close of play,' they explained to the security guard.

'What's all this then?'

A work order was waved in the grey morning light.

'Holes for some sort of monitoring equipment. In the chimneys, to check they ain't moving, John.'

John, whose name in fact was Wesley, scratched his stomach and inspected the work order. 'I ain't been told nothing 'bout this.' But then they rarely told him anything.

'Not a big job. Ten small holes in each spout. We was told you had scaffolding up there already. Right? Authorized by Mr . . . who is it?' The drill operator peered over the guard's shoulder at the flapping piece of paper. 'Name of McManus, that's it. See, it's all signed, John.'

Sammy McManus was on holiday but the paperwork was in order. Nothing unusual. Just another part of the cat's cradle of services required to keep a structure like this in one piece.

'How long all this gonna take, you say?'

'Out of your hair by close of play, with luck, me old mate.'

'Yeah. Sure. OK. Can't be too careful with these old buildings, can you?'

The gates swung open and the green and yellow truck of the Acme Diamond Drilling Services rolled inside. An entirely legitimate crew, who would drill a hole for you in anything, so long as they had a signed work order. Even if it had been stolen. Acme Diamond Drilling Services were *Specialists in Diamond Drilling, Wall & Floor Sawing, Selective Demolition, Concrete Crushing . . .*', plus a number of other heavy-duty services on concrete, so its box in the Yellow Pages said.

335

If you wanted Acme's help, all you had to do was look them up in the phonebook and call.

From their vantage point across the river, McKenzie and Mary watched the figures from Acme crawling across the scaffolding. Throughout the rest of the day and from different spots they continued to observe the crew setting about their work. Not until the last hole had been drilled and the equipment was being stowed did they permit themselves to relax.

McKenzie set aside his binoculars and turned to Mary.

'Should be one hell of a firework display, eh, lassie?'

She smiled in agreement, a soft smile. Then she raised herself onto her toes and kissed him.

They came in through a railway arch that bordered the site. There was only a battered wooden fence in their way, and plenty of cover from the bridge to hide what they were doing. It was also at a point farthest from the main gate and the security guards with their dogs, which on such a large site meant they could have been on the other side of town.

The daylight had gone and low cloud hid the moon. Not that it made much difference; there was so much ambient night light in London that it simply bounced back off the cloud and lit their path. You could read the headlines in a newspaper. Amadeus reckoned they'd have plenty of new headlines to read the following morning.

They missed Freddie Payne. This was, in truth, a five-man job. It wasn't so much the plastic explosive – they needed nearly fifty pounds of PE4, all packed into McKenzie's bergen – double what the textbooks said would be needed plus ten per cent to be sure. The Law of Combat Engineering, which says that you double up on everything because you never get a second chance. The main problem was the audio speaker wire that had been purchased at different outlets down the Tottenham Court Road. It came in great rolls. This is what they would use to wire the charges, since they had decided to detonate the plastic explosive manually. No timers, they wanted to leave nothing behind that might be traced. Each of them carried three of the rolls, Mary included, and there were also radios, wire cutters, ropes, torches, sections of broom handle, even a twelve-volt car battery.

Yet the most difficult work had already been done. The scaffolding gave them ready access and the holes had been drilled. The stolen work order had specified the cutting of ten holes in each of the giant chimneys, on the side that faced into the disembowelled carcass of the old power station. Each hole was about the size of a squash ball.

Because of the loss of Payne they had decided to concentrate on only three of the four chimneys. They took one each, Amadeus, Scully, and Mary, with McKenzie supervising them. McKenzie hated heights, he preferred slithering on his stomach through minefields, although somehow at night it didn't seem so bad. Yet in spite of their preparations the near two-hundred-foot climb up the scaffolding to the base of the chimneys took its toll – not on Mary, whose long and lonely walks across Exmoor had left her with an ocean of stamina on which to draw, but on Scully. He suffered, moaning softly at times, with that dead leg of his dragging behind him like an anchor. They lifted his load up on ropes.

Once inside the gutted walls they could have hidden an entire armoured division, but still they worked quietly. In the distance they could hear yelping, something had disturbed the mutts at the dogs' home. Trains rumbled stubbornly across the nearby railway bridge, and from across the river came the wail of a distant ambulance siren, but inside the power station there was nothing but the soft scraping of rubber soles on scaffolding.

It was not skilled work. Everything had been pre-pared beforehand by McKenzie. A double thumb knot in the end of the grey detonator cord, pushed into the holes at the base of the chimneys so that a foot of the cord was left hanging from the end of each hole like a rat tail.

Then came the sticks of plastic explosive. Each stick seven-and-a-half inches long. One-and-a-half inches in diameter. About half a pound each stick and three to every hole. Pushed home with the wooden broom handle – no sparks! The explosive looked a little like flaky marzipan and as they unwrapped it from its greaseproof paper it smelt sweet, like almonds.

Child's play, so far.

Then the rat tails were joined together with clips, and in turn joined to the speaker wire which they began to snake out like a ring main between the three chimneys.

It was getting cold, but they were all sweating from the climb.

Two fine white wires trailed out of the detonators, which were mated with the speaker wire. The speaker wire trailed down, down, down into the darkness of the power station.

As they dropped one roll of wire down it disturbed a nesting kestrel, which flew with screeches of complaint into the night. The noise echoed back from the empty walls like a shriek of demons. It started the dogs barking once more.

Now they fretted, because they had to wait while their handiwork was inspected by McKenzie. No chances. It took less than a minute for him to check the clips and the connections, but the best part of an hour to clamber up and down the three huge chimneys.

'Christ, Andy, how long does it take you Engineers to organize a firework display?'

'Takes a wee bit more care than falling out o' the back of a perfectly serviceable aircraft, it seems to me. So away and play wi' yersel', sir.'

Waiting around and feeling their sweat dry in the cooling night air seemed a miserable option, so they busied themselves, Scully keeping lookout while Amadeus and Mary occupied themselves by reconnoitring for an alternative escape route. Just in case.

And that was when they realized they'd ballsed it up.

There wasn't enough wire.

They had calculated the amount of wire they would

need from information Mary had downloaded from a newspaper library on the Internet, a comprehensive article about the power station and its endless planning rows, complete with diagrams and dimensions. Except the dimensions had been wrong.

Bloody journalists!

They were almost a hundred metres short. Way short of the safety zone for firing that had been calculated by McKenzie. He'd hoped to fire the charges from the relative safety of outbuildings that stood near the railway arches, but once he had wired the three detonators together there was barely enough wire to get them beyond the main walls of the power station itself. They stood in a small circle around the car battery that was meant to fire the charges, the monstrous brickwork towering above them.

'That's a rare pity,' McKenzie muttered quietly. He was never prone to exaggeration.

'What's to be done, Andy?'

'Three choices, I guess. One: we call it a day and proceed to the pub. Or two: I wrap the bare speaker wires around the battery terminals and pray we don't all get blown to a better world.'

'Three. I'll take three,' Amadeus insisted.

'We make do with just two chimneys. I'll rip the wire off the third, that'll be giving us more than enough cover.'

'Not quite the same artistic effect,' Amadeus replied, 'but it'll do. How long will it take?'

The Scotsman ran his hand through his thick hair. 'Twenty minutes, maybe.'

But they didn't have twenty minutes, not even

twenty seconds. For the dogs they had heard barking were not from the dogs' home but from the security pound. Disturbed by the screech of the kestrel, the Alsatian had alerted the watchman who had looked and listened. Then he had summoned the police.

The night suddenly turned upside down as the immense arc lights that illuminated the power station for special occasions were switched on. Amadeus and the others were caught like dazzled rabbits. Police vehicles were pouring through the main gate, piercing the night with the wail of sirens and the screeching of tyres. Amadeus knew they had failed. No chimneys, now. They wouldn't even have time to make it back through the railway arches.

But it wasn't over yet. The power station site was immense, nearly forty acres of it. Their pursuers were still a little way off; they still had vital seconds.

'The tunnels!' Amadeus shouted, suddenly freed of the hypnotic glare of the lights. 'Mary and I found tunnels in the basement. Full of old power cables heading out under the river. We'll try them.' And he started running, back into the power station, away from the lights and the prying eyes.

It might prove to be less than a total disaster if they could make it through the tunnel. It was head-high and stank with a fetid mixture of stale damp air and rat shit, and its entrance was secured by a metal gate. The gate was padlocked. Raw metal blocking their way.

Fear lends unusual strength. Amadeus snatched up

a length of scrap metal from the floor, used it as a jemmy and twisted it behind the padlock, which soon surrendered, clattering to the ground. Before them, disappearing into the Stygian darkness of the tunnel, stretched huge power cables and pipes as thick as a man's arm, a legacy of the days when Battersea had provided a fifth of London's electricity.

If there was nothing more at the other end, then they had a chance.

It was at this point they realized they were only three.

'Scully! Where the fuck's Scully?'

They were only a few paces into the tunnel, their torches dancing off the walls and floor, rats scattering before them and protesting at the invasion of their underground lair. The beam of a torch exposed a pile of rancid bones, what had perhaps once been a dog, lying in the middle of a stretching puddle. Intruders weren't welcome here. Every noise seemed magnified, echoing off the walls – the scurrying rats, the insistent dripping water from the river above, their own tormented breathing. The sirens seemed a mile away, barely more than a distant wail.

'Where's Skulls?' Amadeus demanded once more.

Before anyone had a chance to speculate, the air around them was filled with terror. It shook. It wanted to be elsewhere. It fled with a great rushing sound, like the death throes of an exhausted space capsule. Then came noise, a great crashing waterfall of noise which beat with the force of axes upon their

342

eardrums and inside their skulls. A semi-solid tide of rubble and dust and dirt pushed its way past them, throwing them to the ground, filling their eyes and nostrils until they couldn't breathe.

Sun Tzu once wrote that the greatest battles are those that are never heard of. Well, screw Sun Tzu. The whole of London was going to hear about this one.

It seemed logical to Scully that he should stay behind and fire the charges. He couldn't run, and if someone had to go down, better it be him. He had so much less to lose.

And he owed everything to Amadeus.

Sure, so Scully had saved him in the Falklands, but that was his job, part of the deal, what he'd signed up for. Amadeus owed him nothing. Yet throughout their time as Paras, Amadeus had always been there for him, not just as an officer but as a leader. A great leader.

Like the time Scully had found himself in a bar in Sardinia, in search of a little R&R after ten days of rigorous NATO exercises. He'd been nursing a drink at the bar when he'd noticed an ape who passed as a US Army artillery officer from Louisiana. Plenty of apes were officers, but this one had succeeded in attracting Scully's attention by standing next to him at the bar and insisting that royalty was incest. Well, perhaps they'd tried that, too, but what Scully couldn't ignore was the further opinion of the officer from Louisiana, expressed at bar-room volume, that this made the

Queen nothing better than a laboratory-bred rat. A German rat at that. So Scully had hit him. Bloody hard. So hard that he'd broken the American's nose, and with it broken his own career, for military regulations insist that striking an officer, even an alcoholic American example, is tantamount to striking a match while sitting in a puddle of petrol.

Scully was dead meat – until Major Amadeus, the Company Commander, had taken the American to one side and explained that Sardinia was full of weird and improbable stories. One story going the rounds was about how a US lieutenant had got himself creamed by a British NCO in a bar brawl – who ever heard of such a thing? A still wilder rumour concerned the attentions paid by that same lieutenant towards two rank-haired young men in the back room of the same bar. Amadeus had carefully and in considerable detail explained how, even in these liberated days, a cokehead from Louisiana with what seemed to be a persistent case of hay fever was scarcely in a position to go round insisting on investigations into what happened to his nasal passages in the back rooms of bars. No, the stories were not to be believed, none of them. The complaint had been dropped.

Amadeus was a great leader of men. A great friend. He'd even been godfather to Scully's only child, a boy, Peter, named after Amadeus, although Scully would never admit as much to his wife.

Pity about the boy. Scully had been on manoeuvres when it happened. His wife was a neurotic bitch with a mouth full of venom and a bathroom cupboard full of pills. Every type of pill. Pills to sleep with, pills to wake up with, pills that relaxed you and pills that made you prance around the sergeants' mess and act like a tart. Pills to fuck with and pills to stop babies with, but God knew why she needed them because after Peter the last thing she was interested in was fucking. At least fucking Scully. Always had a migraine, no matter how many pills she took.

Anyway, Peter had found the pills. He'd been only seven, poor little bastard, and Scully had got a message on exercise in Germany that he'd been granted compassionate leave. Took him totally by surprise. Why the hell did he need compassionate leave?

She was supposed to have been taking care of Peter. Same as she was supposed to have been taking care of Scully. Fucked up on both counts. Then fucked off.

So Scully had so much less to lose than the others.

Which is why he'd stayed behind and touched the bare wires to the battery terminals.

The noise of the three collapsing chimneys could be heard across central London. Nearly a million bricks falling from a height of 337 feet, carefully executed so that they fell inside the walls of the power station where they could do no harm and where the noise would be amplified like a huge drum. Even inside the chamber of the House of Commons, two miles down the river, they knew that something quite extraordinary had taken place, but precisely what no one was sure, not until the cloud of dust had settled.

Yet as the wind blew away the debris and the air

cleared, two things were seen at Battersea. The first was the single remaining chimney, huge, white, illuminated so that it could be viewed from many miles around, pointing like a raised middle finger in the direction of Westminster. A symbol of defiance and contempt. In a campaign that had consisted entirely of symbolic gestures, this struck Amadeus as being particularly apposite.

The second thing to be seen at Battersea was a figure emerging from the dust. Scully had been blown over and beaten by the blast, shaken until he thought the fillings would be rattled out of his teeth, covered in dust and cut by flying debris. But he had survived. There was no point in trying to run. His leg now refused to work, he could barely walk. So he grabbed a piece of metal scaffolding to act as a crutch and, with considerable difficulty, had levered himself to his feet. Then he had walked towards inevitable capture.

It was the young officer's first month as a member of the Armed Response Unit. He'd managed to get all the way through the Lippitts Hill training camp in Epping Forest without screwing up. Absorbed all the lectures, learned how to tuck his trousers into his boots, earned his Marksman classification on a whole bunch of weapons and succeeded in impressing the superintendent. Done it all – except, that is, for the active service bit. Now he'd been thrown in at the deep end, and word had come down from on high that these men were dangerous, enemies of the entire established order. That no risks were to be taken.

Thoughts tumbled inside his head, pushed savagely around by the pounding of the Air Support Unit helicopter that hovered overhead. He could feel the sweat beginning to prickle on his brow, but he had a good sighting through the night scope of his Heckler & Koch MP5. A single-shot carbine in its police variant. A single shot was all a trained marksman was supposed to need.

As Scully emerged from the fog of dust he appeared to be holding something. Something about the size and shape of a rifle. It was at his shoulder, and he was waving it in the direction of the police line. *Christ, the guy was tooled up. Game on.* At that precise and wretched moment, elsewhere on the field another officer stumbled over debris in the dark and fell with a cry. The radio spat into life and the novice's earpiece exploded inside his brain with shouts of 'Officer down! Officer down!'

Inexperience. Fear. Excitement. Adrenaline. Distraction. Perhaps even an in-built desire to do it for the first time, a dark fascination to see how it would feel that the psychologists hadn't unravelled.

So the officer slotted Scully from a distance of almost sixty yards. The soft-point nine millimetre round had a muzzle velocity of thirteen hundred feet a second. It struck the side of the breastbone and began to spin along its axis, dumping its energy and tearing a hole in his chest all the way through to his heart. Blew poor Scully clean away.

SIXTEEN

The destruction of the power station was not the only bomb incident that night. In the early hours of the morning the emergency services received an anonymous phone call through a computerized voice synthesizer. It indicated that a car parked in front of a terraced house in the quiet residential street of Mayday Avenue in Clapham contained a bomb. It also mentioned that the bomber was asleep inside the house.

Sky News received similar information, equally anonymously, about fifteen minutes later.

There was immediate suspicion about the authenticity of the report, given the rather picturesque name of the location. *Mayday Avenue*? But who the hell was going to take any chances after a night like this? So, as quietly as is possible at two in the morning, Mayday Avenue was cordoned off and sniffer dogs sent in.

When they reached the suspect car, the dogs responded with great enthusiasm, running round and round in excited circles. When the VIM check revealed that the car had heavyweight military connections, things began to fall into place. Could this be the car that had transported the explosives to Battersea? Were the bombers inside the house?

Only one way to find out.

An inspection through a night scope revealed that the downstairs windows were encased in metal security grilles. The front door also appeared to be reinforced. Perhaps nothing more than sensible precautions against domestic burglary, but also potentially the signs of fortifications around a bomb factory. There were other problems. Access from the rear was severely impeded by a series of gardens and walls – they wouldn't be able to get a large force of men in that way without disturbing every cat in the neighbourhood. It had to be through the front door.

Oh, but there were so many uncertainties. They had no idea about the internal layout of the house, or who might be sleeping where. If there was a bomb in the car, should they try to disable it first? Or try to evacuate the rest of the street, knowing that it would take hours and almost certainly alert the bombers? No, it had to be simplicity and speed. Delay was not an option, if for no better reason than that Sky TV had already arrived and other news cameras would be hot on their heels. Soon this place was going to be a circus. They had to go straight in.

A bomb-squad Land Rover was driven up as close and as quietly as possible to the front door. One end of a metal chain encased in sound-smothering plastic was attached to the chassis, while the three-foot metal bar that dangled from the other end was carefully dropped through the letter box. It was known as an 'enforcer'. Then the engine of the Land Rover was gunned and the clutch slipped. The metal chain went taut, the Land Rover hesitated as the tyres scrabbled for more grip, then lurched forward several yards. In its wake came the noise of splintering wood, and what remained of the front door of Number 27.

Suddenly Mayday Avenue was filled with the sounds of chaos – the angry shriek of a car alarm as the flying door buried itself in the windscreen, the howling of terrified dogs, the grave-spinning screams of officers as they poured though the hole in Number 27. Then the sound of other doors being smashed in, followed by more screams.

It was over in seconds. Only two occupants and no resistance, which in the circumstances was scarcely surprising. It's damned difficult to resist when you're caught naked in bed with your arms and legs wrapped around each other.

The sounds and sights of that night were captured for posterity and profit by the cameras of Sky TV. They could see it all from their position at the far end of the road, shooting from the bedroom window of a house owned by a quick-witted Asian family who had demanded five hundred pounds cash-in-hand for the disruption. Had they known it they could have bargained for considerably more. The video images were dark and grainy, lit only by the street lamps and lacking the sunlit clarity of the footage from the Iranian Embassy siege, but it was an exclusive on a night when competing newsrooms would slit veins for half as much. Sky had it all. The dark shapes of police in Kevlar-coated body armour scurrying along the road, crouching for every inch of cover. The Land Rover reversing into position. The brief tug of war and its explosive aftermath. The sudden invasion of the house and, only minutes later, the faint image of two bodies being dragged through the remains of the front door and spreadeagled on the pavement outside. Even in the poor light it was possible to see that one was a woman. It was only when the man started struggling that anyone was able to tell that the two were still alive. A boot on the back of the neck rapidly put an end to the protest.

There are many ways for a man to be humiliated. Being caught in the wrong bed is, perhaps, reasonably common, being suspected as a terrorist considerably less so. But being dragged goose-bump naked into the street and left lying face down on the freezing pavement for many minutes is a humiliation afforded to few. Yet then to be raised, arms manacled behind the back, and presented to television audiences around the world, with your career, self-respect and manhood withered in the cold, is all but unique.

For Colonel Abel Gittings, OBE etc, these humiliations had come all rolled up together.

Goodfellowe heard the blast through ears deadened by alcohol. He was drunk and wallowing in it. Not entirely his fault. The diet had lowered his resistance to alcohol, and what little tolerance remained had been finished off by Elizabeth.

It wasn't as if he didn't understand. He wasn't an insensitive, uncomprehending male. She had problems that weighed heavily on her humour and left her distracted, unable to concentrate on the little rituals of courtship. 'It's because I love you that

I don't have to pretend,' she explained. That was good enough for Goodfellowe. If the magic of their moments together had waned, squeezed aside by her money problems, it would only be for a short while. One of those relationship things. Anyway, he'd been distracted, too, with COBRA and all. Power was a great aphrodisiac, but there was the other side of it which could also leave you knackered at the end of the day. No matter, soon it would all be over, they'd be back to normal, and then he would find that memorable moment when he would ask her to marry him and they could put it all behind them, in bed, like they used to. Hell, no rush.

So, late that evening after the final vote, he had dropped in at The Kremlin. He wanted – needed – to say hello. Cheer her up, if he could. Or was it to cheer himself up? Anyway, he arrived.

'Missed you,' he explained.

'Me, too,' she replied, and meant it. She squeezed him briefly but passionately, then sat him down at one of the tables and proceeded to fetch a very special bottle of Crimean champagne, from Massandra, which came with the crisp hint of gooseberries and apple blossom and was the colour of gently baked biscuit. The cork came out with an understated explosion of joy and he relished the moment, playing with the wine, pushing it around his mouth with his tongue before allowing it to trickle slowly down the back of his throat. 'This is superb. Terrific. To what do I owe this pleasure? Guilt?' A clumsy joke which deserved its fate of being ignored.

'Celebration. I think I've found a new financial backer,' she muttered softly.

'That's fantastic. Who?' he responded with enthusiasm.

'He's called Ryman. An old friend.'

'Wonderful!' Then Goodfellowe paused, ransacking his store of recollections. 'Ryman. An old *boy*friend.'

'You've got an excellent memory, Goodfellowe.' She smiled for the first time that evening. It needed more practice, he thought, the first attempt was unconvincing.

'Forgive my stupidity, but why would an old flame of yours want to lend you money?'

'For old times' sake, stupid.' Her lips puckered, she was flirting, the old Elizabeth, teasing him, but the eyes still looked serious, bitter-sweet. 'Don't tell me you're jealous, Tom. It's the first good thing that's happened in ages and I could really do without any menopausal male inadequacy right now.'

Was he jealous? Perhaps. But to him her words seemed an unnecessarily brutal attempt to put an end to that line of conversation.

She had mentioned the name only once before, during a long and deliciously alcoholic evening they had spent at a country hotel owned by a friend of Elizabeth where, in an elaborate game of foreplay, they had left their bedroom strewn with the confidences of their previous entanglements – although, to be fair, most of the confidences had been Elizabeth's. He'd been married so long that his only entanglements in recent years had been with duvets. She'd used her past conquests to goad him, to inflame his

353

male possessiveness to the point where he needed to invade and reclaim every inch of her. If she lived to be as old as Methuselah she was never going to forget the drapes of that particular four-poster. They had loved and laughed, then loved a lot more, and he had forgotten all those names and past indiscretions of hers that had scratched away at him – until now.

'He lives in the South of France,' she hurried on, as though aware that some further explanation was called for but keen to redirect it onto safer, foreign fields. 'Bit of a playboy. Inherited squillions.'

'And keen to help.'

She nodded and held his gaze.

'So what happened between you two? Why didn't it work out?'

'As I said, he's a playboy. I found him in bed with my best friend.'

'Thought you didn't do jealousy.'

'I don't. But I do a fine line in revenge. I put sugar in the fuel tank of his yacht on a night when they were sailing off for one of their little trysts. Left them stranded for hours. They had to be rescued by the coastguard, got lots of local publicity. Unfortunately, she had told her husband she was going to a cookery class.'

'Ouch. And he forgave you after that?'

'The boyfriend? Well, that's all ancient history.'

Until now. Goodfellowe chided himself. He had to be grown up about this. 'Well, if he's willing to help, that would be . . .' – he stretched for the word, almost stumbled – '*helpful*.'

'It would be a loan. I'd have to let him have a share

of the restaurant until I'd repaid it. But he wouldn't interfere.'

'A sort of –' he was about to say 'sleeping partner' until something he was forced to recognize as menopausal male inadequacy gripped him savagely by the throat. 'You've discussed this with him?'

'Of course. We had dinner last week.'

The night of that little white lie, no doubt.

'I'm hoping we can finalize it this weekend. It would be a great weight off my mind, Tom.'

'Mine, too.' Hell, he'd got to stop being such a wimp. This was great news. A new start for Elizabeth, a new start for them both. He squeezed her hand, leaned across the table and kissed her. Perhaps it was the table between them that prevented it from being the long and lingering expression of desire he had intended to show. 'I'm so happy for you. Well done.'

'Thanks, darling. Means me playing hooky next weekend. He can't come to London. I've got to meet him halfway.'

'Where?'

'Paris.'

At which point Goodfellowe had decided to get seriously drunk.

If modern Prime Ministers lead less decadent lives than some of their predecessors, it's perhaps less to do with their virtues than with their diaries, which are crammed. Packed to the point of exhaustion. It leaves them little time to relax, still less time to think. Scarcely time to fit in a good game of cricket or a prayer meeting, let alone a torrid affair.

There is no privacy in Downing Street, even in the upstairs apartment, where the door swings open through day and night as messengers come to demand the attention of the nation's overworked leader. Whatever it might have done for Lloyd George, home turf is no longer suitable for Prime Ministerial mischief. Booking into a hotel under the name of Mr and Mrs Smith is also unlikely to bring the privacy required, while popping round to her place for a quiet evening has its own desperate limitations when two cars crammed with bodyguards have to tag along. So modern Prime Ministers behave themselves, not so much because they are beyond temptation but rather because temptation is beyond their reach. Pity the same can't be said of their Cabinet colleagues.

The nation's leaders are prisoners of their diaries, and all too frequently in their memories the dates become scrambled and details blurred, yet there are some moments they remember with the clarity of finest Irish crystal. Moments such as escaping assassination. Declaring war. That first visit to kiss hands at Buckingham Palace. Viewing the videotapes of what the bishop got up to in the lift of the US Embassy during the Independence Day celebrations.

Jonathan Bendall had woken after only three hours' sleep with the feeling that this would be one of those days he would remember without any need to refer back to his diary. He'd grown used to lack of sleep, to anxiety, to being disturbed by the thought that events were stretching beyond his control. But today things would be different. The breakthrough had come. It was just as he had said, they were bombers and there was blood on their hands. By a stroke of good fortune it was their own blood. Well, that's what came of playing with fire – and messing with him.

He strode into COBRA with a sense of expectation. This was the beginning of the end for the Beakies. They'd been caught, quite literally, with their trousers down – he was still chuckling at the news pictures. He could see the headlines now. **'Beaky's Gone Bonkers!'** God was good. Truly a moment for the memoirs. He made a mental note to pursue his gentle enquiries about literary agents.

'So, Commissioner, to business,' Bendall began, taking his place at the central seat and opening his folder with an officious snap. He was anxious to get on with the matter, like a top spinning at full speed. 'Let's start with our little lovebird, shall we? What have you got for me?'

The capital's chief policeman swallowed. 'Very little I'm afraid.'

The top hummed aggressively. The atmosphere in the room seemed to grow several degrees cooler.

'We're still pursuing enquiries, Prime Minister, but to all intents he is no longer a suspect.'

'But this man's a soldier –'

'Correct. A Colonel Abel Gittings.'

'A bomber!'

'A Signals officer.' He began reading highlights from the file. 'On the directing staff at Camberley – commanded an electronic warfare unit in Germany

– then Military Secretariat – now Deputy Director Defence Strategic Plans based here in Whitehall. Man's got a track record as long as your arm.'

'So'd Philby.'

'Caught *in flagrante*, for sure, but that seems to have been the sole purpose of this little exercise. To set him up. We pulled his car apart, as we did the house of his girlfriend and his London apartment. Now we're doing the same to his family home, although his wife is taking it all rather badly. But so far we've found exactly nothing. Not a sniff of explosives or bomb-making equipment – apart, that is, from the traces of plastic explosive smeared on the *outside* of the car to leave a signature for the dogs. But inside – nothing. He's clean. Almost certainly he has no connection with Beaky.'

'Nothing to do with the cutbacks? That's at the root of all this, isn't it?'

'No more than many. Gittings isn't an axeman, he's merely a very capable survivor. At least, has been, up till now.'

The top wobbled slightly before spinning on.

'So what about the other one? The dead man at Battersea? What about it, Defence?'

The Secretary of State for Defence scanned his briefing note. 'Albert Andrew Scully. Parachute Regiment. Age 42. Regimental Sergeant Major. Falklands veteran. Decorated for bravery, including a Military Medal and a Queen's Gallantry Medal. Impeccable record – until two years ago. He was injured in Germany, disabled out. So he wasn't part of the general cull, strictly speaking.'

'And since then?'

'Nothing. No trace of him anywhere. We're still checking, but nothing so far from the DHSS or the police. He's got no bank account, hasn't even taken out a library book –'

'His disability pension?'

'Goes straight to his wife, and he's had no contact with her either. For two years RSM Scully seems to have disappeared off the face of the earth, until last night. Quite the invisible man . . .' He trailed off. This wasn't what Bendall wanted to hear, not at all.

Another turn of the top. 'Jumpers? Come on, Jumpers. What about the bloody media?'

'They're desperate for news on the dead man but so far we've been able to give them . . . well, practically nothing.' He glanced at Defence, almost sulkily. 'Doesn't help that he's a war hero, not at all.' Jumpers had sleepless eyes and was suffering from the symptoms of incipient flu. The strain was getting to him. His words were imprecise, his enunciation often trailing away as it stumbled between the East End and Night Nurse. 'I've got the Ministry of Defence working on whether we can establish a track record for him as a drunk or wife beater, that sort of thing, but we're still struggling to work out a line to take on the main issue.'

'Which is?'

'Uhh, why we shot a man who appears . . .' – Jumpers sniffed, battling with catarrh. Or was it conscience? – 'well, to put no finer point on it, why we killed a man who wasn't even armed.'

'Because he was a bloody bomber!'

'Precisely, but –'

'But what? Why is there always a but? He blows up half of London and there's a but?'

'You see, the *Mirror*'s wondering why only three of the chimneys went down. It's trying to stand up a theory that he died trying to *stop* the bombs going off. That we shot the wrong man. And several of the newspapers are focusing on the fact that there was remarkably little damage, although I'm encouraging the *Express* to do a feature on the dogs' home. Apparently many of the dogs became hysterical and three have had to be put down. Could provide some helpful colour.'

'Save me.' Bendall buried his head, the enthusiasm drained from his day. He found himself envying the dogs. 'Pass the anaesthetic.'

'Beg pardon, Prime Minister?'

'A joke, Jumpers, a joke. But you're right, it's a bloody awful moment for humour. Is there more?'

'That's it, really. The chimneys fell inside the empty walls of the power station. Just a pile of rubble waiting to be carted off. Apart from the one remaining chimney.' Another sniff. 'I'm afraid that's going to be a cartoonists' paradise. '

'Was the fourth chimney damaged?'

'Apparently not.'

'I want it down anyway. We can't have the bloody thing mocking us from halfway across London.'

'Ahem, I hate to be the one bearing bad tidings, Prime Minister –'

'The *one*?' Bendall whirled once more in the direction of the interruption. It was the Cabinet Secretary.

The Cabinet Secretary remained undaunted, a resolution borne of having hacked her way through the mandarin grove to become the first female Cabinet Secretary in history. She wore a face that was lined but defiant, the marks of a woman who had devoted the best years of her life to men, all of whom had been left in no doubt that she believed she could have done their job far better. Many of them had agreed. So when she talked, they listened. 'There may be no easy means of demolishing the remaining chimney.'

'Why the hell not? The other three put up remarkably little resistance.'

'It's listed. Grade Two. Which means that by law the owners have a duty to rebuild, unless given dispensation to demolish by the Secretary of State for the Environment, Transport and the Regions – which, in light of the enormous expense involved in rebuilding, they will undoubtedly seek. But that would inevitably be bitterly opposed by English Heritage and the conservation lobby who've spent the last twenty years battling to keep the thing standing. Meanwhile, no matter what course of action is proposed, it's my judgement that we can rely on the local residents of Battersea to be split absolutely and militantly down the middle between those who want it up and those who want it down. I can foresee a fresh set of planning enquiries taking years.'

'Your foresight never fails to inspire me, Dame Patricia.'

Bendall was growing giddy. Tops, once they begin to lose their equilibrium, never recover. 'So let me get this straight.' He began counting on his fingers.

'We've got a suspect who's not a suspect. A body who is, apparently, nobody. A national monument that's been turned into the biggest circus site in the city. And nobody's got a clue.' He studied his palms as though trying to read his own future. The top gave a final savage, unbalanced twist, then toppled. 'Well, with apologies to the ladies present, fuck it.'

The blatant obscenity jarred upon the meeting. The complaint of a man in considerable trouble. It made him dangerous, required wary walking. It also had the effect of jarring Goodfellowe to life. He had been sitting quietly, feeling desperately hung over, oppressed and claustrophobic in this day-less room, struggling to keep up with the discussion and struggling even more to sort out his own problems.

Of course he was jealous, he couldn't deny it, he hated the idea of Elizabeth going off to Paris to spend time with another man, but he had also come to realize that he was suffering from something deeper than simply a dose of male insecurity. He was back in that mire of despair where his private life and his political life were heading in separate directions. It was scarcely a new sensation, for his wife, Elinor, had never enjoyed politics. She'd been there at his side, loyally but without any real interest, never truly participating. In truth, holding him back. Not her fault, not anyone's fault, no one to blame, just one of those things. Yet a modern political career is all-consuming, there is no room for the half-hearted, no longer time as there once had been for a politician to read or write great histories in the manner of a Macmillan or a Churchill. The profession of politics is all-consuming; it hadn't consumed Elinor with interest, but it had finally, and tragically, consumed her. As they said, just one of those things.

When, finally, he had crawled out from beneath his guilt and self-loathing, he had found a new start. He had also found Elizabeth. Out of misery had come an opportunity for a second chance, with a woman who was not only interested in his career but almost insistent. She would become one of the great political hostesses, working alongside him, cementing his political alliances as he pushed his way back up the slippery slopes of Westminster, through COBRA, into the Cabinet, then perhaps even into Downing Street. A career that would emerge from the darkness of its recent years.

So why did he feel so bloody miserable? Was it still the malevolent remnants of his guilt? The turning worm of jealousy? The fact that the closer he and Elizabeth got, the more they seemed to be passing each other by like travellers in the night? The fear that on his progress up the slippery slope he would have to sit and sup with men like Bendall, and that he might lose the thing that mattered to him beyond all, his daughter Sam? His wretchedness had to be more than simply his monumental hangover.

His brain felt horridly mechanical and rusted, yet as he sat in this airless room, something moved under the impact of Bendall's obscenity. With a pitiful jolt, some part of his brain collided with another, forcing upon him the enormity of what had happened. They had shot an unarmed man for doing nothing more than ridding the London landscape of a monstrous carbuncle. It was practically a public service, not an excuse for executive execution. A man had died, and by sitting in this room he, Goodfellowe, was partially responsible.

He stirred in his seat, sufficient for Bendall to notice. 'God, you look awful, Tom.'

'Thank you, Prime Minister. But not half as bad as Scully, I'll be bound. Why did we have to kill him?'

'He was trying to kill me, for God's sake.'

'Kill you? With a bit of old iron scaffolding?' Goodfellowe's thoughts were beginning slowly to coalesce. 'Not unless he was trying to break his way into Downing Street and club you to death.'

'Not literally, man. You know what I mean.'

'I just think it's a pity he's dead.'

The room seemed to have grown suddenly stifling for many of those present. The Defence Secretary wriggled uncomfortably and ran his finger around his collar. Dame Patricia began making notes in her precise, minuscule handwriting, as though drafting a bill of indictment.

'I think these things need saying,' Goodfellowe added softly. 'And if they can't be said here, where can they be said?'

There was a moment of silence that was strained with both awe and fear, like children watching parents having sex through an open door. Then Bendall spoke again, his tone full of formality. 'Did you have a *point* to make, Tom?'

'Yes.' Slowly his thoughts were beginning to coalesce, emerging like a chrysalis from its cocoon. 'I think Colonel Gittings must be connected with the case.'

'But he's clean –'

'There's a connection of motive, you see. They're making fools of us' – well, of Jonathan Bendall, at least; they all knew he meant Jonathan Bendall – 'and they've made a fool of the colonel.'

'But why? He's not responsible for cuts in the military.'

'Agreed. Which makes the attack on him seem almost like a bit of – dare I use the word? – private enterprise. A bit on the side. Can anyone say whether the explosives used at Battersea were the same as were smeared on his car?'

Jevons responded. 'Forensics aren't complete yet, but – certainly it's possible. All the early indications are that both were standard Army-issue PE4.'

'So let me get this straight. You're suggesting that after they blow up the power station in Battersea they hightail it over to Clapham and have a go at the copulating colonel?' Bendall sounded incredulous.

'It's a possibility. Worth considering.'

'It's demented! Who the hell would be vicious enough to take time out to arrange for a man to dangle by his balls like that on primetime television?'

Silence. Goodfellowe didn't know, and no one else had yet caught up with him. Bendall was right, it did seem vaguely ridiculous. Then the image of gunge poured into fuel tanks of a luxury yacht came into Goodfellowe's mind, and a flicker of sadness crossed his eyes. 'A woman.'

The suggestion swept them into a confusion that left even Dame Patricia stranded.

'Oh, I see. We're going to run this investigation

on the basis of masculine instinct, are we?' Bendall sneered.

Goodfellowe stared back and knew he despised the man.

'Why else would the phone call about the colonel's car be disguised through a voice simulator?' Goodfellowe responded. 'Beaky's never bothered with that before. So the voice had to be totally distinctive. I'd bet a Ministerial salary that it's a woman.'

The Prime Minister and backbencher held each other's eyes in a hypnotic contest of wills. They both knew that that was precisely what Goodfellowe was doing, gambling with his Ministerial salary.

'So,' Bendall broke the spell, 'Beaky is really Boadicea. From the regiment of Amazons.'

'Try Signals.'

Bendall shook his head slowly, disbelieving, disliking. 'How the hell d'you figure that one out?'

'Look at what they've done. Water. Traffic lights. Fairly low grade stuff. But then telephones. Now bombs. That's technical. Which means we're probably looking for expertise in communications and explosives. Signals and Engineers. So let me ask – how many female explosives experts are there who could make a real mess of Battersea power station?'

The Defence Secretary searched for someone else who might help him, but he was on his own. 'Perhaps about twenty,' he guessed.

'OK, twenty. And how many women officers have left the Signals regiment over the last few years? Probably ten times that number. And if Gittings has managed to make an enemy of any woman, there's got to be a damned good chance she's in the same regiment. Which means Signals.'

'You sure?'

'No. But one of the two's a woman,' he insisted.

'The *two*?'

'The CCTV has only ever shown four. Four of them stuffing up the water system. Four of them knocking over the traffic lights.'

'And at Battersea?'

'After Payne they were down to three. The watchman couldn't see for sure in the dark, but three chimneys, three chimney sweeps. Stands to reason. Now they're down to two.' Goodfellowe winced – God his head hurt.

'Two. And one a woman . . .'

'And if we can avoid shooting her in the back, all the better,' Goodfellowe added. He didn't know why he said it but, like the emerging chrysalis, he found himself driven on. It sounded like an accusation, and everyone knew it.

The Prime Minister and the Backbencher. There could be no doubt about it now, theirs wasn't so much a relationship as a collision, an encounter of fire that one day would burn their relationship to ashes. Maybe that day had already arrived. Every single member sitting around the briefing table was looking at Bendall, waiting for the sign. The Prime Minister clearly should no longer tolerate this insolent man, not if he were to retain his dignity and authority, yet he still needed him. How would Bendall act, from strength or from need? A turning point in the story of both men.

Bendall cleared his throat. 'Check it out,' he instructed. 'Engineers and Signals.' The creases across his face began to lighten. From a cast list numbering in the tens of thousands, they were now looking for a mere handful. If Goodfellowe was right, the odds had shifted dramatically in his favour. 'We need to look for someone with a grievance, or someone who's been acting strangely,' he concluded, attempting to appear as if he had taken charge of the proceedings once more.

The members of COBRA sat with their heads lowered, scribbling as though dutifully taking note of his instructions. None of them wanted to raise their eyes and acknowledge that their Emperor no longer had his clothes.

It was as they were dispersing from COBRA that the Prime Minister took Goodfellowe to one side. The top had finished spinning, now things must lie as they had fallen.

'Trouble is with you, Tom, I don't always like you very much. The damnable thing is, at the moment I can't do without you.'

Goodfellowe considered, then nodded. 'Prime Minister, I think I know exactly how you feel.'

It is the middle of the day, the sun has at last come to London after days of dishwater skies, yet Mary is lying in bed in the small faceless hotel in Bayswater that is all she has left to call home. She is crying softly, shedding tears into her pillow for Scully whom she now knows is dead.

As her tears fall, Mary has no idea how much danger she is in. She is unaware that she is on the list of 286 former women officers of the Signals and REME regiments for whom the security services have been searching frantically during the last twenty-eight hours. She has no inkling that as one by one they have located and eliminated the others, Mary has risen to the very top of their list. She is the one who knew Gittings, who threw a punch at him in the middle of the mess, who had a grievance, who is now acting strangely. Who has left home, but no one knows for where.

Except Barclaycard.

The only advance warning Mary gets is a slight scrabbling at the door before it splinters off its hinges and she is faced by half a dozen armed men in hoods with weapons drawn and pointing at her. She is left defenceless, doesn't even have time to reach for her clothes or even to shout.

She barely has time to realize that it's all over, to wonder whether they are going to shoot her, too. She has only a fleeting moment before they grab her. She uses it to squeeze the hand of Andrew McKenzie, who is lying in the bed beside her.

SEVENTEEN

Mickey heard about it over a cup of tea and an Eccles cake she was sharing with a lobby correspondent in the Press Gallery. He'd got it from a colleague, who had picked it up from one of the assistant press secretaries at Downing Street with whom he was trying to start an affair. Something was up.

A call to the Downing Street press office half an hour later had all but confirmed it. The lobby should expect an imminent summons for an important announcement. A Very Important Announcement. Don't go rushing off for lunch too early, chaps, you won't want to miss this. You'll get the summons as soon as the Prime Minister is free from the meeting of COBRA.

All of which, in Mickey's mind, raised an interesting question. If COBRA was meeting, why wasn't Goodfellowe there?

The answer proved simple enough. He hadn't been invited. Obviously some administrative foul-up. So he hurried across to the Cabinet Office, breaking into a skipping run as he crossed Parliament Street, braving red lights and the wrath of taxi drivers.

His efforts were in vain. The meeting had finished. Even as he sprinted up the stairs inside the Cabinet

Office, the powers in the land were dispersing to their respective corners of the empire with barely the courtesy of a nod in his direction. He'd missed it. Goodfellowe stood breathing fire, feeling the sweat beginning to gather around his collar, his hair looking as if it were desperate to escape. Then Bendall emerged, with Jumpers at his elbow and surrounded by the usual dithering of altar boys.

The Prime Minister spotted the backbencher, frowned as though in reprimand, then extended an arm. 'Tom! Walk with me.'

They traced the private way to the back door of Downing Street, through the ancient Tudor corridors of ghosts and faded glories.

'Glad you're here. Want to thank you for your help, Tom, now that it's over.'

'Now what's over, Prime Minister?'

'Of course, you don't know. We found the last of them a couple of hours ago. Wrapped up in bed together, wouldn't you know. Mobile telephones by their side. Signals and Engineers, just as we said.'

Goodfellowe noticed the use of the plural pronoun. History was being rewritten before it had time to go cold, and by the morning it would have been entirely Bendall's own idea.

'It was good to have you on board, Tom –'

Past tense?

'You're a sour-faced bastard at times, in all honesty you can be a real irritation in the rectal area, know what I mean? I suppose it's your ability to be unconventional that's made you useful. Anyway, it's over. Time to get on with the rest of life.'

Bendall halted his progress and turned to face Goodfellowe in the manner he might use to scold a disobedient spaniel. 'I'm not sure what to make of you, Tom. Never quite know whose side you're on. So far as I'm concerned, there's only one side. Mine.'

'That's very black and white –'

'How black and white do you want it, for Pete's sake? These bastards've brought London grinding to a halt, held the Government to ransom, been responsible for the resignations of two Home Secretaries and completely screwed up my teatimes. To say nothing of what they've done to our opinion poll ratings in the run-up to next week's by-election.'

'Ah, I see.'

'We need a victory, Tom. We need it rather more than I care to admit, and we need it very, very publicly. Time for a little good news, which I intend to announce in about ten minutes. One dead, three in maximum security. Hell, we've ripped the guts out of the bastards! Time to celebrate. And time for you to stop pissing on my parade.'

Bendall took up a brisk pace, intent on leaving his problems behind, sweeping Goodfellowe along in his wake as they entered through the back door of Number Ten.

'I'm sorry to have missed COBRA. Some mix-up . . .'

'No mix-up, Tom,' Bendall responded, still forging ahead. 'You weren't invited.'

'Not invited?'

'Understand me. It's over, finished. I'm fed up with all this discussion. We don't need COBRA any more.

If there's any sweeping up to do, it'll be done on a strictly need-to-know basis. And, my friend . . .' – Bendall smiled, enjoying his little power play – 'you don't need to know.' It was time to reestablish who called the shots. Goodfellowe faltered, fell half a step behind as they passed before Cromwell's disapproving eye.

'You're saying . . . I'm out?'

'Out of COBRA. Out of that loop, yes.'

'But I gave you everything. The water shares. The Signals woman. Without me –'

'I'm grateful, naturally. I'm also a man of my word, Tom. Be patient until the next reshuffle. Your Cabinet job is safe.'

'So long as you're safe.'

'And so long as you behave yourself. Learn to be a team player.' Bendall shook his head slowly, as though the spaniel had peed on the carpet yet again. 'In all honesty, I get fed up with the lack of respect you show at times. I'm the bloody Prime Minister. I don't appreciate all this aggravation coming from a man like you.'

'A man like me?'

'A man who's been given a second chance. A man who's been brought back from the graveyard. A man who ought to be down on his bloody knees with gratitude. A man who's got no right to play the high-minded moralist and have a go at me in front of colleagues just because some bastard gets himself killed in the process of blowing up Battersea power station. No right at all, not while he's off screwing some Westminster barmaid while his wife's in her sickbed. You get my drift, Tom? I'm sure you do. By the way, you're going to have to sort out that little nonsense. Get rid of the wife or get rid of the girlfriend. I'll not have any Minister of mine skulking around in the dark like a mushroom waiting for the press to throw thirty kinds of shit over him.'

'It's getting sorted . . .'

'Good. Great. Nice to know we can do business together, Tom.'

They had come to the entrance to the Garden Room, the basement secretarial room of Downing Street where calm, experienced women translated the frenzied outpourings of the men upstairs into neat documents and coherent English before being transmitted to the farther outposts of Government. On the walls outside hung official photographs of past Commonwealth Conferences where Prime Ministers of many countries sat alongside the Queen. Most of the faces were black, and many had been guests of Her Majesty on previous occasions, mostly locked up in colonial gaols on charges of terrorism or some other form of treason.

'Funny old business, politics,' Goodfellowe muttered.

'Like being roasted on a spit. As they turn you, half of you is overjoyed that things aren't as bad as they were, while the other half's just about to suffer a serious loss of humour.' Bendall indulged the joke, his tone softening. The deed was done, the point had been made. Time to put away his cosh. 'Tell you what, Tom, how about practising to be Prime Minister for five minutes?'

'Does it involve either actual bodily harm or goats?'

'I'm running late and I've got to prepare for the "rejoice-rejoice" bit at the press conference in half an hour. Trouble is, I've got some ambassador waiting to see me. Apparently he wants to convey a personal and very private message from his president. Usually means the president wants a favour; either he's trying to get his mentally retarded son into Cambridge or his sister off shoplifting charges, some such nonsense. If only I were the brutal dictator they seem to think I am, eh? Anyway, I need another ten minutes before the press conference – change of suit, different tie, you know. So can you stand in for me until I'm ready? Entertain him. You've been a Foreign Office Minister so you're used to soothing Johnny Foreigner. Push the boat out – I'll arrange tea in the White Drawing Room, biscuits too. Give him the usual bullshit.'

'Sorry, I've not been Prime Minister before. What is the usual bullshit?'

'The porcelain pieces on the mantelshelf are Meissen, there's a Constable landscape on the wall – not one of his best, on loan from the Tate – but a far better oil of St Paul's by William Marlow, and porcelain miniatures of previous Prime Ministers. Wellington was the one who thought the steam train would never catch on because they'd scare the horses, Gladstone was the one with the whores, Peel was the one who split his party, Disraeli was –'

'Yes, I think I can manage the usual bullshit.'

'So you'll do it.'

'Famous for five minutes. How can I resist?'

'Grand.'

'What's his name?'

'Who?'

'The ambassador.'

'Hell, I don't know. Basil or Boris or some such. Should have it on a card somewhere.' He began scrabbling through the pockets of his jacket.

'Where's he from then?'

'Oh, damn, where is it? That place in the Eisenstein film? You know – the pram and all those steps?'

'Odessa. In the Ukraine.'

'That's it. Odessa.'

Bendall met the Ukrainian ambassador in the gloomy anteroom outside the Cabinet Room and succeeded in apologizing, explaining, and introducing Good-fellowe, all inside sixty seconds. He laid it on with a shovel, not only about his delight at seeing Ambassa-dor Tintulov (he'd at last found the card) but also the historic importance of the press conference he was about to give, as well as the quality of his temporary replacement.

'Tom here is one of the most important men in my Government, Ambassador. Rumour has it that I'm just about to promote him to the Cabinet. One of our best, otherwise I wouldn't entrust you to him. Please make yourself at home. But I must beg a favour – make sure that Tom doesn't make himself too much at home inside Downing Street while my back is turned, eh?'

And he had laughed, smacked Goodfellowe heartily

between the shoulder blades and departed on the run.

Goodfellowe had led the ambassador up the great stairs, past the rogues' gallery of former prime ministers, to the White Drawing Room with its oil paintings and porcelain and too-soft sofas and had waited until the bullshit had all but run out. He had a vague idea that Sir Henry Campbell-Bannerman had used this room as his bedroom when he was Prime Minister and had died here of a broken heart. Goodfellowe was on the point of embroidering some account of how the room was still supposed to echo with the sobbing of his ghost when, from the clamour that arose from below, it became apparent that Bendall had begun his press conference on the steps of Number Ten.

'My apologies for the delay, Ambassador.'

'It is nothing. It is history, so Mr Bendall has said. So why do we not watch?'

Goodfellowe relaxed. A very understanding man, was Boris Tintulov. So they retraced their steps down the grand staircase and came into the hallway of Number Ten with its cold Georgian tiles and empty fire grate, where they took up their position at the window to the side of the gloss-black door. The window was thickly glazed and covered in a heavy net security curtain that muffled the sound, but the picture before them was stark, almost surreal. Bendall stood in the middle of a pool of brilliant light, his back to them, shoulders braced and facing a wall of agitated humanity. Journalists were reaching for him, stretching as near as they could get, everyone anxious to question him first. They seemed to be pointing fingers of accusation, their microphones trained on him like the barrels of guns, while at the very rear stood the unblinking eyes of the cameras with lenses like howitzers.

'In my country this would seem like a firing squad,' the ambassador mused.

'In this country we execute our leaders rather more cruelly. And far more frequently.'

The muffled phrases crept through the windows. '. . . these savage attacks upon the liberty of all Londoners . . . always made it clear that we would never give in . . . a day of sadness that such actions were necessary, but a day of celebration now it is over . . . never shrink from the difficult decisions . . . a Government strong in purpose and principle . . . a country safe in our hands.'

It was as he had reached his peroration about the country being safe in his hands that Goodfellowe began pressing his ear to the window in order not to miss a single inflexion.

'With the passing of this threat, the great city of London has made a fresh start. It is my view that this fresh start should be matched by the Government. I have always said that the greatest threat to any Government is complacency, and no Government of mine will be complacent. So it is my intention to reshuffle the Cabinet, to bring in new ideas, new energy, new impetus. New passion in the service of the people.'

Cries of 'When? When?' erupted from the firing squad. Goodfellowe had his ear pressed so close to the window that he thought he might burst through it, in spite of the fact that it was reinforced and over an inch thick.

'I intend to reshuffle the Cabinet a week today. This time next Thursday. I look forward to seeing you all then . . .'

'Oh, but you can be a brilliant bastard when you put your mind to it, Brother Bendall,' Goodfellowe sighed, reluctant in his acknowledgement of the other man's fieldcraft. With one sweep of his arm Bendall had ensured that he would dominate the headlines not only today but for the rest of the week. He would drip-feed the media with a judicious mixture of leaks and speculation; they in turn would fight over it like dogs on a diet, grateful for every crumb. Bendall would be seen to be in charge of events, offering a sense of fresh direction. It might even win him the by-election that was to be held on the same day, and if not – well, the reshuffle would bury any bad news beyond resurrection. He had saved London, now he had begun the process of saving himself.

The great black door swung open. For a brief moment, Bendall stood in the entrance, silhouetted by the light of a thousand exploding flashguns, hands raised aloft, every inch the Old Testament prophet come to redeem his people and lead them from adversity. Only the pillar of fire was missing. Next time, maybe.

The door closed.

'Ambassador, I must apologize. But I hope you understand –'

'Of course, Prime Minister. Mr Goodfellowe has been a most gracious host.'

'Ah, Tom. Glad you could hear that.' Bendall bent closer, almost conspiratorial. 'You see, I am a man of my word.'

'Why, Prime Minister, did you think I had doubts?'

As soon as he'd opened his mouth Goodfellowe wanted to kick himself. His tone was unnecessarily contentious and now, surely, was not the time to wind up the Keeper of the Keys to Heavenly Office. He recalled the advice given to him by an old mentor about the secret of ministerial serenity. What was it? Mouth shut, mind closed and sleep in your own bed. At the moment he couldn't even manage one of the three.

Goodfellowe's reflections were interrupted by the noise of an anxious pounding of feet that were coming ever closer, drumming their way along the corridor that led from the rear of the house. A private secretary, no longer young and with his bald head shining like a radar cone, was scurrying towards them with one hand on his stomach and the other clamped firmly to his mouth. As he drew near he released both and emitted a low moaning sound that seemed to consist solely of the words 'Oh, dear. Oh, dear.'

'Evelyn, what is all this? Are you sick?' Bendall enquired impatiently.

'It's – it's Beaky, Prime Minister. He's been on the phone again. Says that if you're going to have a reshuffle . . .' He trailed off, gasping for breath.

'Beaky? Screw his mother. Damn. *If I'm going to have a reshuffle – what?* Pull yourself together, man.'

The rebuke seemed to give Evelyn unexpected resources. He stopped hyperventilating and became once more magisterially Mandarin. 'If you're going to have a reshuffle, he says to be sure that the first resignation you announce is your own. By three o'clock next Thursday afternoon. Or else.'

'Else *what*?'

'Or else he's going to take out the entire City of London.'

EIGHTEEN

Just the two of them. In the Cabinet Room. Door slammed shut.

'Four! Four! You said there were only four!'

Goodfellowe begins to protest that it was a reasonable assumption, but Bendall can hear nothing except the explosion of fear that has ignited inside him.

'I just killed myself out there. All that rejoice-rejoice crap. I stripped naked and exposed myself in front of the entire bloody world. Because *you* said it was over.'

'I scarcely –'

'Why did I listen to you? Why? Why?'

'Did no one bother to check Beaky's voiceprint against the guys we arrested?'

The effort is futile. Bendall is beyond listening, beyond the reach of either logic or excuse. Spittle flecks his lips and a wild, watery look has invaded his eyes. 'You, you, you . . .' He tries to unburden himself, to rid himself of the tempest that is raging inside him, but finds himself unable to complete the thought, indeed there is no longer any thought process, he is running on raw emotion. He sputters, snatches at words, at expressions, but finds none of them adequate. The wild look is still in his eyes, a mixture of confusion and, Goodfellowe suspects, a little hate. The knuckles are clenched tight, turning the flesh to bleached linen.

They stand like that for a full minute as though tied to each other. Goodfellowe dares not move or speak; his whole life seems to depend upon the struggle going on inside the other man.

Finally Bendall appears to compose himself. He stops shaking, flexes his fingers to regain the feeling, begins restructuring his disarranged hair with almost feminine care and seems suddenly to be calm. He walks to the door. As he leaves he turns and speaks once more to Goodfellowe with a voice that barely carries.

'Judas.'

Death is a ruffian on the stairs, waiting to pounce and to strike in his own time. He has become the dominant figure of our age, inspiring in equal measure vast outpourings of piety and of profit, although nowadays perhaps profit has gained the upper hand. For the young, Death can be a jovial fellow, the source of endless humour and commentaries, for the young are immortal. They are also blind. It is only as you grow older that the eyes begin to open and you can recognize Death for what he is, the ruffian, lurking, lying in wait, wanting to trip you as you climb the stairs.

Amadeus had never feared his own death. One day Death would come for him, and he had seen enough pain and mutilation to know that at times

Death is welcomed almost as a friend. But Amadeus couldn't come to terms with the death of Scully. Albert Andrew. Follower. Saviour. His brother. In the endless hours since he had killed Scully – for that is how he saw it: he had been responsible for the death of his friend – Amadeus hadn't moved from his concrete prison of a home, the London tower block he so hated. Thank God his wife was away, visiting some relative or lover, he no longer cared which. Perhaps it might have been better had she been there, someone on whom he could focus his anger and desolation, but she wasn't. He was on his own, and never more so than now.

It had started almost as a game, something inspired by the monumental frustration of their lives. They had been swept up in its excitement and pursued the game with a passion – all, that is, except that worthless looter Payne. He had been a mistake. A misjudgement. One of Amadeus's many misjudgements.

Now Mary and McKenzie had gone. He didn't as yet know how, only that they were gone, together, the phone link cut. More mistakes.

Yet this was as nothing compared to the mistake he had made in killing Scully. As readily as Amadeus could live alongside Death, he was finding it impossible to deal with Guilt. Of course, it wasn't his fault alone, Bendall was far more to blame than he, but nonetheless Guilt tormented and tortured him for being the only survivor.

Yet even on his own he was still a soldier. With a job to do.

So when he had seen Bendall on live television, bragging, claiming victory, he knew he owed it to Scully. He had to go on. It was the only way to ensure that Scully's death was not in vain. The only way to deal with Guilt.

But what could one man do? On his own? One man against Authority? Against all the forces under the command of Bendall? One man against the entire orchestrated might of the State?

Why, with the little toys he had picked up in Bosnia, a man could do almost anything he bloody well pleased.

The City of London is unique. It is a small historic enclave also known as the Square Mile that sits at the centre of London town. Arguably it is the most important financial centre in the world. It has more Japanese banks than anywhere outside the Far East, more American banks than even New York. It trades more foreign exchange, sells more gold, deals in more foreign equities, handles more international insurance than any other place on the globe. One pound in every five earned by the entire population of Britain is earned within this fragment of London. The Square Mile is stuffed full of money and power. And, of course, people.

It is also a place of history, a settlement founded almost two thousand years ago by the Romans beside the banks of a meandering tide-washed river they called Tamesis. The Romans defended their town of Londinium behind stout walls of cobble and stone that can still be seen today, and within these remnants of ancient walls you can find not only traces of pagan temples but also the more modern places of worship such as the Stock Exchange and Bank of England, alongside St Paul's Cathedral and sites of less divine judgement like the Old Bailey. Temptation, forgiveness and judgement all rolled up in one.

The tiny enclave of the City of London is the single most important plot of real estate anywhere in the land, a prize beyond all others. That's why it has been a target of invasion, of fire, of plague, of pestilence, of bombardment and blitz. It has always survived. Until now.

'So, do you really have to go?'

There, he's said it. Goodfellowe can scarcely believe himself, but he's gone and said it, and in doing so has betrayed all his lack of confidence in himself, and perhaps his lack of trust in her, too.

He had insisted on seeing Elizabeth. She'd said she was tired and would rather he left it until another time, but he was not to be put off. Got straight on his bicycle and set out for Elizabeth's mews house in Kensington. He felt a desperate need to unburden himself – he had witnessed the most astonishing sight, the spectacle of a Prime Minister setting himself ablaze before an audience of millions, flames that would undoubtedly lay waste to much of the known world. The prospects of many of those around would be turned to cinders, and Goodfellowe had already been set up as the first victim. He had to see Elizabeth.

Yet there's more to it than that. It isn't just Bendall pushing him away, it's Elizabeth, too. She has problems in which he has a right to share, but sharing is the part of love she finds so difficult, and it's beginning to show in other areas. He's suddenly realized it has been more than a fortnight since they last slept together. Somehow they seem to be falling out of the habit. No one to blame, he's been distracted, too, but enough is enough. Or not enough, in this instance. He's feeling bruised, more than a little neglected, and at the same time experiencing an extraordinary sense of intoxication from the turmoil of power he has just witnessed all around him. To put no finer point on it, he feels turned on.

So he has insisted.

When she comes to bed she is naked, her beauty reaching out to him and reminding him of all their shared pleasures, but her hands remain clasped under her cheek like a pillow. She has already explained she is tired. Their bodies cling to separate sides of the bed. Somehow their minds pass each other by, too.

'It's been quite a day.'

'Sure has,' she replies. 'Barely twenty in tonight. This chaos in London is killing me.'

'Bendall thought he'd got it covered this morning . . .'

'Not my empty tables, he hasn't.'

'. . . and by this evening he's up to his neck in alligators.'

'The bank's given me a month.'

'We'll know within a week.'

387

It is as though they have heard nothing, and have lost the desire to continue. They fall into a long silence.

'I might be able to help,' he says at last.

'Seventy thousand would help.'

'That's right. From Mr Ryman.'

She sighs, turns her back to him. Oh, but what a back. How many nights he has lingered awake, gazing at it while she slept, tracing its sensuous curves with his thoughts, kissing it gently, feeling her stir inside her dreams. Is it foolish to be so in lust with the woman he loves? And so in love with a woman lusted after by others?

'Not the jealousy kick again. Not right now, Tom.'

'Am I so wrong to feel that your weekend with an old lover is marginally less appealing than discovering I've got varicose veins?'

'It's wrong that you shouldn't trust me.'

'It's him I can't trust.'

'He's got hundreds of women.'

'And I've got only you. Which is why I fight so hard to keep you.'

'I know,' she whispers, turning once more to face him, no longer angry. Bloody men. 'That's one of the reasons why I love you.'

It seems so long since she had uttered those words. She has often maintained that men are genetically constructed to lie their way into any woman's bed, and therefore expressions of love should be treated as bearing the same sincerity as someone called Vince who works in tele-sales. 'It's what you do that counts, not what you say.'

Fair enough. To some extent he even agrees. So he says it. 'Do you really have to go?' And in saying it he reveals all the depth and tenderness of his bruising, which she's just about to add to.

'Of course I bloody well have to go! You know that. I've got no choice. The restaurant means more to me than . . .' She hesitates, holds back. Even in anger she isn't fool enough to go that far. Bloody, bloody men! 'Means more to me than almost anything.'

'I'd wanted to take you to Paris. Did you know that? Been trying to find the right time to ask you for weeks.'

She strokes his face, still trying to reestablish contact. 'And we will, Tom. We'll go to Paris and anywhere else you want to go.'

'So maybe I could come to Paris with you next weekend.'

The hand is instantly withdrawn. 'Why – *why* do you men always have to be such control freaks? You simply won't accept that I can do this on my own, will you? Well, I can. What's more, I'm going to show you I can. The restaurant is my baby, it's my independence, it's my life. I'm going to Paris and I'm going alone. That's an end to it.'

She has rolled onto her back, gazing at the ceiling. The air feels suddenly stagnant, and her breath is coming in impatient gulps. 'Look, I'll be back Sunday evening. Why don't we have dinner then? We can celebrate and put all this nonsense behind us.'

'I'd like that, very much.'

They are both gazing at the ceiling now, their fingers gently intertwined in truce.

Then: 'How're you getting there?'

'By Eurostar. From Waterloo.'

'When, my love?'

'Just before three p.m. next Thursday.'

To Goodfellowe, lying awake, staring at the ceiling, it seems that the weekend starts disgracefully early in Paris.

As he mounted his cycle the following morning, Goodfellowe realized he had failed. They still hadn't slept together. He hadn't slept at all.

Friday evening. The 250,000 workers of the City move from office to bar and out to their homes in the suburbs. As they depart, the military move in. By Saturday morning armed troops are patrolling the platforms of all Underground and mainline stations and barriers have been erected around the entire City. The Inner City Traffic Zone that has cordoned off a part of the Square Mile ever since the bloody IRA bombing of Billingsgate is pushed out ever further, in places beyond the City limits themselves. Commercial Street, Old Street, the Clerkenwell Road, High Holborn, Kingsway – all become part of the defensive line that has been thrown down around the trading heart of London. Roads of every description, main and minor, are blocked with barriers and sandbags and timber balks, and, of course, manpower. Most of that manpower is armed.

From six o'clock Saturday morning the only access

allowed to the City of London is by foot or by vehicles that carry a military or police presence. Policemen travel on every bus, and all bags are subject to summary inspection. Even the dustcarts carry an armed guard. Delivery vehicles are confined to the hours between eight at night and six in the morning, and are searched with particular rigour.

Men are sent down into the extensive Victorian sewage system. Its brickwork is examined for any sign of recent interference. CCTV equipment is left behind to continue the vigilance.

London has become a city under siege, cowering behind a ring of steel. A Scimitar tank is placed at the bustling intersection between Poultry, Lombard Street, Cornhill, Threadneedle Street and Queen Victoria Street, the great hub where those avenues meet like the spokes of a giant flywheel that turns non-stop, twenty-four hours a day, driving the City onwards – although the flywheel is now slowing perceptibly. A further tank is positioned alongside the Mansion House, for which purpose they have to close Walbrook, and another covers the Stock Exchange.

The intention is also to place a Scimitar on the plaza in front of St Paul's Cathedral, but the Bishop of London objects in the most vociferous terms. God will provide.

The rest is all courtesy of Jonathan Bendall.

Democracy is based on a number of fallacies, the grandest of which is to believe that public opinion is the sum of all individual wisdom. It assumes that individuals are capable of arriving at informed and balanced opinions, which may be true, but completely ignores the fact that when those same informed and balanced individuals come together in large numbers, logic and reason are often cast aside and any gaps left in the framework of opinion are filled with raw, undisciplined emotion. So it was no surprise that the first reaction of Londoners to the Amadeus ultimatum was guided by cool logic. Law and order doesn't have much of a sense of humour and Beaky had blown it. Fascinating chap and all, given us a few laughs and put the politicians in their place, but this time he's gone too far. Bendall is our Prime Minister, whether we love him or mostly despise him, but the fact that we put him there leaves us with a sense of ownership. Anyway, blowing up a couple of ugly chimneys is one thing, blowing up the City of London is quite another.

Although what precisely Beaky had in mind for the City of London was the subject of extravagant speculation. The terminology he had used in his message – that he would 'take out' the City of London – was open to all sorts of interpretation. Did he intend to blow it up, like the chimneys? Or cripple its communications once again? Disrupt its transportation? Flood it with water? Melt the Lloyd's building? Let loose a plague of genetically modified rats? With Beaky almost anything seemed possible.

Speculation became a national pastime, yet speculation never stands still. What began as a matter of serious concern turned with the passing of hours into

Playdough and was bent into all sorts of unintended shapes.

Downing Street was forced to deny it had intervened to stop the BBC playing the record of 'Captain Beaky and His Band'. The twenty-year-old record was back at the top of the hit parade and could be heard almost everywhere, but it was banned from the BBC following the personal intervention of the Chairman of the Governors. It was unfortunate in the circumstances that the Chairman was a close personal friend of the Prime Minister and their families spent holidays together in Umbria, because it encouraged journalists to jump to all sorts of conclusions. People have such suspicious minds.

There were even moments of popular merriment. Londoners have always had an acute sense of the absurd and there were parts of the operation that they found almost comic. So when a car was spotted heading erratically down Birdcage Walk in the direction of the House of Commons, to the authorities it seemed like a serious potential threat. A pursuit was begun by two police cars, complete with sirens and flashing headlamps, at which point the vehicle's progress became still more erratic, speeding onward into the night. The chase ended only when the car failed to negotiate the new chicane into Parliament Square and came to rest with one wheel over the kerb beneath the brooding statue of Churchill.

Yet this was not a terrorist incident. The culprit turned out to be, in the traditional phrase, 'a senior government backbencher', an ageing dunderhead who in spite of years of piteous whining still hadn't made it to the level of junior ministerial milkmaid. He'd been rushing to make a late-night vote, and as he had tried to explain to the arresting officer, his excuse for fleeing in front of the flashing lights of the constabulary was that he'd thought they were a police escort endeavouring to ensure he got to the crucial vote on time. The truth, as became readily apparent as soon as he fell out of his car, was rather more prosaic. He was pissed.

Ah, but he hadn't survived repeated bruising encounters with his electorate for nought. No sooner had the officer suggested he blow into the white plastic pipe of a breathalyzer than the Honourable Member wrenched himself free and fled towards the nearby gates of New Palace Yard, filling the evening air with piteous cries of 'Sanctuary! Sanctuary!' Had he made it through the gates and inside the precincts of the Palace of Westminster he might have been the cause of a constitutional crisis, for by the time the police had obtained authority to enter the protected premises of the Palace to arrest him he would undoubtedly have been as sober as any judge in the land. But he didn't make it. Distracted by the sight of two members of the SO-19 Specialist Firearms Unit in Kevlar-coated body armour with Glock SLPs drawn and aimed in his direction, he lost his concentration and tripped over the kerb. After which he lost his ambition and resigned his seat.

Somehow the constitution survived.

Yet the incident seemed to mark a turning point in the Government's battle for the public mood. The

Government insisted that it had matters under control, but if it couldn't control its own backbenchers how the hell was it going to deal with Beaky? The public mocked; this was, after all, a comic war against a comic character.

The financial institutions, however, did not mock. Trading houses are not noted for their sense of humour, neither are they renowned for their sense of proportion. Panic often seems a more natural reaction. For two trading days, on Friday and the following Monday, the Stock Exchange held its nerve while furiously transferring as many of its computer operations as was possible to disaster recovery sites outside London. No one wanted to be seen to be the first to turn chicken and lose its head.

By the same token, no one wanted to be left behind. On Tuesday the City's collective nerve cracked and every trading screen, no matter where it was located, was drenched in the colour of blood. By early afternoon trading on the Stock Exchange was halted after billions had been wiped off the Footsie.

That evening the London Assembly passed a vote of no confidence in the Government's conduct. The Downing Street press spokesman retaliated by describing the Assembly as a gathering of rats. It was an unfortunate phrase for someone who at the same time was desperately trying to convince anyone who would listen that the ship wasn't about to sink.

Londoners were both spectators and committed participants in the fight, like the townsfolk of Tombstone peering out from behind their shutters at what was about to take place in the main street, wondering how many coffins they would need, and whose name would be on them.

The town was gripped by a heady mixture of anxiety and anticipation about this Fight to the Death. Trouble was, Londoners couldn't decide which one was the enemy.

In the saloons you could get interesting odds. As the days drew on, those against Bendall lengthened. Beaky couldn't win, of course; Hissing Sid had too many marksmen scattered around the town. It was scarcely a fair fight, more an inevitable massacre, but knowing all that he still intended to come out and fight. Wasn't this the stuff heroes were made of? Dead heroes, of course, but that made it all the more fascinating.

Three p.m. Thursday. Not long to wait.

Overhead the Wimp Blimp droned on. And on, and on.

COBRA met every day. Goodfellowe was not invited.

NINETEEN

The Walrus, aka the Chancellor of the Exchequer, focused his shortsighted eyes on the white tile wall a few inches in front of his nose while he relieved himself. It had been a long meeting of COBRA. No progress, little to report, apart from the news about the command vehicles. These were the vans used by the Metropolitan Police as mobile command and communication centres. The present crisis had placed an exceptional burden upon the Met, stretching the thin blue line until the elastic screamed. All leave had been cancelled and police stations stripped to a skeleton staff in order to provide as much manpower as possible in support of their colleagues in the City of London. In much of the rest of the capital, the sight of officers on the street became such a rarity that someone in authority had decided that six mobile command centres should be parked overnight in strategic locations to reassure local citizens and to give at least the impression of a police presence.

By morning, two had been stolen and another left with no wheels, propped up on bricks.

Without looking at him directly, the Walrus addressed the Lord Chancellor, who was standing alongside him, searching within his flies.

'Got to go on backing Jonathan, of course.'

'No question about it.'

'Can't give in to terrorism.'

'Specially not to a cartoon character.'

'A song, Frankie.'

'What?'

'A character from a song. Not a cartoon.'

'Well, yes.' The Lord Chancellor was distracted, still fumbling within his flies. 'You know, when I was a young man the wretched thing was always popping out at the most awkward moments. Now I never seem to be able to find it.' He sighed in relief. 'Ah, that's better.'

'You're not one of the wobblers, then.'

'Wobblers, George? Do we have wobblers?'

'Apparently, Frankie.'

'That's sad. Terribly sad, George.'

'These are sad days, Frankie.'

'I thought Jonathan made a very strong case about the moral imperative of what he's doing.'

'Yes, a very moral cause. It's sad that the voters don't seem to appreciate it.'

'London will get back to normal in a couple of days.'

'Then we can put it all behind us.'

'Well, those of us still left in Cabinet.'

'Yes, pity about the reshuffle. Unfortunate, that announcement. In retrospect.'

A pause as both of them concentrated.

'You'll be safe, George.'

'You too, of course, Frankie. Unless . . .'

''Less what, George?'

The Chancellor turned to face his law colleague directly. 'Sod's law. Heads he wins, and in a flush of victory thinks he can do what he wants. Or tails he loses, and we get a new broom in Number Ten who decides to do some radical sweeping.'

'Been thinking much the same myself. Not much of a reward for loyalty.'

'Little wonder there are wobblers.'

'As Jonathan would say, fuck it.'

They both proceeded to wash their hands with excessive caution.

'Good talking to you, Frankie.'

On Wednesday the Government announced that the following day was to be a bank holiday. The Stock Exchange and other financial institutions would be closed. It was little more than bowing to the inevitable, no one was going to turn up to work in the City anyway.

They also invoked Section 16c of the Prevention of Terrorism Act which gave them authority to prevent the residents of the City of London returning to their homes that evening until the emergency was over. Only five thousand people lived within the Square Mile, mostly within the Barbican complex. Some of the more elderly residents objected strenuously, arguing that they hadn't been moved by the Blitz, weren't going to move for Beaky and would be carried out in their coffins before they'd be moved by their own bloody Government, but overall there was surprisingly little fuss. Most of the residents had already fled to their places in the country or northern France.

It was also on Wednesday, in the morning, that, much to his astonishment, Goodfellowe was summoned to Downing Street. He was still smarting from the last encounter, he wasn't sure he should go. He only knotted his tie and left after Mickey told him not to be so bloody stupid. What had he got to lose?

He found Bendall in the sun-filled garden in his shirtsleeves. He was sitting on a bench beneath the silver birch, holding a drink in his hand. It was clearly not his first.

'Tom. Where the hell've you been? Why haven't you been coming to COBRA?'

'Because I wasn't invited.'

'You haven't been getting invitations? I'm gonna fire somebody for that. Fire the bastards, d'you hear? Of course you were meant to come.' He drank as he lied. 'Anyway, you're here. Sit down.'

Goodfellowe hadn't even undone the button of his jacket. His body language suggested he expected the other man at any moment to try and pick his pocket.

'You know, Tom, I'm surrounded by incompetence. Those other bastards are useless. Useless! Every morning they promise me solutions yet all they come up with are excuses. And now . . . now all they do is sit there and look like mongrels who've just been caught crapping on the carpet. So I looked around this morning and said – "Where's Tom? He's always got some ideas." You know, you should've been sitting around the table, not hiding out amongst the officials. Then I would've noticed you weren't there sooner. I tell you, Tom, I've given them everything they asked for – more men, more resources. Only thing I can't give them is more time. It's getting late . . .' He rolled the glass between the palms of his hands, trying to focus his thoughts. 'I need your help, Tom. You're not like the rest. You're unpredictable, unreconstructed, unrepentant, un . . .' He began stretching for another suitable description.

'Unreliable? I think that's the word the Whips might use. You used a rather more forthright term the other day.'

'Did I? *Did* I? OK, so you don't do things by the book. In the orthodox way. But that's what makes you so important. You're a stubborn bastard, Tom. I need men with a bit of backbone about me right now.' He took a swig of gin, his eyes red from anxiety and alcohol, but also suggesting an inner animal determination to fight. 'I need you, Tom. I make no bones about it. Need you. You've always come up with something. Because you don't think like the others. You don't crawl, don't read out what others have written for you, you don't borrow their words or steal their thoughts. You're the original caveman. And I need something original.'

'Sounds the sort of invitation a man can scarcely resist.'

'Unless I can stop this man I'm dog meat.'

'Not to mention the City of London . . .'

'Find him for me, Tom. You and your insights . . .

maybe you can do what the rest of them together can't. Damned deadbeats, all of 'em. Police, Army, Intelligence – useless! They've given me extra protection, put machine guns in the bloody shower, can't take a leak without some bastard watching me. Done everything – except give me results! That's what I need. Results!' His lips were damp with emotion. 'They've even given the whole bloody thing a code name. Operation Icarus. Scorched wings 'n' all. But when I wake up in the middle of the night, Tom, sometimes I think they're taking the piss, 'cos at the moment the only miserable swine who's going to get scorched isn't Beaky, it's me.'

'Bit like Minos.'

'Who?'

'The king of Crete. It was Minos who Icarus and his father were trying to escape from.'

'What happened to him?'

'He died. Became a judge in the Underworld, I think. Sort of perpetual backseat driver.'

'Damn me, you're frustrating! Always off on a different planet, places where frankly I can't follow. But that's why I need you, Tom. To do what the others can't. To figure out what this is all about – what *he's* about. I've seen you do it in COBRA. Yes, perhaps I didn't realize it at the time, but you're the one who's always been able to keep up with him. Do it again, Tom.'

'In twenty-four hours?'

Bendall lurched forward, closing the gap between them, his eyes and tone conspiratorial. 'Do it and you can have any job in Government you want. Name it and it's yours. Home Office, Foreign Office, Trade and Industry, next door at Number Eleven, even. Anything. Sounds fair enough, doesn't it?'

He allowed it to sink in for a moment, watching Goodfellowe as intently as a roadside kestrel.

'Sounds almost like a bribe, Prime Minister.'

'Sounds to me like the best offer you've ever had, or are ever going to get. You haven't figured it out yet, have you, Tom? I'm your best friend. The man who's going to make everything happen for you. But lose me and they'll bury you, too. May surprise you, old chap, but you're not everyone's cup of tea. And nobody else owes you.'

Goodfellowe was feeling increasingly uncomfortable. While Bendall was sitting in the shade, his own seat was in the direct sun and he was beginning to stifle. At last he unfastened the button on his jacket.

'A few days ago you said I'd betrayed you, called me Judas. Now you tell me you're going to do anything I want.' He didn't try to hide the contempt in his voice. 'How can I believe a single bloody word?'

'Because I'm dying.'

That, at least, Goodfellowe knew, was the truth.

'You know I'm on my way out, Tom, you can smell it. After this fiasco, win or lose, it's only a matter of time. But I'd like another eighteen months. It'll bring me to five years in office exactly, a nice round figure. Sort of historic. Then I'll resign, but I want to be able to walk away, not get dragged kicking and sobbing like all the rest. You must realize how important that is, Tom, for any man. To leave with dignity. Head held high. Is that too much to ask?'

'You'll retire?'

'Eighteen months. Eighteen months in which you can be doing whatever job you want, planning, preparing. Giving yourself the best shot you're ever going to get of taking over from me. Becoming Prime Minister, Tom. What more can I offer?'

The heat was growing more intense, Goodfellowe loosened his tie. 'I repeat. How can I believe a single bloody word?'

Bendall twisted his lips into a sardonic smile, savouring the unfamiliar taste. He wasn't used to his own colleagues doubting his integrity, not to his face. It was another sign of just how weak he had become. His position was falling to pieces. 'OK, Tom. You want to play the tough guy. Fair enough.' Bendall turned to a folder that lay beside him on the garden bench and with almost feverish haste began scribbling on a sheet of paper. He finished and handed it across.

'There you are, Tom. Your guarantee.'

Goodfellowe read, and barely believed. The note was addressed to him. It said: *'It is my irreversible intention to resign as Prime Minister on my fifth anniversary in office.'* The signature was characteristic Bendall, squeezed and bent at a sharp angle, like a set of iron railings that had been hit by a car.

The note flapped in Goodfellowe's hand.

'That's my word. And both your future and your fortune, Tom. With that you can squeeze me for anything you want over the next eighteen months. My life in your hands. It's worth money, too, a hundred thousand on your memoirs. But only if I survive.'

Goodfellowe paused, struggling to comprehend how powerful he had suddenly become. Bendall was tied to him now, whether the Prime Minister found pleasure in his company or not. The paper began to crinkle as he grasped it tight, afraid it might disappear in the breeze. 'Why are you doing this?'

'Because I'd happily settle for another eighteen months. I won't get eighteen hours if it all goes pear-shaped in the City.'

'I suppose I ought to be flattered that you're making such a fuss of me.'

There was a long silence, then Bendall burst into ferocious laughter. 'Special fuss? Of you? Oh, Tom.' He almost choked as he drank. 'How d'you know I'm not making the same promise to every other bastard in London . . . ?'

Goodfellowe is sitting alone in his office, brooding. He's been offered everything, on one condition – that he save Bendall. Yet he can't. He's spent the best part of the afternoon running through every possibility in his mind, and getting nowhere. Bells keep going off inside his head, confusing him. Now he's exhausted. His whole life seems to be stretching out in front of him, yet as hard as he tries to peer ahead he can see no further than a few hours. Tomorrow, three o'clock.

Then there's another ringing sound. His telephone. Elizabeth.

It surprises him. She rarely calls, even after all their time together, and only ever for practical things.

Never to chat. To say hello, how are you, I'm thinking of you. When they are together she's usually a fount of bubbling animation, but it seems you have to be there in front of her to grab her attention. Otherwise it's an out-of-sight, out-of-mind sort of thing. And tomorrow out of the country.

But now she wants to see him – it's her turn to insist. Dinner. Tonight. Before she leaves for Paris. She knows he is hurting. She wants to make it right, to get rid of this jealousy thing once and for all.

'I don't do jealousy,' she has often said. 'It's a sign of distrust. A lack of self-respect.'

Anyway, why should she do jealousy? He's doing enough for the both of them.

He arrives at Elizabeth's mews house in a state of distraction. Half his mind is trying to struggle with the jealousy thing, the other half struggling with the things Bendall has piled upon him. Yet the moment he walks through the door his cares seem somehow irrelevant, for there is candlelight, and home cooking, and Elizabeth who, in her forthright style, insists on taking it all head-on.

'I wouldn't go if it weren't necessary. If there were any other way. But I have to go or I'll lose my business.'

'And if you do go . . .'

'Oh, poppet, you're not going to say something silly like "I'll lose you"? That doesn't come into the question, either. Look, bonehead, he's my backer. You are my lover. Backer. Lover. Got it?'

'You think it so wrong that I should be upset by your going off to Paris – Paris of all places – with another man.'

'What I won't have, Tom, is you telling me who I can and cannot see. I love you, but you don't own me. So what if I once had a relationship with Ryman and cared for him. He's a man I once loved. Another time. Not now. Now is you.'

'And tomorrow?' he almost says, but doesn't.

'If I don't do this dinner, I don't do this deal. Then I lose my home, Tom.'

'Yeah,' he mutters. He knows all about losing his home. Hurts like hell.

Elizabeth feels she has made her point, he doesn't need to be beaten any further. She's going off to Paris to see another man, and if Goodfellowe doesn't trust her that's his problem. Well, not exclusively his, perhaps, a little voice inside keeps repeating that maybe she doesn't completely trust herself either, but relationships are meant to have a sprinkling of spice, a little risk, otherwise they suffocate. She's done the thing with the rose-covered cottage and the slippers and the plans for a future together, and it didn't work, left scars. Made her feel owned, used. Never again. She needs to hang on to her own identity, needs some insurance – and, for Elizabeth, that means the restaurant. So she's going to Paris, and if there prove to be a couple of complicating personal details when she gets there – well, she'll just have to sort them out. Over dinner. In her own way. Tomorrow. Whatever it takes.

As for tonight, she'll sort out Goodfellowe, that

silly, confused, hurting man. Sort him out while he's sitting at the dining table. She knows she's been neglecting him, and this weekend she's about to neglect him some more, so he needs reminding just how good their love can be. Perhaps she needs that reminder, too.

The room is lit only by candles, a gentle light, a light that hides their creases. He's reaching for his whisky when he notices her standing provocatively in front of him. Suddenly she has his full attention. She takes hold of her shirt and lifts it high above her head, posing like a model in a little art studio in a garret overlooking Montmartre – no, forget Paris! Her skin is smooth and dark, just a few freckles at the top of her breasts. She'd once said she would have liked larger breasts but for him they are perfect. Great staying power. Still be there or thereabouts in another twenty years. He lifts his glass in appreciation but the whisky never makes it as far as his lips. She begins slowly to remove every other item of her clothing, rustling, swaying, teasing, as though she is seducing him for the first time, until he feels he wants her as though for that first time, too. Now she is naked, enticingly and unrepentantly naked, and he finds himself breathless – ever more so as she turns her attention to him, undressing him, stripping him, her fingers playing knowingly with every knot, every button and zip, until he has no more defences. Her prisoner. With his own trousers she ties his hands behind the chair.

She begins stroking him, tenderly, first with her lips, then the tips of her fingers, her tongue, her nipples, every piece of her. Then she is standing before him once more and parting herself in front of him with her own fingers until he would have screamed if he'd had breath. Perhaps she isn't as good as she might be at expressing her emotions with words, but there are other languages of love. She seems to know them all.

She takes his glass of whisky, raises it to his lips, teases him with its taste, begins to dribble it down his chin. The raw amber liquid flows off the point of his chin down his neck, feels cold, then begins to trickle down his chest, following a hesitant path across the folds and planes of his body until it is nearing his navel and threatening to run beyond, where he knows it will burn with an ice fire that makes him already gasp in apprehension. But her lips and tongue are pursuing the whisky down, down, down, it trickles faster, then slows, but always her lips follow, running down, racking him between fear and anticipation, tearing him between pain and excruciating pleasure, until the last threads of his breath unravel in one emaciated cry that seems close to agony.

When he is able once more to engage his brain and open his eyes, it is dark, for the candles have exhausted themselves, as has he, and he has forgotten all those silly things that have been worrying him.

When Goodfellowe opened his eyes early the following morning, he found himself gazing at the gentle olive ridges of Elizabeth's back. Right now, in this place and at this quiet time of day, he seemed to have everything he wanted. But he knew it wouldn't last – *couldn't* last. Today was Thursday.

For a start he'd have to get home and change. His trousers were hanging over the back of the dining room chair with creases that seemed like the work of a student of Picasso. Love may be beautiful but there was always a price, and at very least a dry-cleaning bill.

Damnation. Now he remembered last night, and what it was about, and still he didn't want her to go.

Her bed seemed to be the place for so many decisive moments in his life – the place where so often he laid bare not simply his body but also the inner man. This was where the course of his life had begun to change, to turn away from the past and poor, mind-stolen Elinor, towards something new. It was the place where he had dug down deep into his very English psyche and admitted to passions he'd been brought up never even to acknowledge, let alone indulge. It was here, between these sheets, that he had come once more to embrace ambition. He was excessively English about that, too, for admitting to ambition left him feeling self-conscious and even a little grubby. Perhaps that was why he remembered the moment so well. Elizabeth naked, bringing him breakfast. With toast crumbs and a wrinkled newspaper. Oh, and the letter from his old school chum Amadeus. Pity they'd never got round to having that drink, and now perhaps they never would, not once he had become a member of the very Government Amadeus despised so much.

Elizabeth rolled over, in the last throes of sleep.

How much he wanted her, and how much he desired her not to go to Paris. 'If there were any other way,' she had said. And, with the clarity that morning brings, maybe there was. Something he had over-looked. Something that, if he got his trousers back on and went for it, might even stop her needing to go to Paris.

He had wanted to steal half an hour in her arms this morning, claiming her, possessing her, before she went off to Paris, but now he didn't have time. He'd have to skip breakfast today.

The time of Cabinet has been brought forward to nine o'clock. There is little formal business, a deck-clearing operation designed to leave as much time as possible to deal with whatever might lie ahead. Bendall is brisk and the rest of those gathered around the table are demure to the point of invisibility.

'Any comments on this last matter?' Bendall enquires, but there are none. He closes his folder with a peremptory snap, and prepares to rise from his chair. 'Fine. Thank you. Any other business?'

It is a throw-away line, he is anxious to get on. Already his hands are on the arms of his chair levering himself upward.

Then the Lord Chancellor coughs, as though a fly has flown into his mouth and he doesn't have the balls to spit or swallow.

'Prime Minister, I have something, if you please.'

Bendall sits back in his chair, awaiting another expression of solidarity. *Good old Frankie, always ready to give support. There's a security briefing in five minutes but I can make time for this. Then get Woolly to leak it to the midday news.*

'As you know, Prime Minister, we are all great personal friends of yours around this table . . .'

Bendall lowers his eyes.

'. . . and we owe our positions here to you personally. There can be no doubting the intense loyalty we all feel to you.'

A muted rustle of approbation from around the room. Yet good old Frankie is finding it difficult to continue. He has thought about these words throughout a sleepless night, has rehearsed them with colleagues, yet still they stumble in his throat. His hands are clasped together in front of him, knuckles cracking, as though at confession.

'We are your friends. We also have a public duty as Ministers of the Crown. Sometimes those roles sit sadly alongside each other . . .'

But not today, not today, dear Frankie. Today we are four square against bloody terrorism. Four square behind bloody me.

'I hope it might be said that you have no greater admirer around this table than myself, Prime Minister . . .'

A demure Prime Ministerial smile of gratitude.

'. . . and I have taken it upon myself over the last twenty-four hours to consult every one of your colleagues whom you see here. We are unanimous.'

Inside, Bendall trembles with relief. One hundred per cent. The whole bloody lot. Perhaps the rumours that one or two of them have begun to get their braces in a twist are wrong, nothing more than press hysteria. Perhaps old Frankie has whipped them into line. Dear old Frankie. He's about as useful as balls on a cardinal but, by heaven, no one can question his loyalty. Which is more than can be said for many of them around this table. Too many. Still, get through the afternoon, then start a little threshing. Chaff from the wheat, and all that.

'We are united in our determination to beat the scourge of terrorism.'

Alleluia!

'But in the process of defeating terrorism, we cannot contemplate the destruction of the City of London and the devastation that would cause to the entire country. No man, no matter how great, is worth such a price.'

What the hell . . . ?

'Which is why all of us, every one, believes that if this threat is not lifted you must resign. By the deadline of three p.m. this afternoon.'

Bendall doesn't hear all the rest, homilies about hearts full of distress and a place of honour in the annals of our times. He is too busy searching for options. Yet as he looks around the table, no one will meet his eye. They are all against him.

He has less than six hours.

And no matter how furiously he searches, he can't find a single bloody option.

Goodfellowe knew none of this because he was cycling around Shepherd's Bush Green and rejoicing.

It was an unlikely location for a celebration, not a part of London he knew well or wanted to get to know any better, but for the moment it was all he had. Moreover, it was no ordinary celebration, for the touch of inspiration that had brought him here from Elizabeth's bed had worked. Worked! And now, surely, there was no need for her to go to Paris. The good guys had won and he was desperate with impatience to tell her so and to claim his reward. Trouble was, Elizabeth wasn't answering her phone. Must be busy packing. It made him all the more impatient, so he decided to proceed directly to The Kremlin.

He called Mickey to let her know he would be late in the office.

'Where are you? Off stroking our beloved leader's ego again?'

'No, I'm in Shepherd's Bush. Woman business.'

'You didn't have to go that far. I could have set you up right here in the House of Commons.'

'*Elizabeth* business, idiot.'

'Oh . . . And the Bendall business?'

He hadn't forgotten about Bendall, but the matter with Elizabeth had pushed other things out of the way. Anyway, what the devil was he supposed to do? He couldn't work miracles. Mickey was telling him of lurid rumours, about how the press conference called for three that afternoon wasn't simply an opportunity for Bendall to issue another ringing cry of defiance. There was to be the spilling of much blood, so it was being said. Resignations. Ah, the start of the reshuffle, Goodfellowe mused, feeling exhilarated.

414

But no, Mickey was insisting, the whispers around the corridors were of Bendall's own resignation.

Bendall? Resigning? If Bendall were to resign it would be the end of all Goodfellowe's hopes. No Cabinet post and, without that, how would he be able to hold on to Elizabeth? Everything of importance in his life had somehow got round to depending on Bendall. The thought made him queasy. No, it couldn't be, Bendall wasn't the resigning type. He dismissed it as idle gossip.

It was as he listened to Mickey turning the rumour mill that Goodfellowe's eyes wandered around the telephone box in which he was standing. It carried that antiseptic odour of very recent cleaning, yet already it was covered once more in the lurid tits-and-bums cards of the good-time girls offering everything from Swedish lessons to something called Ethiopian aerobics. Goodfellowe scratched his nose but it didn't help. He still didn't understand Ethiopian aerobics. Yet even in this place of squalor the forces of righteousness were not to be denied. A little black-and-white card had been inserted amidst the moral debris. *'If you are tired of Sin, read John 3:17,'* it proclaimed stubbornly. Beneath it someone had scribbled: *'If you're not tired of sin, ring Tray-cee after 3.30 on . . .'* Scribblers had been busy elsewhere, too. One lurid card sought new converts: *'Bored out of your knickers? Get rid of your old M&S, get into a little S&M. Ring Sadie for a stimulating new position . . .'* Beside which somebody had scrawled *'Dyslexics need not apply.'*

In the jumble of notions that were stirring inside his head, one suggestion more irrelevant than all the

415

rest snagged upon the card and its grubby message. That of his old school chum. Poor old Amadeus, he wouldn't be able to play. Couldn't spell, so not invited to the party.

'Shut up!' he ordered.

'What . . . ?'

'Be quiet a minute. Let me think. There's something . . .' He collided with the thought yet again.

Amadeus. Couldn't spell. Not invited to party. Seriously pissed off. Couldn't spell. Couldn't spell any more than, it seemed, could Beaky . . .

It was preposterous. Amadeus? But suddenly his schoolfriend had both motive and mucked-up means.

'Mickey, darling, need something in a bit of a hurry. Our friend Amadeus. What's his address?' But Mickey only had a telephone number. She offered to call it. 'No, don't call him, call up the *Telegraph*'s letter page instead, they'll have the address. Find out where the hell he lives, will you? In a hurry.'

Goodfellowe was cycling back down the Bayswater Road in the direction of Marble Arch, getting soaked in foul-smelling fluid from the windscreen washers of some moron's passing car, when his pager stirred. He wobbled dangerously as he attempted to read and ride.

Oh, save us all.

Shakespeare Tower.

In the Barbican.

The heart of the City of London.

Amadeus is inside the ring of steel.

TWENTY

Betrayal. Not so much an absolute concept as an art form, a point of view, and one that is constantly being updated. Life tells us we should expect betrayal, yet somehow it always succeeds in taking us by surprise. We never learn.

Betrayal can't exist on its own, in isolation, for in the end it's nothing more than the twisted reflection of feelings such as passion, and love, and that strange thing called honour. Betrayal is a mirror-image in which everything becomes confused. What for one man may seem little more than an innocent or idle word can be taken by a friend as a grotesque obscenity, and what, for a woman, may be a practical course of action, is to her lover the most unpardonable offence. It all depends upon the mirror.

Yet unlike the reflection of a mirror, betrayal lingers, eats away at us all like anorexia of the soul. And when we have been betrayed by those we loved and once trusted, it seems as if there is nothing left for us in the whole world.

Except revenge.

Amadeus had woken that morning feeling numb. He had shared his fitful dreams with Scully and all those others he had known who had died for honour and love of their country, and who demanded that they not be forgotten.

He hated this place, this city of dark weathered façades they called the Barbican, a universe of concrete poured into the middle of Wren's great city. Barbican. It meant a Roman fortress. An appropriate place for a final defence of honour.

He had remained inside his apartment since Monday evening, not venturing out, not willing to run the risk of being stopped and questioned by those who searched for him. No one knew he was there. He had lit no lights, sounded no sounds, made no music other than on his Walkman, and then only Mozart and his *Requiem*.

'Day of wrath and doom impending, David's word with Sybil's blending, heaven and earth in ashes ending . . .'

Not that there was anyone left in Shakespeare Tower to hear. The city was inhabited by ghosts. The people had fled.

Now he would ensure they did not return.

The Barbican was little more than two miles from Marble Arch. As he pedalled Goodfellowe tried to maintain a steady pace to quench the alarm that was rising inside him, but failed miserably. His suspicions were ludicrous, extravagant, entirely inappropriate, yet with every turn of the wheels he had this appalling fear that nevertheless they might be correct. His collar was beginning to grow damp and discomforting as he passed the department stores and boutiques of Oxford Street. They stood unnaturally quiet, some firmly closed, others cheerfully advertising an End of the World sale. 'Everything must Go! Before We Get Going!!' Almost twenty past two. Push on!

Goodfellowe knew his fears were preposterous, but nevertheless he knew he ought to share them with others. Filled with misgivings, he pulled over at a callbox and dialled Downing Street, knowing he was about to make an utter fool of himself. He was almost relieved when he got an engaged tone. He tried half a dozen times, same result. The world was about to end and the entire system of government was being overwhelmed by concern. Goodfellowe made up his mind to try again in a few precious minutes but, as he clambered back onto his bike, the appalling truth of his circumstances struck him. The last thing he could afford to do was to tell anyone about Amadeus. For Peter Amadeus was his friend. Amadeus was the man he had invited for drinks inside the House of Commons even as London was being torn apart in search of him. Even more disastrous, Amadeus was the man for whom he had gained vital time by telling COBRA they were a gang of four, not five. They were going to say it was all his fault. Even part of the plot.

Suddenly, being wrong and being taken as a fool seemed the least of Goodfellowe's concerns. Being right about Amadeus would be far, far worse, for in that event they would simply drag him away as a conspirator and each of the security services would take turns in tearing him to pieces. He would never be able to escape the suspicion of collusion, his career would be dead.

No, he could tell no one. He'd have to sort it out by himself.

Onward, driven by lurid imagination and more than a little fear. He was beginning to sweat freely as he passed Red Lion Square. He was making good time, there was little other traffic, and none of it heading towards the City. All the lights seemed to be standing at red, demanding that he stop, but he ignored them, pushing on, pushing on. Up ahead he could see the Tube station at Chancery Lane. He found it shuttered, its mouth gaping empty and black, and this was as far as he could go, for the Tube station stood at the City limits. Beyond it he could see a blockade of barriers, guarded by an elderly constable, and behind him a patrol of camouflaged soldiers, standard-issue SA80s at the ready, thirty high-velocity rounds in the mag. Goodfellowe knew a little about the weapon, a fragment of absurd and amusing clutter he'd picked up at a Select Committee hearing. Apparently the SA80 wasn't all that it might be, since the mosquito repellent issued to the British Army had the effect of melting the weapon's plastic sheathing and turning it into something resembling superglue. The knowledge gave him precious little comfort, however, since this wasn't the jungle. It was Chancery Lane, and the weapons were pointing directly at him.

He came to a stop with his front wheel resting against the first line of defences. The constable, his uniform adorned with the gold insignia of the City of

London police force, took one look at the perspiring and crumpled figure in front of him and reached for the obvious conclusion.

'Not today, sunshine.'

'Oh, hell, here we go again.'

'What was that?'

'It's not what it looks like, Constable,' Goodfellowe puffed.

'Why's that, then?'

'I'm a Member of Parliament.'

'Sure. Makes no difference. You could be Claudia Schiffer but you'll not get through here today.'

Goodfellowe reached into his pocket and waved a plastic photographic pass, a pink and grey ID with an encoded metal strip on the reverse that he was forced to carry in order to be allowed into the Cabinet Office and COBRA. He'd always found its colour scheme ridiculous and rather resented having to carry it, until now.

'I'm part of this operation, constable, part of COBRA. You know what COBRA is? And you must let me through.' Part of COBRA, indeed. Well, true up to a few days ago. It seemed a small exaggeration in the circumstances.

The constable took the pass for inspection, then examined Goodfellowe still more carefully before retiring a few paces to seek guidance from his radio. The instrument at his shoulder spat and sighed as he consulted higher authority, while Goodfellowe was left to wonder at the strangeness of this place, normally a maelstrom of traffic and congestion yet now as quiet as any backstreet of Chernobyl. Even the pigeons were scratching around in puzzlement.

As was the constable. He had crossed to two of the soldiers on duty and muttered something while nodding in Goodfellowe's direction. All three then advanced upon Goodfellowe in a manner that was undeniably smothered in menace.

'We've got that sorted, sir. So I tell you what we're going to do. If you're who you say you are, you'll know the password and I'm instructed to let you proceed.'

He leaned closer to Goodfellowe, his breath heated. 'And if you *don't* know the password, it means you're guilty of deception, personation, theft of Government passes and obstruction of the police in the pursuance of their duty. Might also mean that you're part of this nonsense, trying to bluff your way through. Either way these gentlemen here, under the provisions of the Public Order Act that have placed this area under military jurisdiction, are going to drag you away, throw you in the back of their wagon and take you for a long and *very* bumpy ride.'

Even as Goodfellowe watched, the soldiers stiffened and seemed to grow in bulk beneath their uniforms. The muzzles of their short-barrelled rifles kept staring at him.

'Which specific provision of the Public Order Act?' Goodfellowe demanded, bluffing for time.

'Let's not worry ourselves about which provision, shall we, sir? Just the password.'

'The password?'

'That's what I said.'

There was a moment's silence. One of the soldiers,

young and very spotty, had a bright glazed look in his eye that Goodfellowe found disturbing, as though the lightbulb inside his brain was about to burn out. The muzzle of his rifle was pushed several inches closer. Goodfellowe swore; he was genuinely scared. No one had told him the password. The muzzle of the rifle seemed to be staring angrily at him. There were precious few mosquitoes around at this time of year, so no chance of the bloody thing melting.

Which is what did it. Melting. Glue. Suddenly he was back in the garden of Downing Street, listening to the Prime Minister ranting about incompetence and death and scorched wings, like an ancient king trying to defy fate. It was a guess, but it was all he had.

'Operation Icarus?' Goodfellowe mumbled.

'What was that?'

'Icarus. The password's Icarus.'

The word was still hanging in the air when the two soldiers stepped smartly behind him, blocking his retreat. There was nowhere for him to go. The constable approached still closer, his face serious, his breathing laboured as his lips wrestled with the words.

'I wish you'd said that from the start, sir. Saved us all a lot of trouble . . .'

Two thirty-five.

Head down, pain in his lungs. Goodfellowe pushes forward through Smithfield Market, its silent streets strewn with the unswept plastic and polystyrene of the previous day's trading. In normal times this is a place filled with the cries of porters and the aromas of uncooked meat and roasting coffee, but today – nothing. Only more scavenging pigeons, which scatter in a panic of feathers as he clatters round the corner.

And there it is. He looks up, wipes sweat from his eyes, to see glowering dark towers. He is almost there. At the Barbican. A complex of more than two thousand apartments arranged in blocks and towers around remorseless windswept plazas. A Brave New World of angles and of ugly aerials, built from concrete that weeps soot and grime.

And the tallest and most unforgiving of all the structures that make up the Barbican complex is Shakespeare Tower. Forty-one floors high. Its dark windows looking out sightlessly over the City.

Goodfellowe is forced to abandon his faithful bicycle. He begins running up stairs of cement and across anonymous brick-paved courtyards that seem to suck in winds and turn them round and round in some eternal spin cycle of litter and dead leaves. As he runs, the echoes of his footsteps leap back at him from the empty doorways and stairwells. It's a ghost town.

Two forty-two.

He is by the entrance to Shakespeare Tower. Abandoned, no commissionaire, yet entrance thankfully unlocked. And somewhere, inside, up there, is Amadeus. All doubt is gone now, he *knows* it's Amadeus. Should've known earlier. They'd thought the original letter of warning was written in gibberish to disguise the identity of the author. If only they'd had the wit to realize that it pointed insistently like a finger of accusation, marking the author as someone who was dyslexic, who had once offered Goodfellowe a shilling for a rude picture of the headmaster's wife and who still seems to have one hell of a problem with authority.

The address Mickey has given him says that Amadeus lives on the thirtieth floor. He thumps the buttons of the lift, then thumps the wall in impatience, yet even as he bursts panting from the lift he can see Amadeus's front door is ajar. He knows he won't find him there. He doesn't find any trace of Amadeus, for the apartment is overarranged and crammed with pinks and pastels and little sign that a man of military background lives here, until Goodfellowe opens the door to the smallest bedroom. There he discovers a shrine. The memorabilia of a career spanning many years and several wars. A room crammed like a catacomb. No time to take it all in, just fleeting images of citations and photographs, with something called a Prop Blast certificate swinging disrespectfully from the hook on the back of the door. Weapons, too. A semicircle of combat knives arranged on the wall, and several guns. Probably Soviet, hopefully decommissioned. An Argentinian flag, faded, ripped, covered in ominous stains.

Upward. Eleven further floors, and two more of plant rooms. Lifts. Stairs. Through the door that leads out onto the roof. Two fifty-one.

The rooftop seemed deserted, occupied by nothing more than anonymous pipework and aerials that bent gently in the wind. The air was so much fresher at this height, and the view breathtaking. On every side stood the glass-eyed monuments to Mammon – the banks, the finance houses, the factories of fortune that were the City of London – and in their midst the cupola of St Paul's, standing guard, defiant, as though reminding them to enjoy it while they could, for all things are fleeting.

It was the fresh wind that made him realize he was not alone. The strains of a transistor radio drifted on the breeze from a side of the roof hidden from Goodfellowe by a huge ventilation duct. He turned the corner and found himself staring at Amadeus – and yet again at the barrel of a gun, this time a Czech pistol. It was pointed directly at him.

'Tom.' Amadeus smiled, but the expression failed to stretch as far as his eyes, which were sleepless, disturbed, erratic. 'You were the last one I thought to see. It's been a long time.'

'Perhaps too long, Peter.'

'What are you doing here? Come to apologize for standing me up on that drink?'

'Happily, if an apology is what you want.'

'Ironic. A little while ago an apology is all I wanted. A few words, *politician's* words, even. Not the most priceless of jewels, you would have thought. But it's too late for that now. Still, sorry to have to meet like this.'

'This isn't exactly what I was expecting, Peter.' Goodfellowe was staring at the scene in front of him. Beside Amadeus stood a child's toy, a garish blue-and-yellow plastic shotgun which had a pump

426

action and assorted motifs styled after some kids' TV show. Alongside it, laid out in drill order, were what appeared to be half a dozen multicoloured lightbulbs.

'What *were* you expecting, exactly?'

'I'm not sure. Almost anything. A bomb, a nuclear device, perhaps. Not a children's toy.'

'I'm putting a little theory to the test. We're at about five hundred feet and this toy water mortar claims to be able to launch its little bombs' – he indicated the light bulbs – 'a further hundred feet in the air and for a distance of three hundred feet while they release their contents. Add to that the prevailing wind' – he licked his finger and held it up to test the breeze – 'I reckon the droplets will reach certainly as far as the Bank and Mansion House. Who knows, maybe as far as the river. Kids' stuff.'

'And the devil's work . . .'

'The gun came from Regent Street, and I've used a scuba tank to put the contents under a bit of pressure, just a couple of atmospheres, to make sure it all vaporizes properly. A little hit and miss, but that shouldn't matter, not for my purposes. One block more or less won't make much difference, will it? By the way, old chap, come and squat under that awning, will you? Out of sight?' The barrel of the most un-toy-like Czech pistol was waved at Goodfellowe. 'Can't have you standing about like a distress beacon for all the world to see.'

Goodfellowe crouched, very uncomfortable, his knees cracking in protest.

'Toy water bombs? You plan to destroy the City of London with a plastic water pistol, Peter?'

'Not quite. You see, these little grenades aren't full of water but a little cocktail I picked up in Kosovo from a Russian captain. Buy anything from the Russians nowadays. It's a binary chemical their weapons people have been experimenting with. Two solutions that are harmless on their own, but once mixed together become instantly virulent. Orange rain, they call it. Brought it back as a bit of a keepsake. Never thought about . . . this.' He nodded towards the skyline.

'It'll destroy the City?'

'Iraqis found it did a damn fine job on several Kurdish villages, apparently. Makes the lungs bleed until you drown in your own blood. But there's an unfortunate after-effect. On exposure to the air the compound quickly corrupts. The droplets turn to jelly which doesn't disperse but sticks to everything it touches and degrades very slowly.'

'That's a problem?'

'Sure. It's a persistent agent. This stuff hangs around for a month or more. Doesn't kill maybe, not once it starts degrading, simply causes extreme nausea and temporary disablement. But that makes it very messy, and it's resistant to all the usual anti-agent scrubbing and decontaminants. So you can see why it's a problem. Even when you've taken out the enemy you can't take advantage of it for a long while. Too long.' He paused. 'Although to destroy the City of London, you don't have to occupy it, do you? Just close it down for a month. The Japanese and American money men will do the rest.'

'Destroy the City?'

'That's right. Call in Bendall's overdraft.'

'You think you'd be destroying just banks and companies, for God's sake? Think it through. You'd be destroying lives. The lives of millions. Their incomes gone, pensions lost . . .'

'Tell me about it,' Amadeus spat. 'Your Government does it all the time.'

'But it could never be rebuilt, Peter. This place works on confidence. Cut it to pieces and you can't simply stick it back again afterwards. It would cause a financial meltdown. Hundreds of billions of pounds flooding out of this place at the touch of a button and taking with it the social services, hospitals – yes, and your precious defence budget. The country would be on its knees.'

'It's already on its fucking knees! I'm giving it the chance to stand tall and hold its head up high once more. All it has to do is get rid of one maggot of a man!'

'You'll never get away with it.'

'Why? Because you've arrived? Hadn't noticed you'd brought the cavalry with you. Anyway, nothing's over until the fat lady sings and' – he waved the gun towards the transistor, tuned in to live coverage of the Prime Ministerial press conference due in – what? – seven minutes' time – 'we're only on the overture.'

Goodfellowe rose stiffly to his feet, his knees screaming with pain. 'I can't let you do this, Peter.'

The barrel of the gun was pointed directly at the centre of his heart.

'You've no choice. One step towards me and it's the last you'll ever take.'

'You'd kill a friend?'

'Believe me, I've watched many good friends die over the years.'

'In the national interest.'

'That seems to be the standard political excuse.'

'And *this* is in the national interest?'

Amadeus grew animated. 'What else can I do? Write letters to the newspapers, for God's sake? Go and lobby my *Member of Parliament*?' The words threatened to make him choke. 'You see, that's where it all falls down, Tom. Politicians don't believe in country any more. Or conscience. Only political convenience. You talk about being anchored to your principles, but then the wind changes so you pull up anchor and sail off in some new direction.'

'I don't see it that way.'

'Of course you don't, because you're a politician. An animal that can barely see at all. You stand for election with stars in your eyes but the moment you get elected they put you in blinkers so you don't get lost going through the voting lobby.'

'It's a game of give and take. Teamwork. Like football.'

'It's no game, Tom. It may seem like that at Westminster but out there in the real world it's life and bloody death. You screw up in Bosnia or Kosovo or even in Littlehampton District Hospital, and some poor wretch dies. And how many hospitals have you voted to close in the last couple of years?'

'The world isn't black and white,' he responded, ducking.

'What, there's no difference between right and

wrong? Between deceit and honour? I know that's how politicians like to make it seem with their spin doctors and compromises, but you'll have to forgive me, old friend, Westminster isn't the real world. You talk about being in touch with the people, but the only time you politicians seem to be in touch with the people is when you're pissing on them from inside the palace.'

'Seems to me that you're the one who's got himself morally confused. Setting himself up as the nation's conscience. Who the hell voted for you?'

'It's enough that I swore to defend my country. With my life, if necessary.'

'I took an oath of office, too!'

'Political office? You mean that trough of broken promises? Oh, and you act so proud and so principled while you're at it, even with your noses stuck in the swill. But then you get shoved aside – as you all are. You're sacked. You crawl off to spend more time with your family, your ambitions destroyed. It's only then you discover a different set of principles that had been hiding all the while, new principles that force you to turn on your old friends and become a heartfelt critic of the very Government you were so delighted to serve all those years. Christ, don't you guys ever get sick of spending half your life crawling up the backside of a creature like Bendall?'

Goodfellowe stood silent for a moment, rubbing both his aching knees and his pride.

'Tell me I'm wrong, Tom. Look me in the eye and tell me you're different.'

Me – crawl up to Bendall? 'I thought I was supposed

to be leading this argument, Peter. We seem to have got our roles a little muddled.' He straightened his stiffening back. He knew he was losing this one. 'But you make an excellent point. I suspect we're both fed up with being kicked around by Bendall. So let's do something about that, shall we?'

'Like what?'

'Peter, I'm going to walk over to the radio –'

'Don't move an inch. I'll shoot!'

'Your choice, old friend. But there's something I have to prove to you.'

And Goodfellowe walked, moving across to where the radio had been positioned a little distance from Amadeus to improve the reception. It was only a small affair, the size of a thick book, and from it came the sound of commentators filling the time with empty words as they waited for the three o'clock deadline. In five minutes.

The barrel of the pistol followed him as he moved. Goodfellowe couldn't fail but be aware of the contrast – Amadeus's hand so steadfast and unwavering, his own shaking like a fish in a net as he took up the radio.

'The entire country is waiting for this extraordinary event in just a few minutes' time, when Jonathan Bendall will walk out of the door of Number Ten Downing Street to let us know his decision. In all my years in Westminster I have never known another moment like this, when the fate of not just one Prime Minister but the nation's capital hangs in the balance . . .'

With every ounce of his trembling strength, Good-fellowe hurled the radio as far as he could, watching it sail down in a graceful arc to disembowel itself on the concrete hundreds of feet below, and all the while wondering whether he was about to follow.

'What the f –'

Goodfellowe had risked his life in a gamble to buy a few minutes' time. He felt profoundly sick, yet he dared not pause or lose the moment. 'You want to stop being kicked around by Bendall? Well, what the hell do you think you're doing right now, hanging on his every word? Without Bendall on the bloody radio you won't know what to do. You're as dependent on him as anyone. I thought I might just make the point.'

'The point is . . . the point is that either he will resign, or he won't. If I hear about it at three o'clock or five minutes past, what's the difference?'

'No difference. The principle is still the same. You'll still be sitting on your arse waiting for him to make up your mind for you!'

'I rather think it's Bendall who is waiting on me. I shall destroy him.'

'Funnily enough, I think it's quite the other way around. You may be the saving of Jonathan Bendall.'

'Me? Save Bendall?'

'Resurrect him. Pull him back from the grave. Make him immortal. You see, I happen to agree with you about our Prime Minister's personal qualities. But after this? You won't destroy him. If he decides to step down and save the City, they'll talk about it as the greatest act of self-sacrifice since the crucifixion. He'll be Jesus and John Kennedy all wrapped up in one. A pathetic excuse of a man turned into a national hero. Think about it. Kind of makes you lose the will to live, doesn't it?'

Amadeus was shaking his head as though trying to rid himself of bothersome flies. 'No such thing as heroes any more. Give them a god and you always find there's some editor or other non-believer waiting to turn everything to corruption, to make out that we're all the same sort of lowlife. So Bendall as hero? I doubt it. Anyway . . .' His lips toyed with a restrained smile. 'I'll take my chance. Nice try, Tom, but that one won't float.'

'Then let me try a different boat. Let us set aside Jonathan Bendall, and turn instead to Mary Wetherell and Andy McKenzie. What's to become of them? Or Freddie Payne – although I suspect you couldn't care less for him. Silly, really, what he did, trying to screw a little money out of the system you say you're trying to save. Looks clumsy. Taints them all. But not half as much as they'll be tainted if you let those bloody things off. They'll all of them be accessories before the fact, with the fact being something considerably more unpleasant than the bloody Blitz. Puts them in the same league as Goering and Goebbels in most people's books. So they'll be condemned and then they'll be left to rot.' Time for a slight change of course. 'Correction – *you* are going to leave them to rot. The Commanding Officer who betrayed his own men.'

'Don't you dare lecture me about betrayal! They all knew the risks. Volunteers every one. And victims. Casualties of war, just like you and me.'

'I missed that. Like you and me?'

'Didn't I explain?' Amadeus pulled a contrite face. 'These mortar things start spraying as soon as they're fired. There'll probably be enough undiluted back-wash to ... well, to ensure that neither of us is in much of a position to worry about what happens after.'

Goodfellowe said it softly, yet with passion. 'Shit.'

'Sorry, Tom. I'm used to the idea of giving up my life for what I believe in. But you're a politician. Don't suppose the thought ever entered your head.'

'I am going to die?'

'Possibly. Probably. You're right, it depends upon Bendall. Not my call.' Amadeus was eyeing Good-fellowe curiously. 'Tell me, Tom, how do you feel about that?'

'Dizzy, I guess. Must be the fresh air up here.'

'Or the thought of your life hanging on the whim of a politician?'

'Perhaps it's that I'm a little more confused than you about the principles I'm supposed to be dying for.'

'No need for confusion. It's that stuff we learnt about in civics at school. Justice. Honour. Fair play.'

'Oh God, spare me the lectures about the playing fields of England.'

'Damn you, then try the Falklands! Or the Gulf. The Bogside. Bosnia. Kosovo. All the places British soldiers have been sent to die by politicians who couldn't find the hole in their fucking underpants let alone half these places on a map. The world out there's still a gutter and we need our armed forces to clean it up as much as we ever did. And the only thing our armed forces need, all they've ever asked for, is a little respect.'

'*Respect?* With the City gone and the economy crippled? What sort of dream world are you in? You'll make the military the whipping boy of every third-rate politician in the country. They'll charge around the corridors of Westminster like demented puppets crying, "Never again! Never again!" And there won't be a Chancellor in Christendom who'll resist the temptation to pick the military's pocket at every turn. They'll fillet the armed forces as though they were the last fish on this planet. Save them? You won't have saved them, you'll have shattered them more effectively than a Russian first strike. These aren't principles, these are the excuses of a suicide note!'

'This isn't a bloody election. There aren't always easy options. People must be made to realize –'

'No, it's you who've got to realize. Dying for your country is one thing. Dying for some half-baked idea is totally bloody different!'

'Scully died – and for what? He was willing to risk his life anywhere in the world for his country, but instead he died for no better reason than to save the neck of that scumbag in Downing Street. And that's why he's got to go. What more reason do you want, for pity's sake? Scully is . . .' – Amadeus loses a beat – '*was* the finest, most decent man I ever served with. They killed him. Shot him like a dog. This isn't a game any more, Tom. I'm not fiddling around with traffic lights or telephone systems. There's blood on the ground – Scully's blood – and

I swear it's not going to lie there alone. He deserves more than that!'

Goodfellowe's response was basted in sarcasm. 'Ah, so there we have it. Forgive me, I thought we had been talking about high principle, a matter of honour. But this is nothing but a little piss pot of revenge.'

'No!'

'But certainly. First you pretend you are doing this for your country, yet your country will revile you. You know something, Peter? They're going to stand in great queues to spit upon your name, while Bendall will come secretly at night to dance in celebration on your grave. So then you change your tack and say you are doing this for Scully. *For Scully?* All you'll be doing is reducing Scully's memory to nothing better than a kettle of stinking fish.'

Amadeus is suddenly finding it difficult to breathe, as if he has his head above hot coals. He is confused. 'This is for Skulls. For Albert Andrew. He was my friend. He wasn't in this for any reason. Only because I asked him.'

Goodfellowe's voice has risen to the level of a shout. 'But I thought you said he volunteered. So this is what it's all about. Not about country or conscience, least of all poor old Scully. This is about your own pathetic sense of shame.'

The pistol is still pointed directly at Goodfellowe's heart but it is now shaking, held too tight, and Amadeus's eyes are closed, images of Scully rushing before his mind. He is very near the edge. Goodfellowe is still shouting, pushing.

'Scully was betrayed, for sure. But by you. He

trusted you and you got him killed. That's it. That's all of it. Shame! Shame! Shame on you!'

Amadeus is shaking his head, a jerking motion. Nothing is working properly any more. A straining noise is coming from his throat. He wants to reply, to bulldoze his way through the accusations, but he can find neither words nor wind. It is dark and he is standing over a body, of a young Argentinian conscript with a bayonet in his belly and a soundless scream on his twisted lips. But suddenly he can see more clearly and realizes the corpse is not that of some foreign devil but of Scully, lying amidst dust and rubble. In Battersea. His body is lifeless, except for the eyes. The eyes are staring out, accusing. If anyone had to die it should have been Amadeus. Not Albert Andrew. He was owed. By Amadeus above all others.

Shame! Shame! Shame!

Amadeus has run out of arguments. He can no longer move. Slowly, the pistol tilts away from Goodfellowe's heart, then falls to the ground.

Goodfellowe is shaking, very scared, but his tone grows softer, the lash put to one side. 'Sometimes the best means of attack is to do nothing, Peter. You've left Jonathan Bendall without a friend in the world. He's brought London grinding to a halt and caused chaos to millions. Don't give him the excuse to play the moralizer, to say it was all worth it. Leave him to dangle while his nearest and dearest fight amongst themselves to be the one to finish him off. You don't have to bother. Don't you see, Peter, you've won already? The only thing that can snatch that victory away from you is what you are planning to do now.'

Amadeus is slumped against the wall. He doesn't look as though he has won the greatest battle of his life. His lips mouth the word 'Scully' over and over.

Goodfellowe glances at his watch. Oh, Hellfire! Two minutes to three! He moves across gently, takes up the plastic shotgun, turns to Amadeus.

'Peter, I'm sorry to ask this but . . . I know you normally carry a mobile phone. May I borrow it?'

'Wh-what?'

'Your phone.' Goodfellowe holds out his hand, demanding.

Like a man who has just stumbled bloodied from a boxing ring, Amadeus searches half-aware inside his pocket. At last he finds the phone.

Goodfellowe takes it, retreats, begins punching numbers. For pity's sake let them answer this time.

It's as though his whole life now hangs in the balance. He can still save Bendall. For a while at least. Long enough for Goodfellowe to be granted the status of a national hero, to ensure that his elevation to the Cabinet becomes a foregone conclusion and –

Oh, mother's milk. That time – two minutes to three.

The train.

Elizabeth.

He has missed her. Mislaid her, until this moment. And now she has gone to Paris.

He will have fame. More fortune than he has ever dreamed of. Plus the woman of his dreams.

He is one phone call away from his destiny. All

he has to do is to save Jonathan Bendall and claim his prize. But in making that phone call he will also destroy Peter Amadeus, a man who in so many ways Goodfellowe secretly admires. The body of his friend used as a stepping stone for his own ambition.

It will make him no better than Bendall.

The phone in his hand is ringing insistently. A minute to three. Sixty seconds. Then it answers.

'Downing Street. How may I help you?'

Goodfellowe stares at it for what seems a moment longer than an entire lifetime.

Then he throws the phone as far as he can after the radio.

AFTERMATH

The words of defiance and high principle uttered by Bendall on the step of Number Ten would have carried more weight had he not first, on the dot of three o'clock, had to announce that he was resigning. After that, the media quickly came to indulge in lurid headlines and speculation as to who would succeed him rather than bathing in the dead waters of constitutional principle. The plain truth was that no one liked Bendall and precious few came to his defence.

And when, in the following days, the most rigorous search of the many corners and crevices of the City failed to detect a single trace of either explosive, weaponry or even a mislaid catapult, his noble sacrifice came to seem more a lack of nerve. He'd bottled it. Like a poker player with a knave, queen and king all held in his hand – or at least locked up in the top security wing of Paddington Green police station – yet lacking the grit to call the other man's bluff. For bluff it clearly was. Beaky might have had a shy at a couple of traffic lights and an architectural eyesore, but the City of London? Never! Hell, he was the bravest animal in the land! Which was more than could be said of Jonathan Bendall. A man who had created a crisis out of, well, in hindsight, out of practically nothing.

They didn't stay in Paddington Green for long. The prosecution had a whole confection of suspicions and circumstance, but no hard evidence beyond a mobile phone and an inspired punt on the Stock Exchange that was, of course, no evidence at all. If that were evidence they'd have to lock up at least six former Ministers.

So they were released. McKenzie took up a position with Médecins Sans Frontières and never returned to Britain, while Mary was engaged by a leading firm of City insurance brokers that specialized in terrorism and political risk. She spent much of her time in Latin America negotiating the release of kidnap victims, and fell in love with a prominent Colombian lawyer after obtaining his release from eight months in captivity. Like all her emotional adventures, it didn't work out. Freddie Payne stayed in London, got divorced, then got drunk, and afterwards went skiing near his bank in Switzerland.

Some months after the incident, Goodfellowe found he could no longer resist the temptation to discover what had become of Amadeus. His enquiries revealed that his old schoolfriend had long since left both the Barbican and his wife. There was a report that a senior British Para officer had been killed fighting in Chechnya against the Russians, but it came from a source that had also tracked down Lord Lucan to a cave in Scotland. Yet it might have been true, for no one ever heard of Peter Amadeus again.

*   *   *

He didn't call her for several days afterwards.

'You didn't call,' she said when at last Goodfellowe came round.

'No, neither did you.'

'But, darling, I never do. You know me.'

'Yes, I guess I do.'

They were both circling, already sparring. How typical, he thought.

'Good trip?'

'Excellent. Although I was half expecting you to try and head me off at the railway station.'

'Funny enough, so was I. But I got distracted.'

'Something wrong? You sound . . . different.'

'Things are different, Elizabeth.'

'Why, because of Paris?'

'Not just because of Paris.'

'What, more of your silly jealousy? Bloody men!'

'No, not jealousy – at least, not just jealousy. You knew how much it would hurt me, but I could deal with that. I always have. The point is that I could have stopped you going to Paris, yet I didn't. I was on the way to Waterloo, it seemed the most important thing in my life, yet . . . I got distracted. I suppose I'm always going to get distracted. And what with your distractions . . .' He took a long look around The Kremlin.

'This is an insurance policy, not a distraction,' she insisted. Her voice was beginning to catch with apprehension. He was preparing the ground for something, she wasn't sure what. For once she wasn't in control. 'Anyway, it's all sorted. I got the loan.'

'You didn't need the loan. You didn't need to go to

Paris.' A raised voice, a touch of irritation. 'In truth, the only reason you went to Paris is because you insisted on doing it your way. Throughout all this I've been an irrelevance. You wouldn't let me be involved.'

'There was no other way! Come on, Tom, you know you don't have seventy thousand!'

'You don't need seventy thousand. On Thursday morning I went to see your landlord. A certain Mr Sandman. Difficult fellow. One brown eye, one blue, so I didn't know which one to look at. Foreign, I think. Anyway, I explained to him the foolishness of putting up your rent in the middle of a recession. Told him frankly that it would put you out of business and then he'd get no rent at all.'

'And?'

'Sadly he remained desperately unconvinced. Didn't give a damn. Told me to sod off, in fact, until I told him about his other problems.'

'What other problems?'

'It seems that Mr Sandman has got his claws into several restaurants in central London. He's been trying to turn them into bars. Apparently bars are more recession-proof, people drink through their miseries even if they can't afford to eat. That's why he's been jacking up the rents, trying to force people like you out in order to turn everything into high-profit watering holes.'

Her eyes began to fill with misery.

'However, in order to do that he needs the consent not only of the planning authorities but also the licensing justices. So I explained to him that the whole of the local residents' association in this part of town is on e-mail, which means that with a single touch of a button I can get four thousand objections put in to any planning or licensing application he might make. That's when he began to concede that I might have a case. Then I told him that the four thousand included a couple of hundred Members of Parliament and the chief licensing justice herself. At which point, for reasons which are beyond me, Mr Sandman became overwhelmingly convinced by the logic of my argument.'

'You mean . . . ?'

'The rent's been frozen.'

She uttered a cry of joy and threw her arms round him, but somehow it was an unconvincing gesture and he remained uncharacteristically wooden.

'I could have helped, if you'd asked. But then I could have stopped you going to Paris, if I hadn't allowed myself to get distracted. My fault.'

'Paris meant nothing.'

'No, it meant so much, to me at least, not just because of jealousy but because you were cutting me off. You knew how much that hurt, yet still you went. And that's *your* fault.' He bit his lip until it hurt.

'A relationship shouldn't be a set of shackles.'

'Whatever happened to commitment and loyalty?'

'For God's sake, what is this, a sheep-dog trial?'

'Yes, a bit old fashioned, I agree. But over the past few days I've had a couple of refresher lessons. In commitment that goes too far – and the type that doesn't go far enough.' She flushed. 'You remember when we talked, about motivations being more important than actions? On the whole, I think I prefer the motivations of the sheep dog.'

'But I love you, Tom.'

'When we're together, yes. But commitment needs to be a full-time thing, not something that gets squeezed in between courses.'

'Or punctures.'

'My point exactly. Both our faults.'

'You're being silly. You're always looking for a fight, Tom. Can't resist it. Your bloody nature.'

He wasn't sure if she was talking about his politics or their relationship. It scarcely mattered which. 'There are things we both want too much, Elizabeth. Most of all, perhaps, we want each other to be different to what we are. You want me to be on show in the back of a ministerial car, but sadly I seem condemned to be on my bike in the gutter.'

'And me? What do you want me to be?'

'Perhaps it's that I want you to be in love with me as much as I am with you. And that's never going to happen.'

She could, perhaps, have contested the point. She could have cried, but that would come later, in private. She wouldn't give him the satisfaction of a public display. Instead, very softly, she damned the whole race of stubborn men and their inherent and extraordinary capabilities for letting women down. She should be used to it by now, yet – oh, how it always hurt.

'That's it?'

'That's it.'

'Lucky for me I held on to the restaurant, then,' she offered stubbornly.

'I think I ought to go.'

He rose.

'Even with the frozen rent I would still have needed more capital. Needed Paris.' It was a last defiant charge thrown at him across the room. He turned.

'Oh, I was forgetting. Bendall introduced me to the Ukrainian Ambassador the other day. He's arranging a presidential visit here. Turns out the president is a cousin of your mayor in Odessa. Small world. So I took the liberty of mentioning the problem a very close friend of mine was having with a shipment of wine from that city. The ambassador was charming and very understanding. I think he saw my request as part of the general back scratching that goes on between presidents and prime ministers – you know, giving each other pandas and horses and handing out contracts to each other's sons. I think he assumed you were Jonathan's mistress. Anyway, he promised to look into it.'

'Another political promise?'

'The wine will be with you by the end of the week.'

He turned towards the door.

'Why, Tom? Why are you so angry?'

'Angry?' He paused to consider. 'I'm angry because I can't help wondering whether you slept with him. I ought to be above that, but I'm not. And I'm angry because you think it's none of my business. But most of all I'm angry because I think I shall miss you so very much.'

'I'll see you,' she whispered.

Did she mean it, or were they simply words to fill an awkward space?

He didn't reply.

His hand was on the doorknob.

'And a pox on Paris.'

They were sitting on the Terrace of the House of Commons, enjoying the sun while they ate, watching the Millennium Wheel revolve slowly against the sky. The tables around them were crowded, filled with the frenzied buzz of speculation and rumour that accompanies the installation of any new Prime Minister.

'Thank God you got here, Sam. You're the first grown-up I've talked to all day.'

'What's up?'

'Reshuffle time, and suddenly the farmyard's full of headless chickens hoping to be a big cock by the end of the day.' He tried to make it sound as if it were a matter of complete inconsequence to him, but knew he hadn't succeeded.

'I thought you said you might have a chance . . .'

'That was a week ago.' He shook his head to clear it of regrets. 'So much has happened since then. We've a lot to catch up on.'

'At my end, too . . .'

'But let's start with the good news. Your art course in Italy. I can let you have the money.'

She seemed oddly underwhelmed.

'Daddy, there's a small problem.' A pause. 'It's not eight hundred any more, it's a thousand.'

'And there was me about to tell the good people of Marshwood that we had conquered inflation.'

'It's not for Italy any more, either.'

'Not for Italy? Curiouser and curiouser. So what's it for, Sam?'

She reached for his hand, squeezed it. She was upset. The look in her eye wasn't that of a confident young woman any more but that of the unhappy little girl who used to run to him for help after Stevie's Action Men had taken over the doll's house. 'Something's come up, Daddy, something really important and I . . .'

She wasn't allowed to finish. Their lunch was interrupted by the arrival of Mickey, who seemed uncharacteristically flustered. She squatted at Goodfellowe's elbow in conspiratorial fashion, but as he looked down all he could see was cleavage trying to escape.

'Oh, dear, didn't they have anything in your size?'

'Be quiet. It's all a secret.'

'*That's* supposed to be secret?'

'Daddy!'

'Sorry, Sam. OK, what's this big secret?'

'A summons. From the Prime Minister.'

'I didn't realize George Vertue might need a new secretary.'

'Not me, idiot. You. You are respectfully instructed to get your Marks & Spencer three-button over there as quickly as possible. And say nothing to anyone.'

'Me?' He was about to swear in surprise, but found himself fresh out of breath.

'Rumour in the powder room is that he's fed up with all the altar boys and spin doctors who surrounded Bendall and he wants to balance it out by bringing back a bit of experience.' She picked a piece of lint from his lapel. 'At first I thought they said *elegance* and I was about to tell Downing Street they had got entirely the wrong man, but apparently it's experience they're looking for.'

'Daddy, if you want a new job, it's fine with me,' Sam offered softly.

Mickey grabbed his sleeve and shook it excitedly. 'Hey, Goodfellowe, takes a hell of a lot to kill off an old soldier, eh?'

'Some old soldiers, at least,' he muttered wistfully, his frown a mixture of puzzlement and alarm. 'But do you really think of me as old?'

'Let's put it this way. If you were a party, we'd be on to the jelly and musical chairs by now.'

Sam giggled.

'But maybe that's it,' Goodfellowe continued, still frowning. 'He might want me to resign. Kick me into the House of Lords to make way for someone else. Someone younger.'

'You're ten years younger than he is!'

'But I like Barry Manilow . . .' Goodfellowe had slipped into melancholy, indulging his Celtic roots, which always found it easier to visit the dark side first.

'There's only one way to find out, Daddy. Will you call me later?'

She was squeezing his hand again, and suddenly her words came back to him. She had been in the middle of telling him that something had come up, something that was really important to her. A father

450

and daughter thing that both instinct and experience suggested he was going to find difficult. 'Look, there's half a bottle of Chablis left and I can't go wasting good wine on the whim of any old Prime Minister. We're going to finish lunch, Sam, just you and me. I suspect Downing Street will still be there when we've done.' He turned to Mickey. 'Phone back. Tell them I'm with my mistress and can't possibly be disturbed before two thirty.'

'Should I say which mistress?'

He waved a vague hand. 'Oh, find me one, will you? There always seem to be plenty around this place.'

'Good luck, boss.' Mickey kissed him on the cheek and wiped away the lipstick with a manicured thumb before leaving.

Goodfellowe returned to his lunch and swallowed a large mouthful of wine. 'I suspect it's going to be one of those days. Again. So, what were you saying has come up, Sam?'

She remained silent, concentrating on chasing a slab of vegetable terrine around her plate.

'You said it was something really important, that's what you said. Sounded as though it was going to cost me a hell of a lot of money.'

She pushed the plate aside and studied the grain on the wooden table in front of her. 'It's Darren and me. We . . .' She looked up at him, needing to gauge his reaction. 'This is really awkward. I'm sorry, Daddy, but we've got ourselves into a bit of trouble.'

'Oh, Sam! Darling, don't tell me you're . . .'

'The Big P.'

'You're . . .' He couldn't find the words, neither could he stop himself gazing with horror at her stomach.

'No, Daddy! I'm not pregnant. What the hell do you think I am, an amateur?'

'Then . . . ?'

'Big P. Prosecuted. For obstruction. It was during one of our demonstrations to save the streets. I didn't want to tell you unless . . . But the magistrates found us guilty.'

'And now you need a thousand pounds?'

'For the fine and the costs. Sorry, Daddy, I hope this won't embarrass you. But I think it's worth taking a few risks in order to save London, don't you?'

Goodfellowe laughed until he thought they might hear him in Heaven.

ACKNOWLEDGEMENTS

This book has taken me more than a quarter of a century to write. When I was a student of security studies in America, I wanted to write a thesis about the vulnerability of modern cities. Manhattan Island in New York seemed a classic example. However, in the climate of domestic dissent created by the Vietnam War, I was dissuaded from going ahead with the project on the grounds that it might have given the wrong kind of people 'too many ideas'.

The security of cities continues to be a problem – indeed, it's one that is growing. As cities become more technologically sophisticated, so they grow more vulnerable. I still have no desire to give too many specific ideas to those wrong kind of people, so although this is a book about bringing London to its knees and, like any writer, I have wanted to make the book as authentic as possible, in several instances I have modified my description of the attacks in order to alter or leave out vital components of any such operation. *Whispers of Betrayal* is to be read for fun, not as an instruction manual.

This book has been a particular source of pleasure for me. One of the many privileges of being a writer is the extraordinary number of people who are willing to let you invade their lives and drink deep of their experiences. I've had more help on this book than perhaps any I have ever written. In particular there are a large number of former military men, real-life versions of Amadeus and Scully, who gave freely of their time and who I hope will enjoy the finished results. It's a cliché to suggest that the inspired bits are theirs while the faults and fumbles are all mine, but in this instance it is almost entirely true. Paul Ford explained to me how things go bang, Alasdair Hutton talked to me about the insanity of jumping out of the back of aeroplanes, and Jasper Archer introduced me to the Guards (although I hasten to add that he is an entirely different creature to the tormented Freddie Payne). Ian Patterson has been an immense source of strength, humour and wisdom, introducing me to any number of specialists, including David Wills and Dan Tomlinson, who allowed me to drag him around London late at night conjuring up all sorts of lurid scenarios. All these men are of great talent, many are still young with a lifetime of service ahead, and I was hugely impressed by the quality of men and women who have been through the military. But that's the sad point – they've been through it and quit. An exceptional number of gifted men and women seem to have drifted out of the British armed forces in recent years, largely, I suspect, because of the incompetence of their political masters. That has been the country's great loss.

I've had fun with many other aspects of this book. The splendid restaurateur, Patrick Wynn-Jones, MBE, has been kind enough to allow me to base The

Kremlin on his excellent restaurant, Pomegranates, near the Houses of Parliament. Liz Brooks of the Dyslexia Institute very kindly introduced me to the difficult but no longer impossible world of word-blindness. Thanks to the work of the Institute, the Amadeuses of this world have a much better chance of fulfilling their potential than ever they had. My old university chum David Broadbent allowed me to lean on his experience of modern Eastern European wines while another university colleague, Anthony Browne, introduced me to Christopher Burr, a Master of Wines who told me fascinating stories about the vineyards of Massandra and the classic vintages of the Russian Tsars. The ultra-modern world of computers presented me with a greater challenge, but Jennifer Klinec and Simon Dodd guided me through their virtues and vulnerabilities. I received advice and inspiration in considerable measure from David Welch and Peter Dobbs, while my former newspaper colleague Chester Stern tried to steer me around the many obstacles I created for myself in the area of policing a modern city like London. I owe Mary Wetherell an apology for taking her name and appending it to an entirely different character, but I hope she will have some fun with the results.

Other friends have always been there to help me with my books. People like Andrei Vandoros, Jim Spicer, Jeremy Hanley, John Whittingdale, Tamsin Rosewell, Anne and Bernard Jenkin. I couldn't do the books without them, but then neither could I have much fun in life without them.

Two people in particular need a special vote of

thanks this time around. Tim Hadcock-Mackay and Torquil MacKenzie-Buist have helped me and my family immensely through this last year and enabled me to bring *Whispers of Betrayal* to completion. They have been not only splendid supporters but also the greatest of friends. I have spent a sometimes chaotic but extremely happy time with them, finishing off the book at their lovely dog-filled house in Ashcott. It will always be a special memory.

Finally, this book is dedicated to Jill Dando – not in the way I would have wanted, but fate is cruel. She was a very special person and always immensely kind about my books, but then she was kind about almost everything and everyone. Her memory continues to burn brightly not only for her fiancé Alan Farthing and her family, but for countless others. I am one of them.

MD
January 2000

MICHAEL DOBBS
The Buddha of Brewer Street

'A rattling good yarn to keep you warm on long winter
nights'   *Sunday Express*

A new Dalai Lama, the infant god-king of Tibet has
been born. Now, around the child explodes an international conspiracy that leaves a trail of death in its
wake, from the slopes of Mount Everest to the heart of
London's China Town.

It is an unlikely battleground for a backbench MP – but
then, Tom Goodfellowe is the unlikeliest of heroes – his
career is going nowhere, he is permanently overdrawn
and his love life is a disaster. Just when things couldn't
get any worse, a mysterious Tibetan monk walks into his
chaotic world and draws him into a murderous race
against time.

On the outcome of their quest hangs the fate of millions
and the survival of one of the world's great religions.
The odds look hopeless, but Tom is a born fighter, and
the best of Goodfellowe is yet to come.

'Slick moving, fast and distinctive'   *Mail on Sunday*

'Parliamentary intrigue, political scandal and government
treachery . . . Dobbs demonstrates why he is the master'
                                    Times Literary Supplement

ISBN: 978-0-00-649798-1